SKIES
OF THE
EMPIRE

VINCENT E. M. THORN

Cover art and design by Fabrice Bertolotto.

This book is dedicated to Alexis

For saving my life and making this possible

SKIES
OF THE
EMPIRE

CHAPTER ONE

"Get that thing out of my sky!" the captain's voice boomed through the pipeline. She sounded angry rather than frightened, and Cassidy wished she could feel the same in that moment. Sailing during a storm was no easy task on its own, with the winds pushing them in every direction at once. The thick clouds and rain made navigation a nightmare. But having to fight a dragon in such conditions was just insane. Cassidy's body trembled as she aimed the harpoon gun. The ship occasionally buckling in the wind gave her a discomforting glimpse of the distant ground. Usually, the sight wouldn't bother her — one could hardly be afraid of heights after ten years of living in an airship — but at that moment, she couldn't help but worry she would soon have an intimate meeting with the jagged rocks below, which left her heart sinking into her stomach.

She had a difficult time keeping the gun steady in the heavy wind. She managed, however, despite how sore it made her arms. Tracking the silhouette as it glided behind the thunderheads, she saw the dragon as it burst from the clouds, met with a flash of lightning that illuminated its scales, revealing them not to be black as Cassidy had first suspected, but a deep, rich green. The sudden roar of thunder that followed caused the entire ship to shake worse than the winds, though only for a moment. The beast charged the ship along the port flank, directly toward her. Once she had the shot lined up, she pulled the heavy trigger beneath her fingers, hoping to fire down the monster's open throat. Instead, the harpoon sailed through the air and grazed the face of the beast. It took a few scales and drew blood before veering off into the gloom, but it failed to penetrate or deal any permanent damage.

The creature roared in pain, and a bright, reddish-orange glow emanated from its cavernous maw as it drew nearer. Cassidy whispered a curse that was swallowed by the winds, but before the beast could reach the ship or loose its flames, cannon fire blasted from above. The beast was struck broadside, and it roared again as the sudden impact sent it flailing.

Cassidy took the opportunity to rearm the grapnel, setting loose the cable from the failed harpoon, then setting a new one in place. The dragon climbed and caught up with them. She fired the second harpoon, seeking its heart. The dragon's massive tail knocked the projectile out of the way as it struck the ship, giving it a violent rock. Cassidy pulled the lever to once more release the cord and reloaded the weapon as two more cannon shots — one missing, the other hitting its hind leg in a shower of blood — forced the beast to retreat again.

Cassidy waited. The wind continued to batter them about. She heard a series of shots from the rotary gun on the starboard side. She heard the engines cut and go into reverse and the ship turned hard, nearly causing her to slip from her seat. The dragon was far faster and more maneuverable than the ship, but it did not seem to care which side of the vessel it was attacking, giving the crew the advantage of being able to position freely. Once it was back in Cassidy's sight, she lined up the shot. Her arms were sore and weary from holding the gun against the gale, and her palms were sweaty inside her gloves. Her heart beat faster and harder than any drum she had ever heard. The dragon's maw glowed again. It fired, and so did she.

The harpoon sailed through the jet of fire, and just as the flames splashed against the hull, briefly transforming the frigid, wet air into a sauna, the hooked blade struck its mark, lodging deep in the dragon's shoulder. The monster's blast was cut off prematurely as it let out another cry of pain, this one far louder yet less rage-filled than the previous outbursts. The line pulled taut, bucking the ship, as the dragon tried to fly away.

Despite its superior size, the ship was towed by the dragon even as the engines chugged in vain to pull the other way. The captain's voice rang out in the pipeline again, only this time, anger was replaced with excitement. "Damn good shot, Cassy! Get up here and make sure it doesn't break away!"

Cassidy didn't reply. Instead, she hopped from the gunner seat and bolted to the ladder. She gave a quick, mock salute to Lierre, the engineer, who nodded as she put out the last of the fires. Once on the main deck, she darted to the helm. The captain only relinquished her position when Cassidy physically had her hands on it, and she quickly discovered why; in the wind, the wheel pulled heavy, and she nearly lost control of it.

"Keep that rope slack as you can," the captain called over the gale. "We want to stop that thing from getting out of range, but it will rip that anchor right off the ship if you fight it."

"Aye, aye, Captain!"

The captain left. Cassidy turned the ship from full astern to full ahead and cranked the wheel hard to port until the ship aligned with direction as the dragon. She released some of the air from the balloon and dropped until they were sailing at its level. The dragon swerved and tackled the ship, nearly knocking her from the wheel, but she held her ground.

Kek called over the pipeline. "It's out of cannon range," he informed her. "Turn further to port."

As she began to make the turn, the wheel fighting her for every inch, Cassidy shouted back into the copper pipe, "I know where the damn cannon is, you ground-dweller!" It took throwing her entire weight on the wheel to get it to turn as far as she needed, and it nearly wrenched itself back when she tried to straighten her hold.

"I love you, too," he replied, his words punctuated with a loud cannon blast and another roar of the dragon. The dragon dived under the ship and flew up the starboard side, only to get snagged on the cable and shot by Nieves and the rotary gun, causing it to retreat again to the underside.

A bell rang in the lower deck, signaling another fire. "Nieves," Cassidy called over her shoulder, "go help put that fire out!" Nieves did not hesitate to follow the order.

The dragon started to pull the ship down, so Cassidy released more air from the balloon to keep as close to level as she dared. It was only when she did so that she realized how dangerous that would be; the dragon was leading them into the mountains.

She dropped the engines to standard speed and turned the wheel hard to port, narrowly avoiding a rock wall. The dragon pulled the ship through a narrow passage between two mountains, clearly hoping to elude them. Its wings were beating harder; it was desperate. That meant it was almost down, but it also meant it was more dangerous.

With the winds less chaotic — though by no means calm — in the pass, Cassidy brought the engines to hold, letting their target pull them along so she could focus on steering clear of the mountains. Instead, the monstrosity turned around, diving at the ship. The talons at the top of the dragon's bat-like wings griped the beak-head and the railing with a thunderous *crunch*, its snout right in Cassidy's face. She looked up in terror, releasing the wheel. She felt its hot breath wash over her. The creature's teeth were each half as tall as she was and were flecked with dried gore. She tried to run, but the rain had battered the ship and the floorboards beneath her boots were slick, and she fell.

Panic enveloped her as she looked around in vain for shelter or cover. *Pissing blight,* she thought. The dragon's maw opened, bright embers glowing in the back of its throat, the light reflecting on the water and obscuring her goggles until all she could see was bright orange. Then, a gunshot rang out from above, and the dragon's eye exploded in blood and smoke, causing the creature to panic and thrash about. The fire in its maw released in short bursts rather than a solid jet, catching fire to a several patches of the deck. Cassidy scrambled to her feet and looked up to see the captain dropping down from the balloon, pistol in one hand, sword in the other, her purple coattails flapping like a banner behind her. She landed on the dragon's head, one foot on each massive horn and her sword skewering the dragon's other eye, before jumping down to the bridge.

The dragon broke off from the ship, trying to flee to safety, but it remained snagged by the harpoon, pulling the *Dreamscape Voyager* along. "Full ahead," the captain ordered, standing next to the pilot.

"Aye, aye," Cassidy said breathily as she slammed the telegraph to full ahead.

The captain shouted into the pipeline, "We've almost got her now! Let's show that overgrown lizard who the real queen of the skies is!" Once they cleared the canyon, Cassidy turned hard to starboard, giving the cannon a clear line of sight. Kek fired three consecutive shots, and one tore through the dragon's wing, another punching its side. It beat its wings more fiercely than before, but it didn't matter; it was done for. It began to plummet to the ground, threatening to either drag the ship with it or rip out the harpoon gun.

"Release the cable!" the captain ordered into the pipeline. Someone obeyed, and the ship reoriented itself. "Let her down gently, Cassy," she said afterward. Cassidy cut the engines and began letting the air out of the balloon in slow, short bursts. The wind caused them to drift, but the closer to the ground they floated the less severe it became.

Kek climbed down from the cannons with an ice canister to help put out the fires. Once Nieves and Lierre arrived with their own, the flames were quickly doused, and only a few char marks suggested there was ever an issue.

"Alright, gather 'round," the captain ordered, waving everyone to where she and Cassidy stood. "Kek, you're on scales."

"Aye, aye," he answered, combing his blond hair back with his fingers.

"Nieves, you get teeth."

She merely nodded.

"Cassy, you're on stomach duty."

Cassidy sighed and accidentally increased the speed of descent for a moment, but she quickly corrected it. "Aye, Captain."

"It's your turn, don't kill us over it," Nieves replied, a smirk tugging her lips, though she tried in vain to keep her face straight. Cassidy tried to suppress a grimace at that. Dragon attacks were just infrequent enough she hadn't been keeping track of the duties that came with bringing one down.

"She's right," the captain reminded her before turning to the engineer. "Lierre, how bad was the damage?"

"Superficial, mostly," she said. "Won't even slow us down."

"In that case, you can help Cassy."

"Aye, aye," Lierre said, forcing a smile.

"And, as always, everyone pitches in on the hide," the captain finished.

With about thirty meters of space between the ship and the ground, Cassidy stopped the descent. Kek was the first to the ladder, Nieves behind him — Cassidy caught her muttering something to Kek about looking at her ass before following. As Lierre followed her, Cassidy supposed Kek might have preferred the view *she* had.

The engine deck smelled of charcoal, and Cassidy was a little sad to know that once they started flying again — because the deck was open to the winds — the scent would not be noticeable for long. Scorch marks covered the inner walls and floor of the port side, but Lierre was right; there was no permanent damage.

Lierre lead everyone down through a trap door to the lowest deck, where the lifeboats were stored, and into a small room containing a platform boxed by metal rails. A set of levers and a winch sat on the floor on the edge of the room. The engineer grabbed several harnesses from the wall, passing them around. Cassidy latched hers to the winch, as did the others. From a shelf, each crew member grabbed a large, leather sack.

"Everyone secure?" Cassidy asked.

"I am," Kek answered. He added, "If you're worried about it, though, you can always hold me tight the whole way down."

"Thanks, but no," she replied dryly. "You two ready?"

Nieves nodded, and Lierre gave the all clear sign. Cassidy pulled a lever. The railed-off section began to descend with a loud hiss of steam and turning of the motor. After a long descent, they came out under the deck. Beneath them they could see the dragon that had earlier terrorized them, now a broken mess cast against the rocks, red-black stains of its blood contrasting against the mud and the grass and stones below. Once the platform came to a halt, still another twenty-five meters from the ground, Cassidy grabbed hold of the harness, giving herself plenty of slack to work with, and jumped from the ship. Her body jolted when she stopped, but she held on. She looked down, then loosened her grip to descend at a steady pace.

She was the first to touch down, mere feet from the dragon. The splash of mud was unpleasant, but worse was the feeling of solid ground beneath her feet. It was a surreal and uncomfortable feeling, standing static, the wind holding no sway on how she moved. The heat was also stifling, and after the heavy rain the air was sticky as well. She'd always hated it on the ground, from the first time her foot had ever touched solid rock. *How could anyone have ever lived down here?* she wondered as she approached the fallen beast.

Kek landed atop the dragon itself and gave a long, low whistle. "I am a damn good shot," he boasted, looking to Cassidy.

"Sorry, I'm not going to stroke your ego, Kek," Cassidy replied, but she couldn't help her giggle. "We got to get to work."

"Right, right," he said with a sigh. He pulled a knife from his boot and started to pick the scales off, tossing them in his sack.

Cassidy unsheathed her own, much larger knife from her belt, and took a deep breath as she approached the dragon's belly. Lierre landed beside her just as she plunged the blade to the hilt into the body. Blood dribbled out along with the smell of rotten meat, which earned a groan from everyone. Cassidy gagged as she cut the corpse wide open, intestines and other viscera spilling onto the ground at her feet and intensifying the stench. "I hate this part," she said quietly as she knelt, the black-red and pink and purple lumps of flesh and guts fouling her air.

Lierre got on her knees beside her and together they began to rummage through the insides. Even through the thick leather of her gloves, Cassidy could feel the hot, slimy coating of what she was running her hands through. She found the first lump, cutting it open to reveal partially burned woods, a few bones, and what looked to be partially digested meat.

"Good thing I missed breakfast this morning," Lierre commented, her Castilyn accent making even so simple a statement sound almost lyrical.

Cassidy's eyes watered as she felt bile rising in her chest. "I wish I had," she muttered once she forced it back down. She tossed the useless pile away, sifting through more. She found a half-chewed pair of pants connected to a charred boot by way of leg. She searched the pockets, finding several wet pieces of paper, two partially melted gold coins, a wrench, and a busted pocket watch. The papers were damaged beyond legibility, but the rest of the contents she placed in her bag before continuing.

"Daen's tits!" Lierre shouted, throwing a substantial lump to the side before shivering. "I just found a *head*."

"A human head?" Kek called down.

"No, a lettuce head," Lierre answered angrily. "*Of course* it's a human head!"

Cassidy nearly laughed but discovering more partly digested *something* killed her desire to do so. When she had exhausted her current pile, she stood up, approached the giant corpse once more, and — holding her breath —plunged her hands into the wound, gathering what she could from the insides and yanking them out to the ground. Most everything hit the mud with an audible *squelch*, but the secondary stomach — which was larger than she was — dangled off the lip of the entrance, still held by its connective tubes, and the primary one was still inside.

She groaned.

Kek must have wanted to distract himself from the fact that he was directly above the rancid mess, because he called up toward the head, asking Nieves how tooth pulling was going.

"It's fine," she called back, her voice strained as she tried to persuade the teeth to budge.

"I was really hoping you'd say, 'it's like pulling teeth'," Kek said, his voice rife with mock disappointment.

7

It was Lierre's turn to groan. "That joke stopped being funny the third time," she told him, throwing what looked like a large bone she'd pulled out of the pile at him, barely missing his head.

"I don't think it was ever that funny to begin with," Nieves replied.

"You laughed just like everyone else," Kek protested.

"Sure, but it wasn't *that* funny."

Cassidy held her breath again as she cut the secondary stomach open, the acids and juices pouring onto the ground.

"Ugh, that smells even worse than before," Kek whined. Cassidy let loose her breath when she felt she could hold it no longer and had to inhale the foul air.

"At least your face isn't in it," she told him. She reached her hand into the fleshy sack, opting to simply push everything out and pick out the valuables as she saw them. Hunks of meat and bone piled up, and eventually her attention started to drift.

After a minute or so, she was brought back to attention when a piece of shattered cannonball landed on her foot. She cursed incoherently in all three languages as she hopped in place, the pain almost blinding. The more rational side of her mind tried to calm her by reminding her that her boots were sturdy enough to prevent any serious damage. But that side of her mind was of little comfort to the fact that, serious damage or no, it still hurt, a lot.

Eventually the pain subsided, and she limped back to her work.

"I didn't know you spoke Rivien," Kek said, seemingly impressed by her profanity.

Cassidy blinked the tears from her eyes, wishing she had clean hands to take her goggles off. After a moment, she answered, "I can also ask where the head is, and order lunch."

"Eh," Kek replied. "The cursing is much more useful."

"Also, your Castilyn is way off," Lierre said, playing up her already thick, musical accent. "It's *merde,* not 'marry-day'. *Chatte* was right, though," she added after a pause.

"Thanks," Cassidy replied sardonically. She returned to work.

The rain stopped and the clouds dispersed, making way for the sun to heat the already too-warm surface. The rancid bile at Cassidy's feet grew even more rank.

Digging her way deeper into the dragon's insides, Cassidy found what she was looking for. "Finally!" She exclaimed, extracting a round, glassy gem with swirling red and gold patterns along it. The matching firegland was still fixed into the stomach lining, but it came free with a vicious tug. Stepping back from the dragon and her crew, she struck one of the stones against the other. A marvelous jet of golden red sparks sailed out and created a thin arc of fire that flew nearly as high as the ship before sailing down, striking the mud and fading out.

Nieves came from the front of the dragon and tossed her sack full of dragon teeth on the ground. "Good work. Just remember to keep them away from Kek, or he'll put them both in the same pocket," She said, eying the blond man with a sly smirk.

"It was one time!" Kek shouted defensively. "It's been ten years, let it go!" This time the smell and viscera were not enough to keep Cassidy from laughing. That was cut short, however, when she felt her harness begin to pull. That wasn't good.

A call from above confirmed that. "Trouble inbound. Gather what you got; we leave now!" Cassidy shoved the fire glands in separate pockets of her trousers and tied her salvage pack shut as the winch above reeled the harness in. Once she was halfway to the ship, she saw what they were fleeing; a mass of briars grew towards them, crawling across the land at several meters a second. Small, rainbow-patterned wisps of light spiraled between the encroaching thorns.

Cassidy's harness snagged, stopping her ascent. She heard the captain issuing orders, but she couldn't quite make them out. She tried to climb up her rope, but with her baggage she had trouble, and her gloves were still slick with dragon guts. She tossed the sack up to the platform to free her hands but was unable to climb when she felt something grab her right ankle.

She looked down and saw the briars had reached up and ensnared her. She shook her foot violently trying to dislodge them, but their thorns sank in, tearing through the leather of her boot like parchment and cutting into her skin. She screamed in pain as the unnatural plant wrapped her leg, sending wispy fingers reaching out at her from within. The thorns dug into her calf as the stalk climbed toward her thigh. She reached into her pockets, pulling the fireglands back out. She struck one against the other; the sparks cast off from the gems ignited the briars, causing them to recoil as though they were living, thinking creatures. With her free foot she scraped the tendrils from her leg and struck the stones together again, burning more of the assaulting plants.

A vine of thorns shot out from the mass, gripping her left wrist, forcing her to open her hand and causing the fire gland to fall. "No!" she screamed, reaching out in vain. Struggling against the briars pulling her back, she forced her hand back to her leg, extracting a small knife from one of her pockets and twisting her wrist to cut the demonic limb that had seized her. It took some sawing but finally released her as her blade snapped through the last fibers.

She tucked the remaining firegland in the front of her shirt and took to climbing while she was still free, seeing her friends above pulling the ropes to help her along. Despite the assistance, she was struggling. Her heart beat faster than she ever felt possible. Sweat ran down her face in rivers. Her leg began to grow numb and burn all at once. Each pull that made her climb felt an hour apart.

She finally placed her hands on the platform and was immediately pulled up by the others, all working together. Once she was safely aboard, someone hit the lever to pull the platform up. Her head was spinning. She heard discussion, but it was so distant and muffled she could not determine who was saying what, only that they sounded like they were panicking.

She closed her eyes, suddenly feeling as though she hadn't slept in weeks.

When she opened them, she was faced with a swirling sky above her. It was made of overwhelming color and filled with stars of bright silver. She stood. She had no difficulty with that. Distantly she heard music, sweet music that seemed to mask lament. She looked at her surroundings; she was on the *Dreamscape Voyager*'s deck, but there was no balloon keeping her in the air. She heard no engines. She walked to the edge, seeing that despite those facts, she was indeed sailing far above the ground.

The ship floated above an almost familiar forest of red and yellow leaves, but the stars and unfamiliar clouds of shifting colors killed any feeling of recognition in the landscape. The sky shifted between various combinations of gold and red and purple, but neither the blue or green or gray of the skies familiar to Cassidy. Clouds and stars formed unrecognizable constellations and patterns, and strange celestial bodies filled the sky between them, leaving no emptiness in the sky.

She heard a voice, small and gentle, whisper in her ear. "You smell as the other," it said. It sounded feminine. "But you are not her. You are not the one who sails the Dreamscape. Who are you?"

"My name is Cassidy," she answered, looking for the source of the voice.

"You lie." The voice sounded intrigued, rather than offended.

"It's a nickname, not a lie," Cassidy argued, looking around.

"How is it not? You said it was your name when it is not. That is a lie."

"It is not a lie, because it's what I choose to call myself."

"So, you lie to yourself, too?"

"It's not a lie," Cassidy insisted. Why was she arguing with a disembodied voice? "If anything, it's more like an abbreviation."

"But what you said was 'my name is Cassidy'. That is untrue, isn't it?"

Cassidy sighed. "If I say 'yes', will you stop harassing me?"

"The only thing I did is ask who you were," the voice countered. "It was you who lied."

"Fine. My name is Cassandra. But please, call me Cassidy."

"I shall consider it."

"I guess that's good enough," Cassidy conceded. "So, who are *you*, and what do you want from me?"

"You may call me Hymn," the voice answered.

"Hymn? Like a song?"

"That is correct."

"So, Hymn," Cassidy asked, looking around, "just who are you?"

"I gave you a name," her disembodied voice replied. "If that means nothing to you, perhaps a better question to ask is *what* I am."

Cassidy paused as she stalked the deck, looking out beyond it. She had heard tales of a place like, she was sure. It was the dreamscape, the namesake of her ship. The motherland of sirens, of wisps, of nightmares. And most terrifyingly of all, home of the Fae. That the voice spoke narrowed the possibilities already, but its aversion to lies was a damning indicator.

Cassidy's hand darted to her trouser pocket to pull out a piece of iron, be it a wrench or knife or coin, but she discovered then that she was naked as the day she was born. Reflexively she covered herself with her hands. "What do you want from me?"

"I find you interesting," Hymn answered casually, as though that were all the answer she would need. Cassidy looked up and down and to all sides and still could not find the source of her voice. The helm of the ship creaked as it turned hard to starboard, back the way it had come.

"I'm interesting?"
There was no answer.
"Hymn?"
Silence.

The wheel straightened itself up, sailing out into an inky black void in the sky that sounded of roaring thunder and smelled of static and rain. The void extended around the world, surrounded the ship, and consumed it.

CHAPTER TWO

The first thing Cassidy noticed when she woke up was the feeling of the ship beneath her flying through the sky. It felt right, constantly shifting ever so slightly in the wind. It felt real, the weight of the ship around her, supported by the engines and the balloon. So unlike that dream. It was right. It was real. It felt good.

She slowly became aware of her more immediate surroundings. She could feel she was in her bunk, her blanket wrapped around her like a cocoon. It took her several minutes to open her eyes, but when she did, she was greeted by the golden-red kiss of the sunset cascading into the room. She rolled onto her side to try and get up, only to fall back asleep. When she woke up again, however — this time awakened by the growling and gnawing pain of her empty stomach — she pushed the blanket off and embraced the icy air on her skin. She'd been stripped to her underclothes at some point. A flash of indignant annoyance rose from her chest but faded quickly, replaced by gratitude when she remembered that she had been wearing clothes soaked with dragon innards.

She rolled out of bed, bracing herself for the fall from the top bunk, only to find herself on the bottom, touching the floor almost immediately. She stood up, and her leg gave out, causing her to stumble. She caught herself on the top bunk and steadied herself before kneeling to inspect her leg. It was bandaged from foot to thigh, but the wrappings were tight and fresh. Her wrist was similarly bandaged.

She stood up, more slowly this time, keeping her leg steady, and walked over to her storage trunk. She flicked it open and extracted a set of neatly tied clothes tied together with twine. She set the pile on top of Nieves's bed — the one that sat alone with no bunk above it — and dressed. She started with a white shirt with sleeves that covered to her wrists. Usually she would roll the sleeves up in all but the coldest conditions, but she felt she should cover her bandages to keep them from snagging on everything she crossed. She only buttoned the shirt most of the way, stopping where the shirt had once broken under the strain of her bust, leaving her dark cleavage on display.

She donned her corset next, a brown leather one with straps and buckles, which she found much easier on her hand. After that was secure, she threw on her stockings, adjusting them around her bandaged leg, and stumbled into a pair of trousers, fastening it with a belt that had a set of extra, stylish straps draping down over her leg. Sitting down, she slipped on a pair of knee-high boots with an upturned trim. After tying her hair back with a leather cord, she completed her ensemble with a pair of iron-rimmed goggles, which she situated on her forehead. A few of her red locks draped over them, hovering in front of her face.

She returned to her trunk, taking from it a set of tools, her spyglass, and a pistol. After the unsettling dream, she was grateful for their solid weight on her hips.

She was surprised to find her crew sitting in a circle the breezeway outside the cabin. Kek was speaking enthusiastically about something. He had his hands cupped, about a foot from his chest. "And I swear, she had *the* most massive — Cassidy!" He interrupted himself upon seeing her. He rose, brushing passed Lierre to run up and hug her. "Are you alright?" He asked, taking half a step back, but keeping a grip on her shoulders.

"I'm fine, Kek," she answered awkwardly. "Why are you acting so weird?"

"No reason," he said, though Cassidy learned his reason when she felt his hand caress her butt.

"Shove off," Cassidy said flatly.

Kek obeyed quickly, jumping backward. "Yep, she's alright," he said, standing on the other side of Nieves.

Lierre came in to embrace her, much more enthusiastically. "Captain said we weren't to bother you until you could get yourself out of bed," she said. "We've all been worried, though. How do you feel?"

"A little groggy," Cassidy admitted, still not sure what to think about all the concern. "Hungry, too. But I guess that's normal, since I obviously missed lunch." She looked out to the darkening sky. "How long have I been out? Six hours?"

Lierre looked to Kek, who shook his head like he didn't want to say anything, then to Nieves, who answered, "You've been out three days. Well, in and out, but still."

"Three *days*?" Cassidy exclaimed. "What the fuck happened?"

14

"You don't remember?" Kek asked, leaning in, looking at her like there was something on her face. "What's the last thing you *do* remember?"

"A Fae spirit interrupted our scavenging, we escaped, and I got worn out from the fight," Cassidy said, recalling the events. "Nothing about that should merit three days of sleep."

Kek looked incredulous. "Cassidy, do you remember the most important detail?" he asked, then he nearly shouted, "You were *touched* by the Fae! You could have died! Or gone mad."

Lierre shuddered, looking like she was holding back from covering her ears with her hands. "I wish you would stop *saying* that!" she said sharply, stomping her foot down.

"Point is, you had a fever running since we pulled you back on the ship," Nieves finished, giving a sideways look to Kek.

"You were also thrashing and screaming for a while," Kek added, earning a swift jab in the ribs from Nieves.

"Screaming?" Cassidy asked.

"Sounded like you were having a nightmare. You kept screaming 'him'," Kek said. "You thinking about some guy at port, or something?" He added suggestively.

"No, it's been a pretty dry year," Cassidy murmured absently. Realizing what she said, she felt her face grow hot. Returning to the subject at hand, she added, "No nightmares."

Kek whistled. "A year, eh?"

"Drop it," Cassidy replied. "So, what were you guys talking about when I came out?"

"Ah, yes," Kek answered, musing lacing his voice. "Well, Captain said you'd settled down, but we had to wait for you to wake up on your own, so we started swapping tales. I was just telling the girls about what I got up to the last time we made port in Revehaven to pass the time. I just started. Pull up a seat."

Cassidy shrugged and grabbed a bucket from the engineering storeroom, overturning it and setting it in the circle with the others. Once everyone had their seat, Kek leaned in. "So, like I was saying," he said, "Revehaven. Of course, this was right after the incident with the harpies' nest, so I just wanted to get off the ship and drown myself in ale. Maybe literally, if I could afford it. Well, I don't make it but two streets when I run into this tall woman in a red dress, and I swear by the Mists, she had the most massive, beautiful —"

Cassidy's attention slipped. She had actually wanted to hear the story for a while, curious as to why she had returned to the ship the following morning to find Kek asleep on the gangplank, naked and covered in gravy and bruises, being licked by dogs. But, try as she might, she could not focus on his words. Instead, something else he had said echoed in her mind. *You were touched by the Fae.*

She'd heard all the stories, of course, of those who had similar encounters. No sailor worth the iron on her ship didn't know the songs by heart. Few of them were very pleasant. Madness was a common theme; it was said among many sailors that those touched by the Fae see their death at every turn, and paranoia grows until everything and everyone is a perceived threat, until the affected has to be put down like a feral dog. Other stories told that once the creatures taste a person's blood, they hunt them, night by night, plaguing them, until eventually they kill them in their sleep. Sometimes those stories ended with everyone around them dying, too.

But all of that is just the talk of drunken sailors, right? She tried and failed to convince herself of that. She had seen what the Fae left behind, seen their vestiges in the distance. And all the laws surrounding them existed for a reason. So, knowing what she knew, how could she rightly dismiss the parts she wasn't so sure of?

Her stomach growled suddenly.

"So, she pushed me out the window — Cassy, was that your stomach?"

Cassidy blushed. "Well, yeah, when was the last time I ate?"

"Fair point," Kek said. He pulled something wrapped in parchment from his coat. "This'll tide you over 'til supper, I think."

"Thanks, Kek," Cassidy replied. She unfolded the wrapping to reveal a half-eaten mushroom. Not feeling overly picky, she ate it like it was her last meal. It was very dry, and she could barely taste the too-thin slice of meat stuffed inside, but she savored it all the same. "So," she said between bites. "You got pushed out a window?"

"Yep," he replied proudly. "And by the Dread Mother's own luck I landed in a passing cart filled with bags of flour."

"How high did you say this room was?" Nieves asked. Cassidy was grateful to have her asking for details, because she didn't want to admit she wasn't paying attention.

"Third story, in one of those tight, clustered places on Clock Street," Kek reiterated. "You know, that really narrow, winding one with the —"

"Yes, yes, with the clock tower," Nieves said, waving her hand to prompt him to get on with the story.

"Right," he said, clearing his throat. "So, I already couldn't feel my legs *before* getting shoved out the window, I can't even explain how I feel after, but after a while I manage to roll out of the cart and immediately get pulled into a shady bar by this thug who slams a leather delivery bag in my chest, telling me to deliver it to a man named Veni. *Or else.* So, by this point, I'm tired, confused, sore, and now I'm being threatened, too! I explain to him I don't know who Veni is, or who he's working for, but he won't have it!

"He says to me," he sucked in some air and did his best to make his voice deeper and dimmer, an effort Cassidy found hilarious, "Don't give me that piss. I got your description this morning. Blond hair, pale skin. Short." Kek couldn't hide his bitterness at the last one, earning an undignified chortle from Nieves.

"By the Mists!" Lierre exclaimed, sarcastically adding, "They described you so expertly!"

"I'm not that short," Kek protested under his breath. A little louder he said, "I'm just as tall as you, Lierre."

"Our height is normal enough for women," Lierre answered, patting affectionately him on the shoulder. "For men? Not so much." Kek made a face somewhere between a glare and a pout that made Cassidy giggle.

"Why didn't you tell us you delivered to shady folks on the side?" Nieves added. "There must be some good iron in that."

"Ha." Kek shook his head. "Not a single copper, actually. So, after the guy threatens to break my legs, he tells me where I can find Veni, which led me mountainside, into Dust Town." That earned simultaneous, sympathetic groans from Cassidy, Lierre, and Nieves. "Right," he agreed. "So, I head down that way, thinking I'm probably being followed, so I don't bother looking for a guard.

"I'd never been to Dust Town before that day, and I really don't want to go back," Kek murmured. "So, the very first thing I notice is this beggar, just sitting in the middle of the street, stroking his . . ."

Cassidy tried her best to keep listening, but her wounds started to burn incessantly, whisking away her thoughts. She cradled her injured wrist into her lap and rubbed her leg with her free hand.

People very rarely survived direct attacks by the Fae, and she'd never heard a *trustworthy* account of what injuries caused by them were like. As a result, she didn't know how long she could expect to be in pain; she had heard of cursed wounds that never healed. A tinge of worry crept across her mind. What if this interfered with her ability to work on the ship? The idea that she might have to stop flying with the crew terrified her. The *Dreamscape's* crew was her family.

It's a fresh wound, Cassidy, she told herself, taking slow, steady breaths to calm herself. *Of course it still hurts. It's going to heal, like everything else.*

As she tried and failed to refocus on Kek's story, her mind returned to his mentioning of Hymn. That must have been what he meant. Not 'him.' So why had Cassidy been screaming her name? It made a certain sense that in three days she would dream more than the little bit she remembered, so it was possible she could have kept dreaming of the Fae.

But is that all it was? she wondered.

She was brought back from her thoughts by the ringing of the dinner bell.

". . . winning me a hundred iron marks!" Kek finished as everyone began to rise.

The others insisted Cassidy be first up the ladder, in case she fell. She tried to protest, insulted by the notion she couldn't make the short climb to the deck, but Nieves grabbed her by the shoulders, whisked her round and pushed her into the iron rungs. She gave Cassidy a quick slap on the rear on her way up.

"I'll remember that," she muttered. In spite of her protests, she did find the climb more stressful than usual, her wounds straining as she made the journey, but it wasn't nearly enough that she could not make it. Arriving on the deck, she saw that the captain had set all the chairs around the burner, a pot of bubbling stew at the heart of it, and a stack of wooden bowls and spoons beside it.

The captain herself sat at the far center of the circle, her legs crossed, showing off the pistols strapped to her thigh-high boots. She wore her purple leather coat undone, showcasing her white lacy bodice underneath. Her black, wide-brimmed hat sat askew atop her head, her raven hair cascading from beneath it.

"Glad to see my First Mate up and about," she said. She had a wide smile across her face.

Though Kek had followed Cassidy up the ladder, he was the first to sit, choosing to sit to the captain's left. "Captain," he said respectfully.

"Mr. Valani," she replied with mock formality. She removed her hat and dropped it to the side. Cassidy sat to the right of the captain. Nieves sat in the free spot by Cassidy, leaving Lierre the seat between her and Kek.

"Captain," they both greeted warmly.

"No sense waiting, dig in," the captain ordered. Kek was the first to grab a bowl, taking the ladle from inside the pot and scooping up a serving for himself before returning to his seat, followed by Nieves and Lierre. Cassidy rose, serving herself. As she leaned over the steamy concoction, the sweet smells washed over her. She could distinguish the myriad of meats and vegetables mingled with the rare spices acquired across their journeys, all rising up and filling her senses, far more potently than she was used to. She attributed that to her hunger and eagerly filled her bowl.

Only once Cassidy returned to her seat did the captain rise. She always served herself last, and never took a bite until the rest of the crew had. Cassidy once asked why that was, and her answer was that it was every captain's duty.

"So, what were you little birds gossiping about?" she asked as she served herself.

"Kek was finally telling us what happened last time we docked in Revehaven," Nieves answered, mouth half full.

"To think I missed it," the captain said as she sat down, a frown tugging on her lips.

"I could start over if you like?" Kek offered.

"I'll spare the girls that," she answered. "But if you're still telling, I'll ask the others to catch me up later."

Kek swallowed a mouthful of stew. "Right, so I'd just won myself a hundred iron marks in a game of Snakes, and as I'm collecting my winnings, I immediately attract the attention of two very beautiful women — one of them with skin about as dark as Lierre's or Cassidy's, black hair and silver-blue eyes, the other tan with — now that I think of it, if Nieves grew out her hair and smiled once in a while, she'd be a dead ringer for her." Nieves made a face at him but said nothing as she continued to eat. "Proving my point. Anyway, these women dragged me away and threw me in a carriage."

"They just carried you away, did they?" the captain asked, an eyebrow raised. "No effort on your part, Valani?"

"Did you miss the part where I had just won a hundred iron marks?"

"I suppose that would do it," she replied. "Continue."

"So, they tell the guys pulling the carriage to head 'home,'" Kek said, pausing his story occasionally to take a bite of his dinner. "Miss Silver-Eyes undoes my belt, and at that very moment her partner starts kissing —"

Cassidy took a bite of soup, and once more her attention slipped. She felt badly, because she was genuinely interested in how these events came together, but at that moment all she could think about was how absolutely wonderful the food was. The savory blend of river eel, rabbit, potatoes, and the various spices from all over the Empire came together so perfectly that for a moment, she forgot everything else. After she swallowed her first mouthful she began to wonder. She'd eaten this before — in fact, it was usual practice to simply throw the last remainders of everything into the pot when their stores ran low, and it was usually a very underwhelming experience. So why was it affecting her so much? She wanted to attribute it to the fact that she hadn't eaten in days, but she was still paranoid about what — if any — affect the Fae had on her. Did they somehow enhance her senses? She'd heard stories when things like that happened. They usually ended with the afflicted person turning into a monster.

The growl of her stomach told her she was probably over-thinking it, so she continued eating and tried yet again to focus on Kek's story. She gave up after a while, realizing that she had missed too much context.

The orange sunlight was confined to a small pocket of the horizon, the rest of the sky a green-black shroud. None of the moons had yet shown themselves, and the stars were only just beginning to break through the darkness. As a result, the crew's fire left them night blind.

Cassidy looked out into that darkness, thinking back to her dream, of the *Dreamscape* being swallowed by a similar void. Once more she wondered what happened after that, and why she had been shouting for Hymn.

She shook her head. Why did it matter to her? It was a fever dream. There was no Hymn, it was just a name she thought up in a dream her panicking mind clung to. *Right?* Despite her attempts to rationalize, sailors were superstitious by nature, and she was no exception.

She sat silently, her thoughts repeating and lingering until eventually she stopped thinking altogether. She sat in stillness and gazed at the pot of stew. Distantly she was aware that she had finished her bowl and wanted to fix a second helping, but she held the empty dish in her hands. From miles away she heard the laughter of her crew as Kek's story unfolded.

". . . and that's when Cassidy found me."

She jolted, giving an unintelligent, "Huh?"

"I said, that was when you found me," Kek said slowly.

"Oh, right, that."

"Were you listening at all?" He sounded indignant.

Cassidy flushed and looked down.

"Take it easy on Cassy," the captain said, patting her on the shoulder. "Poor girl's been through a pretty rough ordeal."

Kek waved a hand dismissively. "Of course."

"I did want to hear the story," Cassidy whispered. "Sorry."

"Don't sweat it," he replied. "Maybe another time. Does it hurt, any?"

Cassidy got up to serve herself another bowl. "A little," she replied. "Burns a bit." She added after a few a few bites. "I'd be lying if I said I'm not a bit worried about what will happen."

"Navin's breath, Kek," Nieves snapped, "I told you not to spout that superstitious tripe."

The captain patted Cassidy's shoulder again. "You'll be fine, I promise."

Somehow that put Cassidy's mind at ease, at least a little. Though she offered no explanation, Cassidy knew she could always trust her. So she nodded.

"Given all you've been through, I'll understand if you want to rest rather than stand watch tonight," the captain said.

"No, I've slept enough," Cassidy said, rising. "I can still do my duty."

The captain smiled, her gold-amber eyes shining in the firelight. "Glad to hear it."

The crew stayed at the dinner circle long after they'd finished the stew and turned off the burner, idly chatting. This time Cassidy joined in, laughing and contributing to each discussion as they came. It was almost as though nothing had happened.

The moons had risen, brightening the sky and illuminating the land below. It was early autumn, so the trio aligned neatly, forming an arc with the smallest, Turye, resting just above the horizon to the west, the second, Meia, mirroring it to the east, and Jiqun, the largest, sitting above them in the middle of the sky. All were full tonight, and the clouds were scarce, so they could see for miles in any direction.

Lierre was the first to turn in, announcing her departure with a yawn and goodnight wishes. She offered Cassidy one more hug before taking her chair to the storage room under the aftcastle and disappearing down the ladder. Kek followed a few minutes later, and Nieves not long after him, leaving Cassidy and the captain.

Cassidy took her chair away, as well. She decided it was as good a time as any to check the inventory. There were mushrooms and enough dried meat to last them until they made port, and there was no shortage of water, though they'd run out of brandy and mead. They were down to their last two ice canisters and had nearly spent all their harpoons and cannon shells in the dragon attack. The cargo they were carrying in from Cielhal was accounted for, and what they could salvage from the dragon battle had been cleaned and sorted. She was glad to have missed that particular duty.

As the captain brought her own chair and the cooking pot into the storeroom, Cassidy reported the low supplies.

"Thanks, Cassy," she said. "If we're low on ice canisters, we better not let Kek make breakfast tomorrow."

"Not that we have anything for him *to* cook and set on fire," Cassidy noted.

"He'd find a way."

Cassidy giggled at the thought.

Stepping back into the moonlight, Cassidy stared out into the horizon. She could see the silhouette of the highlands far to the north, a series of forests and rivers decorating the landscape of Asaria between the sea and their destination. She stood by the edge of the ship, looking down at the river they flew over. Despite the distance — they were flying amidst the clouds — she could see silver wisps dancing along the river. What she could not see was what attracted them down there.

"Oh, Cassy?" the captain called.

"Aye, Captain?" She turned, and the captain threw something at her, which glittered like gold in the moonlight. Cassidy caught it and realized immediately it was the firegland.

"Without a set, it's not worth a lot," she told her. "Might as well keep it."

"Thank you, Captain," she said, admiring the now-clean gem. She always found fireglands to be beautiful. She tucked it between her breasts, figuring she'd get a chain for it later, and took to looking toward the horizon for any signs of trouble.

"So, what did you dream?"

Cassidy thought about exactly what to say as she watched the world move beneath her. "I was on this ship," she said finally. "But we were in a different place. The ship and I, I mean. The balloon and the engines were gone, but still we sailed the sky.

"It was strange," she noted. "The sky was unlike anything I'd ever seen. Stars and colorful clouds, and moons enough that you could see at least a couple in every direction. The voice of a Fae spoke to me."

"Sounds exciting," the captain said wistfully, taking her place at the helm.

"It was frustrating," Cassidy replied. "She kept calling me a liar."

The captain snorted loudly.

"What?" Cassidy asked indignantly.

When her laughter subsided, she let out a relaxed sigh. "It's nothing," she said, though her lips were still curled into a smile, as though she were holding onto a private joke. "So, other than being called a liar, what happened?"

"The ship turned and sailed into a dark void," Cassidy recalled. "I don't remember anything else."

"Three days you had to dream and that's all you have?"

"Sorry to disappoint, Captain," Cassidy replied sarcastically. The captain shrugged. "Do you think it means anything?"

"I've had my own encounters with the Fae, Cassy," she said, her voice laced with musing. "And I can tell you one thing's as sure as the sun rising in the morning; a dream with the Fae is no dream at all."

Cassidy wasn't sure how to answer that, so she hooked onto the Captain's comment about her own experience. "You mean when you stole the gods' winds?"

Asier laughed. "No, nothing so grand. I've crossed them few times, all long before we met, Cassy. Once before the war, twice during. The stories don't quite live up to the truth, I think."

"What happened?"

The captain paused, then leaned against the wheel, palming one of the spokes absently. "You've heard the stories of my service to the Empress," she said, and though she kept her tone conversational there was a glimmer of sadness beneath. If Cassidy were not so familiar with the captain, she'd have missed it. "Most of them are about as accurate as a blindfolded drunk playing darts. But some," she added, growing quieter, "some ring true.

"The first time, though, I was just a little girl, must have been nine or ten," Asier continued, "living in Revehaven. My friends dared me to touch the mountainside. Not the mushroom gardens fenced off with enough iron to build a ship, but the true earth and stone."

Cassidy whistled at the proposition.

"Well, even back then a challenge wasn't going to scare me off, and I lived in the lower part of the city anyway, so I said I'd do it.

"We found an area where no one was looking to stop us, and I climbed off the city street and down onto the support pillar. Ah, the look on their faces," she laughed. "I'd eat my hat to see that again. So, there I was, still technically in Revehaven, and yet at the same time, a world away, a massive piece of iron beneath my feet the only thing connecting me to the city I knew. Consequently, it was also the only thing stopping me from plummeting to my death. Didn't think about that at the time, though. I climbed down the sloped anchor, right up to the side of the mountain, and slapped it with the flat of my hand. One of the boys watching . . . we called him 'Squeak' from then on, because of the sound he made when I did that."

"Couldn't you have just climbed *up* from where the city meets the wall?" Cassidy asked.

"You know, I thought about that a lot afterward," Asier replied. "But when you're young and foolish, the most dangerous ways seem the most fun." She cleared her throat before resuming her tale. "So, I'd just proven myself the bravest person any of my friends had ever met when I noticed something. Several meters beneath me was a cave. So, being the insufferable showoff I *used to be*," she emphasized the last part to wave off any commentary, "I found some footholds in the mountain and climbed down. You'd think with the way they

were screaming I'd cut my own head off and started juggling it."
Despite understanding the concern, Cassidy laughed at the visual.

"Keep going," Cassidy insisted.

"I made my way down, nearly slipping a couple times, and
entered the cave." The captain adjusted the wheel slightly when she
felt them start to drift, but otherwise paid little heed. "By that point,
I could hear my friends above crying, 'Elyia, no!' and 'Come back!'
and someone was actually crying, until I entered the cave, and
everything became quiet. I can still remember the wind, faintly
whistling against the cave entrance. It was so soft I almost missed it
over the sound of my own heart pounding in my ears."

"And you found your first Fae inside?"

"Of course, that's why I started the story, wasn't it?" Asier
snapped playfully. "Don't interrupt."

"Sorry, Captain."

"Right. Anyway, I went deeper into the cave, and everything
became surreal, like walking into a dream." She paused, taking a
breath. "I can still feel the sense of vertigo, the sensation like I was
walking in water, the way my head was spinning. I kept walking. My
curiosity fueled me, and this was like no adventure I'd had before."

Very distantly off the port bow Cassidy saw a ship's silhouette
against the sky where the moon had colored the black sky green. She
raised her spyglass and determined that whomever it was, they were
not on approach, heading southwest.

"Anything interesting?" Asier asked. When Cassidy shook her
head, she carried on with the story. "Anyway I kept going forward. I
don't remember being scared, exactly, but I must have been. After
all, I was a child, in a cave, and it was dark. But I kept going all the
same, because the novelty and the excitement were too much to
ignore, and before I understood what happened, I had walked into
the Dreamscape.

"Though I could see and touch the rock all around me, I was
certain that it was starlight lighting my way. And there, at the end of
the tunnel, I encountered *her*.

"A black oil lamp in the Rivien style sat on a stone like a prized
museum piece. There was a red glow coming from within, along with
a voice like pure music. For a few years afterward I thought I had
been enthralled or possessed, but I'm sure now I was merely in awe
of the magic and beauty."

"So, what'd you do?" Cassidy asked.

25

"I did exactly what little girls are always warned not to do," Asier said. "I spoke to her."

Cassidy made a noise somewhere between a chuckle and a snort.

"Of course, being a child, my first stupid question was, 'are you real?'"

Cassidy laughed harder. The captain laughed with her.

"She answered by throwing the question back to me," she said, "'Are *you* real?' I talked to her for what felt like hours, about how long she'd been trapped there, and all the foolishly silly questions a ten-year-old can think to ask. She must have been very lonely, trapped there," she added sadly, "because I honestly think she was glad for even my company. Of course, she may have just been patiently waiting to make a deal."

Captain Asier adjusted her hat to scratch at her scalp. "And we did make a deal," she admitted finally.

"*You*," Cassidy asked, taken aback "made a deal with a Fae?"

"Oh, aye," Asier said, casually as if discussing the weather, rather than breaking one of the greatest laws in the Empire. Cassidy must have been making a face without realizing it, because she added, "It's easy to look at a story like *The Sorceress and her King* and ridicule the sorceress for trying to outsmart a goddess, or to listen to *The Priest and the Gambler* and boast, 'well if *I* were the thief, I'd make my demands of the Fae very specific so they couldn't make me regret it,' or even to look at these stories and say, 'just don't make deals with the Fae.'

"But here's the thing, Cassy," she concluded. "There's a reason all those stories exist, why we need parables and warnings. It's because we *know* Fae cannot lie or break their word, and they are clever and charismatic."

Cassidy swallowed. "So, what was the deal?"

"She said if I set her free, she would reward me," Asier said simply. "Gods, that was dumb. I learned later, much later, that if a Fae offers you a trade, you should haggle. But I was ten at the time, and she seemed nice, and rewards sounded pleasant. I guess it worked out well enough, all things considered, but it could just as easily have blown up in my face."

"So, what happened?" Cassidy asked.

"I freed her," she replied. "She poured out of the lamp like smoke and took the form of the most beautiful woman I had seen before

or since. She wore a sensuous red dress, and the smile she gave me....
Well, after that, she gave me my reward and disappeared."

"And what *was* your reward?"

"Knowledge," Asier replied. "Private, personal knowledge.
Knowledge many people think they want but can't escape once they
have it."

Cassidy considered pressing for more information, but the
emphasis Asier put on the words *personal* and *private* stilled her tongue.
Instead, she asked, "Did you ever see her again?"

"No, and twenty-five years later, I'm still not sure if I should be
grateful or disappointed."

Cassidy leaned against the gunwale. "So, what were the other two
encounters?"

The captain looked away, ahead.

"Those memories are . . . less fond," she said. "If it's all the same,
I'd rather keep those locked away."

"Of course, Captain," Cassidy replied. "I didn't want to trouble
you."

"No trouble, Cassy."

They stood in silence for a while. The captain remained at the
helm to keep the ship on course, correcting the occasional drift.
Cassidy marched around the deck to keep an eye on the horizon for
any other signs of movement or storms. After a while, she climbed
the stairs of the aftcastle, continuing her rounds. She sat at Kek's
cannon for a minute, resting her leg as she looked out. She could see
a storm brewing far to the west, but that would not affect them. She
reported as much to the captain.

The rest of the night passed in a similar fashion, with Cassidy
pacing the deck, looking for any signs of trouble. She and the captain
spoke every so often, making plans for when they reached port,
remarking on the smooth weather, debating whether or not
gryphons had gone extinct. Cassidy was sure they had. Hours passed
this way, until eventually the light of the sun began to illuminate the
sky in the distance. The sky was still a dark gray, but morning had
noticeably arrived, and Cassidy's shift was over.

She bid the captain a good morning and moved to the ladder.

"Fetch Kek and Nieves," the captain ordered, not taking her eyes
off the sky.

"Aye, Captain," she answered, climbing down. Her wounds still
troubled her as she made her decent, but it was easier than going up.

She walked past the engine compartment, wondering briefly how she could ever dream of the ship without that beautiful, rumbling machine.

She kicked the door to Kek's room, having learned not to just barge in on him years ago. From inside she heard a muffled, "I'm up."

"Your watch starts in about . . . now!" she yelled through the door. From inside she heard the customary thud of him falling out of his bed, so she turned to her own shared cabin.

Opening the door, she saw her bunkmates sleeping soundly. Nieves was sprawled, uncovered, across her bed, her clothes piled haphazardly at her feet and goggles still on her forehead. Lierre, oddly enough, slept on the top bunk, which had always been Cassidy's customary space, due to the engineer's fear of rolling off the bed in her sleep.

Careful not to wake Lierre, Cassidy nudged Nieves awake. She blinked a few times, saw Cassidy, and nodded. Without standing she pulled her trousers up and started working on her boots.

After stripping her own boots off, Cassidy undid her belt. With all the added weight from her tools, her trousers fell around her ankles with a loud *thud*. She removed her corset and shirt, discarding them just as lazily and crawled into bed. She fully expected after three solid days of sleep she would be struggling and tossing and turning all morning. She fell asleep the instant her head touched the pillow.

CHAPTER THREE

It was only just past dawn, at the start of autumn. Despite that, it was hotter in the blighted desert than it had any right to be. As a result, the *Scorpion* was traveling at full speed just to mitigate the blistering heat, for what little good that did. Zayne wondered, not for the first time, why the meeting had been called here, of all places.

He looked ahead, and it was not long before he saw his destination. Amidst the endlessly empty miles of barren desert stretching out to the horizon, five hundred ships formed a circular wall around a volcanic plateau. The Dragon Nest it was called. Once they were close enough to see the black and green banners that bore the Imperial Crest — a jade phoenix circling around itself — Zayne ordered the ship to standard speed. The last thing he needed was to be shot down as a perceived threat.

I know we need to come here eventually, he thought to himself, *but Daen's spit, why do we need to plan this job right under the watchful eyes of the Empire?* As they drew nearer, Zayne eyed the ships nearest their side of approach; every one of them was lined from stem to stern with cannons, some three decks high. He also noticed most of them were without engines and had iron anchors to keep them from drifting too far. Those would be the conscripts. He made a point of avoiding those, instead finding an officer's ship; while those were far fewer, they were easy enough to find, as they had they appeared to have freedom of movement.

The one they approached was a vessel with three decks, the word *Justice* emblazoned on the side. Zayne tucked his thumbs behind his belt as the ship turned and positioned itself alongside the *Justice*, close enough to lay down a gangplank. He stood on the port side, looking over at the other crew. A score of men and women, young and old alike, stood in the black uniform of the Empire. Some seemed uncomfortable in it, nervous as rats cornered by a cat. Others wore it like a second skin, standing proudly as though they had worked their entire lives to end up in this pit.

He was not surprised by either; volunteers were promised five thousand iron marks for every year's service at the Nest, with their families receiving a significant stipend should they die prematurely, so it a tempting offer to the poorest dregs across the Empire. Additionally, officers who remained at the Nest tended to advance in the ranks at a faster rate than those stationed anywhere else, provided the casualties under their command stayed low enough. So it was, the Nest was the perfect post for the foolishly ambitious. The third group, the conscripts, consisted of men and women charged with the highest crimes, offered the choice between execution and fifteen years at the Nest. Most chose execution. As he waited for the *Justice*'s captain to greet him, he wondered at the circumstances that brought him here.

The other ship's captain made her appearance several minutes later. She wore a red coat with twin tails and black trimming, adorned with medals of iron and gold, with gold tassels hanging from her epaulettes. She stood directly across from Zayne, her arms behind her back and her feet shoulder-width apart. She had a strict intensity to her, and though she was not tall, she held herself in such a way that she stood out amongst the crew. She was also a bit young for the honors she wore, marking her as one of the foolishly ambitious, yet successfully so — a dangerous person to cross.

"I am Captain Jarva Hawkwind," she informed him. "State your name and business or be blown out of the sky."

"Captain Zayne Balthine of the *Scorpion*," he answered, trying and failing to smile, resulting in a half-scowl that made his face feel odd. "The ship called the *Martyr's Demise* is here on business. I am here to meet with her captain." He extracted a piece of parchment bound with a red ribbon. "I have permission to take my ship into the formation to meet her."

Hawkwind turned to a pair of deckhands and nodded her head to the side, causing them to run off. A minute later they returned with a gangplank. Zayne moved back to let it fall where he had been standing. Hawkwind and two others — both tall, heavily muscled men — came aboard, and out of the corner of his eye Zayne saw one of his crew reach for his pistol. He stopped that with a wave of his hand.

The *Scorpion*'s captain handed the parchment to Hawkwind. She unrolled it, reading it with an overly business-like demeanor. This close to her, Zayne realized her nose had recently been broken and put back into place. Her knuckles were also bruised, and Zayne suspected she had come out on top in whatever fight she'd had.

"We'll have to inspect your ship, Captain Balthine," she said. "Have your crew report to the deck. I'll tolerate no foul play or trickery while I am aboard. Do I make myself clear?"

Zayne hated being given orders, especially by strangers, and most especially on his own ship, but the thought of all the surrounding ships opening fire on him at once kept his tongue in check. Instead, he approached the helm and opened the pipeline. "All hands on deck," he ordered. He closed it. Only two crew members had been off the deck — seeing to it that their cargo would not be found during this inspection. When they arrived, Hawkwind nodded, and she and her bodyguards began their patrol. When their backs were turned, Karn reached behind his back, clutching the pistol tucked under his belt.

Once they had gone down to the lower deck, Zayne grabbed the filthy man by the scruff of the neck and dragged him to the side of the ship, slamming his body into the gunwale and forcing him to look down at the distant ground.

"Are you out of your fucking mind, Karn?" He demanded, whispering sharply in the man's ear. "You were seriously about to pull a pistol on an Imperial Captain, in a *hive* of Imperials? Do you realize that we are surrounded by enough cannons to blow you clean out of your mother's memory? See that sand down there, Karn? *Do you see it?*" The man nodded frantically, his cap falling into the distance, revealing his balding and scarred scalp. "Endanger this ship and crew again, and I will take your pistol, blow a hole through your knees, and throw you overboard! Do you understand?" Karn nodded once more, but Zayne shoved down on him. "Do you understand?" he repeated, louder.

"Aye, Captain!" The man whined, terror rife in his voice.

"Good man," Zayne said, pulling the man back up to his feet and patting his shoulder. "I appreciate the rest of you remembering to show our guests the proper and *legal* respect expected of you," he said to the rest of the crew, who said nothing. Jacques and Flea looked terrified. Nanette merely gave him an exasperated look.

After nearly an hour, Hawkwind and her cronies returned to the deck. "Everything appears to be in order," she said. She seemed frustrated by her search, clearly having expected to find something amiss. Zayne was used to it; mercenary ships had that reputation, and it was well earned.

"Of course it is," Zayne replied. "I trust this means we're free to move in?"

"Aye," Hawkwind answered begrudgingly. "You'll find the *Martyr's Demise* at the highest ring of ships," she said, pointing up, "on the inner-east side. Do not stray, or you will be fired upon."

"Of course."

Once Hawkwind and her guards returned to their own ship, Zayne took to the helm, firing up the balloon to rise. As they climbed, he observed the infamous Nest itself, taking in the faults and cracks that spewed acrid smoke and simmering heat. There was an uncomfortable, anticipatory silence in the air. He watched as the various crews, conscripted and otherwise, and tried to keep an eye on the plateau for any changes. A few men eyed the *Scorpion* with greedy eyes, but most kept their eyes down, waiting.

The *Martyr's Demise* was easy to spot; unlike nearly all the ships in the formation, it did not wear Imperial banners. Across its hull in white paint was a depiction of Daen, the Goddess of the Desert; the mural portrayed her as a womanly specter with draconian claws and fangs. A similar rendition of Daen was emblazoned on the *Scorpion*. But most notably, hanging from the figurehead and crucified across the bow, was the bone-white corpse of a dragon.

"Do you think they see the dragon as an insult here?" Zayne asked Nanette as he guided the *Scorpion* toward it. The slender woman turned away from the Nest to observe the *Demise*.

"What do you mean?"

"Do you think the Imperials stationed here see that as Dardan boasting?" He clarified. "Specifically, that she was able to bring down a beast they failed to."

"I don't think they care," his first mate said.

"You think not?"

"Aye."

She wasn't looking at him. "You're mad about Karn," he observed.

"You could have handled it better," she said tersely.

"He could have gotten us all killed. As a first resort."

"And threatening to blow out his knees before dropping him? Seems excessive."

"I'll apologize to him later," Zayne answered. "After I deal with Dardan." Zayne brought the ship to a halt when he was close to the

Demise. The ship drifted, bringing them even closer. "Stay close," Zayne instructed Nanette. "I want to leave as soon as this is done."

"Of course."

Zayne ordered Flea and Karn to get the gangplank laid out, walking across to the other ship as soon as it was in place. No sooner than he had set foot onto the *Demise* did the *Scorpion* rise and fly away. Zayne noticed he was the last of the Great Captains to arrive. The others were gathered in a circle, watching him.

As he took his place in the circle, he eyed the others in sequence.

Closest to Zayne was Ject, Captain of the *Silent Song*. He was a wiry man with a short, trimmed beard. As always, his jacket hung open to display his collection of scars and a masterful tattoo, which created the illusion that his chest had been cut open to expose his heart. The effect was more convincing in low light, but it was still a work of art in the daylight.

Nyrien was the Captain of the *Forgotten Promise*. She was taller than most women, and lean. Zayne suspected she had once been beautiful, but her scars warped her face and left her with a perpetual sneer. She was also unpleasant to be around, so perhaps the scars kept her honest.

Lancen, Captain of the *Second Chance*, stood beside Nyrien, though only in proximity; the two despised one another. He was far and away the shortest adult Zayne had ever seen. He was also the only captain present without any visible scars; he avoided fighting when he could, preferring negotiation. When that failed, he made sure someone else took the blows.

Zayne had expected the next woman in the circle to be the middle-aged Captain Eveth, but instead it was a younger woman with long, sand colored hair he didn't recognize. Compared to the others, she seemed relatively relaxed and in high spirits. That either meant she had no idea what the meeting was about, or she was someone to worry about. And her presence alone told Zayne she was dangerous.

Completing the circle was Dardan. She was the founder, leader, and chief employer of the Daughters of Daen, who had called for the meeting in the first place. The captain of the *Martyr's Demise* was the only one sitting rather than standing, and rather than wearing a black coat like everyone else, her features were obscured by a voluminous black shroud of silk draped over her face and body. Only her pale left hand was visible, and it was clutched tight around the grip of an iron lantern with fogged glass. An orange flame danced inside. She always carried that lantern with her, no matter how bright the day, and the sight of it always made the back of Zayne's skull itch.

"Captain Balthine," Dardan greeting him. Her voice was deep and sultry, but Zayne heard something else in it. It always seemed like there was a second voice whispering the words as she spoke, just on the edge of hearing. He tried his best to ignore it, but Dardan always had him questioning his senses and feeling uncomfortable. He supposed she liked it that way.

"Captain Dardan," he responded as neutrally as he could, offering only the faintest nod. He faced the unfamiliar girl. "Where is Eveth?"

"Dead," the replacement said placidly with a bob of her head. "Harpies swarmed, back in the spring. Del Thanris," she added, offering her hand, "current Captain of the *Illusion of Justice*."

"Shame, I rather liked her," Zayne admitted as he clasped Thanris' forearm, and she returned the gesture. Being killed by harpies was a terrible way to die.

"Mourn on your own time, Balthine," Nyrien snapped. "You've wasted enough of ours already."

"Oh, yes," Lancen replied, "It was *his* fault for being halfway across the Empire, when you were already here, hoping for the opportunity to lick the boss's boots."

"Enough!" Dardan snapped, causing a silence to ring out. For a brief instant, Zayne was sure he saw the flame in her lantern turn from orange to blue and back. "All of you, stand over there," she said, tilting her covered head to indicate a place by the starboard bow. There was a nervous pause to see who would obey the order first. Thanris was the first to start walking, followed by Ject, and the rest followed. "It will start soon," Dardan informed them.

Zayne was tempted to ask what would begin, but he figured it out quickly enough on his own. The daily awakening of the dragons. He waited in anticipation, staring at the massive landmark. The hush from before returned, intensified now as he was a part of it. Minutes passed in stillness.

When those minutes stretched on, the tension souring into tedium, Nyrien broke the silence. "Is anything actually going to happen?"

It was as if the dragons had been waiting for someone to ask. A bellowing roar sounded as the ground began to quiver and shake. Several of the faults and breaks in the landscape widened, and jets of steam blasted from the cracks. An explosion rang out. Stone and ash and liquid fire shot into the sky.

Shrieks filled the air. *Dragons.* The first dived from the spewing lava, stretching its wings as droplets of molten stone rolled off its scales like water. The blue-scaled beast roared defiantly. Then the cannons started. Thousands of concussive blasts sounded as the guns arranged in a spiral formation fired down at the mountain unleashed their explosive fury. The azure beast was felled after no fewer than ten iron shells ripped through its body, leaving it in bloody tatters to drop like a stone.

Where the first fell, three more emerged from the volcano, one green and two red. Emerald scales glinted as the former climbed skyward, only to be shredded by the onslaught. One of the reds plummeted immediately as its wings were punctured, but the third weaved around the heavy fire in its efforts to flee the trap.

The geyser of molten rock fell away, revealing a horde of dragons emerging from the volcano's depths.

They flew in chaotic patterns Zayne struggled to track. Even with a dedicated fleet unleashing hails of heavy iron upon them, the sheer scope of the nest was staggering and overwhelming. Spewing torrents of flame, the dragons paid blood for blood.

One ship shattered when a dragon with crippled wings crashed through its burning hull, its crew and dashing them across the plateau below. A gray-scaled beast flew forsook the melee and shot skyward over the blockade and nearly escaped. It reached the *Martyr's Demise* in its climb, and the beat of its mighty wings sent Zayne and the others tumbling across the deck. He floundered for purchase on the black floorboards before the gale died down and the monster was gone.

The chaos seemed to last an eternity, but it may have been only minutes. It took him a while to register that the fighting had even stopped. His ears were ringing, and he wondered briefly if the encounter had left him deaf. Once the smoke cleared, he saw the aftermath of a massacre. There were holes in the formation, and some of the ships remaining appeared to have been crippled. From the distance, he could scarcely distinguish individual dragon corpses, much less see the men and women that had fallen, but their blood

35

stained the rocks below as flakes of ash slowly descended. A glance in any direction revealed that despite the efforts of the Imperials a, handful of dragons escaped the slaughter to freedom and would soon vanish on the horizon.

The ringing in Zayne's ear faded and silence pervaded the scene. Until he heard the familiar and disquieting laughter of Dardan. The shrouded woman banged her lantern on the table in lieu of clapping, and the noise was painful against the tense and somber quiet.

"Such a wonderful display of power, don't you think?"

Zayne considered the question and wondered whether the silence of the others was equally contemplative or if they were just scared and confused. "The Empire's, or the dragons'?" He finally asked.

Something in the shroud shifted, and Zayne suspected Dardan was smiling. He didn't like it.

"Death on such a scale," Dardan mused. "Blood spilling on the rocks, and countless lives snuffed like a candle. Daen herself would be pleased."

Zayne could not help but notice the woman had evaded his question. He was beginning to think he was better off not knowing.

"With all due respect," he said, "I trust you did not call us from every corner of the Empire to watch that gory fireworks display, charming as it was."

The shroud shifted again, and this time he could feel Dardan's scowl directed at him. It was less unsettling than the smile, though he still felt like a dozen pistols were trained at his heart. He hated being around Dardan. Every fiber in his body screamed when she was near, a primal reaction that made him burn with a desire to flee. Her every action set his nerves on edge. He wondered if the others felt it.

"I did not think you to be the squeamish type, Balthine," Dardan said, earning a chuckle from Nyrien.

"I'm not," he replied tersely, shooting a glare at Nyrien. "I just want to get to the point. I passed up some good work for theft and smuggling. *Honest* work," he added pointedly.

"Of course," Dardan said. She seemed to ignore the barb, but he wasn't going to count on that. "I trust that means you brought my cargo?"

"Of course," Zayne assured her, unable to fight the sneer on his face. He reached into an internal pocket of his coat and extracted a square, cloth-wrapped bundle. Almost too eagerly, he tossed it to

Dardan. Despite the shroud that should have obscured her vision, she snatched it out of the air with ease.

"Excellent." The company leader unwrapped the package and opened the small, wooden box within. Small, color shifting lights that blurred at the edge like fire rose up from the box, dissipating in the air. "A seed of the World Tree," she said, and there was a sly smirk in her voice that made Zayne queasy. She snapped the box shut and repeated, "Excellent."

Zayne tucked his thumbs behind his belt, keeping his fingers as close to his pistols as he dared without tipping his hand. He wanted nothing more than to wash his hands of the whole affair.

"There is still much to be done," Dardan continued, tapping her long, boney fingers against the lantern. "And Balthine, you volunteered yourself for the suicide mission."

"My specialty," Zayne answered sardonically, all the while wondering, not for the first time, *How did I get myself in this mess?*

CHAPTER FOUR

Cassidy dreamed she was in that other world again. The sky was a canvas of spiraling mist and distant clouds the likes of which she had never seen and woven within were those alien stars and foreign moons.

As before, she stood alone on the *Dreamscape Voyager*. Just like the last time she dreamed, there was no roar of the churning engines. And now, as then, there was no balloon holding the ship aloft. There was, however, a mast and sail like a pre-Ascension ship's, features that did not exist in the waking world.

She was fully aware of the fact that she was dreaming, which was an oddity in itself. That made her feel a tremendous sense of vertigo. But despite knowing she wasn't awake, everything she touched felt very real. She was clothed this time, wearing the gear she had stripped out of before bed. She could not help but notice, however, she was missing all her tools and most of the coins in her purse. She wondered at that, questioning if the Fae's well documented aversion iron would apply in a dream.

"Hymn?" Cassidy called into the surreal environment. "Did you bring me here, again?"

"I did not," came the reply. This time when Cassidy turned to look, she saw the source of the voice immediately.

Hymn was definitely of the Fae. Cassidy gaped, having never seen anyone so striking before. She was at once everything Cassidy had ever pictured from tales, and so much more. Her eyes were large and narrow, and the colors reversed so her pupil-less irises were stark white surrounded by deep blue sclera with swirling patterns. Her skin was lighter than any Cassidy had ever seen, practically alabaster, and seemed to glow like moonlight reflecting off silver. Her ears were sharp like knives, and long enough to reach the back of her head. Her stark black hair flowed to her ankles and moved as though she were under water. The effect was shared by the sleek dress and detached sleeves she wore, which seemed to be made of the night sky itself, with small star-like lights glimmering between a spectrum of blues that shifted tone from every angle Cassidy looked at it.

If Cassidy had ever thought to personify the very concept of dreams, she might describe the Fae before her.

"What is wrong?" Hymn asked in a sickly sweet and patronizing tone. Despite the condescension, her voice was rich and musical, and there was something warm in it that felt safe. "Do I intimidate you? Or am I so beautiful words are lost to you?"

Cassidy shook her head, as much to clear it as from embarrassment. She knew the Fae *should* intimidate her, but that wasn't what she was feeling. At least, it wasn't *all* she was feeling. "Sorry," she said, glancing away, taking in the strange night. "If you didn't bring me, who did? Why am I here?"

She turned back as Hymn moved toward her. The Fae didn't so much walk as glide, adding to the sense that she existed under water, and her dress and locks blurred at the edges like smoke billowing around her. "Cassandra, you are drawn to this place as a moth is drawn to a flame," she said, reaching out and touching Cassidy's cheek. Her hand was like silk, cool and soft. Oddly, Cassidy felt no desire to recoil, despite everything she knew of the Fae. "What do you remember of our last encounter?"

Cassidy looked around. "We were on this ship," Cassidy said. "You called me a liar," she added, receiving a playful smile from the Fae. The look sent a shock through her muddled mind, and fear took root. Not panic, but a rational sense of danger. "And the ship turned around and sailed into a great void," she added at last.

"That is all?" The Fae cocked her head to the side, and her raven locks floated around her briefly.

"That's it," Cassidy answered cautiously, unsure as to the significance. "So, why am I here?"

Hymn removed her hand from Cassidy's face and touched her sleeve, pulling it back to reveal a set of deep cuts not fully scarred-over. Woven into the healing flesh was a purple thread of pale light woven that seemed to pulse in time with her heartbeat.

"You are marked by the one whose path you crossed," she said. "She calls you through your dreams that she may find you, for she is blind, and limited in her capacities where you travel awake. Perhaps she intends to devour you," she added nonchalantly.

Cassidy furrowed her brow. "The Fae from the mountain pass? Why?"

"You escaped her," Hymn said simply.

"Why did she want me before?" Cassidy asked, "And who *is* she?"

"I cannot answer the first question," the Fae told her. "As for who she is, she is known by many names and titles, though your kind best know her as the Goddess of the Wood."

"Faeorn?"

"That is one of the names attributed to her," Hymn acknowledged, nodding.

"I'm being hunted by . . . a god?" Cassidy asked flatly. The Fae merely shrugged. She flowed over to the helm and settled against it, her arms folded under her breasts, leaving Cassidy to her thoughts. She had never put much stock in the gods; to her, they were just names to invoke when frustrated, symbols for mercenaries to use to scare the superstitious, and stories passed on from when men still lived on the ground. She didn't deny they existed, but she had never considered she might fall under their gaze, as the Iron Veils warned.

"So, if I'm being pursued by Faeorn," Cassidy said, trying not to feel overwhelmed by the prospect and failing, "and she's not you," she added, "why is it that you're and not her?"

The Fae gave a long-suffering smile, like a teacher praising a slow student. "At last we come to the heart of the matter," she said. "I wish to make a deal with you."

Cassidy's heart pounded. In addition to bringing death and madness, the Fae were notorious for their bargains, which often led to death and madness. And Fae were incapable of lying outright and could never betray their word — that was common knowledge — but they would certainly not consider the *spirit* of a contract, so long as they were satisfied whatever deal they struck. Failing to uphold her end of such a bargain could easily get Cassidy killed, or worse. In fact, whatever *her end* entailed could be disastrous on its own. She took a hesitant step away from the Fae and narrowed her eyes. "What do you have in mind?"

"I will agree to protect you from the one you call Faeorn," Hymn told her. Her voice was comforting, almost hypnotically soothing, like a lullaby. "On the condition that when the time comes, you will protect me from my own enemies."

Cassidy opened her mouth quickly, feeling the word *yes* forming on her tongue almost on its own. But before the sound could escape her throat, she stopped herself. "That deal weighs rather heavily in your favor," she said, remembering her captain's advice. She stepped forward and looked Hymn in her beautifully strange eyes. She swallowed a lump in her throat as she considered what to say next.

Finally, she went decided. "Protect me from *anyone* who wishes harm on me," Cassidy offered, "and I will agree to your terms."

"You ask too much, Cassandra," Hymn answered.

"More than you?"

"Anyone at any time could wish you harm, and yours is a path that crosses many others," the Fae said. The color in her eyes and in her dress was changing, bleeding from blue to red like wine suffusing water.

Cassidy could not be sure, but she thought she was making the Fae nervous. Did Hymn need this deal more than Cassidy? She decided to test her luck. "I don't know how many enemies you want me to protect you from either, or who or even *what* they are." The Fae's color shift intensified as wispy threads of vibrant ruby permeated Hymn's ensemble and cast a furious glow. Cassidy staggered backwards.

There was a thundering blast in the distance, far ahead of the ship. Cassidy looked toward the source, seeing a black void similar to the one that had stopped her dream before. Hymn glided back into Cassidy's line of sight, standing so close Cassidy could feel her own breath brush off the Fae's skin and blow back in her face. She saw the detail in the swirls in Hymn's eyes, saw they were patterns of clouds and stars like the ones in the sky and her dress. Any coy levity she had been affecting was gone, replaced by an intense stoicism.

"I promise to protect you to the limits of my power," Hymn said. Her voice was no louder than before, but she spoke the tiniest bit faster, and there was a small note of what might have been desperation in her tone. "So long as you agree to do the same for me." Cassidy bit her lip. She had just begun to replay the words in her head when Hymn gripped her firmly by the shoulders. "There is no time for you to search for riddles. This is your only chance. Do you accept my bargain?" There was a groaning in the wood as shadows rose like smoke between the floorboards. The darkness amassed into a shape Cassidy almost recognized.

"I accept!" she said quickly. She felt Hymn clasp her wound.

"Then it is time for you to awaken," the Fae told her, and Cassidy was consumed by darkness.

CHAPTER FIVE

Cassidy leaped out of bed as though she'd heard a gunshot, tripping over her blanket as she tried to discard it. She was in her cabin. The light peering through her curtain suggested it was midday. More importantly, midday in the real world. As she picked herself off the floor, her entire body felt stiff. Her neck cracked at the slightest shift of her head. She gathered the clothes she had discarded that morning and put them back on. It felt good to have the weight of her tools on her again — most welcoming, she noted, was the pistol on her hip.

Unless she had been asleep for another few days, which she doubted, they were still en route to the capital, though they were scheduled to make port soon. She grabbed her dueling sword out of the corner and slid it into her belt. Lierre and Nieves appeared to have taken their blades as well, which they typically only bothered to do when disembarking.

No one waited for her outside the door this time. She didn't see Lierre in the engine compartment, so she climbed the ladder to the deck. Captain Asier was at the helm, as though she hadn't moved since Cassidy had turned in the night before. Kek was talking beside her.

". . . get her once we're in — oh, she's already up," he said, nodding his head in her direction.

The captain turned and smirked. "Well, I never thought I'd see the day," she announced. "Cassy, awake before the lunch bell!"

"I thought I'd keep you on your toes," Cassidy replied, trying to keep the laugh out of her voice.

She joined them, looking ahead to see the silhouette of Revehaven. Like nearly all cities, it was built above and around its namesake mountain range, with tiered streets forming what appeared from the distance to be intricately designed orbs atop the peaks. As they drew nearer and could see the multiple levels for what they were, they seemed less spherical but more impressive; the city was a series of nested platforms anchored into the sides of the mountains, and no matter how many times Cassidy visited and revisited the sight, it never stopped being awe-inspiring. Like a man-made sunset.

The captain guided the *Dreamscape* to the section of the city nested above second-highest mountain in the range, as was her custom, aligning with the vast harbor. Hundreds of ships were in port, dozens coming and going at any given time. Despite the sheer scope, traffic was guided efficiently by the City Watch, which operated from quick, three-person boats that maneuvered easily around the much larger crafts and it wasn't long before they were directed to a berth. Once the *Dreamscape* docked, Lierre and Nieves appeared from the aftcastle, laying down a gangplank. Almost immediately, member of the City Watch — a portly man with an over-sized, graying mustache — approached, stopping just short of coming aboard himself.

The captain reached into her coat pocket, extracting identification papers and trade manifests. Cassidy accompanied her as she presented them to the old man. As with all Watch officers in the Empire, he wore a dark blue uniform of military cut with red trim and a copper sash across the chest, in which he had holstered two pistols. He had a dueling sword on his hip, the level of polish and perfection on its hand guard suggesting either it had never been used, or the man wielding it was exceptional. Looking him over, Cassidy discredited the latter possibility.

The port authority examined their documents thoroughly and dispassionately.

"Very good, Captain Asier," he said finally, returning her documents. She folded the parchments and tucked them back in her coat. "Your docking fees have been waived for the extent of your current visit."

The captain raised her eyebrow. "They have? Why?"

"I can't say," the Watchmen said with a shrug. "I figured you have a benefactor."

"It would certainly seem so," she answered. There was a mixed sense of musing and suspicion in her voice. The officer walked away, apparently unconcerned by the unusual situation. Had he been bribed to forgo the customs search, too?

"That was weird," Asier muttered. She looked up at the city skyline as if answers could be found there. "No matter. Cassy, see that the coin we'd set aside for port gets split evenly between you and the others."

"Aye, Captain," Cassidy said.

The captain turned and called up to the deck, "The rest of you, get the cargo ready for pickup." Cassidy joined her crew mates at the doors at the base of the aftcastle, entering the captain's cabin after the others walked into the storage.

The captain's cabin was far larger than the crew cabins, and with that, it was far more cluttered; a table sat bolted down in the middle of the room, featuring dozens of wind maps strewn about its surface. A dagger was pinning one of the papers down, as though the captain had been fed up with it. Books were piled everywhere, as Asier had a tendency to set them wherever she happened to be when she finished with them. Trophies and relics of the captain's previous life hung from the walls, most encased in glass frames. Weapons were common pieces. A bed large enough for two people rested in the back beside the door that led to a balcony.

Cassidy considered what she would do with so large a cabin if she had her own ship. She had grown used to living economically with Nieves and Lierre, and even the notion of having the crew cabin to herself, like Kek had, was beyond her.

In the drawer of a writing desk near the back of the room, Cassidy found the purse they had set aside to use for the docking fees. She spilled it out in her palm, whistling at the amount. Twelve gold ravens and six iron phoenixes. An iron coin was worth ten gold coins of the same weight, so there was no way she could split them evenly between four people, so instead she divided the gold as instructed, set one iron coin for each of the crew and left the remaining two for the captain.

She put her share in her purse and assigned each of the remainders to different pockets on her person, then joined the others in the cargo room. Two large trunks and a couple of crates had been moved to the front, and Nieves and Lierre were bringing two more.

"This crap is heavy," Kek whined, sitting on one of the trunks to catch his breath.

"Is it now?" Cassidy asked, reaching into her pocket. "I don't suppose you'll appreciate this added weight then, will you?" She handed Kek his share of coin.

"What's the occasion?" he asked, looking into the glittering pile.

"Apparently someone already took care of the docking fee," Cassidy told him. "Captain told me to share the spoils."

Lierre dropped her crate beside Kek's trunk. "She's always so generous," Lierre praised as she accepted her handful of coins. Looking at the handsome amount, she added, "How long was the captain looking to dock?"

"No kidding," said Nieves. "I know prices have gone up since last year, but this is ridiculous."

"She probably just wanted to be ready for any surprises," said Cassidy. I'll be right back to help get this stuff moved," she added before retreating. The captain was sitting on the gunwale reading a broadsheet — probably local news — though her eyes looked unfocused. "Captain, these are yours!" Cassidy called to get her attention. She didn't toss the coins until the captain's attention was fully on her.

Looking at the coins, she looked up at Cassidy. "Whatever for?" She sounded genuinely confused.

"You said to split the fee evenly," Cassidy told her. "That's the remainder we couldn't split."

"Oh," she replied, pocketing them. "Thank you, Cassy." With that she returned to whatever she was reading, and Cassidy returned to help the others.

With all the cargo at the front of the room ready to be moved, Cassidy bent to start with one of the trunks. She picked up one side, Kek the other, and she realized immediately that Kek had not been lying about the weight.

They dropped it by the gangplank, Lierre and Nieves close behind them with the second. The crates were mercifully much lighter, though by no means comfortably so. It took a few trips, but eventually they had all the cargo lined up.

"Alright, Cassidy, you go tell the clients that their cargo has arrived, and —" she hesitated when she saw two men approaching the ship. They wore short, black coats with asymmetrical, green silk capes that hung off one shoulder and under the other arm. *The Royal Guard? Here?* Cassidy wondered. As the captain moved to greet them, Cassidy followed.

"Elyia Asier?" One of them asked. He was a man of middle age, his beard graying slightly. He had a scar that ran from the end of his nose over his lip.

"*Captain* Elyia Asier," she corrected.

"Of course, Madam," the man said with an apologetic bow. "Titles aside, we must ask you come with us."

The captain crossed her arms. "On what charges?"

"No charges," the guard assured her, holding up his hands. "We aren't representing the law here. But we were told to tell you — what was it?"

The other guard, a younger man, scratched his stubble with a gloved hand. "We were told to tell you there would be amber peonies."

"Right, that was it. We were told you would know what that meant."

The captain withdrew her hand from her weapon. "Very well. Change of plans; Cassy, you'll stay here until all the cargo is picked up. Kek will be the runner. Once it's all collected, or if anything's not picked up by sundown, you're free to go for the night." She handed Cassidy a folded piece of parchment from her coat.

"Aye, Captain." It was a copy of the list of contacts for the pickups.

Cassidy watched her go with the Royal Guards. The way she walked, with her head high and her stride confident, Cassidy might have thought they were *her* personal guards.

Kek stepped up to her. "What was that about?"

"No idea," Cassidy admitted. "Sorry, Kek, but you've got work to do."

He looked crestfallen. "What's that?"

"Nothing major," Cassidy promised, "but I'm stuck here to make the trades, so you've got to tell the owners their cargo's in. Once you've told them all, you're free to run off."

"Aye," he said with a sigh. Cassidy handed him the list.

"Lierre, Nieves, you're free to go," she said. "We meet at the *Dog's Watch* later, right?"

Nieves nodded. "Kek thinks he can win his coins back from me," she said, walking up to him, nudging him in the ribs with her elbow.

"I've got a plan!" Kek insisted. Lierre chased after, and the three soon fell out of earshot, leaving Cassidy alone. As she had the night before, she reflected on her dreams. Unlike before, however, she knew she could not dismiss them. They were far too lucid, far too real. And the captain's comment about dreams of the Fae not really being dreams stuck with her.

"I promise to protect you to the limits of my power," she whispered aloud, recalling the Fae's inverted eyes glowing that fierce red. She wondered what those limits were, for both of them. In her

46

dream – if she could call it that, anymore – Cassidy had forced Hymn to make a deal that benefited them both equally, as the captain had suggested, but she had no idea what she had actually agreed to.

It occurred to Cassidy that she may have heaped *more* onto herself, as she still did not know what a Fae might need protection *from*. Dealings with the Fae seldom ended well for the mortals involved, or so the stories often said. She could not recall a single story when they did. She was almost certain she had never heard one *to* recall. And then there were the legal issues to consider. She placed her hand gingerly against her throat as the thought of dropping from the gallows bored into her skull.

CHAPTER SIX

Zayne would have given his left arm if it would get him out of the desert any faster. As it was, the Scorpion was flying full speed ahead, and he refused to look back until the shadow and carnage of the Dragons' Nest was far, far behind him. He didn't even step away from the helm until he could see the ocean on the horizon. It was late in the day by that point, and his eyes were heavy. He sat down on the port gunwale and buried his face in his hands.

He was alone on the deck and was grateful for the temporary solitude.

Suicidal. *That was the word she used, wasn't it?* Zayne reflected. He forced himself to laugh. It was hollow, but it's all he had at the moment. He'd done 'suicidal' jobs before, but that was not the problem. In the past, 'suicidal' just meant 'really hard'. This time, Dardan really was feeding him to the Dread Hounds.

He reached into his coat pocket and extracted an apple. He took a bite, the softened fruit crumbled dryly under his teeth.

Maybe I could be a farmer, he thought to himself. It was a dangerous enough profession to keep him from getting *too* bored, and he already had the ship. *I could fake my death, change the ship name, and give it a new paint job. Something respectable, like the* World Tree *or* Giver. Would the crew go for that? He could not just send them on their way if they didn't; they would run crying the truth to Dardan before Zayne could say 'good riddance.'

I could always kill them, Zayne considered, looking down at the apple between bites. He could see the tracks of his teeth along the inside of its flesh. *No, Nanette wouldn't like that.* He could hear her now, saying something like, *You're the captain of this vessel, you're supposed to look after them, not kill them.* And she'd probably remind him every day until one of them died.

"Fae-touched woman!" He cursed, rising to his feet to throw the apple remains as far into the desert as he could.

"Losing another argument to me in your head?" Nanette called. He turned to see her climbing the steps from the deck below.

"Yeah," he admitted, sitting back down but avoiding her gaze.

"You shouldn't take it out on the food, you know," she told him, sitting beside him. Zayne noticed she had applied a fresh coat of perfume — the scent of a desert flower, the name of which eluded him. "Apples are very expensive. So, what was I telling you?"

"That I'm supposed to be looking after this nest of bilge rats, rather than killing them."

Nanette nodded. "I am full of sage and useful advice," she said evenly. "So, why were you thinking of killing them?"

"What would you say to the idea of being a farmer?" Zayne asked, evading the question while he could. "Or a fishing woman?"

"Dangerous work. And either one would bring us much too close to the ground, for far too often." She folded her arms. "This is about the job, isn't it?"

"Aye," he answered, turning his body to look out at the desert behind them.

"However expendable she claims you are," she said disdainfully, "you and I both know you're a vital part of this band. You're the best captain she's got."

"Lancen is far cleverer, and Ject is more accomplished, and Nyrien is favored," Zayne replied.

"Lancen is a coward, not clever," Nanette said coolly. "And once we get this job done, you'll cast an inescapable shadow over Nyrien and Ject."

Zayne snorted derisively and stared out at the expansive desert. He thought back to his brief encounter with Hawkwind, and the question he had posed himself just before meeting her. *If things had been different, would it have been me unknowingly waving my future murderer along?* But things *hadn't* been different, and as such, he was the murderer and Hawkwind was the soldier.

CHAPTER SEVEN

The day passed slowly. Most of their clients had unloaded their goods within a couple hours, but Cassidy was left waiting for what felt like the rest of the day for the last delivery. Out of boredom, she struck up a conversation with one of the guards stationed on the wharf — he had been a friendly sort, though she learned more than she ever cared to about the man's wife and daughter and the schools on this side of the city. After a time, however, his shift ended, and he was replaced. The woman taking his place wasn't rude or callous, but she didn't seem comfortable with prolonged conversation, so Cassidy started walking the deck to keep moving. She practiced the acrobatic jumps and tumbles she had once been taught by a group of performers she had met in Melfine. It passed the time, but not nearly as well as she would have liked.

The sun was low in the sky, glowing orange and red like a wildfire before the last client finally arrived. He was a plump, balding, bespectacled man, wearing an obscenely rich coat that did not come close to fitting his girth. Accompanying him were two much younger, taller gentlemen with admirable figures: one was richly tanned with shoulder-length black hair. The other had a lighter complexion and shorn blond hair. Both wore their sleek overcoats open with no shirt underneath, showcasing their smooth, muscular frames. Cassidy had to refrain from making a low whistle, settling for a smile.

"Are you Mendrin?" She called down as they drew near, trying to keep her eyes on the overdressed man. However, the way he managed to look down his nose at her despite being on lower ground seemed like permission to feast her eyes on his employees instead.

"*Lord Cobinth* Mendrin," the man corrected. His voice was nasally, and he spoke breathily with an odd inflection that grated on Cassidy's nerves. "My family is quite significant and influential here in the Capital! In fact, my cousin's wife's mother was nearly the Champion of the previous Empress, you know! And my younger brother's fiancé is an attendant of one of the Empress' handmaidens!" Behind him, Cassidy could see his employees mouthing along with the words and making overly dramatic poses. It took all her self-control to keep a straight face. "Now, then, is this the, *uh*, ship called, *ahem*, the *Dreamscape Voyager*?"

"Aye, this is her," Cassidy said, caressing the railing affectionately. "Best ship in the skies."

"Yes, yes, spare me your life story," Mendrin said, waving his wrists to speed her along. "You have cargo from the Barony of Cielhal, do you not?"

Cassidy raised her eyebrow but said nothing about his manners, or the fact that the Empire didn't recognize Cielhal – or any other territory – as a *barony*. "Of course, it's right here. Ten iron marks for delivery."

"Ten! That's outrageous! Scandalous, in fact!"

Cassidy folded her arms. "Do you know what lives in the skies between Cielhal and Revehaven, Cob?" The man sputtered. Cassidy wasn't sure whether it was to protest the nickname she had devised or because he wasn't used to being talked back to, but she didn't give him the chance to interrupt. "Basilisks," she said, holding up one finger, adding another with each subsequent threat, "phoenixes, manticores, wyverns, pirates, harpies, and *dragons!*" Putting her hands down, she leaned over the bow, staring the man down. "Lives are risked out in those skies, and if you don't respect that we ask for compensation, maybe you should buy your own damn boat and make the trip yourself!"

"You—, I'll report— I'll! You'll—" the man fumed. The way his face reddened brought Cassidy's mind back to her dream of Hymn, and how her dress had shifted in color in much the same way. Where the Fae had been unparalleled in her beauty, however, the pompous noble before her was nothing short of a medical nightmare with thick, purple veins straining against thin, reddening skin. "Fine, Nyuran take you! You!" he snapped at his men, "Pay this thief and bring my property back to the rickshaw!" He handed off his purse to the longer-haired gentleman, and the pair climbed the gangplank to meet her.

"Right over here, boys," she said, eying them both appreciatively. She was pleased to notice they were returning the favor. When the blond reached for the trunk, she put her foot on it to hold it down and held out her hand.

The other man laughed. "Don't worry, we aren't going to run off without paying you," he said, spilling coins out of the purse into his rather large hands.

"I don't trust your boss," Cassidy said evenly, counting the coins as they spilled out. Once the money made its way into her pockets, she made him sign the manifest. She watched enthusiastically as they hoisted the chest by either end and carried it off the ship.

Once she was alone, she returned to the captain's cabin, closing the mahogany door behind her. She removed a false panel from the inside of the door, taking from it the long-necked iron key. She ducked under the writing desk, sliding a well-read copy of *Legends and Truth of the Fae* out of her way. She pulled up one of the floorboards to reveal a second hidden cavity, this one containing a small chest. The key clicked in the chest three times before it popped open.

Cassidy poured the iron into the chest, the coins clinking loudly as they were added to the pile. She did the math in her head to write down later. After locking the chest, with another three clicks as she turned the key the opposite way, she tucked the chest back in its hiding place.

She yawned and stretched. Finally, the day was done, and she was free to depart. Flooded with a sudden vigor, she decided to forgo the gangplank and jumped down to the wharf from the gunwale, diving into a roll when her feet made contact. A guard standing nearby jumped and reached for his sword.

"Easy, there, kiddo," she said with a smirk, though the guard didn't look much younger than herself. "Just getting some exercise. The *Dog's Watch* is that way, right?" she said, pointing a short way down a nearby street. She didn't need to ask – it was her favorite bar in the city – but she wanted to get the guard to lighten up and talk. He didn't. Instead, he merely nodded dumbly. She gave him a sympathetic smile. "Don't work too hard," she offered, turning around. She immediately turned back, "Unless someone tries to steal that ship. Then I want you to work harder than you've ever worked in your life!" The nervous look on his face made her giggle, and she ran along Peddler's Street.

Peddler's Street had an official name, but Cassidy could not be bothered to remember it. Everyone, local or otherwise, called it Peddler's Street, due to the numerous merchant stalls lined up in doorways and on the corners of alleyways. As she walked the crowds, she heard vendors hocking goods that alleged to be from every corner of the world. Some were real treasures, while others were impressive forgeries.

"You! Sailor from Dawnhal!" someone shouted at her.

Cassidy stopped abruptly to find an older woman sitting on a stoop wearing a garish, silk turban of a dozen bright colors on her head, and equally varied gemstones draping over her wrinkled forehead. *A fortuneteller*, she concluded.

"You'll have to do better if you want my business," Cassidy told her snidely. "Red hair like this," she said, twirling a strand around her finger, "with dark skin like mine, of course I'm from Dawnhal. You'll have to dig a little deeper if you want to awe *anyone* with your 'visionary powers.'"

The first time Cassidy had made port in Revehaven, she had been conned by a fortuneteller who had correctly guessed her favorite food and the name of her childhood pet. Cassidy realized six months later – in a moment of idle reflection on the other side of the world – that the fortuneteller had probably overheard Cassidy tell Captain Asier about those things earlier in the day. So, she had lost money that could have gone to a good meal, and all she had to show for it were vague statements about the future, which probably could have applied to anything if she remembered them.

"So cynical," the woman said with a smile. Her accent was thick, vaguely Rivien, her voice deep and smoky. "I would like to read you, child," she said. "But fret not; for you, I would do it free of charge."

Cassidy raised an eyebrow and considered. She had never heard of a fortuneteller, or anyone on Peddler's Street, doing a job for nothing. She dismissed it as a crafty way of getting publicity. "No, thank you, I have some friends to meet in town."

"That's a shame, I was hoping to read a girl who made a deal with the Fae."

Cassidy stopped dead in her tracks and looked around to see if anyone else had heard that. No one so much as glanced at them. Cassidy moved to the woman's stoop as she got to her feet and invited her inside.

"Madame Venitha," she introduced herself, ushering Cassidy through the doorway.

It was exactly what Cassidy expected from a fortune teller's hovel; a small living area had been stripped of all conventional furnishings save two small, overly padded stools and a table, atop which rested a glass ball, inside which sat a candle. Thin silks of various colors were draped across the room, strategically placed in front of candles to create the illusion of otherworldly color. The façade was already weak, but it fell even flatter in comparison to the actual Fae realm Cassidy was almost certain it was trying to impersonate.

Still, somehow, she knew about Cassidy's deal with Hymn. She sat down at the table opposite the fortuneteller. "How do you know?" Cassidy demanded.

The fortuneteller leaned in over the ball. "I could see it in your eyes the moment you walked by."

Cassidy began to grind her teeth. She wasn't sure if she was angrier at this charlatan for wasting her time or herself for buying into it, or worse for confessing – if only to this one woman – that she had consorted with all that was considered evil and wrong in the world.

"My eyes have been different colors since the day I was born," Cassidy snapped. People often remarked that she must have been Fae-touched because of them, though as she got older people stopped vocalizing such thoughts. *Still*, she thought, *I should have known that was what this was about sooner.*

"Yes, yes," the woman replied dismissively, "your left eye is green like your mother's eyes." She almost sounded impatient. Amidst her surprise, Cassidy noticed the woman wasn't as old as she had initially thought; she was wearing makeup to appear wizened when she was middle-aged at most. "And your father's eyes were a light brown bordering on yellow, which is reflected in your other eye."

Cassidy sat with her mouth agape.

"I was not referring to the coloration," said Venitha. "Though, I suppose I could see why you would assume so. I imagine you had no shortage of rocks hurled at you as a little girl." Cassidy nodded to acknowledge the statement; it was and accurate, and not so unusual in smaller cities. "No, there's more to your eyes, dear. An intensity. A vitality. To someone with my talent, it is like a bonfire on a clear night."

Part of Cassidy's mind wanted to dismiss the woman, but she had already proven she knew more than she should. "So, what does this 'bonfire' tell you?" she found herself asking.

The older woman smiled. "Give me your hand, child," she said. Cassidy hesitantly presented her right hand, palming one of her pistols with her left, her thumb on the hammer. If the older woman noticed Cassidy's actions as she took her hand, she gave no indication. There was an odd flicker of green light by her ear. Cassidy blinked. *What was that?* When she looked behind her, she saw green bottles on a shelf and berated herself for being so jumpy.

Cassidy felt a jolt of static when the fortuneteller's fingers brushed her own, causing them both to twitch. The other woman's hands were cold and bony. Cassidy heard a muffled whisper before she spoke. "You walk in the shadow of greatness," she said as her fingers traced the lines in Cassidy's hand. "You have it in you to be greater still, but you must be vigilant not to linger in the comfort of the shade." She moved her fingers in a spiral pattern starting from the center of Cassidy's palm and trailing outward.

"You will be brought low by a scorpion," she continued, "and its venom will consume you until the end of your days." Cassidy raised an eyebrow but said nothing. A frightened part of her was tempted to dismiss it as cryptic nonsense, to deny any kind of mysticism, but the fortuneteller had said enough to convince her she was the genuine article. And there was the fact that she wasn't paying so much as a copper token for the experience. So she decided not to be too rude and settled in to listen.

The fortune teller closed Cassidy's hand. "Yours is an interesting destiny," she said finally. "And we will meet again."

Cassidy raised an eyebrow. "That's it?"

"That's it," the fortune teller answered flatly. She stood up and pushed her chair in. "After all, you aren't paying me, so why should I tell you everything? Or anything?"

"But you're the one who volunteered!" Cassidy protested.

"I wanted to *read* you," the older woman reminded her, a sly smile twisting her lips. "I never promised my services. If you want to hear the rest, that will be five copper doves."

Cassidy opened her mouth to protest, but she supposed she hadn't been promised anything. She closed her mouth and glared at the woman, who wore a self-satisfied smirk.

"Go enjoy your evening, Cassandra," the woman said, leading Cassidy out the door.

"Wait, how did you —" she began, but the fortuneteller cut her off.

"After everything else, you think I wouldn't know your name?" she asked, all but shoving Cassidy out into the street. "We shall meet again, child," she repeated before slamming the door, leaving Cassidy alone on Peddler's Street.

Fae-touched woman, she thought to herself, nearly missing the irony. She realized then that she would have to find new insults, lest she spend the rest of her life unintentionally cursing herself. That was an unsettling and sobering thought. A miserable pit formed in her stomach.

She continued up the street unmolested, making her way toward the bar. The sign that swung over the door was a hand-painted plaque depicting a rather vicious dog with a pocket watch in its mouth. The paint seemed fresh, and the front door appeared to be made of a different, sturdier wood than the last time Cassidy had seen it. The blended aromas from ale and whiskey and smoke from inside accompanied the stenches of piss and sex that wafted into the streets, which filled Cassidy with an odd sense of nostalgia. Only after catching a whiff of the familiar smells did she pick up the sounds of an off-key harpsichord, a chorus of deplorably tuneless singers, and the general din she'd come to expect from the place.

She pushed the door open and entered and was soon greeted with varied cries of "Cassidy!" and "Cassy!" and "You bitch!" all of which she met with waves toward the general directions of the criers. The *Dog's Watch* was packed as ever, thick with smoke and the heat of crowded bodies.

It took Cassidy a few minutes to spot Kek, who sat at the corner of the bar with a busty, black-haired woman on his knee and a perky blonde woman leaning into him from the adjacent chair. Cassidy looked for Lierre and Nieves, preferring to settle with them so as not to interrupt Kek, but when she saw no sign of either, she navigated through the throng toward the blond gunner.

". . . shot right through three of the monsters' hearts in one blast," she heard him saying as she neared, holding his pistol up demonstratively. "Harpies? They don't scare me!"

Cassidy smiled to herself, shaking her head until she was close enough to draw their attention, and a cruel joke came to mind. She forced the sternest face she could muster, and in an accusatory tone she called out, "Kekarian Valani!" That caused Kek to whip his head toward her in confusion. "I can't believe what I'm seeing! You're gone six months, and rather than seeing your poor, sick wife, you come here to the bar to see your floozies? Jun will not be happy!" As if on cue, the women showering Kek with attention looked at one another before rising and walking away. Cassidy claimed the newly vacated seat next to her friend.

56

Vincent E. M. Thorn

"That was uncalled for!" Kek whined, turning his stool around and taking a swig of his ale.

"I needed some room," Cassidy said defensively, though she wasn't completely able to suppress her smirk. She looked toward the crowd and saw the women that Kek had been favoring had found a new mark; the blonde was cupping the front of the unsuspecting man's pants while the black-haired woman cupped his coin purse. "Besides, they didn't seem interested."

"They *could have been*," he protested. After another drink, he slammed his cup down. "Also, *Jun*?"

"What's wrong with Jun?" Cassidy asked.

"Too common," Kek replied with a dismissive flick of his wrist. "If you're going to tie me down, make her exotic!"

The bartender approached them. He was a bald man with a thick mustache that drooped past his chin, but with no beard to speak of. "Cassidy," he greeted her warmly, "honeyed mead, a box of smoke, and soup o' the day?"

"Aric, you always know what I want to hear," she replied, reaching into her purse and setting a silver falcon on the table. "And keep the mead flowing!" She turned back to Kek. "Exotic, huh?" she asked. "How about Arianne?"

Kek pursed his lips contemplatively and downed his drink. "I knew a girl named Arianne, back in Melfine. Cute, but her teeth were huge!"

The bartender set a pewter cup and a box of cigarettes by Cassidy's arm. The mead smelled wonderful, even amidst the multitude of scents.

"You're saying Arianne is not good enough because her teeth are big?" she asked, her voice rife with mock accusation, before taking a drink. "Fine. Josca?"

"No chance, but that reminds me," Kek replied, "I met an old woman named Josca a few streets over today, runs a menagerie of some sort, and she has raised the smallest spiders I've ever seen. They weren't much bigger than me!"

Cassidy raised an eyebrow. "Kek, a spider *egg* is bigger than you."

"I'm telling you, Cassy, she managed to grow them small, somehow."

"I can't imagine why anyone would want to keep spiders, I don't care how small they are," Cassidy muttered, taking a cigarette from the box. "Got a match?"

Kek shook his head.

"Where's Nieves?" she asked, looking around.

Kek craned his neck to try to see over the crowd, pointing toward the other side of the bar. Cassidy looked, surveying the crowd, and sure enough she saw her distinctly cut short black hair, followed soon by the rest of her. She appeared to be playing dice games against a man with a wide-brimmed black hat and a green coat.

"She's going to leave a few coins short," Cassidy said aloud.

"Are you kidding?" Kek replied. "I've never known Nieves to lose a dice game in her life. Have you?"

Cassidy shook her head. "Not yet," she admitted. "But she will tonight, to that man. I can feel it in my gut."

"Want to wager?"

Cassidy considered. She usually hated gambling, because she hated to lose, and she especially hated losing to her crew mates, who she would see the next morning. But she had a strong feeling.

"All of next week's cleaning duties say Nieves won't profit against the green-coat."

Kek raised his eyebrows. "You're on!" They clasped hands.

"Okay, so Nieves is gambling," Cassidy said. "Where's Lierre?"

"Last I saw, she was talking shop with some local mechanic," he answered. "And somehow that led to them going upstairs." He added in a much softer voice that Cassidy barely heard, "maybe I should start looking for engineer girls."

"And of course, I left my matches on the ship," Cassidy muttered.

"I can help with that," replied a deep, somewhat familiar voice. She turned to see one of Mendrin's men, the black-haired one. He held up a matchstick.

"Fancy seeing you here," she said, bringing the cigarette to her lips. He struck the match against the bar and lit it for her. She blew a billow of smoke to the side before thanking him.

"It's the least I could do," he replied, pulling up a stool next to her. "After all, beautiful women should not have to endure my uncle's rudeness."

"Cob is your uncle?" she asked, unable to hide her surprise.

That earned a laugh. "Sadly so. Malivai," he added by way of introduction. He offered his hand, and she took it with a smile.

"Malivai," she repeated. "Call me Cassidy. You don't take after your uncle, I see."

"I try not to," he told her with a warm chuckle. Cassidy tried to place his accent; it was *almost* Castilyn but tempered with Asarian. He'd probably lived in the Empire most of his life. "But enough about my misfortunes, what brings such a beautiful woman to this unfortunate place?"

"I happen to *like* it here," she told him. "You run into some interesting people," she added, leaning close.

There was a near-tavern wide cheer, "Asier!" followed by a series of individual shouts of "Elyia" and a few rude epitaphs. Cassidy spun in her stool to see the captain. She had a girl in tow, which was odd; Asier usually found her company with older women.

The captain looked around and quickly spotted Cassidy and Kek. "Cassidy Durant!" she half-shouted. She glanced sideways at Malivai and said, "Six months you've been gone, and you haven't even seen to your husband! What would he do if he saw you flirting with a random dock worker?" Cassidy sputtered incoherently.

Malivai cleared his throat. "I was just leaving, Madam," he said. He added to Cassidy, "It was nice meeting you." With that, he disappeared into the crowd. Kek was snickering.

"That was uncalled for," Cassidy whined.

"Sorry, but we need to talk."

Aric brought her a bowl of soup, and when he saw the captain, he threw his arms out as if to hug her but made no move to close the distance between them. "Captain Asier!" He shouted happily, "Welcome back! What'll you have? On the house!"

The captain smiled. "Grape brandy for me and my friend here," she said, referring to the girl. Cassidy examined the newcomer. She had long, black hair that framed a heart-shaped face, light bronze skin, and piercing blue almond-shaped eyes. Something about her struck Cassidy as unusual, and after a thorough look over, she realized what it was.

She's so clean! At least, her face and her hands were clean; no signs of dirt or sweat or calluses or even a chipped nail, but she was wearing a more typically marred coat and pants that didn't seem to fit her quite right.

"Who's the kid?" Kek asked. Cassidy took the opportunity to start eating.

The captain grabbed the girl by the shoulders and all but pushed her between herself and her crew mates. "This is my niece, Miria, and she's the newest addition to our crew."

Cassidy nearly choked on a piece of charred meat. She and Kek shared a glance, and he looked as dumbfounded as she felt. The crew hadn't changed since Nieves signed on nine years ago.

"Don't look so surprised, it's rude," the captain told them. Cassidy resumed eating but continued to examine the girl. Miria was a teenager, best Cassidy could tell, putting her at about the same age she and the rest of the crew had first signed on. But Cassidy was certain none of them ever looked so nervous and helpless. She looked like she was struggling to keep her head up.

"So, Miria," Cassidy said between bites, "what brings you under the wings of our beloved captain?"

The girl's eyes widened a little, as though she had not expected to be addressed. She looked over at the captain, who merely nodded. She turned back to Cassidy. She said something too quiet to hear, then after a few moments repeated herself just loudly enough to compete with the din. "She promised my mother years ago that I would be a member of her crew, once I was old enough to fly." She said no more.

Again, Cassidy and Kek traded looks, this time with a shared gleam of curiosity.

"Where are the others?" The captain asked. Cassidy pointed over the crowd to where Nieves was still tossing dice — she seemed angry and intent — and Kek pointed directly up to indicate Lierre was probably still upstairs. "We can wait to introduce them, then," Asier replied, though she sounded disappointed.

Cassidy put her bowl to her lips and downed the rest of her soup. "You're from the higher parts of the city, aren't you, Miria?"

The girl nodded quickly. "You could say that," she replied.

"Up near Clock Street?" Kek asked.

"Yes!" she answered enthusiastically. "Absolutely!"

"I knew a woman who lived on Clock Street, once," Kek told her nostalgically. "Threw me out of a window."

Miria looked confused, and a little frightened. "Why?" she squeaked.

"Well, it's a long story, but it all started the last time we docked here in Revehaven," Kek began.

Cassidy was eager to have a second chance at hearing the story, but a flicker in the corner of her eye pulled her attention away. She turned to see a silver-blue light outside the window, which cast a silhouette like a crooked a finger to beckon her outside. Looking around the tavern, no one else seemed to notice the sight. A burning prickle agitated the cut under her arm, and a tightness welled up in her chest.

"I'll be right back," she said to her companion, not listening for their replies as she wove out through the crowd. Once outside, she looked around and saw the glow of the light disappear around the corner of the building into an alleyway. She chased it down, her fingers on her pistol. The light led her around another corner, one she knew to be a dead end. She drew her weapon as she rounded the corner, aiming it directly at –

The light itself.

Cassidy stood in silence; her finger hovered over the trigger as her barrel pointed at a small ball of blue light floating in the air in front of her. The ball chimed like a bell several times before it shouted at her in a familiar voice. "Do not point that thing at me!"

Cassidy stared incredulously for a moment before lowering her gun. "Hymn?" she asked.

"Did you think I would be anyone else?" The Fae spirit asked.

"Last time I saw you, you were taller," Cassidy replied dumbly. The ball of light turned around slowly in one direction, then the other, revealing little wings, like those of a dragonfly. Cassidy squinted, barely able to discern a form in the light. She could see Hymn, though her dress seemed to emit an almost blinding silver and blue light, making her difficult to perceive. The Fae seemed to be examining herself.

"Yes, I do seem considerably shorter, now," she agreed.

Cassidy reached out a hand to touch Hymn, but she flew circles around her, eventually landing on the back of her hand. "I would rather you not try to grasp me, Cassandra," she said sternly.

"Sorry," she said awkwardly. "What are you doing here?"

"Looking for you."

Cassidy furrowed her brow. "I pieced that much out for myself, thanks," she said sharply. "Why?"

"I am here because of the deal we made," the Fae replied just as tersely.

Cassidy's mind was spinning, having a hard time believing that a Fae was standing on her hand in the middle of an alleyway in the Imperial Capital. It simply did not happen. And yet, here it was. She wasn't sure if her heart was beating too fast to follow or if it had stopped dead. It felt like both. Despite her overwhelmed confusion she managed to say, "I guess it would be hard for us to protect each other if we only saw each other when I slept."

"Indeed it would," the Fae acknowledged, and there was an edge to her voice, like she was talking to a child. It almost made Cassidy want to squash the little light with her other hand. She refrained, and Hymn continued in a much less patronizing tone. "I have been following you since the Silver River. Your ship is fast and covered in iron, however, so I only just caught up."

"All ships are covered in iron," she answered automatically.

"I have noticed that."

There was an awkward silence.

"So," Cassidy said after a moment, "you're just going to follow me around?"

"I find myself lacking in other choices," Hymn conceded. "I suspect simply being here will keep me away from my enemies, for the most part, so this is not the worst arrangement that could be made."

Cassidy raised her hand, causing the unsuspecting Faerie to wobble slightly. "So how can you hold up your end of the bargain?" She asked, eying her new tag-along. "I mean, you're smaller than my fist right now."

"I am quite capable of a great many things, Cassandra," the little ball of light said flatly, a tremor of red rippling across the blue for an instant. "You shall see as we travel together." She paused. "You may also notice some changes of to yourself as a result of our bond." The light became blue again.

"Changes?"

"I cannot say with certainty," Hymn replied slowly. "It is not the same for every union, and such things are very rare. My kind and yours seldom make lasting and involved contracts."

Cassidy nodded. "Yeah, all the stories I've heard of Fae dealings are quick trades or favors. But you say it does happen?"

"Clearly. You and I have formed such a union."

"Clever," Cassidy said, rolling her eyes. "I mean, there's a precedent, so you've seen this before?"

"I . . ." she paused. "I have never personally done this, so I cannot say."

From nearby, Cassidy heard the moaning of a man who had been sleeping in an empty crate.

"We can talk later," she decided. "I'm going back inside." She looked at Hymn, realizing the little ball of light would stick out and likely make a scene. "Would you wait —"

"I will not," the Fae said firmly. "It was not easy to catch up to you, I will not let you get away from me now."

Cassidy sighed. "Fine," she said, "but . . . can you . . . turn off this light? Or hide?"

Hymn floated quietly for a moment. Then she flew down the front of Cassidy's shirt.

"Hey!" Cassidy screamed, unprepared for the strange, tickling warmth that passed over her breasts and hovered beneath them. "Not there!"

The man who had been sleeping in the alley made a confused noise.

"There is nowhere else I can hide without being separated from you," Hymn insisted, her faint light peeking up from Cassidy's cleavage.

"This – but – no!" Cassidy sputtered, "This is indecent!" She reached for the Faerie, who returned to hovering a short distance in front of her.

"Do you have a better solution, Cassandra?"

"Cassidy," she insisted, scratching at her scalp again. Her nails tugged against the leather cord that kept her hair back. Then it struck her. She let her hair down, allowing it to drape over her shoulders and back. "Can you hide in here?" she suggested.

The Fae moved quickly again, vanishing in Cassidy's hair. She could feel Hymn sitting against the nape of her neck. The sailor had never thought herself ticklish, but it took remarkable self-control not to shiver and swat at the new addition to her personal space.

"This is not quite as good a place to hide as the inside of your shirt," she informed her. "However, if you are more comfortable with me here, it will have to do." Physically, Cassidy was actually *less* comfortable now, but there was still decency to think about.

"Alright, stay out of sight," Cassidy reminded her.

"I will do the best that I can, Cassandra."

"I told you to call me Cassidy."

"I said I would consider it."

Cassidy grunted, but said nothing more as she walked back to the tavern, trying not to appear too stiff and uncomfortable, and she was sure she was failing miserably. Walking with a Fae. *Next thing you know,* she thought to herself, *I'll have a pet dragon and have babies with a siren.* In an effort to alleviate her anxiety, she tried to think of the logistics of that.

When she returned to the *Watch*, she was greeted by several voices in the crowd that seemed to have forgotten her earlier entrance. She waved automatically at them and after navigating the crowd took her seat back at the bar.

"... woke up the next morning to Cassidy kicking me in the ribs," Kek said, pointing at Cassidy as she drew near.

She wanted to insist that she had only nudged him with her boot, but what she really wanted was to finish her cigarette. And maybe another. And after that, maybe the whole box, and partner it with all the mead in the bar. She found the cigarette she had been smoking sitting in an ashtray. It had gone out while she was away.

"Captain, can I get a light?" she asked.

"Cassy, I'm disappointed," Asier said with chuckle, reaching into her pockets. "Leaving the ship without matches! Next you'll tell me you —" she turned to look at Cassidy and stopped. "What is it?"

"What's what?" Cassidy said nervously.

"You look like you've seen a ghost," the captain said simply.

Kek turned his attention away from Miria and nodded. "Aye, she's right," he said, though he seemed to think it was funny. "You're shaking." He paused.

"I'm fine," Cassidy said, calmly as she could, though even she noticed the tension behind it. "Just been a long couple of days, that's all." Bringing the cigarette up to her mouth, she added, "so, a light?"

"I can help with that," bellowed a man from nearby. She turned in her stool to see a massive, square jawed sailor wearing a worn, brown jacket, with goggles on his head to hold back his wavy, red mane and highlight a crimson scar that smoothly traced his widow's peak. He was accompanied by two large, men wearing identical brown jackets.

"I see I left a nice, clean scar," Cassidy said, fingering her own forehead in reference. "Miria, this is Captain Jevar Altis. Or as we like to call him, Little Jev."

"But he's giant!" Miria squeaked.

That earned a raucous laughter from the three newcomers.

"Such a cute lass," Jev said after regaining his composure. "Finally expanding your crew, Asier? Or just replacing this piss pot?" He added, waving his hand in Kek's direction. Kek retorted with a rude, one-handed gesture, not even taking his mug away from his mouth.

"Kek's staying, so don't try and take him anywhere," the captain said, taking a swig of her drink.

"Wouldn't dream of it. I'd rather have your first mate."

"You know I'm not going to jump ships, Jev. So why are you here?" Cassidy asked flatly.

"I just wanted to apologize for how things ended between us last time," he told her.

Cassidy looked at his scar again. "Glad I was able to put some manners in that thick skull," she said, giving the man a mock punch to jaw.

"Not an easy thing," Little Jev admitted, "but we Dawnhal sailors got to stick together, eh?"

"I suppose so," Cassidy agreed, though in truth she never felt the need to tie herself to home. As far as she was concerned, the fact that they were both sailors did more to tie them together than the fact that they had the same hair.

"So, you said you needed a light?" Jev asked.

Cassidy looked at the cigarette still in her hand. "Oh, right, yes, sorry, thanks," she said as the older man struck a match. As he brought the flame close to her, it flared as if dropped in oil, catching Little Jev's sleeve on fire.

He screamed and stumbled back, crashing into a table where a group of scar-ridden men and women were playing a game of cards. The table collapsed under his weight, coins and cards went spilling in every direction. A cup of dark liquor dumped out on Jev's face.

When the red-haired man pushed himself to his feet, a bald woman with a tattoo of a naked rivermaid said something Cassidy could not hear and punched him square in the jaw, knocking him back into his friends.

"This, my dear," Cassidy heard Asier telling Miria, "is the beginning of what we call a 'tavern brawl.' It's an occupational hazard. Finish your drink quickly." Miria picked up her mug to obey just as one of Jev's crewmates slammed face first into the bar.

Jev's other friend roared and spread his arms wide as he tackled the bald woman, ensnaring both her and a man with biceps the size of tree trunks at the same time. The three of them crashed into a billiards player. Cassidy watched as the chaos rippled out, and the brawl erupted.

Asier, Cassidy, and Kek each placed two iron coins on Aric's bar. As Asier noted, bar fights weren't uncommon, and it paid to have the bartender vouch for you when the Watch came down. The tavern owner slipped the coins into in his pocket, offering a nod and sought safety under the bar.

Jev weaved around a burly man's fist until he tripped over Cassidy's stool. The attacker missed the falling Jev, and his fist flew straight for Cassidy's face. Cassidy caught the fist with both hands, just shy of hitting her in the nose, and Kek and Asier slammed the brute on either side of the head with their empty mugs. He dropped like a sack of potatoes. Cassidy kicked him in the nose for good measure.

A whirl of light passed across Cassidy's vision as someone attempted to swing a cue stick at her. The assailant fell haplessly to the floor. Cassidy kicked him once in the groin to stop him from getting up. A billiard ball flew at her face, but when she held her arms out to block it, it clacked as though struck, and its trajectory changed, lilting slightly upwards before falling harmlessly towards her. She grabbed the ball out of the air, confused.

"Hymn?" She asked quietly.

"Do not question me now," the Fae said sharply in her ear. "There is an attacker to your right."

Cassidy whipped her head to see who Hymn was talking about, finding a broad-shouldered woman with a body adorned in intricate tattoos taking a swing at her with an eager fist. Cassidy threw the black ball in her hand, striking the assailant in the knuckle. She recoiled in pain, but her momentum kept her going, so Cassidy struck her square in the jaw with her fist to stop her. Pain sent a shock that tingled up her arm and all along her spine.

"Pissing blight!" Cassidy yelled, shaking her hand. She stared at the woman, who was now flat on the floor. "What in the Mists is your face made of?"

"Behind you," Hymn told her.

Cassidy spun around in time take a heavy punch to the cheek, whipping her head to the side. She slipped on spilled drinks and tumbled over a fallen brawler. Her ribs struck one of the billiard tables as she stumbled away.

"Jump!" Hymn ordered. Before Cassidy could ask why, she saw a large shadow closing in on her, so she took a deep breath obeyed. What she had expected was scramble onto the table and out of the way. Instead, an explosive blast of air beneath her feet launched her directly over a falling man, who crashed bodily into the table and made it collapse.

She fell aimlessly and landed on something soft.

"Oomph!" It was Jev.

"Sorry," Cassidy grunted, though she wasn't sure she could be heard over the din. She picked herself and tried to get her bearings. The entire bar was in chaos, which was typical enough during a brawl. She stumbled around the fight, ducking the odd swing and made her way to the back stairs for a respite. She was disappointed. A man tumbled down the steps. He crashed hard into the wall at the bottom, and Cassidy realized he was shirtless and only wearing one shoe.

She looked up to see Lierre, her hair slightly disheveled and the left leg of her trousers half-tucked in her boot. She had an extra tool belt, too.

"Cassidy!" she called enthusiastically, offering a friendly wave. "Is that a fight I hear?"

"Aye," Cassidy said. She offered a look to the man Lierre had assaulted. He had a black eye marring an otherwise unremarkable face.

"That's good, I would hate to make a scene," she said, taking the steps and kicking her now-former paramour in the kidney, earning a groan.

"What did he do?"

"This bastard said I was *almost* as good as his *wife*!" Lierre answered, kicking him again, getting another groan. "The nerve!"

With the raucous brawl behind her, Cassidy couldn't pick out her friend's tone well enough to figure out if it had been the discovery that the man had a wife, or the unfavorable comparison that had set her off. She decided it didn't matter and asked, "Can I get a shot in?"

"Be my guest," Lierre replied, stepping back up one step. The air left the man's lungs when Cassidy's boot connected with his ribs.

Hymn jingled in Cassidy's ear. "Cassandra, move to the left!"

"Did you hear that?" Lierre asked looking around. Cassidy heeded the warning and pinned herself to the wall as someone swung a chair down on Lierre's injured love, inspiring a grunt that devolved into a gurgle.

Cassidy punched the man with the chair square in the nose, hearing a satisfying *crunch* as he fell back, though now both of her hands hurt. She cursed, shaking it off as Lierre gave one last kick to the man she'd thrown down the stairs.

"Let's regroup and get out of here," Cassidy suggested. "Preferably before the city guard shows up." Lierre nodded, and they clasped hands to charge into the fray. They soon found Kek. Someone had him gripped by the front of the shirt, slamming her fist repeatedly into his face.

"Kek!" Lierre called out, "Where's the captain?" Kek pointed vaguely behind them, toward the harpsichord, distracting the woman punching him long enough for Cassidy to punch her in the side of the head, laying her out.

Dusting himself off, Kek said, "I had that under control, you know."

"Yes, your face looks much better like this," Lierre agreed, a slight giggle bubbling up under her words.

"That looked awfully personal," Cassidy said, kicking the woman in the ribs as she tried to get up. "What'd you do, Kek?"

"I . . . may have accidentally found certain parts of her anatomy with careless hands," he answered defensively. He paused. "And my face. Tavern brawls are confusing, I get lost so easily."

"Cassandra, behind you," Hymn called.

"Did you hear that?" Kek asked.

"You hear it too, then?" Lierre asked in turn.

Cassidy whirled around in time to stop a large, bald man from stumbling back into her. She shoved him away forcefully.

"Seriously, Cass, what was that?" asked Lierre.

"Later," she answered automatically. "Where's the captain?"

"By the harpsichord. Didn't you see me point?"

As if on cue, the disjointed sound of something slamming multiple keys on the harpsichord broke through the din. Cassidy turned to see Asier bashing the face of a man with a half-shaved head into the instrument. Miria was crouching behind her.

Cassidy led her crew mates to their captain, Hymn calling out occasionally to lend instructions as they navigated the brawl.

"Captain!" Cassidy shouted as they drew near. The captain didn't seem to hear her, but when they met eyes, she dropped her victim flat on the floor.

Asier made a couple of hand signs. *Where's Nieves?*

Cassidy replied by shaking her head and shrugging. She wasn't too worried about Nieves; that girl never had the patience for a brawl and was likely outside waiting for them. Asier must have felt the same, because she nodded. She held up her middle, third, and small finger on her left hand and tapped them to her chin twice before grabbing a broken stool leg and smacking an attacker in the face with it.

"Through the back window," she relayed to Lierre. She then turned to Kek. "You and I are going to give the captain a path." Kek nodded.

"Cassandra, you must evade," Hymn called.

"Seriously, Cass, what the Mists is that?" Kek shouted at the same time Cassidy managed to say, "Evade—?" before a billiards cue smashed across the side of her face, throwing her to the ground.

Her skull reverberated, her eyes watering. Her vision was filled with spots. She pushed herself up to her knees and found herself face to face with Little Jev, who was pushing himself up out of a beer puddle beside her. He mumbled something at her that sounded vaguely like "What the piss, Durant?" but could just as easily have been incoherent slurs.

Someone picked her up by the shoulders and she felt the floor beneath her churn like a longboat in a storm. She hurled before looking up. She saw a blond bloom staring at her through the blur. "Mph ulgg nugghh," she said.

"Good talk, Cass," Kek said in her ear, though he sounded far away. She blinked away the tears and moaned. She found her feet and looked around. There was a warmth in her face.

"You are bleeding," Hymn whispered in her ear, "however, you have not been dealt any permanent damage."

Cassidy tried to speak only for a warm bubble of thick fluid to spill out over her lips. She coughed and the rest of the blood in her mouth spilled onto the floor. She thought the fight was winding down, but it might have been her imagination. Asier and the girl were slowly making their way through what remained of the fray toward her and Kek. Against the blurred and dizzy scene, Cassidy saw something that stood out in its odd clarity.

A bearded man with shorn black hair in a ragged, brown coat stalked behind Captain Asier. He shifted deliberately, and Cassidy saw the knife he pulled from an interior pocket. The world seemed to move with a deliberate slowness as she watched. The stranger turned to the captain, knife at the ready, while Asier was preoccupied with a drunk who had staggered in her way. Cassidy reached out blindly and grabbed something. It fit neatly in her hand. She threw it. A strange tinge of static bit her fingertips, realizing too late she had thrown a knife.

The blade spun gracefully through the air. The iron edge seemed to glow a faint red. Cassidy's heart raced. She reached out, as if she could undo her action, to stop the disaster she could see coming.

The blade *twitched* in its flight.

The wooden handle struck the attacker square in the temple, throwing him off balance with a loud grunt. The world seemed to quicken again. Cassidy sucked in a deep breath. She could have blinded, or killed, someone with that move.

"Nyuran's breath!" Kek exclaimed. "You just . . . .. He went down like a sandbag!"

Asier made her way over to them, unhindered by her would-be attacker, with Miria in tow. "Nice shot, Cassy," she praised offhandedly. "Let's get out of here."

Someone had already broken the window, so Cassidy climbed through it. Her wounded leg protested as she hit the cobblestones. Miria was prodded out by the captain, and Cassidy gingerly took her arm. The girl had a nervous air about her, but Cassidy was surprised to find she had a strong grip and didn't need much help. Kek was next, groaning. Asier came last, looking around.

Nieves was sitting on a nearby barrel in the lamplight while Lierre was pacing beside her. Seeing Cassidy and the others, they moved, and the group huddled close together. "Who's the girl?" Nieves asked at the same moment Lierre asked, "Are you okay?"

Asier put a hand on Miria's shoulder and smiled broadly. "The newest member of our little family," she said. "Miria, this Castilyn beauty is Lierre Myrlin, engineer extraordinaire," Lierre pretended to be modestly embarrassed, "and that angry looking woman behind her is Nieves Tarhant, the best damn sawbones you'll find outside of Rivien."

"Flattery, Captain?" Nieves asked with a hardly suppressed smirk.

The captain ignored the comment. "Ladies, this is Miria, my niece." Lierre gave the nervous girl a hug that threatened to smother her with her impressive bosom, and as soon as she released her — dizzy and disoriented — Nieves gave her a hearty handshake. "With that out of the way, I think we should get back home for the night. Lead the way, Mr. Valani." Kek nodded and began the trek back to the ship.

The captain patted Miria on the back to follow, casting a look at Cassidy that said *we need to talk*. When Lierre and Nieves departed, Asier tilted her head to beckon Cassidy to follow her. They put some distance from the tavern — not a minute too soon, as the local Watch was on the scene to break up the fights. After a few turns down unremarkable alleys, Asier leaned against the wall of an unlit house and crossed her arms under her breasts.

"That was some dangerous shit back there, Cassy," she said bluntly. "Show me."

A knot formed in Cassidy's stomach and her chest went cold. "'Show you,' Captain?"

"Don't play games," Asier said. "Show me the Fae."

Cassidy could feel a tingle on the back of her neck where Hymn was hiding.

"How'd you know?" Cassidy asked. She choked on the words, her throat feeling constricted.

"I know the signs. Three times, I told you." The captain uncrossed her arms and placed a reassuring hand on Cassidy's shoulder. "Cassidy," she said calmly, but seriously, "I'm not going to turn you in. You should know that by now. But I need to know we aren't in danger. Why is it following you?"

Cassidy looked at Asier's amber eyes. She looked worried, and that sent a shiver down Cassidy's spine. So she told her. She repeated what she'd said her about the first dream. She told her about the deal in the second. She told her about chasing Hymn down the alley and her insistence on staying close. All through the story, the captain had stared silently, intently, at her, her eyes urging Cassidy on every time she faltered in the telling.

". . . and that's when I came back to the tavern."

The captain's amber eyes burned like embers in the night, boring into Cassidy. The minute dragged on endlessly. Cassidy feared the captain would tell her she was no longer welcome on her ship, or that she had to die for consorting with the Fae — a high crime in any country. She had said she wouldn't report her, but that wasn't all encompassing. Tears threatened to spill as Cassidy waited for the verdict.

Asier finally relaxed her arms and sighed.

"Gods stay blind," she prayed softly. "You should have told me sooner. This is a lot to take in. I won't tell the others. But you should." The terror Cassidy felt must have been clear on her face because the

71

captain added, "No need to rush it. But it's better they hear it from you before they find out. Besides, we're family, Cassy. I understand it's scary; it's huge. But... think about it; what if it were Kek, rather than you?" She smiled, and Cassidy smiled too. She was right, of course. She always was. "Now, where is it — she — hiding? She must be close."

"It's okay, Hymn," Cassidy said. "You can trust the captain."

There was a moment of stillness before the brilliant, blue light emerged from beneath Cassidy's hair. Hymn floated just behind Cassidy's shoulder.

"So, *Hymn*," Asier said peering into the light. "Can't say I've ever heard of you."

"I would have been quite surprised if you had, Dreamscape Voyager."

Asier narrowed her eyes at the Fae for a moment. "That's my ship's name, not mine."

"To the Dreamscape, you are one and the same."

Cassidy raised an eyebrow at the Fae but was ignored.

"No matter," Asier said tightly. "I want to hear from your mouth that you are not a threat to my crew or myself."

"Every word Cassandra has told you has been truth," Hymn said. Cassidy could faintly see her crossing her arms through the light she emitted.

"You're dodging the request," Asier said. "Promise me you're not a threat to my crew, or you'll see firsthand what happened to Lucandri."

Hymn's ball of light flickered red, gone so quickly Cassidy might have missed it if she'd blinked. Cassidy felt a deep cold sink into her body. *Shit,* she thought dismally, *what happens if Hymn tries to get me to fulfill my oath by fighting the captain?* She would never turn on Asier, but she knew there would be consequences if the Fae pressed the issue. She just didn't know what those consequences would be, and that terrified her.

"I promise that I am not a threat to your crew, nor to yourself, Dreamscape Voyager," Hymn said stiffly, "so long as your crew and yourself are not threats to Cassandra or myself."

Cassidy felt sick. Hymn was pushing it, she was sure.

The captain, however, smiled easily and gave a small laugh. "Cassy is part of my crew," she said.

"I am no stranger to human greed," Hymn said. "Kin and kith are no promise of safety."

"A fair point," the captain conceded soberly. "Still, if you're with Cassy, you're on my side. Welcome aboard."

CHAPTER EIGHT

Zayne sat in the captain's cabin, pouring over the maps of Revehaven for what must have been the thousandth time. The Empress' palace sat under his tapping finger as he tried to get a sense of things. *Suicide*, Dardan had said. Gods, but that was putting it mildly.

There was a rap at the door.

"Enter," he called, not looking up. Karn stepped in, reaching to remove the hat he no longer possessed. He covered up the action by scratching at his balding, black hair.

"Captain," the deckhand said nervously, "Miss Nanette said you wanted to see me?"

Of course she did, Zayne thought bitterly. Since the incident at the nest, Karn had kept himself a deck away from Zayne. For his part, Zayne had been quite comfortable with the arrangement.

"Aye, I did," he lied. Annoyed as he was, he couldn't undermine Nanette's authority by contradicting her. "I wanted to apologize, Karn," he said, fighting the desire to gag as he said the words.

"You — you what, sir?" Karn looked positively confused. Zayne raised an eyebrow, considering the man. He was stocky and reasonably tall, though he hunched in an attempt to appear smaller. Balding and ragged as he was, Zayne might have pegged him as middle aged, but he wasn't even thirty. All told, he looked more like a vagrant than a mercenary.

"You heard me," Zayne said bluntly. "I am sorry about threatening to throw you overboard."

"It would have been in your rights," Karn murmured.

"Yes, it would," Zayne agreed. He hesitated. "But that doesn't make it acceptable behavior. Hence the apology. However, I expect you to exercise better judgment in the future."

Karn hesitated, then said, "Aye, sir."

"Good. Before you go, can you hand me one of those books? *The History of Revehaven?*"

"The what sir?"

"The book. *The History of Revehaven,*" Zayne answered flatly.

74

Karn stared at the stack of books on the shelf by the door. He seemed distressed, looking between them and Zayne frantically.

"Can't read, Karn?"

A pause. "No, Captain."

Zayne leaned back in his chair. "Oh." He had meant it as an insult, but if the poor bastard really couldn't read, that changed things. "Here I was, thinking Dardan assigned you here to spy and read my letters." He forced a chuckle, trying to pass it off as a joke. But the suspicion had been real.

"No, sir," Karn said.

Zayne sighed. "It's the one with the blue wooden cover." Karn lugged the fat tome over to Zayne's desk, dropping it with a *thud* on top of one of the sprawled maps. "Thank you, Karn. You may go, now."

"Aye, sir." He seemed to be in a hurry to leave.

The book was every bit as dull as it was massive. Zayne skimmed it quickly, looking for references to the Imperial Palace. He finally found a sketch of the external structure. The surrounding text mentioned the date construction began, then listed in almost fetishistic detail the births, deaths, marriages and expenses accrued during the almost three generations of its construction. But never once did it occur to the author to mention any functional characteristics of the place.

He'd wasted his time. He pushed the book aside and went out to the deck for air.

Nanette was at the helm. Her black long coat clung to her slender arms and back before billowing out at her hips. Her black hair was tied in a tight tail that started slightly above her head and ended just past her waist. Her sun-kissed skin was bathed in moonlight. Zayne admired the sight before approaching.

"Change of plans," he announced. "Adjust our course to Andaerhal."

Nanette gave him a sidelong look, and after consulting her compass, map, and wind-chart, turned the ship slightly to port. "May I ask why?"

"The Royal Family doesn't seem to be particularly forthcoming with their floor plan," Zayne said wearily.

"How rude of them," Nanette said dryly.

"I know!" Zayne fired back. "You'd think they'd want to be more accommodating of thieves and the like. Anyway, we can't do this blindly, so we need a better map."

"And you'll find one in Andaerhal?"

"The primary chapter of the Architects' Guild is in Andaerhal. They will have a copy. Maybe even the originals."

"Your plan is to steal from the Architect's Guild?" Nanette asked incredulously.

"Too much work," Zayne said with a dismissive flick of his wrist. "Besides, I probably wouldn't even know how to find anything in their library. My plan is for someone to hand me the plans. We'll be on the move before the day is out."

"Bold," Nanette said quietly. "Do you have a contact who can just *hand them to you?*"

"Not yet," Zayne answered reluctantly. "But that won't be a problem."

"If you say so. It's not far, so we should make it by dawn."

As Nanette had predicted, the *Scorpion* reached the city with the gray-pink dawn. Andaerhal was small, perched on the very edge of the Imperial Sea. The industrious town was built atop a lone mountain surrounded by lowlands and empty sea, rather than being cradled between several peaks the way most Imperial cities tended to be. Seen and smelled from a great distance were the smokestacks from the foundry district — Andaerhal was the cheapest source of many of the Empire's ironworks, due to its proximity to a chain of massive iron mines. More than a quarter of the people in the city worked those foundries, and suicide rates were high.

It wasn't long before they found an empty berth at the harbor. As soon as they made landfall, however, the *Scorpion* was greeted by no less than ten heavily armed members of the local port authority.

"I just love our reputation," Zayne said sardonically, thinking about the oversized portrayal of the desert goddess on the side of the ship. It was considered ill fortune to draw the attention of any of the gods, and painting the face of one on the side of one's ship was a surefire way to do it. The fact that the mercenary band he was stuck with was named 'The Daughters of Daen' probably didn't help matters. Only the wicked would invoke the gods thus, was the general opinion, and Daen was the most wicked of all.

Zayne was first down the gangplank, and he offered his documents without a word of complaint. The leader of the security detail took the papers with a sneer. "What's your business in Andaerhal, Mercenary?" he snapped.

"Shore leave," he answered, pulling the friendliest smile he could from his bag of tricks, and patting the man on the arm.

"Don't touch me, scum," the guard spat, and Zayne held his hands up in mock surrender, his smile waning only slightly. "Docking fee's gone up this morning, isn't that right, Gilly?"

An acne-ridden guard just shy of his middle ages snorted. "Exactly right, Caen," he said with a smirk. "Damn shame, too. If you'd have been here just a little earlier, you'd get in for a low rate of two silver falcons. Now it'll be six."

"That's quite the rise," Zayne said, affecting a disappointed tone. "Well, nothing to be done about it," he added, pretending to reach into his coin purse. He dropped the coins he'd stolen from the guard out of his sleeve into his palm. He looked at his hand. Seven silver coins only slightly larger than his thumbnail sat in his hand. He pulled one away and poured the rest into the guard's hand.

"Pleasure doing business with you," the man named Caen said as he handed Zayne back his papers and slipped coins back into the pocket Zayne had stolen them from.

"And with you, Officer," Zayne said, his smiling remaining until the guards entered the crowds of the docks. Nanette approached with her arms crossed under her breasts in a disapproving gesture.

"What'd it cost us?" she asked.

"They paid us a whole silver for the privilege of our ship gracing this pitiful harbor," he replied.

Nanette rolled her eyes. "Why do you insist on doing that?"

"Doing what?"

"Picking pockets," she said bluntly.

"It's a victimless crime," he argued. "Besides, they were trying to rob us. 'Docking fees just went up', indeed."

She raised an eyebrow.

"Don't give me that," he said. "Besides, it keeps my hands quick." He shrugged, weighing her purse in his hand to demonstrate.

She punched him.

"Ow!"

"You could have been quite a pickpocket back home," Nanette said sardonically. She retrieved her purse and offered Zayne a shake of her head.

"You know, for all my father liked to accuse me of being a thief," Zayne said as they began to stroll into the city, "I never stole a damn thing before the day he died."

"Yes, yes, I know," Nanette said wearily, "You just wanted to be a magician, you've said it a thousand times."

Zayne frowned, "Right, sorry."

Nanette sighed. "Don't worry about it."

As they left the harbor, Zayne asked, "Do you trust those three to guard the ship?"

Nanette folded her arms. "They're our crew," she said flatly. "Why?"

"I don't trust Dardan," he said, "Those three were assigned to us by Dardan."

"We had a shortage of crew; they needed a ship."

That was the story, but Zayne was still skeptical. "I'd still rather have a crew I can trust. Like what we had before Salaa and the others died." Nanette nodded. "I miss them," he continued. "Salaa especially. A damn fine captain. A good friend."

"That she was," Nanette agreed. She seemed to realize at the same time Zayne did that they were getting maudlin, and silently agreed to shut up about the past.

As they made their way through the city, they pretended to be interested in the local culture. Nanette would point out decent looking taverns, Zayne would make commentary on vendors and entertainers. It might have been unnecessary, but if any curious watchers had taken note of their arrival, Zayne wanted them to disregard them as tourists.

After meandering through crowded streets, the pair finally arrived at the House of the Architects Guild. It was the most grandiose building in the square, appropriately enough, though it seemed strange and culturally out of place; it was constructed of alabaster stone shaped into spires and arches, rather than a timber structure with tiered levels, and there didn't seem to be any pillars supporting the roof, at least on the outside. In all, it would look more at home in Castilyn than in the Empire.

There was a bookstore across the street, which Zayne and Nanette promptly ducked into. He pretended to be enthralled in a history about the Rivien Council of Princes, while she found herself a copy of *The Priest and the Gambler*, a story Zayne vaguely recalled from his childhood.

From over the tops of their books, Zayne and Nanette watched as petitioners and guild members filed in and out of the stone building. It wasn't hard to pick the architects from their clientele; the gray suits pinned with the guild emblem gave them away. As they watched the architects filing out, they would occasionally mumble remarks to one another: "He's too confident," "He looks too new," "Is that a bird's nest on her hat?" "Too happy," "Too noticeable."

After two hours of people-watching, they finally spotted the perfect mark; he was a spindly man on the brink of his middle ages. He looked dower enough to throw himself off the harbor. "You know the signal," Zayne said quickly. He rose from his seat and dropped Caen's last coin in the bookseller's hand. She handed him a handful of copper coins in exchange and he walked out with the book. He caught up with the spindly architect — which wasn't hard because he was shuffling his feet and didn't seem interested in going anywhere.

"Ah, yes, Uncle, it's so good to see you!" he called out, affecting a Castilyn accent, throwing and arm around the man's shoulders.

"What the—"

"What a pleasure it is, you're absolutely right," Zayne assured him as he guided him along the street. "You know, the Rivien people have an expression for days like today. 'Visit rarely and be more loved,' they say, but you know, I can't even begin to tell you how you've been missed of late."

"Who are you?" the man asked, and he was too confused to hold any anger in his voice.

"Oh, Uncle, can't you see the resemblance?" Zayne replied with a laugh, flicking his long, black hair with a flourish like a cape.

"You Sehra's boy?" he asked after a moment. Zayne merely shrugged and smiled. He guided the man to a tavern he and Nanette had picked out beforehand.

"Gods and nightingales," he said with a wistful sigh. "How long has it been?"

"Well, I don't —" Zayne all but pushed him into a seat. Sitting across from him, Zayne had a full view of the tavern while the old man's view consisted of the wall.

A rather buxom barmaid bounced over to their table. "What can I get for you, gentlemen?" she asked in a chipper voice.

The man across from Zayne stuttered slightly, eyes darting between Zayne, the waitress, the waitress' breasts, and back again.

"Don't be shy, Uncle," Zayne insisted, "I'm buying. Have whatever, it's such a joyous occasion!" Out of the corner of his eye he saw Nanette pick a table in the opposite corner, back to the wall like himself.

"I . . . I suppose I can enjoy a nice apple brandy," he conceded, though his voice was heavy with confused caution.

Zayne smiled warmly. "Make it two," he said. People always seemed more agreeable when you drank what they drank.

"Good choices!" the barmaid said. She leaned in a poor attempt at seduction. Well, it had the old man distracted well enough.

"You probably know what's best," Zayne said. "Two orders of whatever you recommend." She curtseyed and bobbed away.

The architect watched her intently as she went into the kitchen. He then turned back to his escort. "What's all this about?" he asked.

Zayne shrugged, saying, "You looked like you were having a rough day." And wasn't that just the understatement of the decade? "As for why I'm here, well . . . can't I just try to see my favorite uncle?"

The man looked uncertain. "I don't . . ."

He was interrupted by the return of the barmaid, who set two mugs on the table, her breasts threatening to escape from her low-cut top. Zayne kept his eyes in the cup, ignoring the churning in his stomach and the shadows in his mind.

Zayne reached into his purse and extracted a gold coin. "Keep it flowing," he said. He took a swig from his mug, though it tasted like swill and ash in his mouth. He spit it back into the cup and pantomimed taking a hearty gulp.

The old man kept trying to ask Zayne about his identity, and why he was there, but Zayne diverted him each time, pressuring the architect to talk about himself until eventually, around his third mug, he was ranting about the lack of artistry that had been plaguing the Architects Guild for years, how the guild's standards had been on the decline as they induct anyone with the coin rather than what he called 'the Eye', how he was pretty sure the reason his wife left him was that she had been sleeping with the guild master — "I could never prove it," he'd said, "but I saw that smirk of his" — with

Zayne merely nodding along. He offered the occasional sympathetic comment or outraged agreement, but otherwise, let him talk. When the food arrived, Zayne pecked at the fried hawk with a side of mushroom gravy. It was a very flavorless affair, but it was conventional, and a gave him something to do while his hostage prattled on.

Zayne eventually learned — through the architect referring to himself while recreating conversations with unflattering impressions of other people — that his name was Aden, and as the drinks flowed, he seemed to have come to the conclusion that Zayne's name was Haeden. He didn't much like the name, but at least the man had given in to Zayne's gaslighting. He was a taken aback at how quickly this tack was working.

When the man finally came to a pause, Zayne slammed a stripped leg bone on his pewter plate. "Those bastards," he declared, gauging his reaction by Aden's tone, rather than his words.

"Exactly so! Twenty-five years I've dedicated to the guild! Twenty-five! And what do I have to show for it?"

"Uncle Aden," Zayne said kindly, and Aden reacted to Zayne using his name with a look of warmth. Or maybe he was too drunk to feel anything else; Zayne could not be sure. "You are a brilliant man, and there are brighter days to come."

"You think so, boy?" Aden asked.

Zayne nodded. "Of course," he said. "Now, let's not be so down. To family!" he said, raising his mug. Aden didn't seem to notice Zayne hadn't even finished his first cup.

"To family!" the old man exclaimed. "You're a good lad. I know your mother always disapproved of me, but you don't seem too much like her."

"She could let jealousy get the best of her," Zayne said carefully.

Aden guffawed. "Indeed she could. You've really helped me today. Is there anything I can do to return the favor?"

"Funny you should mention it," Zayne said, lounging in his seat. "You have access to the full archives of the guild, right?"

"I do indeed."

"Well, I'm writing a book." The lie came to Zayne easily. "A grand tale of adventure and heroism. But I want it to be just right, and I'm having trouble writing a scene wherein the stalwart hero rescues the beautiful princess from the clutches of an evil tyrant. It keeps coming across as too hollow, too straightforward. I need to get a sense setting. Is there any chance that, maybe, you could get me a copy of the floor plans for the Imperial Palace?"

Aden's brows furrowed. He took a sip of his brandy. When he spoke again, his voice was sober and serious. "So, that's what this is about. You want into the palace. Are you an assassin, or just an overly ambitious thief?"

Zayne's pulse quickened. "Uncle, I —"

"Quit feeding me that lie," the older man said bluntly. "I didn't believe a word of it to start with; I may be old, but I'm no fool." His eyes, previously laced with sadness and drunkenness, were now sharp with anger.

Zayne placed a hand on one of his pistols, pulling back the hammer with a loud click. Aden must have noticed, because he breathed in sharply. Zayne dropped his fake accent. "I thought this was too easy. So, what will it take you to provide me with the plans?"

"Those plans are for the eyes of the Master Architects only," he said bluntly. "And I can imagine what a velvet-tongued liar like yourself would use them for."

Zayne felt a pang of guilt but didn't let it show. He thought about crafting another lie, but in the end, he decided to take a different approach. "What if I killed the Guild Master?"

Aden opened his mouth, probably to protest, but the words died in his mouth. Either he was drunk enough to consider Zayne's proposal, or his hatred of the Guild Master was enough to do it. Whichever it was, Zayne had his hooks in the man.

"Think about it," he said simply. "I can kill the man who has caused you so much grief, who has so brazenly *disrespected* you." He paused. "It would be easy. And no one would ever think of your role in it. All you need to do is give me a few sheets of parchment the world will never miss."

The man considered for a few minutes. "I suspect if I refuse, you'll just kill me," he said wearily.

"It's a possibility," Zayne agreed vaguely. He didn't relish the thought, but his choices were few; Aden couldn't be free to report him, after all. He watched the old man swallow the last of his brandy.

"You have a deal. *Nephew*."

Zayne cursed the moons. There was sparse cloud coverage, and Jiqun had only just begun to wane. As a result, bright light exposed him as he climbed the over-designed Guild House, using decorative trims and the stone gutters as handholds. He was able to duck in cover behind the occasional grotesque or decorative spire, but as he climbed, his black coat stuck out like a knife in a pincushion against the alabaster stone that defiantly reflected the moonlight.

Halfway up, he found an open window and quickly pulled himself inside. He turned back to ensure no one had spotted him and closed the window. He stood in a mostly bare office; several easels lined the wall, each with unfinished projects upon them, and a cramped desk had three chairs on either side of it, but otherwise it was wide, empty space.

It wasn't the Guild Master's office, so he moved on. He opened the door slowly to ensure no one was in the hall before he darted for the stairs at the end of the hall to his right. He kept one hand on his sword and drew one of his pistols with the other. The staircase was a steep and tight spiral, and after his previous climb, his legs were burning in protest. The door at the top was locked. Setting his gun aside, he reached into his coat to extract a pick. After a few moments of fiddling with the lock, he heard the gut-churning sound of the pick breaking. He muttered a handful of randomly chosen curses and slammed his shoulder into the door, which did nothing. Finally, he grabbed his pistol and blasted the lock off, doing his best to ignore the sudden ringing in his ears it caused.

So much for stealth, he thought to himself.

He kicked the door open to reveal the decently sized, well lit, and nicely furnished room beyond. An elderly man with half-circle spectacles sat behind a large oak desk. The man stared at Zayne with a steady expression. Seven guards in dark green capes – six men and a woman – stood in a line with pistols trained on Zayne.

The seated man adjusted his spectacles. "It would seem Master Aden was correct," he said conversationally. "The assassin has arrived."

"That *bastard*," Zayne spat. He eyed the guards. "You hired the Emerald Falcons for protection? I'm flattered. And on such short notice, too?" The Emerald Falcons were a guild of fighters, usually commissioned by traveling nobility. They were among the best paid mercenaries in the Empire, with a reputation to match. He had never seen them in action, and a pit formed in his stomach at the notion of fighting seven of them.

Zayne leaped back, pulling the door shut just in time to hear the deafening cracks of pistol fire. He crouched low and held his breath as the door above and around him had holes blasted in it, splinters showering in every direction.

He counted. Six shots. He couldn't wait for one of the others to reload, so he had to risk the seventh shooter. *Gods, please don't tell me they have more than one gun apiece,* he thought as he shouldered the door open.

He drew his second pistol and leveled it on the first man he saw. He pulled the trigger. He didn't check to see if the shot connected; he just threw the weapon at the next man in line, cracking him in the head. That man's pistol fired aimlessly, blasting a hole in a nearby drawing board.

Zayne drew his third pistol and fired, hitting the next Falcon in the hand, blowing it clean off his wrist. Once more, he threw his spent weapon, only for it to sail harmlessly off the mark.

Shit.

He drew his sword, a slim dueling blade with a cross-guard hilt. The remaining Falcons unsheathed their own, and Zayne could not help but notice how stylish their weapons were. Even at a glance, each was unique to the owner; some were gilded, and others were silver, but all intricately designed with swept hilts. He immediately wanted one.

He rushed at the man he had hit in the head, deftly blocking a too-weary slash. He reached out with his free hand and untied his opponent's belt. He ripped the leather strap free and retreated. The Falcon's scabbard and a few pouches fell to the floor, sending coins scattering across the floor. The man tripped gracelessly.

A more alert duelist dove at Zayne, blade poised for his chest. He lashed the belt like a whip, wrapping it around the end of his attacker's blade, and tugged it off course. He went for the opening, but the Falcon was ready and moved his body around Zayne's strike.

Zane let out a hiss as the Falcon's blade cut his hip. On an intellectual level he knew it wasn't a fatal strike. On a more primal level, however, he knew it hurt. A lot.

He stabbed blindly, feeling his sword punch through the Falcon's solar plexus. His body went limp, and as Zayne retracted the blade, it slumped on top of him.

He wanted to spew up when he felt that last burst of hot breath on his neck. He thought the blood pouring out on his hands would burn him. In the recesses of his mind, a dead woman stared up at him in terrified confusion. He shook the memory away and shoved the body to the floor.

He stepped out of the way of a slash that threatened to take his arm. He reached into a hidden pocket in his coat and threw the contents at his attacker. Copper and silver coins scattered in the air, glimmering in the light. The man flinched as they bounced off him. Zayne whipped his blade and slit his throat. Dark memories threatened to invade again, but his blood was up, and the battle swept his unwanted thoughts aside.

Before the Falcon could fall, Zane wrapped an arm around him and held his body tight to use as a shield. The woman and the newly one-handed man struck together from his left while the man with no belt and the last Falcon came around to attack from the right.

Zayne hurled the corpse at the woman, and his wound flared in pain. The body landed on her sword and she stagger into her partner. Zayne ducked beneath a slash and grabbed a fallen sword as he pinned the cape of the beltless man to the floor with his own.

He hefted the new blade, trying and failing to ignore the twinge in his side before he switched hands. "This is much nicer," he noted aloud. He didn't have much time to admire the weapon, however, before he nearly lost his head to an aggressive overhand strike. He jumped out of the way, the pain in his side bringing him to his knees upon landing.

He narrowly rolled out of the way of another strike. He narrowly parried blow after blow against a better-trained fighter as he fumbled around the room for something – anything – to give him an edge. He grabbed a candelabra with his free hand and swiped at the Falcon's cloak, catching fire to it. The man didn't seem to notice, so Zayne threw the candelabra aimlessly away, and searching desperately for a way not to die.

Slipping on his own blood, Zayne crashed to the floor. The burning Falcon stepped heavily on his chest, forcing the breath from him. By The man Zayne had pinned was free, having shed his cape, and the other two were on their feet as well. The man pressing down on Zayne had both hands on his weapon and was poised to bring the blade down on Zayne's face. *Daen, please don't let me die like this,* he prayed halfheartedly. *Not yet.*

The man's burning cape erupted into a full-blown conflagration. He panicked and dropped his sword. Zayne reached up and caught it by the blade, cutting his own hand in the process. The burning man flailed, so Zayne was able to throw him off and roll to his feet. He hissed as his wounds stung with fresh agony.

The Falcons had apparently split their attentions between him, their burning friend, and another fire that had started when Zayne had blindly thrown the candles. He allowed himself a wry laugh, but it died when the cut on his side stung again.

"Tagren, Luc," the woman shouted, "stamp Jainin out!"

Jainin. That name triggered old memories and sparked an ember of rage in Zayne's heart. The darkness pressed in on his mind again, and he saw the red haired woman again, her death mask seared into his eyes, only this time, another memory burned alongside it, one that made his blood boil and pushed his muscles forward, like a swig of bottled battle lust. He blindly barreled through the woman's attack as she tried to behead him. She fell hard to the floor with a crack.

The room was ablaze, now, and Zayne's opponents were little more than silhouettes against bright flames. With his stolen sword, he stabbed and slashed at the Falcons. As they fell, Zayne struck at the burning man. Though he could no longer make out the man's features through the flames, Zayne imagined oak red hair and beard and a self-important sneer. He knew he wasn't seeing the stranger even as he drove the sword into him again and again. He also knew it was senseless to keep attacking him. But the actions of his body were far away, the vibrations running up his arms with each slash and cut were flights of fancy, and his hammering pulse belonged to someone else, for all it mattered.

When Jainin stopped screaming, Zayne stopped. He fell to his knees and gasped for breath. The woman pushed herself up and roared as she moved to deliver the killing strike. He could only watch, drained as she came, thrusting her sword like a spear. He saw his reflection in the polished iron.

The charred floor gave way under her feet with a devastating *crack*. She disappeared and her sword skittered to Zayne's knees. He took it, sliding it into his sheathe – the blade was too long, but he could do nothing about it now. Wary of suffering the same fate as the Falcon, he crawled slowly to the desk, the other stolen sword still in hand. The Guild Master hid under the oak bulwark, trembling and holding his knees to his face.

"You," Zayne said between breaths. "Give me. The plans. To the Imperial Palace." The man continued to shake. "Aden. Betrayed us both. But I still need. Those plans."

The Architect didn't move, so Zayne stabbed him in chest. The body twitched when he pulled the blade out. He thought he could suppress the need, but with his battle lust fading, nothing quelled his revulsion to blood. He turned and spewed watery bile. The acrid smoke made it hard to catch his breath, and he started coughing. He coughed until he thought he would be sick again. He kept on heaving and coughing even as he crawled across the floor to a window. He felt for a latch. Unable to find one, he stood up into the stifling darkness as smashed the window. As the smoke poured out around him, he realized he couldn't escape that way. Even if he could see the ledge, anyone on the ground would be looking, now.

He crawled along the remaining floor, feeling for the strongest boards, and turned to the staircase. The stairs and most of the building were solid stone, and despite the numerous collections of paper and furniture, he guessed – hoped, really – that it wouldn't be too long before the fire ran out of fuel. The building would stand. More importantly, the records he wanted would probably be safe. Hopefully they were kept a vault. Pulling the door open, he heard a rumble that made his stomach drop out. A fist of raw heat slammed him in the back, sending him cascading down the stairs. He bounced heavily and painfully off wall and floor, down the spiraling staircase, stopping about halfway between floors. A gout of flame shot over his head, twitching like a dog's lapping tongue before flickering away. He forced himself up and ran.

He heard the clamoring of frantic, confused people roused unexpectedly from their rest. He passed a few guildsmen who were scrambling behind the crowds. When he made it to the main dormitories, he blended into the crowd as best he could. Despite the panic, the guild house had been built with multiple stairwells to prevent major congestion in case of an event just like this, and Zayne had no trouble blending into the crowd as they retreated downward, though it took him longer than he would have liked.

Once outside, he hugged the side of the building as he broke away from the small mob, escaping the notice of the Watchmen tasked with calming the growing crowd and assessing the situation. He limped through a tangle of alleyways before finding the back entrance of the tavern where he and Nanette had agreed to meet. He knocked twice. Twice more. Three times. Once. Nanette opened it.

"Did you really need to set a blasted fire?" she whispered before she took in his injuries. "A set up?"

"Yes, and yes," Zayne answered quietly as she ushered him to a stool, which he very slowly sat down on. The owners of the tavern didn't know they were there, and they intended to keep it that way. As a result, they had to work by moonlight. Nanette carefully brought a washbasin for Zayne to clean up. "Emerald Falcons," he said.

"Liar."

"Oh, am I?" He handed Nanette one of his new swords. She turned it over, admiring its gleam in the moonlight.

"I like it," she said casually, setting it aside delicately.

"Me too," Zayne answered. He pulled his coat and shirt off and took a spool and needle from one of his coat's hidden pockets. He fumbled with them due to his cut hand, and Nanette took them from him. She started by stitching up his sides. "We need – ah! – to find that little bastard and get those plans."

"So he told the Guild Master about the assassin, huh?"

"Probably figured if I failed, he'd be rewarded as a hero, or something. Considering the – ow! – Falcons, I doubt he expected me to win." Zayne sat in relative silence as Nanette finished up, giving only the occasional hiss. Once the job was done, Nanette wrapped his hand.

"Let's go, before the owner wakes up," she advised. Zayne nodded and the two of them moved into the street.

The fire brigade was on the scene, and while a thick billow of smoke slowly emanated from the Guild Master's tower, Zayne could see no other signs of fire. The crowd had mostly congregated across the street, and while some curious watchers had gathered, most were the architects, waiting until the Watch said it was safe for them to return to their home. Aden was easy enough to find. Like most people who didn't have practice hiding their guilty conscience, the backstabbing guildsmen lingered in the back of the crowd. Zayne nodded to Nanette, and they split up. When Nanette was a step behind Aden, Zayne approached from his side.

"Uncle Aden, I'm so *glad* you're okay," he said caustically. The man gave a little yelp that was cut short when Nanette placed a hand over his mouth and the two of them dragged him into an alleyway.

They found a perch that was deserted, save for a homeless tramp sleeping in the corner, and Nanette threw the architect to the ground. Zayne kicked the man in the same spot he himself had been cut. "I thought we had a deal, *Uncle*."

Zane expected him to say something along the lines of 'let me explain', or 'it wasn't my fault.' Aden, however, surprised him by tactlessly shouting, "How did you survive?"

"I had a lot of anger," Zayne said, narrowing his eyes. He kicked the man in the ribs.

"But the Falcons are —"

"Good, to be sure," Zayne interrupted. He sat on his haunches, feeling his nerves pull hard as he stretched his wounded side. He hoped the pain added to his intensity rather than detract from it. He loomed over Aden as much as he could. "They're also dead. Now I want you to listen to me very carefully, because I don't much like people who betray me. I did your job. So as soon as the Watch gives the all clear to return to the Guild, you and I are going into the Archives. You will give me the plans I asked for. And if you even think about betraying me again, I will kill you."

CHAPTER NINE

Cassidy walked with Miria along the bow of the *Dreamscape Voyager*. The girl was still nervous walking along the gunwale. She would occasionally look out to the ground far below the docks, invariably stepping back whenever she did. She had slept somewhat fitfully, too, commenting about dreams of falling. But it was her second day aboard and those moments were growing further and further apart, and she was learning the ship relatively quickly. Cassidy led her to the ladder to the lower deck.

"Even though you're not our engineer," she explained as they descended, "it's important you learn as much as you can about the job. Every member of the crew needs to be able to step into every position, just in case." Lierre was checking the propeller motors for obstructions when they found her. "Lierre," Cassidy called.

"Hey, Cassy," she answered without leaving her work. "Damn birds nesting in the mechanisms again."

"Perfect!" Cassidy exclaimed.

"Perfect?" Lierre turned to look at her. Her goggled face was smeared with soot and sludge, as were her arms and the exposed cleavage on her chest. "How hard did you hit your head the other night?"

"Pretty hard," Cassidy admitted. "But this isn't about that. Now's the perfect opportunity for you to show Miria the works."

"Ah, yes, Miria!" Lierre waved her over. "Put your goggles on, you don't want this in your eyes." Miria obeyed, and as Lierre turned her attention to the propeller, Cassidy went looking for Hymn.

The Fae was somewhere on board, Cassidy was sure, but finding her was difficult. A large portion of the ship was decorated with iron filigrees or plating, specifically because of threats of the Fae, so most nooks Cassidy could easily dismiss. Still, she had only seen her twice since coming aboard, and never when there was enough privacy to talk to her.

She climbed up to the aftcastle and sat down on the steps. The captain, Kek, and Nieves were all out for supplies. She scanned the deck, hoping to find Hymn's telltale blue glow. She finally spotted a glimmer in the space between two boards beside the starboard gun. She jumped down and knelt by it.

"There you are," she whispered.

"Yes," Hymn said dismally from inside her nook. "I am here."

"What's wrong?"

The light shifted from blue to a red and back. "I do not like it here," she said simply.

"In that hole?" Cassidy asked.

"In your world," Hymn snapped. "There is iron everywhere. Iron coats your ships, it is in your currency, it is even in some of your clothes, and not simply as armor or weapons, but as buttons or pins. Everything reeks of it."

"It was your choice to come here."

"You are wrong. I am here because it is the only way to protect you. The word of my kind is binding."

Cassidy peered into the hole for a moment. "Sure, but here's the thing; you made the deal with me. I didn't put a gun to your head."

Hymn was silent for a while. Cassidy was about to speak again when she finally answered. "Please leave me be."

"If we're going to be stuck together, we might as well be friends," Cassidy suggested.

"I do not require friendship to protect you, Cassandra," the Fae said. "Our bond is stifling enough as it is. So, I ask again, please leave me be."

Cassidy scowled at the glowing light. "Fine," she said, "be a bitch." Hymn's light flashed red for a moment but was blue again so quick she might have imagined it. Cassidy stormed off, offered a look to the overcast sky before returning below deck.

"– is why you always make sure every motor is clean and clear before takeoff," Lierre said. "This part should be able to spin freely, like so, when not in use."

"What's that sticky stuff?" Miria asked, her voice echoing in the works.

"Tar, mostly," Lierre explained. "It builds up pretty slowly from regular travel. But if we ever need a smokescreen, you can be damned sure it'll gunk up the whole thing." Miria pulled her face from the works, and her face was already almost as dirty as Lierre's. Comparing the soot-covered face before her with the pristine face she had met at the *Dog's Watch*, Cassidy couldn't help but laugh.

"What?" Miria asked, pulling her goggles up, leaving a section of clean, olive skin untouched by the surrounding grime, which made Cassidy laugh even harder. Lierre followed her gaze and joined in. Miria looked indignant until she saw Lierre's face, identical in its grime, and started to laugh as well.

She then took a handful of grime and wiped Cassidy's face with it. Cassidy let out a shocked gasp and Lierre emptied her own hand on the other side. "Hey!" She squealed. She slipped her gloves on and scooped up some tar and slapped Lierre with it, then Miria.

"Oh, no," Lierre cried sarcastically, "I am now dirty! Whatever will I do?"

Once the laughter subsided, Cassidy had Miria help clear out all the motors while she went to ready the storeroom. As she made it up to the deck, she heard a call.

"Excuse me, Miss Durant?"

Cassidy made her way over to the gunwale. She hadn't been expecting any callers. She looked down at the dock below to find Malivai standing on the docks. He was wearing a shirt today, which was a bit of a disappointment, but it was tight enough to be forgiven.

"Malivai," she greeted him with a smile. "What brings you here?"

"I wanted to apologize for any . . . uncomfortable advances I made the other night," he called up awkwardly. "It was not my intention to insult a married woman."

Cassidy raised her eyebrow, then started to laugh. "Oh, right that. Look, could you come up here? I don't want to shout over the docks."

The man nodded and made his way up the gangplank.

"Now first thing," she said with a smirk, closing the distance between them. "I'm not married. Never was. That was just my captain making a bad joke to get me and my crew mate alone."

"Oh," Malivai said, clearly torn between relief and humiliated confusion.

"Second of all," she said, easing her arms under her breasts, swaying in what she hoped was a seductive manner. "I wasn't at all offended."

"Ah, well, good," he said. He cleared his throat. "In that case, how would you like to join me at the opera house tonight? There's going to be a performance of *The Priest and the Gambler*, and the performers are all from Rivien."

"Ooh," Cassidy cooed, "an opera. I don't get invited to anything fancy like that very often. But I'm afraid we're setting sail today, just as soon as Captain Asier gives the order."

"That's disappointing," he replied.

"It is. But... *maybe* we can do something right now that would keep you in my thoughts during the long voyage to Nasradaan?"

"That's, er, very tempting, Miss Durant," Malivai said awkwardly.

"Cassidy," she corrected.

"Cassidy," he agreed. "Very tempting, but you seem to be, um, busy."

She raised an eyebrow at that. "Pardon?"

Malivai ran a fingertip along his cheek. Cassidy repeated the gesture and smeared engine grease and tar along her face.

"Oh, right, that," she said with a chuckle. "In that case, maybe next time I come back to Revehaven?"

"Maybe so."

"Cassidy?" Miria called from below. She climbed up the ladder quickly, and she seemed to be in a panic. "There's a bird! Lierre said to get you!"

Cassidy sighed. "Duty calls," she said to Malivai, whose eyes seemed to be stuck on Miria, his mouth agape.

"Right, right," he said in a distracted tone, his gaze unflinching locked on the girl.

Cassidy scowled. "She's too young for you,'" she said, giving him a forceful shove. "I'm sure you can find your way ashore."

"Oh, sorry," he stammered, his face flushed. "I should... I better go."

She didn't watch him go as she stamped toward the ladder. "I'm sorry if I interrupted something," Miria said sheepishly, "but Lierre said it was really important!"

Cassidy took a deep breath before she started down after the girl. "Not your fault," she said. "Come on; let's take care of this thing."

When they arrived on the lower deck, they were greeted by the sight of Lierre brandishing a pipe wrench with both hands, swinging it wildly at an eagle roughly the size of a large dog. The eagle pecked tentatively at Lierre, who swatted at it with the wrench, both reaching just shy of their marks but giving no quarter.

Cassidy drew her sword in her left hand and her pistol in her right, pulling back the hammer as she raised it. "Alright, Lierre, I've got this." Lierre slowly backed away as Cassidy stepped between her and the avian aggressor. The bird squawked and Cassidy lunged, flicking the tip of her blade. The bird hopped back slightly and to the side to avoid the cut but didn't fly away. Cassidy swung at the beast, and it ducked under her strike with a graceful bob of its head. She kicked the unwelcome guest in the side, and it spread its wings and started flapping wildly, squawking in outrage. Cassidy skewered one wing and fired directly into its beak, blowing its head clean off. The body flopped unceremoniously onto the floor.

"Alright, then," she declared, holstering her gun. She pulled her sword from the wing and wiped it off. "Miria, have you ever plucked a bird?"

"Plucked?" the girl asked uncertainly.

"You know, pulled all its feathers out so we can cook it?"

"Oh. No, I haven't."

Several conversations with Miria had begun that way since her arrival. Cassidy was very tempted to ask what the girl *had* ever done before coming aboard. But the girl was a quick learner and always eager, so Cassidy couldn't bring herself to be annoyed. "Well, take it to the deck for now. Nieves and I will show you later. Then you can finish up with Lierre."

The girl offered a timid salute like the one Cassidy often snapped at the others, and Cassidy couldn't help but rustle her silky hair before departing – earning her a shout of protest.

Cassidy climbed back topside. She cleaned and reloaded her pistol before she returned to her original task of preparing the storeroom. By the time everything was in its proper place, Kek and Nieves had returned, each pulling a rickshaw full of supplies up the gangplank.

Kek stared briefly at the grime coating Cassidy's face, but said nothing about it. Nieves, however, asked, "Did you lose a fight with a factory?"

Cassidy snorted as she helped unload the supplies. "I'll have you know; I've never lost a fight with anyone or anything!"

"Except that time at the Ivory Tower in Melfine," Kek offered.

"Special circumstances," Cassidy argued.

"And the time we were boarded by those Rivien pirates," Nieves said.

"I was outnumbered," Cassidy said weakly.

"Or that time you stabbed *me* instead of the idiot you were dueling," Kek added.

"Okay, that one does not count!"

"I'm pretty sure you ended up on your ass after that mess," Nieves said. "So, I say it does."

"Oh, just piss off!" Cassidy sputtered even as she helped Nieves with the boxes of medical equipment. Once everything was situated, Kek started swabbing the deck while Cassidy cleaned her face and hands from the rain barrel strapped down next to the gunwale. She was just finishing up when the captain stepped aboard carrying several sheets of parchment.

"Kek, why are you swabbing?" she asked as she walked the deck. "I thought it was Cassidy's turn."

"Lost a bet," Kek said mournfully.

Asier looked like she was suppressing a laugh. "So she dropped the day's chores on you, eh?"

"All *week's* chores," Cassidy corrected. She looked at the stack of parchment in Asier's hands. "Are those the trade manifests?"

The captain nodded, handing them to Cassidy. Their cargo for this voyage consisted primarily of orders from various shops and businesses – everything from a few specially made clockwork trinkets to chests full of clothes woven by the best seamstresses in the capital – but they were also carrying personal effects, such as letters and gifts, from people trying to connect to friends and loved ones in Nasradaan, who didn't want to wait for the government's official postal service to make its rounds.

"Ten days of double duty," Asier mused loudly so Kek could hear her as he pushed the mop along the deck. "I hope it was worth it."

"I'm sure he thought it was a sure thing," Cassidy said genially.

Asier nodded. She dropped her voice to a whisper. "So, where's your *friend?*"

Cassidy's eyes drifted over to the nook she'd last seen Hymn residing in. "I think she might take offense at us calling her my friend," she said bitterly. "She seems to want to be left alone."

Asier looked at the spot where Cassidy was staring. "I wonder what was so terrible," she said, "that she would be so desperate."

"You mean to agree to my terms?"

"Exactly. The Fae are neither humble nor powerless. That she would turn to a human for protection suggests she was desperate."

"Yeah," Cassidy agreed. "She definitely seemed pretty desperate when she took my hand." She found herself unconsciously rubbing her bandaged wrist, and promptly tugged her sleeve down to stop herself. "She wanted to put me between herself and some vague enemy." That reminded her of something else Hymn had said. "What interest would Faeorn have in me?"

Asier tensed at Cassidy's mention of the name. "The gods delight in testing and tormenting mortals," she said after a moment's deliberation. "They may have just picked you out at random. And you've never been so pious as to hide from them."

Cassidy shrugged uncomfortably. "Makes as much sense as anything else," she conceded. "Wrong place wrong time?"

"Possible. Well, the whys and wherefores of gods aren't worth thinking about," Asier said as she took on a more casual tone. "Just keep to the skies and face whatever storms may blow, like we always do."

Cassidy nodded, trying not to let her worries get to her. "Aye, Captain."

"That's the spirit. Now, since your chores are taken care of, why don't you and Lierre get us ready to set sail?"

"Aye, aye, Captain." Cassidy approached the helm and spoke into the pipeline. "Lierre, get those engines hot."

"Aye, aye," came the response. A few minutes passed before the engineer called up again to announce the ship was ready to depart.

"If you're ready, Captain," she said with a smile.

Asier smiled back. "Get us out of here, Miss Durant." Cassidy saluted before heating up the balloon, enabling them to rise above the port. A flip of the telegraph caused the engines to churn and roar, the propeller blades causing the ship to fly astern. She guided around the patrol skiffs with minimal effort and aligned the bow with the open sky to the southeast before switching to standard speed ahead. A nearby trading vessel with a less-than-attentive pilot nearly smacked into their port side, but the *Dreamscape* was small and maneuverable enough that Cassidy managed to narrowly avoid the inevitable infraction. Even over the roar of both ships' engines and the noise of the harbor, Cassidy could hear the shouting of the other ship's captain. Whether she or the other pilot was the target of the curses she wasn't sure. She also found she didn't much care.

Once they cleared the traffic of ships at the docks, Cassidy slammed the telegraph to full ahead. Far below the valley at the base of Revehaven, a field of green stretched for miles, sweeping out until it reached the forest to the south and the mountains behind it. Cassidy caught Miria staring out at it, her hands clenching the gunwale tight as she leaned out, apparently seeing the vista from this perspective for the first time.

"Different than the view from Clock Street, isn't it?" Cassidy called to her over the roaring wind and engines.

The girl turned to Cassidy, her hands still holding onto the side as if for dear life. "What?" she asked, her brows furrowed in confusion. "Oh, right," she added. "It's so pretty."

Cassidy chuckled to herself.

"Now, now," the captain said with a smirk, "you acted just like that when I first took you away from Dawnhal." Cassidy looked back at Miria, staring breathlessly at the world below and silently acknowledged that she had. It was several minutes before the wonder seemed to settle in Miria. When she stepped back from the gunwale, Cassidy dropped them to standard speed and waved her over.

"Miria, why don't you fly us for a bit?"

"Me?" she asked nervously. "But I've never even been on a ship before. I don't –"

"Nothing to worry about," Cassidy said, stepping away from the helm. "I told you, you need to be able to step into any job," she added. When Miria awkwardly stepped up to the helm, Cassidy guided her hands to the wheel. "Very simple," she said, "turn it starboard to veer toward the starboard side, port to veer toward the port side."

Miria experimentally tugged the wheel and the ship shifted course slightly. "If it's that easy, why isn't everyone a pilot?" she asked after a moment.

"Oh, there's more to it, certainly," Cassidy said. "But, right now, with no obstructions, ships, or other threats in sight, it's really all you need to keep us on course." She tugged lightly on the cords for the balloon controls but didn't pull them. "This one," she said, tapping one, "heats up the air in the balloon, raising us up. This one," she tapped the other, "lets the air out and brings us down." She tapped on the telegraph. "This is labeled, though I argued getting it replaced with one written in Rivien to mess with you," she said with a smile. "If the lever is all the way up, that's full speed ahead. All the way down, full speed astern, and here in the middle –" she pulled the lever down one notch. After a moment, silence enveloped them. "– stops the engines.

"The more complicated aspects of flying stem less from equipment and more through what you know and what you feel," she said. "So, what I want you to focus on," she stood behind the girl and pointed over her shoulders, "is keeping the bow of the ship pointed directly at the point where those two mountains meet. I'll have you change speeds a few times, but I want you to focus on keeping us as straight as possible."

"Yes – um –"

"The correct way to acknowledge an order is to say 'aye, aye'," Cassidy advised. Captain Asier was not the most formal ship captain in the world, but there were certain protocols that she insisted on, if nothing else because she asserted that they were good habits.

"Aye, aye," Miria said. She gingerly pulled the lever to standard speed ahead, causing the engines to roar back to life and the propellers to savagely beat at the air. Cassidy looked at Asier, who stood behind her watching intently.

"I'm not used to teaching," she said defensively.

"You did very well, Cassy," the captain assured her. "Let's leave her to it for a while." Cassidy followed Asier up the aftcastle, where Nieves was keeping watch. "So, Nieves. What do you think of our newest crew mate?"

The sawbones turned to face the captain. "She's . . . earnest," she said, casting a look to the new girl. "May I speak freely?"

Asier crossed her arms and cocked her head. "Of course," though her tone suggested she would evaluate Nieves' words harshly.

Nieves noticed, so she spoke hesitantly. "Don't get me wrong, she's a nice girl and seems to legitimately want a place here. And she's not slow to pick up the trade," she added at the same time Cassidy noticed Miria correcting the ship's drift.

"Hurry up and get to the damn 'but'," the captain said impatiently, and despite not being the subject of her ire, Cassidy felt a sharp chill in her chest.

Nieves swallowed something in her throat. "It's just . . . Captain, I don't understand why she's here at all." Perhaps not wanting to risk angering the captain anymore, she added, "Not that I think she's unwelcome, Captain, I just thought we had a well-balanced crew already."

Cassidy realized she was holding her breath but was too scared to let it out. She had thought the same things Nieves was saying, but she wasn't about to voice such thoughts. Nieves herself looked like her pistol went off on its own accord. The captain, however, relaxed a little.

"I suppose I should have at least given you some warning," she said. "Fact of the matter is, this is a promise I made back when the *Dreamscape* came into my possession. I just had to wait until she grew old enough."

They each took to watching the skies, chatting amicably, first about how well Miria was adapting to her new home aboard the ship, then to what they were going to do in Nasradaan, and the political climate in the border city. As the sun reached its zenith, the captain ordered a full stop. Miria nearly jumped out of her skin at being addressed, but she did as she was ordered. The sudden quiet left Cassidy's ears ringing.

"Something wrong, Captain?" she asked, looking off the port side to see if Asier had spotted something.

"Nothing's wrong," Asier assured her. "Just feel like a couple of exercises are in order. Cassy, get Miria a pistol. Nieves, get the crate I stashed in the cargo."

"Aye, aye, Captain," they said simultaneously, running off the aftcastle. Cassidy followed Nieves into the cargo room, opened the supply locker, and took a pistol that looked identical to her own but with a rose worked into the metal. She also grabbed a powder horn, a cleaning rod, and a leather bag of shot. Nieves was sliding a crate along the floor.

"Oh, come on!" she heard Kek shout. "I just got this part of the deck cleaned!"

"Quit your bellyaching, Kek," Nieves said. "Honestly, what kind of gentleman doesn't help a lady with something like this?"

"Oh, because I'm a man I'm just good for moving heavy things? Sexist!"

Cassidy scuttled past their argument in time to see Kek helping despite his protests. She handed Miria the weapon. The girl held it in an open hand, as if it frightened her. That was a good start, Cassidy supposed. Unlike *some people,* she thought, shooting Kek a look even though he was too distracted to notice.

"You ever fired a gun?" she asked, suspecting she knew the answer. When Miria shook her head, she started walking her through the anatomy of the pistol. "Pretty basic," she promised. "The flint sits in here, so when you pull the hammer back it's sitting up like this," she said, demonstrating. "When you pull the trigger, it'll strike this part, sparking. The gunpowder inside will explode, firing the bullet. But, don't count on it waiting on you to pull the trigger. As my father once put it, 'every gun is a hateful thing, and wants nothing more than to kill whatever looks at it funny, so never point it at someone if you aren't entirely sure they wouldn't be better off with their brains on the outside.'" Miria visibly paled and nearly dropped the gun.

Cassidy caught it and added. "Careful. Dropping these things is a surefire way to . . . well, get them to fire. Now, this one's unloaded, but never count on that." She taught her the proper ways to hold the weapon, aim, and store it and the powder. Only when she was satisfied with how she could handle it did Cassidy show her how to load it.

"So, Captain," she asked. "What's our target?"

Asier approached the crate Nieves had been sent for and cracked it open. She extracted a bright, orange pumpkin a bit bigger than Cassidy's head.

"Nyuran's milk," breathed Lierre, who had come up during Cassidy's rundown. "That's a really expensive target." Cassidy nodded in agreement. Farming on lowland was dangerous for any crop due to the risk of attacks from the Fae and other creatures, but it was widely acknowledged that the months pumpkins could be harvested coincided with the Fae being at their most active. As a result, they cost a fortune. And here they had a whole crate full, and they were going to shoot them.

"Expensive, yes," the captain agreed. "But effective. Even at a distance you'll see the mess these make. Miria, take a step toward the railing." Hesitantly, the girl did so. "Kek, when I give the word, I want you to throw this as far as you can."

"Aye, Captain," Kek said. He looked like she'd asked him to throw his coin purse over the edge, and Cassidy couldn't blame him.

"Miria, you're going to do as Cassidy taught you and shoot it."

Miria nodded, then remembered to answer with, "Aye, aye, Captain."

"Now!"

Kek threw the massive gourd with both hands, letting it arc over the side. Miria held the pistol with shaking hands, following the pumpkin with the barrel, and fired. The crack echoed down to the valley and all around them. Smoke erupted from the weapon and set Miria to coughing. The pumpkin sailed gracefully to the ground without notice. Cassidy watched it career until it was just a tiny orange dot against the green, which then splattered into smaller, harder-to-see chunks.

"Not to worry, Miria," Asier assured her. "You can't expect to be a marksman after the first shot. Cassidy will get the next one, so watch how she does it." Miria nodded, and the captain shouted, "Now!" Kek threw another pumpkin, and Cassidy watched its arc and set up her shot, the barrel of her pistol resting on her right arm. As the target began to fall into her sights, she pulled the trigger. The shot rang out like the last one, echoing and making Cassidy's ears ring, but this one was accompanied by a sizable chunk of the pumpkin being obliterated and its innards flying in the breeze.

Miria stared quietly at it as it fell, and Cassidy was worried she would lose heart. Instead, she looked up at Cassidy and asked, "So you just focus on where it will be a full second later?"

"Exactly."

"Do you want me to reload, Captain?" she asked. Asier nodded and she began to reload. It took her longer than Cassidy, but she did it properly.

Asier shouted, "Now!" and Kek threw the next pumpkin. This time when Miria fired, she grazed the edge of the target, causing it to spin on its way down. "Better," the captain praised. "Remember, guns are unreliable the farther you are from your target, and the winds out here can make even a perfect shot veer off, so be sure you shoot quick, before it's too late." Miria reloaded again and Kek threw again. She missed that one but hit the next three. That satisfied the captain, who ordered the remaining pumpkins be saved for supper. "Now, put the gun someplace safe." Miria obeyed.

When she returned, Asier tossed her a sword. The girl caught it deftly and held it more gracefully than she had the gun. The captain passed one to Cassidy as well. It wasn't a proper duelist's weapon, but a training blade with dull edges and a safe point.

"Life out here is dangerous," the captain said, "and you probably won't have time to reload during a real fight. You'll use a sword a lot if you want to survive out here. You might even see some action in the cities. So, show me what you can do."

"Aye, aye, Captain," Miria said.

"Miria, don't hold back," the captain said. "Cassidy, same to you. At the ready."

Cassidy obeyed and sized up her opponent. Miria held her sword in the style favored by Imperial fighters, which was good for sweeping arcs. Cassidy, however, favored a style recognized in southern Castilyn, wherein she gripped a section of the hilt between her middle and forefinger, which focused on punching with the sword. Miria was right-handed, and if Cassidy's own experience was anything to go by, she'd likely never fought a left-handed opponent before.

Cassidy didn't want to hurt the girl, or humiliate or discourage her, so she decided to let the girl get a few shots in before ending it. She was considering moving her sword to her right hand when the captain said, "Begin!"

Miria moved like a bullet to clear the distance between them, her sword a flash of iron Cassidy barely saw coming. Cassidy blocked the strike, but Miria had already backed away and attacked at Cassidy's right. Cassidy found herself parrying a series of blows, each only in the nick of time, and she couldn't launch her own attack before the young girl moved again to strike.

Cassidy leaped back and swung at the girl's legs, but Miria practically danced away from her attack before putting Cassidy on the defensive again. She had severely underestimated the girl. She knew her sword well. A flash of blue shined at the edge of Cassidy's eyes and she felt a spark of static between her fingers and her sword. She stifled a cry and met Miria's attack with one of her own. Her heart beat so rapidly in her chest it hurt. Her perception slowed.

Cassidy swept the girl's feet with a kick, but Miria recovered gracefully and guided Cassidy's following thrust away before stabbing at Cassidy's ribs. Cassidy slammed her shoulder into Miria's to throw her off balance. Instead of following through with another attack, Cassidy broke off to take a deep breath. The girl was faster than her by a long way.

There was something strange about Miria's fighting style. Cassidy watched the girl circle and it clicked; she was fighting too clean. She didn't kick or throw a punch. In fact, she kept her left hand behind her back the entire time. As Miria slid past her guard, Cassidy grabbed the girl's arm and shoved her off, going for a strike. The girl gasped, but she recovered after only the slightest stumble and knocked Cassidy's sword away with a flick of her own. Cassidy raised the blade for a quick jab, and Miria tried the same. The practice blades met point to point, bending harshly as their forward momentum carried them forward. Another flash of blue light was accompanied by another jolt of static against her fingers. Miria's training sword snapped under the tension and Cassidy's smacked her in the shoulder, ending the bout.

Miria was panting like a dog, and Cassidy wanted to laugh, but she was breathing even harder. Kek, Lierre, and Nieves stared between the two of them, dumbstruck. The captain merely looked thoughtful.

As her vision swam, Cassidy had a thought she found silly: *So that's what she'd done before coming aboard.* She lost consciousness immediately after.

CHAPTER TEN

Cassidy woke to the chiming of tiny bells. She groaned as her eyes fluttered open, a brilliant blue light hovering in her vision. *Hymn,* she thought sullenly. Her muscles were aching, and her head was pounding. She listened to the sounds of churning engines and propellers and was grateful not to find herself in the Dreamscape, if nothing else. She checked her surroundings; she was in her bunk. Or, rather, she was in Lierre's again. She supposed no one wanted to put her dead weight on the top. She took a deep breath and swung her legs off the cot. No one had undressed her this time, which was a relief even though she was slick with sweat.

"Hymn," she repeated aloud. "What happened?"

The Fae wasted no time. "Your friends know about me, now."

Cassidy's eyes shot open. "Shit," she said. "How? Why?"

The ball of light floated aimlessly. She must have been looking for a safe place to sit, because she eventually settled on the bed across from Cassidy. "You are able to tap into reserves of power as a result of our bond," she said once she was situated. "During your battle with the one called Miria, you did so, perhaps unaware, to match her superior speed. Doing so pushed your body beyond what it was capable of doing, resulting in stress that left you deprived of air and energy –"

"So I passed out," Cassidy finished.

The ball of light momentarily turned red. Then it faded back to blue. "Yes. After that, I moved to ward you of any more attacks and sustain you, thus exposing myself."

"Aw," Cassidy cooed, "I'm touched."

"I did so to keep my word," Hymn said flatly.

"And now I'm over it," Cassidy said in the same tone.

"Your friends' reactions were interesting," Hymn said. "The one with golden hair, the one you call Kek, attempted to catch me and demanded to know what I had done to you. The Healer attempted to help him. The plump one clutched you and seemed on the verge of tears.

"The Dreamscape Voyager put a swift end to all of the commotion," she finished. "And here you are." Cassidy wasn't sure she would ever get used to hearing Asier called by the ship's name. She held her head in her hands, trying to think past the throbbing in her temples.

"How long was I out this time?" she asked.

"Less than one hour," Hymn replied. Whatever faint relief Cassidy felt at that news was promptly buried by realization. She hid her face in her hands and took a deep breath. *They know,* Cassidy thought. Asier had been right; she should have told them herself. She stood up and approached the door apprehensively; she knew what she would face on the other side: distrust, disgust, fear, resentment, accusations. She took another breath and readied for the worst.

She opened the door. Lierre wrapped her arms tightly around her, so tightly it sucked the wind out of her. "Oh, you poor dear!" she exclaimed. "The captain told us what happened! It must have been so frightening!"

Cassidy found she could hardly breathe. She returned Lierre's hug. "Yeah," she agreed vaguely. "I was definitely frightened."

Lierre stepped back and Nieves took her place in front of the door. She slapped Cassidy across the face and shouted, "What the fuck, Cass?" Before Cassidy could figure out if she should be contrite or slap her right back, she pulled Cassidy in for a hug as well. "We were so worried about you, you dumbass." Tears formed in Cassidy's eyes, and only partly because of how her face stung. Another pair of arms wrapped around her and Nieves. "Kek," Nieves said without moving, "I swear if your hands drift south, I'm going to throw you overboard."

"No promises," Kek replied, though he didn't sound like he meant it. "Cassidy, I don't think Nieves can handle another scare like that." Nieves growled. "Maybe you should stop, for her sake."

"Kek."

"Okay, okay," he said, "for all of our sakes."

Lierre rejoined the hug and Cassidy suddenly realized she couldn't move. She didn't even want to. Tears streamed down her face and yet all she could think about was how stupid she had been for thinking her friends would reject her.

"I'm so sorry," she said between gasps.

"Um, excuse me," called a small voice. Cassidy looked up and saw Miria awkwardly wringing her hands. "Captain Asier wishes to see you at the helm."

Cassidy pulled away from the others and wiped her eyes. She looked to the others and nodded. As the others moved up the ladder, Cassidy was left alone with Miria.

"You . . ." she hesitated. "You fight really well."

Miria's eyes widened. "Thank you," she said, just barely audible over the rumble of the engines. They walked to the ladder together. "I was angry, during the bout," she added. "I thought all your grabbing and kicking was cheating. But As – Captain Asier explained that out here, there is no swordplay."

"There's just survival," she and Cassidy finished in unison.

Cassidy nodded and motioned for Miria to climb ahead of her. "Everything out here is life and death," she said. "but that's not as bad as it sounds." She followed Miria up to the deck.

Once the whole crew was assembled around Asier, she brought the ship to halt. "Cassy," she said with a grin, "glad to see you decided to wake up today instead of next week."

"I like to keep you guessing," Cassidy replied. Kek chortled, though it seemed halfhearted.

The captain's smile faded as she looked at Miria. "You sure you want to do this?" she asked. All eyes turned to Miria, who nodded uncomfortably.

"Yes— er, aye, Captain," she said. "Cassidy had a secret taken from her, so it's only fair."

"You can't take it back when it's gone," the captain said with the slightest hint of a warning, but she seemed pleased all the same.

"I know," Miria replied. She paused, looking at each member of the crew. Curiosity itched in Cassidy's mind. "The reason Captain Asier took me on – and the reason I'm so . . . green," she paused again, swallowing something in her throat. *She's doing this on purpose,* Cassidy thought bitterly as her curiosity turned from an itch to a burning. Finally, the girl let out a deep breath. "My full name is Yushiro Miriaan, and I am the daughter of Empress Yushiro Shahira and heir to the Asarian Empire."

Cassidy stared dumbstruck for a moment. It wasn't that it was unthinkable. In fact, it made a certain kind of sense. Still, knowing Captain Asier was once in the employ of the Empress was one thing. Being told a member of her crew was the crowned princess of the entire Empire was much more difficult to comprehend. Cassidy was busy piecing together all the oddities that suddenly made sense when Kek started laughing.

"Damn, you almost had me!" he said with the slap of his knee. "You nailed the dramatic timing. How long were you and the captain planning that one?"

"Kekarian," Asier said sternly.

"Aye, Captain?"

The captain merely glared at him. Kek withdrew immediately.

"So," he said sheepishly, "she's really –"

"She is."

For her part, Miria, or Miriaan, looked like a weight had been lifted from her shoulders.

"That's where you learned to fight," Cassidy said dumbly.

"Yes," Miria acknowledged. "Er, I mean aye. Swordplay was the most enjoyable pastime at court, and I had nothing but time."

"You've been waiting for years to take on a bloody *princess*," Kek said, suddenly looking at Miria like he'd never seen a girl before.

"It was the cost of the ship," Asier said casually. "Now stop staring at the poor girl, it's rude."

Kek obeyed awkwardly, but Cassidy heard him whisper "The princess," in an awe-inspired tone.

"I hope this doesn't change things between us," Miria said.

"It won't," Asier assured her. She looked to the crew. "Will it?"

"No, Captain," Cassidy, Kek, Lierre, and Nieves all answered in harmonized unison. Cassidy added, "She's one of us, through and through." Miria smiled at that, and Cassidy clapped her on the shoulder.

"Now that that's settled," the captain announced, "let's get back on course."

CHAPTER ELEVEN

Zayne leaned back in his chair as he stared at the floor plans for the Imperial Palace. "*Suicidal,*" Zayne said with a wry laugh. "Maybe I should skip the mission and just hurl myself overboard," he said to the drawings. He dismissed the thought; despite his misgivings, he had a plan coming together. *A good plan,* he allowed himself to acknowledge. He was starting to think he could actually do it. Breaking into the most heavily guarded building in the Empire might even prove to be the easiest part. Getting *out* with the prize, however . . ..

There was a banging on the door and Jacques' voice called from the other side. "Captain, you'll want to see this."

Zayne frowned, rolled up the plans, and tucked them into a hidden compartment in his desk. He tried to think about what could be so important; Jacques would have been forthcoming about an attack or an Imperial patrol – at least, Zayne hoped he would. Maybe he was luring him out to a mutiny. He allowed himself a chuckle at the thought. Just in case, he grabbed an extra pistol from the desk and slid it into an interior pocket of his coat. Even that simple action tugged at his stitches and made his bruises ache.

Thinking himself ready for anything, he opened the door and set foot into the moonlight. The entire crew was gathered around the port side of the ship with their backs to him, so if it *was* a mutiny, it was the most poorly thought-out mutiny in history. Nanette held her spyglass.

"What's the attraction?" Zayne asked, pulling his coat on tighter to cover a shiver.

"Something strange," was all Nanette said.

Zayne approached cautiously, searching the horizon, and spotted what it was quickly enough. A massive ship, four decks tall, completely enclosed, and without weapons. It floated aimlessly in the sky like a bloated cloud. "A luxury cruiser," he noted.

"Aye," Nanette agreed. "But notice what's missing?"

Zayne stared at the ship. "No lights," he said. "No guard ships."

"And I'm not seeing any movement aboard, either," Nanette said, handing him the spyglass.

Zayne gave a cursory look to confirm her words. The ship was named the *Golden Duchess*. A luxury ship was bound to have a decent haul. "How's our time?" he asked.

"After the detour in Andaerhal," Nanette said, "I'd say we're about half a day behind where you wanted us, and we've still got the Black Gulch ahead of us."

"Another hour or two won't hurt anything," Zayne said. "Bring us in."

The other ship was drifting with the wind. When the *Scorpion* lined up with it, Zayne ordered Karn and Flea to tether the ships together. No one called for them to stop. No one stood on the deck. "Karn, Nanette, guard the ship. Jacques, Flea, we're going to investigate."

"And take the plunder, right, Captain?" Flea asked eagerly.

Zayne sighed. "Aye, we'll take the plunder if there's no one aboard. Or if they attack us, because fair's fair." He looked to his crew. "But I swear by Daen's fury if either of you *provoke* someone into attacking us, I will shoot you myself."

Flea nodded eagerly, while Jacques merely grunted in agreement. Zayne drew a pistol and waved for Flea to go first. Jacques followed him to the door of the aftcastle while Zayne observed the deck. His first assumption when faced with an abandoned ship in these parts would have been a harpy swarm. However, there was no blood, no signs of struggle. Not so much as a splinter out of place. He approached the telegraph. The ship had been flying at standard speed before the engines had gone still.

"Sweep for traps," Zayne advised. He himself searched for anything out of the ordinary. Well, aside from the lack of crew, passengers, or guards. All he found was a moderately-sized locket. He held it up to the moonlight. It was a cheap piece, made of shabby copper with no monogram, insignia, or even basic design. Inside was a painstakingly folded letter.

The letter was written in the flowing script of Rivien rather than the angular and exacting Imperial language. As Zayne read, he became convinced that whoever had written the letter was not Rivien himself and had probably used a very cheap translation book.

> *My Precious Ilham,*
> *I commit to the gods that your intention for our first reunion is prosperous. I have done as you have appealed, and*

brokered passage aboard the Yellow Duchess, *though it cost me dearly. We shall appropriate aboard and finally ignore the hate between our families.*
  Forever my love,
  Rune.

Zayne shook his head and tossed the note into the wind. *No clues there*, he decided. He supposed it would have been odd if the note *had* been an explanation of events. The parchment danced away from the ship and turned around, catching on the gunwale.

"All clear, Captain," Jacques said quietly.

Zayne eyed the door that would take them inside. His fingers itched beneath his gloves. Rubbing them nervously, he ordered Flea to take point – mostly because if things went bad, he'd rather sacrifice Flea in the event of an ambush – and they opened the door. They descended the stairs to the second deck, which consisted of a narrow corridor with another staircase at the far end. Nine doors lined the left side of the hallway, while only one interrupted the wall to their right.

Flea looked to Zayne, who nodded his head toward the lone door. The scrawny man clutched his pistol like he was afraid of dropping it. He took a deep breath. Then he flung the door open, waving his weapon in every direction. Nothing shot the idiot, and nobody screamed. Flea crawled inside and Zayne pressed himself to the wall, motioning for Jacques to do the same.

"All's clear, Captain," Flea whispered.

Zayne kept low and quiet as he entered the large room. His first impression was "pink." The curtains were pink. The walls were pink. There was a bed large enough for twelve people which was pink, and the scattered blankets and pillows were a different shade of pink. The *floor* was pink. The massive vanity by the wall was white, but the trimmings were very pink. Perhaps the only thing in the room that didn't fit the theme were the piles of clothes gathered at the foot of the bed. Trousers and skirts, blouses and dress shirts, corsets and waistcoats were all strewn about. Flea was already searching the pockets.

As with the deck and the corridor, there was no one in the room aside from the three of them. Zayne looked around. He felt an itch between his shoulder-blades.

"Next room," he whispered, crossing the hall. Flea stuffed his pockets with coins and pocket watches before stumbling across the hall. They opened the first door on that side. This room was less garish and spacious, no larger than an average bunk. The room contained a bookshelf, a writing desk, a feather bed with the covers only lightly disturbed, a rather expensive looking storage trunk, and a clock. A man's trousers – small clothes nested inside and belt still half-fastened – shirt, waistcoat and socks were piled beside the bed. Jacques was the first to start searching the pockets this time while Zayne looked at the books. They seemed the kind of books chosen by a host who wanted to cater to a lot of different tastes, but probably didn't read themselves; a book about the Castilyn War shared a shelf with an almanac of wind-charts and a collection of children's fables.

Jacques stood up quickly to stuff his pockets and kicked a book that had been hidden underneath the occupant's clothes. Zayne picked it up and examined the cover before flipping it open. The book was titled *Life Before the Skies* and was a theoretical account of what society was like prior to the invention of airships. Zayne stopped at a page that contained a detailed sketch of a man's reflection reaching out of a mirror to grab him when his back was turned. Despite being a mere drawing, the face of the thing in the picture emitted pure malice, and a chill ran down Zayne's body.

He slammed the book shut but couldn't shake the dread that clung to him like a cold sweat. He closed his eyes and saw the malicious face in the mirror. "Let's move on," he said. It took all his self-control to remain poised and confident.

The remaining rooms were little different. No signs of struggle, leaving the unsettling impression that the occupants had merely gotten up, stripped their clothes off, and wandered off. They approached the next set of stairs. Apprehension mixed with relief when Zayne heard whispers coming from below.

"Alright, just like before," Zayne said quietly. "Flea, you go first. Jacques will follow, and I'll guard the rear."

Flea scratched his head, listening to the sharp whispers. "All due respect, Captain," he said nervously, "but I ain't too fond of that order."

"Fine," Zayne said exasperatedly, "Jacques will go, you go in front of him, and I'll follow."

"Aye," Flea said nervously. "Wait, Captain, that's the same–"

"You're damn right it's the same bloody order," Zayne said. "And you'll follow it, or I leave you here."

Flea hung his head. "Aye, Aye." After five steps, the stairwell made a turn. Zayne waited until Flea disappeared around the corner before motioning Jacques to follow. He didn't hear any sudden gunshots, so he slowly crept after them. He found them crouched by a sealed door. The whispering on the other side seemed frantic. Zayne remained a few steps above and leveled a pistol.

"Open it," he ordered. Flea took a deep breath – an act Zayne found himself mirroring – and flung the door open. The whispering stopped. Beyond the doorway was thick with shadows. Rancid air rushed out to greet them. Flea looked to Zayne, who glared back at him, and stepped into the murky darkness. Jacques looked only a little more well composed, stopping to swallow something in his throat before following suit. Zayne took another deep breath and shook the image of the evil drawing from his mind. He followed his crew.

The room beyond the door was a spacious dining hall. Three grand tables sat in rows, bathed in the moonlight and buzzing with flies. Food sat on every plate in various stages of being eaten and covered with fat black flies. Zayne approached a hardly touched plate of spoiled meat. Forks, knives, and spoons were dropped haphazardly, the chairs all pushed away from the table gracelessly – with a few even toppled over – but the spread on the table was sitting static, as if merely forgotten.

"Ow!" Flea shouted. "Watch where you're walking, you fat-footed galoot!"

Zayne turned to see Flea standing quite by himself on the far side of the room, trying to break into a wine-cabinet. Jacques was still by the door removing a painting from the wall, presumably to look for a hidden safe or the like.

"What are you talking about, Flea?" Zayne asked, picking up a spoon and dropping it into the cold goo that once had been soup. The spoon didn't even sink at first.

"This lummox—" he started, but when he saw Jacques wasn't near him, he swallowed. "Nothing, Captain, just nervous." Zayne grunted in acknowledgment, doing his best not to give away how unnerved he was.

There was a loud crash. Zayne whirled toward the sound and pulled back the hammer of his pistol. Jacques had dropped the painting on the floor. Zayne cursed the man silently and stepped around the room. He found the servants entrance and stepped into the outer walkway. The engines were silent and cold, as he'd expected. He stepped down a set of stairs that led to the engineer's compartment. As with the rest of the ship, it was abandoned. The coal shovel lay on the floor next to the burner. There was a large stockpile still ready to be burned. It seemed the engineer had abandoned ship as readily as everyone else. He peered in the shadows and realized the coal-covered boot prints led right up to the gunwale.

"Piss and blight," Zayne whispered to himself, bracing himself against the nearest wall. *Mass suicide,* he concluded. He ran back up the steps and barged into the dining room, paying no heed to the stench. When he kicked the next door open, Flea nearly jumped out of his skin and Jacques fired his pistol at the floorboard. Zayne ignored them, marching down to the last level. A desire to get answers and get out overrode his sense of caution. His boots thudded loudly on each step.

The last corridor was ten rooms, five to each side. Zayne carried a pistol in each hand, now. He took a deep breath. He kicked the first door. The room inside was much like those upstairs, only larger. The bed was made, and the books were on the shelves, completely undisturbed. He kicked the next door across the hall. It was a mirrored scene, save for the blankets on the bed having been cast aside. He continued, not bothering to investigate each room like he had above. He knew what he was looking for, now. He hoped he wouldn't find it.

He kicked the seventh door in the sequence and stopped in the hallway. A candle-lit altar sat against the far wall where the up-turned bed had once resided. A marionette, complete with a bloody handprint over its mouth sat amidst the candles. In the puppet's hand was a planchette and in its lap was a spirit board. The room had an unsettling color to it; despite the orange fires of candlelight, there was a halo of purple and blue light touching every shadow.

"Captain, what's gotten–" Jacques started, but he stopped when he saw what Zayne was seeing.

"Captain? Jacques? Don't tell me you've gone dumb," Flea called, approaching. When he saw the room, he let out a girlish squeal and backed into the wall.

Zayne heard a whisper coming from the marionette. "Jacques? Flea?" he asked without turning from the room.

"Aye, Captain?" Jacques asked, his voice betraying the slightest tremor of discomfort.

"Empty your pockets of everything you've looted," Zayne ordered, staring at the puppet. It seemed to be staring back. "Now." To his great surprise, terror outweighed their greed and he suddenly heard the clatter of coins and pocket watches and other valuables hitting the floor. Zayne leveled one of his pistols at the marionette and found his hand shaking. His finger twitched on the trigger, and he found it heavier than he was accustomed to. The blood on the puppet's mouth started to resemble a beard, and the once featureless thing had a very familiar face.

Black-haired bastard, it whispered with its eyes. *You'll hang for it.* For a moment, Zayne wasn't on a ship at all, but in a house clear on the other side of the Empire, staring into the washroom, the body of a red-haired woman sprawled naked across the floor and covered in blood and deep gashes.

He pulled the trigger, breaking his trance. His first shot missed by a hair's width, causing one of the candles to flicker, but the second pistol rang true, striking the puppet in the forehead. It screamed as its face exploded in splinters and purple flames. The candles erupted into jets of fire. The walls caught fire. A banshee shriek rang out from the spirit board as the flames consumed the room.

"Run!" Zayne called, only to find when he turned around that Jacques and Flea were already at the stairs, tripping over one another. *My crew,* he thought sardonically. He followed suit, the flames spreading around him. The stairs started to crumble as he climbed the steps two at a time. The stairs collapsed in front of him as he moved toward the dining room. He leaped and caught the floor, pulling himself up. Smoke and flames left him near blind as he charged through the dining room. He slammed his thigh into a burning table.

He let out a yelp and charged, choking on the smoke. The ship groaned around him and the floor buckled. Zayne fell to his knees and crawled the rest of the way to the stairs. He scrambled up, only finding his feet when he reached the top. The fire spread from each of the rooms, but Zayne ignored them as he ran straight ahead. The flames licked at him, but he knew better than to fixate on that. At last he reached the deck. The *Scorpion* was still tethered to the larger ship, though Nanette was crouching over it with a dagger, ready to slice it at a moment's notice. She made eye contact with Zayne and in a distant part of his mind he registered her relief.

Perhaps unnecessarily or perhaps not, he jumped the last few feet onto his own ship and Nanette cut the rope. Zayne all but stumbled to the helm and slammed the ship's telegraph to full ahead. The *Scorpion*'s engines roared to life, and Zayne imagined the ship was eager to flee as he was. At long last, Zayne tried to catch his breath, only to break down in a fit of coughing and wheezing. His knees hit the deck.

Someone started hitting him with a coat. He opened his mouth so he could demand to know why when he realized he was on fire. After everything, he was too tired, too resigned to fight it. He almost lost consciousness before a sudden cold washed over him. He sat frozen and shivering as Nanette blasted his coat with an ice canister.

Now that the danger had past, he thought about the *Golden Duchess*. Someone had deliberately used Fae evil to kill everyone on board. He was sure if it would have affected them, too, given a chance. Maybe it had. Looking on that puppet, it had been like looking into the face of his father.

CHAPTER TWELVE

Eleven Years Earlier

Zayne's breath caught and his muscles tensed when the door finally opened. He looked at the clock through the crack in its glass frame and withheld a sigh. They had waited an hour, standing behind their chairs as expected, and the miserable drunk had barged into the house as if none of that mattered. He saw his mother release her own held breath while his brother and sister kept their heads down, staring at their empty plates.

"Welcome home, father," Zayne forced himself to say, unable to keep the bitterness from seeping into his words. His mother cast him a worried glare as the old man tossed his coat in the general direction of the stand and flopped into his chair. He put his feet on the table, mud splattering beneath them. His mother quickly walked around the table and wiped it away.

Jainin tapped his iron prosthetic fingers on the table, the way he always did when he was annoyed. And he was always annoyed. "Well, sit down."

Nanette was the fastest to obey, as though she were a lightning bolt. Cenn was only marginally slower, sitting still as a statue, his brown eyes wide with terror. Zayne obeyed at a calmer pace, trying to keep himself, and his father, in check.

The red-haired man tapped his iron fingers on the table hard enough to scratch the finish on the wood. "I've had a long day, woman," Jainin said, "hurry up!" The breath that wafted across the table smelled like a brewery.

Zayne interlocked his fingers and leaned into his hands to keep his scowl from showing. That backfired, however, when the old man's iron index and middle fingers struck against his elbow. He let out a sharp breath of pain.

"Elbows off the damn table, you ground-dwelling heathen!" Jainin said sourly.

Get your muddy feet off the damn table, you drunk shit-for-brains, Zayne wanted to shout. He looked to his mother, whose darkened, knowing eyes pleaded at him to stay silent. She removed the lid covering the pot. She carved at the meat — the man at the market said it was mutton and charged a great deal for it as a result, but Zayne had his doubts. It tasted suspiciously like basilisk meat. Then again, he'd never had mutton before, so *maybe* it just tasted the same — and set it on Jainin's plate, along with a ladle of carrots, turnips, and potatoes.

He took one bite and snorted. "It's cold."

Zayne's mother mouthed the beginnings of words as she looked for a delicate answer, but Zayne spoke first. "We thought you would be home an hour ago," he said, louder than he should have. He didn't even see his father's hand fly before it struck the side of his face, the cold iron hitting him just below his eye.

"One more outburst like that and you won't eat," Jainin warned him.

Nanette hopped out of her seat and walked over to him. "Are you okay, Zee?" she asked, putting her hand on his cheek.

"Sit back down!" their father demanded. The little girl all but jumped back to her seat.

"I'm okay, thank you Nettie," Zayne said with a forced smile. He dropped the smile the moment he turned away from her. Zayne raised his plate so his mother could reach it as she served, accepting his meal with a gracious, "Thank you, Mother." He took a bite and could not understand what Jainin was complaining about; the food was plenty warm.

"Where's my wine?" Jainin demanded after a few bites.

"I'll get it," Zayne's mother offered. Zayne could see her silently cursing herself for forgetting.

"Make one of the juniors do it, Malinda," his father retorted. "Sit down, already. You," he added, pointing at Cenn, "get me my damn wine." In his panic, Cenn dropped his fork on the floor as he rose, a small piece of meat skewered upon it, earning a disapproving grumble from their father.

"So how was your day, dear?" Malinda asked as she finally took her seat beside her husband, opposite Zayne.

"Dismal," Jainin said, "'every day I deal with delinquents like him," he pointed at Zayne with his thumb, not even deigning to look at him, "all with the notion they can do what they like. The ingrates should be grateful I don't send them all to the gallows!"

"Surely that's a bit harsh," she replied, her voice soothing and sympathetic.

"Harsh? No, every last one of those little blighters is a . . . is a blight! A blight on Dawnhal's integrity! . . . What's taking you so long?" he added at Cenn, who had to climb atop the counter to reach the wine shelf. The young boy dashed back to the table with a bottle in one hand and a glass in the other. He set the glass by Jainin's boots, pulled the cork stopper, and started pouring as the old man continued raving. "No respect for the law, any of them! Should just shoot them when they enter my courtroom. Especially the black-haired ones," he finished, and this time he did look at Zayne, his eyes narrow and filled with disdain for the fact that his eldest son was not his mirror image.

"What does hair color got to do with anything?" Cenn asked, not realizing he was overfilling the cup.

"Outsider blood with no respect for the laws and traditions of —" he noticed before Cenn that red wine was flowing over the edge of the glass. "Stop spilling the wine you little —" he kicked the wineglass over, causing it to crash to the floor with a sound that Zayne equated with his and his mother's hopes for a peaceful night. "Look what you made me do!" He said, planting his feet on the floor to rise.

Malinda scrambled to her feet as well, placing herself between Jainin's swinging hand and Cenn's face, getting smacked hard in the stomach.

Zayne heard his mother force a word out, disguised as a grunt, the moment she was struck, "Go." Zayne took his cue and rose, darting around the table behind her, picking up his little brother in the crook of his arm and reaching for his sister's hand with his free one.

"The fuck do you think you're going?" Jainin demanded, and Zayne felt something hard strike his back and heard the shattering of a plate, but he kept running, pulling his siblings close to his chest so their father's only available target was his back. Warm liquid struck his back a second before the supper pot struck the floor behind him, but he didn't stop. "Don't you run from me, Boy!"

Zayne reached the stairwell and was relieved to see the bedroom door already ajar. He pushed through and closed it with his body, holding it closed as the loud and angry pounding shook him. He didn't loosen his grip on his brother and sister, who in return had their arms wrapped firmly around him. He did, however, slump into a seated position.

"It was an accident," Cenn cried into Zayne's chest, soaking his shirt with tears and snot.

"I know," Zayne whispered as soothingly as he could, hoping he was heard over the sounds of the old man's fists on the door and the shouts of, 'Let me in, damn you!'

The door stopped shaking, only to be replaced by a sound that chilled Zayne to his core: his mother's cry of pain before several *thuds* down the stairs. "*Why do you get in the way, woman?*" Jainin shouted, his voice as clear as though he were in the room with them. Zayne could not hear his mother's reply, but he could guess it when the judge replied, "*Stop? Stop? Can't you say anything else? None of this would have happened if you hadn't got in the way! I must discipline my child!*"

There was another cry from their mother. It sounded far more distant than the shouts.

"*Do you want him to end up like your black-haired bastard?*"

There was another pause as Malinda replied.

"*The fuck he is! His hair is black as the night sky! I know he ain't my son! Don't you lie to me!*" Something heavy crashed into something else, the sound of breaking glass ringing out as if to compete for attention.

"It was an accident!" Cenn repeated, sobbing harder. Nanette was crying too, though her tears were silent and accompanied by more tremors.

"I know," Zayne said again, petting each of their backs. He took a deep breath. "Daen, strike that man down," he whispered. Cenn didn't seem to notice, but Nanette clutched his side.

"Zee, you mustn't!" she cried into his shoulder. "Mama says you mustn't ever call the gods for nothing!"

Zayne opened his mouth to argue, to tell his sister to stop being naive, to tell her that the attention of the gods would be worth it if it meant never again being subject to their father's rage. But then he closed it. She needed his support, not his derision. "You're right, Nan," he said, stroking her scalp. "I'm sorry."

The shouts grew incoherent, and eventually there was a stamping of boots down the stairs, and the door slammed.

"Alright, little ones," Zayne whispered, hoisting his siblings up. "It's time for bed." It was still early, but it was a testament to their fear that they didn't argue. He set them on the floor, and they crossed the rooms to their beds, where he tucked them in. "Mama needs my help to clean up," he told them. "But if you're still awake when I'm done, I'll read you a story, okay?" Cenn nodded enthusiastically and Nanette smiled in spite of her tear-reddened face.

"Tell us the one about how Elyia Asier saved Dawnhal!" pleaded his sister.

"I wanna hear one about monsters!" Cenn argued.

Zayne forced himself to smile. "Tell you what," he said, "I'll tell you about Asier saving us from monsters." He turned and let the smile fall from his face as he crept out of the room, seeing a broken vase at the head of the stairs. He picked up the larger shards delicately and made his way carefully down each step. His mother was gathering all the food from the floor. He knelt to help her. They worked in a relative silence, throwing the pieces of her hard-made meal back into the dented pot.

After they moved to scrubbing the floor, Zayne finally said. "We need to get out of here."

Malinda gave him the half-amused, half-suffering look she always did when he brought it up. It broke his heart to see her try to smile with a split lip, and her face was starting to swell and change color. "And go where, my dear?"

"Anywhere," Zayne said firmly. "Traders go to Melfine all the time. We could make a fresh start."

"With what money?" his mother retorted. Her tone was affectionate, if a little patronizing. "Your father keeps a tight grip on what he earns."

"I've been working down by the docks for months, now," Zayne informed her, "saving my coins, getting to know the ships. It won't be long before I can get us passage on a vessel bound for Melfine, or . . . literally anywhere but here."

"But Dawnhal is my home," Malinda argued.

Zayne wrung out his rag as he thought through his reply. "And it's always been mine, too," he said as he resumed scrubbing, "but we aren't even safe under our own roof, here." He took a deep breath, adding. "The twins are almost six. We can't keep taking the blows for them forever." Saying that reminded his body of the plate that struck his back. He reached back as best he could, but the muscles felt swollen.

Malinda didn't speak. Her lips formed a tight line as she scrubbed the floor harder.

"We will get out of here," Zayne promised. To himself he added, *even if I need to invoke* all *the gods to do it.*

CHAPTER THIRTEEN

Since being outed to the crew, Hymn spent much of her time by Cassidy's side rather than confining herself to nooks in the woodwork. Despite that, however, she remained tight-lipped and indifferent to Cassidy's attempts at friendship. More damningly, Cassidy decided, was the Fae's insistence on calling her Cassandra. The crew was wary of having her aboard. While they didn't go so far to avoid Cassidy to avoid Hymn, there was a tension whenever they spotted her. After a while, though, they had taken to simply ignoring the sulking Faerie, difficult as that might have been.

The sun was low on the horizon, and the captain was dishing out everyone's supper. Nieves had taken the leftover pumpkins and the bird Cassidy had bagged before leaving Revehaven and made a very thick and delicious chowder. She had even made enough that the crew was enjoying it for the second night in a row.

There was a companionable silence as Cassidy took to eating. She considered the glowing blue orb floating by her shoulder. "Would you like some?" she asked Hymn. Kek looked over at her apprehensively. There was a distinct shift in the nature of the quiet as the others ate at a more deliberate pace.

The blue glow that was Hymn remained silent for a moment, and Cassidy figured she was ignoring her and resumed eating. Only after Cassidy had had a few bites, Hymn asked, "What do you expect in exchange?"

Cassidy raised her eyebrow. "For a bit of my soup? Nothing. I just thought you might be hungry." She paused. "Do the Fae even get hungry?"

"We do not require food to sustain ourselves," Hymn informed her. "However... it *can* be of comfort." Without another word, Cassidy held out a spoonful to the Fae. Hymn's glow changed briefly to a light pink and back again. She gingerly approached the spoon, enveloping it in her light. When she backed away, it was empty. "Thank you," she said quietly. "For your consideration."

"No trouble," Cassidy replied as she started eating again. She looked at the others. Asier acted as though nothing was amiss, but the others were clearly unsettled. Cassidy set her bowl on her lap and broke the silence. "Say, Miria. You ever hear the story of how our captain broke the Castilyn Blockade and captured the queen at the end of the war?"

Asier gave a wry laugh and hid her face. "Not this again," she said wearily.

Miria looked up from her own bowl. "My mother told me she bribed the captains of a dozen –" she began, but Kek scoffed.

"She didn't ask if you knew what happened," Kek told her. "She asked if you heard the *story*."

"Is… is there a distinction in there?" Miria asked. She seemed a little flustered at the interruption.

"Oh, yes," Kek said with faux seriousness. "See, princess, you're a sailor now, so you need to learn that when it comes to your exploits, or your crew's, you should never let facts get in the way of a good story."

"A proper story should be incredible!" Cassidy agreed.

"It should be romantic!" Lierre added.

"And impossibly heroic," Nieves chimed in, only slightly less enthusiastically than the others.

Miria's brow furrowed, as though she wasn't sure if they were screwing with her. "Alright," she said calmly. "I'll bite. What's the *story*?"

"I'm glad you asked," Kek said with a smile.

"Oh, for fuck's sake," Asier muttered, practically burying her face in her bowl.

Kek set his bowl aside, stood up, and placed one foot on his stool. "It was the last year of the war, and the Castilyn Armada was gathered around Tal Joyau. Hundreds of thousands of ships with their cannons facing the north encircled the city. They expected the full might of the Imperial Fleet to bear down upon them."

"Instead," Cassidy said, taking advantage of the natural pause in Kek's cadence, "it was five ships that charged at the armada!" She stood and started walking around the dinner circle. "Five of the fastest ships ever constructed; The *Night's Wish;* the *Clockwork Hydra;* the *Temptation;* the *Never World;* and of course, spearheading the charge was the *Jade Phoenix*, captained by our very own Elyia Asier, the empress' personal champion." Out of the corner of her eye, Cassidy could see Asier pretend to blush modestly.

"Seeing such a small force amassed against them," Nieves continued where Cassidy left off, "the Castilyn forces suspected a trap, but they could not resist such tempting bait. So a small contingent broke off from the armada to sink these ships before they reached the city's borders."

"What they couldn't know," Lierre chimed in, leaning into Miria as if to whisper, "was that Captain Asier had stolen the storm winds from Nyuran herself! The five Imperial ships danced around the enemy like eagles. And they fired their massive cannons with such coordination the Castilyn ships fell out of the sky in perfect sequence." She tapped her spoon against her bowl to indicate a pattern.

"Only then did the battle truly begin," Cassidy said, gesturing grandly as she spoke. "While the other three ships lured the enemy warships into fruitless chases and skirmishes, the *Night's Wish* and the *Jade Phoenix* shot straight through the blockade, picking off ships as they passed, the stolen winds saving them from enemy cannons, flamers, and rotary guns. In trying to stop these ships, the Castilyn Armada did more damage to itself than a hundred Imperial Warships."

"And thus they made it," she continued. The story always made her quiver with excitement whether she was telling it or hearing it. Sometimes she would find herself thinking about it and be reminded how amazing it was that she served under such a legend. "Beyond the armada lay Tal Joyau, a city of splendor and beauty to rival Revehaven. The *Night's Wish* focused on capturing the city while Captain Asier –"

"Admiral," Asier interrupted sweetly.

Cassidy hardly missed a beat as she made the correction, "– while *Admiral* Asier led the *Jade Phoenix* straight into the heart of the enemy capital. She dove from the ship directly into the throne room of Queen Isabel Lancastian XIV." Cassidy drew her spoon like a sword. "'I am Elyia Asier', our dear captain proclaimed, 'Champion of Empress Yushiro Shahira, and I speak with her voice. Isabel, send your greatest champion, that I may end this war without undue bloodshed.'"

Lierre, being the only Castilyn aboard, usually played the role of Queen Isabel when they told the story. This telling was no exception. "'What madness is this?' the queen asked, outraged and terrified all at once, 'What madness that you think I shall not simply execute you for your insolence?'"

Cassidy leaned forward, "And our captain, the legendary bodyguard of the empress, stepped forward with her sword outstretched and said, 'Do not be a fool, Isabel. Your city is mine. This war can end with a duel of honor or the wholesale slaughter of Tal Joyau.'"

"The queen was furious, yet she smiled, believing Captain – Admiral – Asier's luck could hold no further," Lierre said, "and she leaned back in her throne. 'I shall send your head back to your precious Shahira in a box, along with whatever kindling is left of your *Phoenix*. I accept your challenge. But know this; you will face all three of my champions.'"

Cassidy smiled with pride just thinking about the words she was about to say. "And our captain stared down the three *chevaliers*, Queen Isabel's greatest duelists, and said cold as the north winds, 'Ready your white flares, Your Majesty.'

"The duel ended in mere moments," Cassidy continued. "The greatest swordsmen in the kingdom were felled in six quick motions, while the empress' champion bore only two cuts across her chest." Asier undid the top two buttons of her coat to show Miria the crossing scars over her breasts as confirmation. "She took the sword of one of the fallen, climbed the dais to the queen, and demanded her surrender."

"That night," Kek said, clearly eager to finish the story he had begun, "a thousand white flares were fired from the palace, signaling that Castilyn had surrendered the war."

"I was there," Lierre added, her excitement tempered as reality set in. "There were so many flares that the streets lit up like noon."

"And the rest is just politics," Asier finished unceremoniously.

Miria sat there, staring, wide eyed. "That was . . . quite a story," she said after a moment. "My mother read me the reports, but . . . your story felt more *real*."

Asier chuckled. "Ironic," she said, "but a good story beats a report any day. That's the thing, Miria: whether or not a story is true is irrelevant; what matters is that it is *alive*." She leaned back, considering. "In actuality, there were *fifty* ships on our side, not five, though I'm sure you knew that. I don't know how many ships they had, but I doubt it certainly wasn't hundreds of thousands."

"And the duel?" Miria asked.

Asier smiled and offered a small shrug. "The fight wasn't as easy as it sounds." She slurped the last of her soup and rose. "Nieves, Cassy, you're on first watch tonight. The rest of you, clean up after you're done."

124

There was an echoing murmur of "Aye, Captain" as Asier set her bowl away and retired to her cabin.

The rest of supper was peppered with light conversation. Miria wanted more stories, but Cassidy and Kek couldn't settle their argument about which stories were better. Nieves took the opportunity to tell Miria about the time Cassidy was so drunk she got turned around in an honor duel and stabbed Kek in the leg. Cassidy insisted that Kek got in the way. Kek politely reminded her that he had been sitting down at their table at the time, and equally politely told her to do something very unpleasant with her excuses. Laughter was shared by all except Hymn, who had settled on Cassidy's shoulder. Cassidy wondered briefly if she was asleep. *Do Fae sleep?* she wondered idly.

The conversation took several turns, from talk of pirates to the time they had been hired to ship what had to be the world's largest collection of smelly cheeses from the southern edge of Castilyn all the way to Revehaven – the hold had smelled of cheese for months – and Miria told them of her life at court, about the gossips and the sycophants, and performed unflattering impersonations of the stuck-up fools she encountered regularly. Cassidy recognized one of the subjects of mockery as Cob Mendrin, and she let out a particularly unladylike laugh when Miria stuck her nose in the air and declared, "My uncle's wife's sister once had the honor of emptying the empress' chamber pot!" At one point Kek asked if there were any available women at court, to which Miria offhandedly replied that his smell would drive them away.

When finally they wound down, Kek and Lierre made their way below deck while Miria helped Cassidy stow the chairs and dishes. "Cassidy?" she asked before she headed down below. "I know why I'm here, but how did you and the others end up with Elyia? Er, sorry, I mean, Captain Asier."

Cassidy bit her lip, thinking back. "You know, some days I wonder the exact same thing," she said after a moment's consideration. "Seems like a lifetime ago. Luck, I suppose. The captain made port in Dawnhal about the same time I was looking for someone to set sail with. I was ready to sign on to the first ship that would take me on, didn't care where I was going or who I'd be going with." She allowed herself a short laugh. "You know, there are a few heretical tribes among the Rivien that don't believe in luck.

They say there are still gods – nameless ones – who look out for us, even after the others betrayed us. They would argue it was fate."

Miria furrowed her brow. "So, you mean my mother didn't choose this crew?"

Cassidy scratched at her scalp, unsure why Miria would assume such a thing. Then it hit her. *The captain agreed to take her on before she ever met us.* "No," she said, "the captain brought me aboard because she needed a second set of hands. It was actually kind of funny, she flew the *Dreamscape* from Revehaven to Dawnhal completely alone. Somehow." She leaned against the helm. "Let me tell you, sailing with just the two of us was exhausting, and I was so relieved when we recruited Kek. I can't imagine how she ever managed by herself."

Miria hesitated another moment. "So, you really weren't hired on just to look after me. Your acceptance, treating me like a real crew member . . . none of that is lip-service?"

"Not a word of it," Cassidy assured her, unable to keep her confusion completely out of her tone. "Shit, none of us even knew the captain was still working for the empress. We were told those days were –" Miria walked up and surprised her by throwing her arms tightly around her.

"Thank you," she whispered into Cassidy's shoulder.

Cassidy was taken aback and barely had the wherewithal to return her hug. She patted the girl awkwardly as she did so. "Of course, kid." Cassidy thought back to Miria telling them about life at court. She mentioned sycophants, and gossips, and admirers, but Cassidy realized in that moment what the princess had *not* mentioned. "We're all friends here," she promised.

Miria pulled away from the embrace, and her eyes were glistening with the threat of tears, but she was smiling. "Thank you," she repeated as she climbed down the ladder.

Cassidy watched her go before taking her place at the helm. She set the ship at standard speed and focused on keeping course. Nieves was making her rounds with the spyglass, checking the horizons. The night was darkened by clouds, and only the largest moon still illuminated the sky.

As the night wore on, Cassidy found herself wanting to scratch at the bandage around her wrist. "How long before I can take these damned stitches out?" she complained.

"Not long," Nieves said vaguely. "Probably would have done so by now if you hadn't popped a couple in your little pissing match with Miria."

"Pissing match?"

"Captain said 'see what she can do,'" Nieves replied. She put the spyglass to her eye. "Can't see a damn thing tonight," she muttered. Then, a bit louder, she said, "but no, you had to prove a point. 'Cassidy doesn't lose fights.' Well, that's what happens. The scar on your leg will probably be thicker and misshapen, now, to boot."

Cassidy frowned and rubbed at her leg. "Damn it," she muttered.

"Cassandra is lucky that worsening scars was the only long-term damage she suffered," Hymn said from Cassidy's shoulder. She then turned to Cassidy. "Drawing on the power of our bond like you did could have taxed your body to its limit."

"And *now* she speaks!" Cassidy shouted. She thought back to the fight, the burst of energy, the slowed perception. "Maybe if I'd have known I *could* do it, I might not have done it."

"I sincerely doubt that," Hymn said nonchalantly.

"What the fuck does that mean?"

"I think you know exactly what it means, Cassandra."

"Call me Cassidy," Cassidy snapped. Through the blue light, she could swear she saw Hymn wearing a smug grin.

"I have already told you; I shall consider it."

Cassidy felt her grip tightening on the wheel. "Fine," she said between clenched teeth. After a moment's silence she turned to face the Fae. "So, how do I avoid doing it next time? Or how can I know I'm doing it?"

"The same way you know when you are breathing," Hymn said. "It is a natural act and therefore a feeling you must learn to recognize."

Cassidy took a breath and started thinking of everything she was feeling. She was cold, but that was the night wind. She was overly full from eating. And her wounds were itching incessantly. Against Nieves' suggestion, she unwrapped her wrist. The stitched-up wounds wove around in arm in a barbed spiral, but there was a strange pattern in the mix that obviously hadn't been carved by the briars. Separate from the lacerations was a fresh-looking scar that was too deliberate and shapely to be natural: three crescents nested inside one another, the largest facing opposite the other two, with what appeared to be a flower in the center of it all. When Nieves had reapplied her stitches, they had bent and warped. The sawbones had said they resembled a brand more than a cut, and now Cassidy found herself agreeing.

"I don't *feel* anything thing unusual," she said, rewrapping her bandages, "but I can *see* you've done something."

"Perhaps you are simply incapable," Hymn said offhandedly.

"Incapable?!"

"It is a word that means unable to —"

"I know what it means, you... you... tiny lantern!"

Nieves was snickering. Cassidy shot her a glare.

"So, can this bond of ours do anything other than make me almost kill myself?" she asked.

"I suspect so."

"So spill," Cassidy demanded.

Hymn's light seemed to slump. "Very well, Cassandra. If you wish to see what else you can do, you should unsheathe your sword."

Cassidy looked to Nieves. The sawbones shrugged and watched interestedly. Cassidy slowly drew her sword, watching as the Faerie slowly drifted away from the weapon.

"Focus on the iron in the blade," Hymn instructed.

Cassidy did as she was told, looking intently on the gray blade. It was a simple weapon, covered in scratches and there was a slight chip in the edge. "What about it?" she asked.

"You must focus on the iron," Hymn repeated.

"It's just iron," Cassidy said irritably.

"Focus," Hymn said again.

"What the fuck *about* the iron am I supposed to be focusing on?" Cassidy shouted.

"Take that anger and direct it at the blade," the Fae said calmly.

Cassidy pursed her lips. She was angry alright. The whole exercise must have been a Fae joke. It was just a sword, a piece of iron. She felt a jolt of static beneath her fingers followed by a flash of heat. She shielded her eyes from a sudden burst of light. Her sword was on fire. When she realized three and a half feet of fire danced in her hand, she shrieked and started waving the weapon erratically, trying to put it out. "What — shit! Shit!"

"I'll get an ice canister!" Nieves called, bounding for the storage room.

Cassidy swatted aimlessly with the sword for several moments before Hymn started fluttering around her face to get her attention.

"Cassandra, please calm yourself. You made the fire; you can control it." But Cassidy could hardly focus on the Fae's words.

"Why is it on fire?" she demanded.

"Listen to me, Cassandra," Hymn said slowly.

Cassidy chose to continue panicking until Hymn flew closer and smacked her across the face. Despite being no more than a hand's length in height and much thinner, the Fae somehow mustered enough force to knock Cassidy's head aside, as though she'd been struck by a full-sized hand.

"Right," she said slowly. "I'm sorry." She held the sword out at arm's length. "How did I do this? And how do I *un*do it?"

"You fed your anger into the iron," Hymn explained. "To extinguish the fire, you must draw it back out." It was at that very moment that a blast of snow smothered the sword and Cassidy's left arm. Nieves was holding an ice-canister, poised to blast her again if need be.

Cassidy looked at the sword, which was now covered in ice. "I guess that works just as well," she said. "So, can I do that with any iron?"

"No, you cannot. You are only able to affect iron you have had contact within a span of… ten seconds, I believe."

"Interesting," Cassidy said, wiping her blade off. The thin sword had been blackened, but otherwise seemed unremarkable. She bent the blade and found it flexed as well as it ever had. She held it up for Nieves to see.

"This seems very dangerous," she said. She made a move to grab the sword but held herself back, as though it would bite her.

"Yeah," Cassidy agreed. "Very."

"Cassidy?"

"Yes?"

Nieves made a gesture of rubbing her nose. Cassidy repeated the gesture and when she pulled her finger away it was covered in blood. "Damn it." She wiped the blood off her face with her sleeve. It was strange, the air didn't feel that dry.

Cassidy sheathed her sword and checked their course. They had drifted farther than Cassidy would have liked, but it was easily remedied. Nieves paced the deck and checking the spyglass. Hymn hovered over Cassidy's shoulder, and the Fae's light did little to help Cassidy adapt to the night, but she assumed it couldn't be helped so she didn't bother to complain. Besides, Hymn made it easier to check charts and her watch.

Her eyes were heavy well before midnight, but she stayed focused on her job until her watch ended. At the hour, she brought the engines to full stop and checked the wind charts and maps, cross-referencing them with what little she could physically see below and ahead of her.

"I think we're about an hour's flight north of the Hammer-struck Shore," Cassidy said to Nieves. "If the winds are favorable, we'll be able to cut above much of Black Gulch," she added hopefully.

Nieves nodded in agreement. Black Gulch was considered by most sailors to be a blight on the Empire. Spanning a thousand miles in any direction, the Gulch was a maze-like chain of massive mountains and plateaus. Storms were almost constant farther inland – and even when there were no storms, the upper winds were harsh and unforgiving – meaning ships often had to choose between going around the Gulch or through it. Going around was a lengthy delay that most ships could scarcely afford. But going through carried its own risks; the 'black' of Black Gulch was derived from the color of harpy wings. There were more harpy nests in the region than anywhere else in the Empire. Probably anywhere else in the world. "We'd better get our rest, just in case," Nieves said gloomily, shoving her spyglass in her coat. Cassidy agreed.

"You wake Kek and Lierre. I'll fetch the captain."

Nieves nodded and vanished below deck as Cassidy made her way to Asier's door. She knocked once and the captain's voice called out, "Enter." Cassidy obeyed. Hymn followed her inside. Cassidy thought she saw the Fae almost relax as the light she gave off shifted in a strange way. She wondered why, until she saw the glowing creature set down on the table. The captain's cabin had considerably less iron decorating the surfaces than the rest of the ship.

Asier was dressed in a red shirt and a black waistcoat and was sitting at her writing desk. "Midnight already?" she asked absently.

"Aye, Captain," Cassidy replied.

The captain rose from her chair and stretched. She took her coat from a peg on the wall and threw it on, along with her hat and gun belt. "Well, Cassy," Asier said with a smile, "I have a feeling today will be big. You'd best rest up."

"Aye, aye," she acknowledged. She didn't tell Asier that she was almost ready to fall asleep on the floor right there, but she definitely felt it. She offered Asier a salute before making her way below deck. When she reached the bottom of the ladder, Lierre and Miria were sharing a yawn in the passageway.

"Enjoy your watch," Cassidy said wearily.

"Oh, yes," Lierre said sardonically. "It'll be grand."

Choosing to ignore Lierre's sarcasm, Cassidy turned to the princess. "Miria, you aren't on middle-watch," she said. "Why are you up?"

Miria looked down at her feet. "No reason," she mumbled. "Couldn't sleep."

"Well, you should try anyway," Cassidy advised. "We're going to need you alert when your watch starts."

"Yes– er, aye, Cassidy," Miria agreed, turning back to their shared cabin.

When she shut the door behind her, Lierre whispered to Cassidy, "I think the poor dear had a nightmare."

Cassidy looked out to the distant shore, but she was unable to see it in the gloom. "I can't say I'm surprised," she said. "That place is the stuff of legends, and none of them good."

"Aye," Lierre agreed. "Give Kek's door a kick before you turn in; he really should be up by now."

"I'll take that under advisement," Cassidy promised. When she passed Kek's door, however, the blond man opened it and darted down the passage, barely saying 'Morning' before he was gone. "Rude," Cassidy said aloud.

"I believe it is because he does not like me," Hymn said conversationally.

"Maybe if you weren't such an abrasive bitch," Cassidy suggested as she ushered them into the cabin. Nieves was already face down in her cot. After Miria joined the crew, a fourth bunk was installed, directly above hers. In the two weeks since the princess had come aboard, Nieves had hit her head six times.

"I believe your people have a relevant expression. It is to do with pots and kettles."

"I know the one," Cassidy said. She climbed up to her cot without undressing and closed her eyes. She didn't want to be caught with so much as her boots off in the Gulch. "Though, I think it's a more popular expression in Castilyn than in Asaria."

"Whether Castilyn or Asarian, they are still your people," Hymn argued. Cassidy felt the Faerie land on her knee.

"You think so?" Cassidy asked, though by that point she was too tired to think very hard about how she replied, much less what Hymn was saying.

"Regardless of whatever tribes, cabals, nations, or brotherhoods you form," Hymn said, "you all herald from the same world, and you are all human."

Cassidy chuckled softly. "If that were enough," she said idly. Whatever sleep-deprived, profound statement she was going to make slipped out of her mind and was replaced by the comforting cloud of sleep enveloping her. She fell swiftly into a dream of piloting the *Dreamscape Voyager* over the distant desert mountains of Rivien. She dreamed of a sunset striking the back of a distant mountain, coloring the cloudy sky with a myriad of reds and oranges and casting beautiful shadows of different shades of blue and purple.

Hymn stood beside her, not as the miniature version of herself that hovered at her shoulder, but as the tall, beautiful woman Cassidy had first met inside the Dreamscape. Cassidy didn't find anything strange about that. Her dress and her backward eyes were glowing the same gradient of red as the sunset, rather than their usual blue, though stars still shone in the distant sky within her strange dress. They did not speak to one another. Both were content to watch the glorious sunset as the airship coasted silently above the land.

As the ship drifted along, dusk turned to night. Stars filled a suddenly cloudless sky, and many unfamiliar moons rose in strange patterns across the sky, at various stages of their cycles. They varied greatly in size; some seemed as small as Cassidy's thumbnail, others as large as her fist. The night sky was a deep purple with clouds touched in red, and Hymn's dress seemed to be a continuation of the sky itself.

They sailed in silence and a gentle breeze tussled Cassidy's hair. The engines weren't roaring, the propellers weren't clattering, yet still the ship moved at a fair pace across the sky. Below them, the desert gradually gave way to grass, which in turn gave way to trees that slowly but surely became a forest.

A song rose up from the woods. It was bittersweet and strange, the notes rising and falling with the wind. Wisps danced between the trees. They flew near a massive tree, one with a trunk that must have been sixty feet around and towered above the rest of the forest canopy.

At the foot of the tree, laid out in a small nook, was a young woman. Despite the great distance between Cassidy and the ground, she could see the woman clearly. She looked remarkably like Hymn, though her black hair was tinged with gray and red. She wore a dress not unlike the one Hymn wore, though the sky within the bizarre folds was gray and starless.

Hymn was no longer at Cassidy's side. Instead, she was far below, looking over the other woman. Cassidy moved over to the edge of the ship and found herself walking on the forest floor. She stepped over roots and stones and stood a few feet from Hymn. She had her hands folded in front of herself, looking at the woman lying in the tree. She stooped down and touched the strange woman's cheek. The color bled away from her left sleeve and she recoiled. A brief flash of blue moved along the gray dress, falling like a leaf until it vanished far within the gray sky. The color returned to Hymn's dress.

The Faerie turned to Cassidy and it seemed as though she had only just noticed her. She looked different from what Cassidy recalled. Older was not quite the word Cassidy would have chosen, but it was the only word she could think of that fit. Her face was both familiar and not. Only her inverted, star-filled eyes were exactly what Cassidy recalled, despite the changing patterns and color, and yet she had never expected to see sadness there. "Cassandra," she said. Her voice carried a note of surprise tangled strangely with grief. "I was not aware you were following me," she said. She looked around. "I should not be in this place. Nor should you." She reached into her sleeve and extracted an elaborately formed hourglass filled with blue sand. The sand inside was flowing in reverse. "There is probably still time to return to your dream before you must awaken."

Hymn walked past Cassidy, and when she turned to follow, they were already aboard the *Dreamscape Voyager*. Hymn's dress had returned to its usual blue.

"Hymn?" Cassidy asked as the ship began to move. "What was that?"

"That was a personal matter," the Faerie replied. She stepped away from Cassidy, moving toward the bow.

"That woman looked like you," Cassidy said.

"Did she?" Hymn asked. "Cassandra, I apologize for interrupting your dream. It seems our link has many uses, but we can take advantage of it another day. You need your rest."

The moons and the stars gave way to the cloudy sunset and the forest was lost again to desert and Cassidy forgot the experience in the Dreamscape. She took the helm and sailed into the sunset. The crew was there, and they milled about working at their duties, but they were nearly colorless and blurred at the edges. Compared to the iron sharp clarity with which she saw Hymn, it was almost too obvious she was dreaming them. Still, it was a familiar dream into which Cassidy allowed herself to be swept. She rocked with the motions of sailing through the desert. Together, she and her crew adventured and explored the skies.

The dream was cut short, however, when she felt a hand on her thigh. She opened her eyes to find Lierre shaking her.

"The captain wants all hands," she said.

Cassidy nodded and groaned into her pillow while Lierre set to waking Nieves. Cassidy tried to remember what happened during her dream of the desert, but it was lost to the fog of awakening. All she could remember with any clarity was when Hymn took her into the Dreamscape. She hadn't known that would happen.

The Faerie was still sitting on Cassidy's leg. Cassidy wondered if she slept, too. She eased herself up to give Hymn a chance to move before she threw her legs over the side of the cot. Nieves smacked her head on Miria's newly installed bunk, prompting a laugh from Lierre and Cassidy, and a string of incoherent curses from Nieves.

While Cassidy and Nieves climbed the ladder to the deck, Hymn flew alongside Cassidy the entire time. Lierre entered the engine compartment and started shoveling coal. Topside, Miria was at the helm while Kek and Asier each had a spyglass in hand and were on watch.

The only sound was the *chug* of the propellers and the rumbling of the engines, which were usually a comforting sound, but in the Gulch, they induced a certain paranoia. "Trouble, Captain?" Cassidy asked.

Asier's attention remained on the horizon, but she shook her head. "Not yet, but the day's not over."

Cassidy looked up at the sky and took in a deep breath. "Storm's coming," she said.

"Aye," Asier said. "Once it hits, I want you on the helm, and once it passes, I want us over the Gulch."

"Aye, aye, Captain." Cassidy looked toward the land, focusing on the spires of stone they were flying through. "Any nests?"

"Old ones," Asier said. "I doubt we'll be lucky enough to avoid them forever, though."

"Should I bring out more guns?"

Asier seemed to consider that. "No," she said. "Not with the storm inbound."

Cassidy cast her eyes downward. At the bottom of the hills, mountains, and rocky towers was a river that snaked its way southwest, effectively marking their path. The Gulch was wide enough in most places for five ships to fly side by side with room to spare, but in others it was considerably tighter. Cassidy had to guide Miria twice through passages that left maybe ten feet on either side of the *Dreamscape*.

It was about noon when the storm finally struck. It started with a few fat telltale drops of rain that quickly turned into a torrent. Cassidy took the helm as Asier had ordered and kept the ship as far from the rock faces as possible. The winds battered at the ship, causing it to swing and sway and creak. Cassidy held tightly to the helm. Nieves had strapped herself to the rotary gun for security while Mira clutched the railing of the stairs of the aftcastle. Kek was on the aftcastle, but Cassidy couldn't keep an eye on him while she struggled to keep the ship from slamming into a nearby cliff. As the storm raged, it was all Cassidy could do to keep the ship steady, and she had given up on making any kind of progress through the Gulch. Lightning struck close enough at one point that the thunder's reverberations caused the ship to swing hard to port and knocked Cassidy to her knees.

The storm lasted two hours by Cassidy's watch, and when it was done, she was soaked to the bone. Kek came down from the aftcastle with his boots making a loud *squelch* with each step. Miria had vomited at some point during the onslaught and was cleaning her mouth. She still looked a little storm sick.

Cassidy fired up the balloon and brought the ship just under the clouds, which still did not put them above every possible obstruction. Below, the Gulch was gray and covered in fog. Cassidy eyed the river and set course to follow it. She shivered as the cold winds whipped at her wet clothes. The clouds broke away slowly, giving way to beams of sunlight that did little more than accentuate the shadows of the Gulch.

Asier ordered Nieves to get some extra pistols and shot, as well as a bar of wax. She sent Miria to get everyone a spare coat; they were all oversized and shapeless, but also dry and warm. She had Kek monitoring the starboard horizon while she eyed the port. Cassidy called Lierre over the pipeline for an update. She was miserable, but unharmed, and she'd kept the bellows dry. The wind moaned as it passed between the canyons and fissures. As they moved along, Cassidy came to recognize specific features of the rock.

"Miria, you'll want to see this," she said as she began to follow a bend in the river. Kek and Nieves took a place by her side and Asier stood beside Cassidy. Cassidy opened the pipeline again. "Lierre, Arrelan is right around the bend if you want to stop working for a minute."

"Aye, and thank you, Cassidy," Lierre called back.

The view of a steep bluff was slowly replaced by a sweeping valley where many rivers met. As they rounded the bluff, the natural rock formations gave way to precisely carved marble and alabaster and stone in carefully arranged patterns. Towers climbed the cliff side, and streets and homes stretched along its length and down its face. The city stretched from high in the hills into the valley, and though it was weather-worn by untold centuries of storms and long since plundered by treasure hunters and collectors, the walls stood high and shone under the beams of sun as if to defy the end that had come to the cities of the ground so long ago.

"It's beautiful," Miria said as she stared at it in obvious wonder.

"Once, this city was as grand as Revehaven," Asier told her. "That there," she pointed at a particularly high building with a domed roof made of what seemed like solid marble, "was once the Palace of Arrelan, one of the nine great cities of what we now know as the Black Gulch. "It was once said the city was so rich that each month the king would host a feast so grand that not one soul in the city would go hungry." She pointed to the statue of a dragon in the city square. "They worshiped dragons, which protected them from harpies."

Cassidy leaned over to whisper in Asier's ear. "You made that one up, didn't you?"

"I honestly can't remember."

Cassidy smiled, both at the captain's joke and at the look at Miria's face, and wondered briefly if she had been so enraptured the first time she had seen Arrelan. Then, looking down, she realized she must have, because she was *still* in awe of its beauty.

Cassidy took them around the city, still following the river. As the day wore on, with the awe of the city behind them, a tense gloom fell over them while they looked for danger on the horizon. The sun was low when Kek finally spotted something. "Captain, out to starboard," he called. Asier ran to his side and Cassidy cast a look that way. Even without her spyglass Cassidy could make out the silhouette of a ship.

Asier twisted her spyglass. "That ship is being swarmed," she said. "They need help."

"Are you sure that's wise, Captain?" Kek asked. Cassidy couldn't help but notice the slight tremor in his voice.

"Kekarian! If it were us, we'd want all the help we could get, wouldn't we?"

Kek hung his head. "Aye, Captain."

"Nieves, the wax," Cassidy ordered. Nieves nodded and pulled the large bar of amber-colored beeswax from her pocket. Cassidy opened the pipeline. "Lierre, all hands on deck. Harpies."

The engineer was up the ladder with remarkable speed. Miria had been on the aftcastle but joined the others when she heard the call. Nieves broke off two pieces of wax and handed them to Kek, two more for the captain, and two for Lierre. They rolled the wax into balls and stuffed them in their ears.

"Miria," Cassidy asked. "This question may sound out of place, but it's very important; are you drawn to women?"

"I – what?"

"Harpies are siren-kin," Cassidy explained. "So, if you are drawn to women, you need to plug your ears. Now."

"I – I never thought about it," the princess said awkwardly. Cassidy looked to Nieves, who answered by breaking off two more pieces of wax and handing them to Miria. Cassidy showed her how to form the wax and helped her stuff her ears.

"We get new blood and *still*, you and I are the only ones not rendered deaf," Nieves complained.

"I hate it too," Cassidy muttered. "It'd be nice to be able to call out in a fight, for a change."

"Alright, Cassy," Asier said, louder than usual, "get us in."

Cassidy nodded and saluted and returned to the helm. She turned hard to starboard. As the ship grew closer, Cassidy could see the details of its design. It was a little bit larger than the *Dreamscape*. Painted along the side of the ship was a white, ghostly woman with sharp teeth. Its figurehead was a rivermaid with her arms spread along the sides of the bow. As they drew nearer, Cassidy realized it was not a carving, but an actual rivermaid corpse, pinned and anchored to the ship, with spikes in its hands, tail, and throat, in addition to other bindings holding it down. Its eye sockets were empty, its mouth open in a snarl to reveal spiny teeth.

At the same time she saw the rivermaid, she heard the Siren Song. The music was a sweet, repetitious chorus that seemed to echo across her memory. It resonated in every thought she had. The song seemed to come from the wood under her hands, from the very air she breathed, from the ship beneath her feet. The song was so strong she could feel her heart thrum to its tune and her bones shake as she struggled to stay on course. But at the same time, it was not painfully loud.

She offered Kek a look. He was still affected by the song, despite having deafened himself to it. He was shaking and rubbing the front of his trousers with the bottom of his palm. Lierre, similarly, was squirming in place and hugging herself to keep herself together. The captain merely stood with her arms crossed, her fingers digging into her shoulders. Miria was nervously rubbing her own throat. This was the hardest part for them, Cassidy knew; when the fighting started, they would have something to focus on other than the song, and they were deaf to the worst of it. But while they waited, they had nothing but to let the waves of sound wash over them, and while they couldn't hear, they could still *feel* the music.

A thought occurred to Cassidy. "Hymn, does the siren song affect you?"

"No," Hymn said flatly. "The children's song does not affect my kind. This is folly, you know," she added.

"Maybe," Cassidy agreed. All told, she didn't much relish charging into a harpy swarm, herself. "Still, it's the right thing to do."

"If that is what you believe, so be it," Hymn replied sardonically. "I have sworn to protect you, but I cannot do the impossible. You must fight to your fullest."

"That was my plan," Cassidy muttered irritably.

"If you fight like you did in that tavern, our friendship will be short lived indeed."

Cassidy opened her mouth to protest. She stopped when the Faerie's exact words hit her. She chuckled, and a smile forced its way across her lips. "Well, I also have to protect *you*," she said. "So, you'd better not hold me back." Cassidy dropped altitude to bring them level with the other ship. The swarm was a rapid blur of movement, and Cassidy couldn't track any of the frenzied creatures long enough to count.

Harpies bore a passing resemblance to human women, like a shoddy recreation; they had the faces of women, though their teeth were more like needles and their eyes and thin lips were solid black. They had full heads of lustrous black hair that moved and flowed counter to the air or gravity, as if underwater. From the waist up, their naked form might be mistaken for women in their prime, only their complexion was too sickly, their skin the color of eggshells rather than any range of human flesh, and blackened veins made them unpleasant to behold. Feathers covered their forearms like opera gloves, and wings sprouted at their wrists, just above their talon-like claws. From the waist down, they were much more avian, with black feathers coating bowed legs, a second pair of wings jutting out along their calves. Their feet were another set of talons, thicker and longer than those at the ends of their wrists.

Despite their wings, Harpies seemed to swim, rather than fly like more mundane winged creatures. They darted through the air, wriggling like eels as they harried the crew of the black ship. The swarm encircled them and took dangerous swipes at them with their talons while they swatted at the monsters with swords and occasionally fired pistols.

Asier was the one to bring the *Dreamscape*'s crew into the battle. Her shot rang loud and true, cutting through the song and showering the opposite crew with the black ichor of harpy blood. The song was momentarily replaced by a deafening shriek as Cassidy and the rest of the crew fired a volley of shots that dropped a handful of the winged creatures out of the sky.

The harpies' song resumed, and Cassidy felt the weight of the music fall upon her like an anchor. Fighting against the pressure in her body, she drew her sword in her left hand and dropped the pistol she'd fired, taking another from her coat. One of the beasts broke from its kin and crossed the gulf between ships first. Cassidy fired. The bullet landed in the creature's shoulder and it slammed bodily into Cassidy, pinning her to the deck.

"Cassandra," Hymn called, "focus on the bullet while you're still connected to it!" Cassidy flailed, unable to ask Hymn what she was talking about. The harpy raised its head off her shoulder, its jaws open wide. It drove its teeth at her.

Shit! The bullet, the bullet! She thought frantically. A painful snap of static jumped between her body and the harpy's. A flare came to life, bursting out of the creature's wounded shoulder. It screeched in deafening terror. Cassidy's coat caught fire right above the breast as the it flailed, scratching and pushing off. It flew away. Cassidy tore her coat off furiously and stamped it out. She readied another bullet and fired it in the fleeing monster's ass. Cognizant now of the Fae trick, she felt the metal at the edge of her mind. She ignited it. The harpy's panic intensified as its feathers caught fire. The flames soon engulfed it, and its cries died out as it dropped from the sky.

Three more broke from the swarm and picked her out. They began to circle her, crooning their hypnotic song. She swung with her blade, striking one along the side of the face. Its song grew louder and more intense, as if to answer pain with domination. Cassidy could feel her arms and legs grow heavier. A voice whispered in the back of her head. *Stop fighting,* it said. *Open your arms, enjoy the song and stop fighting.* She ignored the voice and pushed through the sudden lethargy that washed over her. She stabbed at one of the sickly creatures, aiming between its almost human breasts, but missed as it swooped, striking the belly instead. *Stop fighting,* the voice pleaded, but Cassidy twisted the blade in the creature's stomach, and with a firm grasp of her ability, she set the sword on fire. The harpy shrieked in her face, drowning out the chorus of its sisters. Blood trickled out of Cassidy's ears.

As the harpy died, Cassidy could hear the song again, but it was muffled, as though she were underwater. She staggered as she cut through the next, her sword still ablaze. The fire extinguished after she cut through the third harpy and its body skittered across the deck in two parts.

"Cassandra," she heard Hymn through the blood in her ear. "Behind you." The words barely had time to process in her head when she turned. A massive talon scraped across her arm, and the brunt force of the harpy's weight knocked her down.

She pushed herself up. Blood trickled down her arm but more concerningly, fat drops of red were falling like rain from her face. She found her footing to confront her attacker, only for the harpy's face to explode in black ichor. She blinked. Then, she looked for her savior and found Miria. The girl stared blankly, clearly amazed by what she had done.

Cassidy could have kissed the girl, but she settled for pushing her out of the way of an attack. Instead of Miria's neck, the harpy's fangs bore down on the barrel of Cassidy's pistol, cracking audibly. Cassidy ran her sword through the monster's throat. Her heart was pounding, and she found herself struggling for breath. She was about to fall when Kek caught her. He fired his pistol at an oncoming beast before helping her to the stairs of the aftcastle and setting her down on the bottom step.

"Can you reload for me?" he shouted.

"Yeah," she groaned. "I–"

"What?" Kek yelled. "Can't hear you. Ear's plugged."

Cassidy pulled her gloves off and tried in vain to clean the blood from her own ears. "Give me the gun," she said.

"What? Cass, take the gun if you can reload it."

Cassidy snatched his gun and started to reload as took heavy swings at incoming harpies with his sword. Her hands were shaking, and she dropped a ball, which rolled out of reach. She took another from her pack and dropped it in, tamping it down. She handed him the pistol and started on her own. She tried to breathe through her nose but found she couldn't. When she wiped her nose, her hand came back soaked in blood. "Shit," she muttered. She gasped for air every few seconds.

Kek fired again and traded pistols with Cassidy before a harpy's talons struck him across the chest and knocked him back into the staircase.

"Kek!" she shrieked. She scooped up a handful of powder and shot in one hand and threw it at the assaulting harpies. She felt the static snap across her fingers rapidly as she ignited all the iron balls, which in turn caused the gunpowder to explode. There were bright lights and thick plumes of smoke accompanied by sizzling cracks. The surrounding harpies around her shrieked as they burned and retreated. She cradled Kek's head, shaking him gently. When he groaned, she released a breath she didn't even realize she was holding. She embraced him and whispered, "We'll make it through, I promise."

She grabbed his sword and stabbed blindly at an oncoming harpy. She thought she missed until the burning black ichor sprayed across her face. When she pulled away and blinked away the fog of weariness, she found she had been right before; she had missed, and someone else had killed her assailant. Through the smoke she saw a tall man with long, black hair that waved in the breeze. He dropped the smoking pistol that had saved her life and lashed out with an ornate dueling sword. In a flourishing sweep, he severed the head of another winged beast.

Cassidy took advantage of the diversion to check on Kek, who was still groaning. She tugged at torn sleeve, ripping out long strips to bind the worst of his wounds. "I'm ruining a nice shirt, so don't you die on me, you son of a bitch." She tried to shout – more for her own benefit than his – though it came out as a raspy whisper. She grabbed a pinch of powder and set to reloading a pistol. The stranger who had saved her life was fighting off two of the creatures, claws catching steel and struggling for dominance. She leveled the gun across her arm. She was forced to shut one eye because her vision was doubling horribly.

"Cassandra," Hymn called from somewhere, "aim a little farther left." Cassidy obeyed. "Now!" Cassidy pulled the trigger. She barely heard the shot. The stranger punched one of the harpies in the teeth at the same moment the back of its skull exploded. Cassidy thought he looked pretty surprised, but he still had the wherewithal to turn on the next creature. He pierced the creature's wing, but it latched onto his arm with one talon and wrapped both its feet around his body, squeezing with its razor-like claws. Cassidy staggered as quickly as her feet would carry her. She threw an arm around the harpy's scrawny neck, and pulled down, choking it with all her body's weight.

She felt something in her wrist snap and pop. She let go and shrieked until her throat went raw. She was barely aware of the harpy falling down dead beside her. She was blind with tears and blood and smoke. She was faintly aware of the warmth of Hymn's touch against her skin, her pulse resonating with the wounds that were all screaming for her attention.

She wasn't sure how much time had passed before she could push herself up, but by then, the battle was ending.

CHAPTER FOURTEEN

Zayne found himself staring at the sky. He was unsure how long he had been looking at the red swirling clouds above. Long enough to forget himself, at least. He decided the cloud he was facing looked like a bird with the head of a dog. His head was pounding, and his mouth was dry. Blood – both his own and the harpies' – was drying against his skin, coating his hands and face in a disgusting crust along with the gun smoke.

And he was smiling.

He had fully expected to die without hope for rescue or record. Not unlike Salaa. There had been very little warning – *And damn Flea for his inattention*, he thought to himself – so the harpies were already upon the ship before Zayne even knew there was a threat. He was fortunate enough that Jacques had fired a shot too close to his ear, rendering him temporarily deaf. After that, he had had time to come up with a pair of makeshift earplugs, using strips of an old rag. But even without their song, harpies were deadly, and overwhelming. And yet the gods must have heard his desperate prayers, for they sent the mystery ship as if from the Dreamscape itself.

He pulled the cloth from his ears and was relieved to hear the wind and nothing else. He turned around, taking in his rescuers. They were gathered around the dark-skinned woman who had saved him at the last. *On my list of things that I thought I would never see,* he thought wistfully, *someone holding a harpy in a chokehold is pretty high. Probably right above someone saving me.*

"*Fuck!*" the dark-skinned woman hissed. She was sitting on the stairs leading to the aftcastle while a skinny woman with cropped black hair was dabbing at her wounds with a wet rag. A blond man was holding one side of her while a plump girl with even darker skin held her down. Zayne noticed that the one who had saved his life had red hair that defied her skin color. She was from Dawnhal, there was no doubt.

"Stop whining," the skinny one was saying. "Your stitches ruptured. Really bad, this time." Zayne was about to approach when he saw the woman's corset was torn open. There was a bloody cut along her naked breast. Unwelcome memories drained the strength from Zayne's limbs. His stomach roiled. Dark walls closed in on him.

He turned away from the triage and focused on the open air. He was above the Black Gulch, as far across the empire from his nightmares as he could fly. Steadying himself, he looked to two women who stood apart from the carnage. One was a young girl, perhaps fifteen. Behind all the dirt, ash, and different kinds of blood, some might have called her pretty; she had a heart-shaped face and almond-shaped eyes of dazzling blue. She was of little interest to Zayne, however, who focused on the older woman next to her.

She was maybe ten years his senior and had a cool, collected stance about her, even after the heat of battle. She stood turned to her injured crew mate, but her amber colored eyes were fixed directly on Zayne. He couldn't read the expression, but he assumed it was calculating and judgmental. Like most who looked at him, really. Maybe she regretted coming to the rescue after she'd spotted his ship's heraldry.

"I am Captain Zayne Balthine," he said, approaching the woman, "of the *Scorpion*. I owe you a debt for the rescue of me and mine." He offered his hand.

The woman looked for a moment like she might spit on his gesture, but that melted away to a sincere looking smile. "Captain Elyia Asier," she replied, clasping his wrist, "of the *Dreamscape Voyager*. You know, the reason civilized people do this is to prove they *don't* have a weapon up their sleeve."

Zayne's head spun too hard to catch the reprimand. "You're *the* Elyia Asier?"

"I'm *an* Elyia Asier, to be sure," she replied with a smirk. "Not that I've ever met another one."

"The Empress' Legendary Bodyguard?"

"That's the one."

Zayne's jaw dropped. Asier put one finger on his chin and made him close his mouth. "Well," he said dumbly. He stood there, trying to formulate his thoughts. *What a strange day.* "I can't believe you – I mean – it would be an honor if you and your crew would join me – my crew – for supper, as thanks for saving our hides."

Asier looked over at her crew. "Nieves," she called.

The woman with the cropped hair did not look up from the Dawnhal sailor when she replied, "Aye, Captain?"

"How's Cassidy?

"I can speak for myself, damn it!" the Dawnhal woman shouted. "Ow, *shit!* I mean, Captain."

"Doing rather well, all things considered," the woman called Nieves replied.

"Will she be walking tonight?"

"If she stops *squirming while I have a needle,* she might."

Asier turned back to Zayne. "We need to patch our wounds," she said, "and clean the blood. I suspect you need the same. After, though…." She paused. Her eyes darted between him and the sky. "We would be glad to share a meal," she said at last.

Zayne offered a bow. "It is I and my crew who are honored." He stepped away and made the mistake of glancing back to the girl from Dawnhal. It was only a glance, but once more he saw her torn corset and shirt, and the naked breast baring a gash and covered in blood. The bile rose in his throat. He crossed the gangplank back to the *Scorpion*, grateful that someone had set it down after the battle – he doubted he could make the jump again in his current state. He walked as quickly as he could into his cabin, slammed the door behind himself, and promptly vomited on the floor.

He scrubbed the floor clean, grateful he had eaten lightly. He filled his washbasin and stripped from the waist up. He scrubbed at the blood and sweat and ichor that clung to him. He scoured his hair and his face and every inch of his body until the water was completely black and opaque. Then he poured it out and started again. He repeated the cycle five times before he was satisfied. He identified several cuts earned in the fight, but decided they weren't life threatening. To his surprise, the stitches Nanette had given him after his encounter with the Emerald Falcons were still mostly intact.

There was a knock on his door. "Enter," he called. Nanette opened the door and shut it behind herself.

"There you are," she said. She was still covered head to toe in harpy blood.

"I'm not exactly hard to find," he pointed out. "This boat only has so much space."

"Karn is dead."

Zayne took a deep breath. How had he missed that? He wanted to say the news didn't bother him. He wanted to think they would be better off without him. But he found he couldn't. Instead, what he said was, "Damn it."

He hadn't trusted Karn much. He'd liked him even less. They hadn't worked together long enough for Zayne to know about any redeeming qualities the man might have possessed. Despite it all, however, the news was heavy. "Damn it!" he repeated, louder than before. He slammed his fist into the door.

"Zayne, calm down," Nanette said.

"Calm down? Nanette, a member of my crew is dead!" He turned away from her and kicked a stack of books. "I haven't been captain for a year! In less than one year I got someone killed! Salaa would—"

"Salaa's dead, Zayne," she said, poking a slender finger into his chest. "Or have you forgotten?"

"Of course I haven't," he replied.

"And even when she was alive," Nanette continued, "how many people did she lose? Look at me, I'm asking you a question."

Zayne thought about it. "Seven, since I signed on."

"Twelve," she corrected, "if you count the day she died."

"Your point?"

"My *point* is that Salaa was a good Captain, but she wasn't perfect, and if you spit clean your goggles once in a while, you'd see that. Death happens out here, and we've burned our share of friends. But as long as the *Scorpion* flies, we keep moving forward."

Zayne took a deep breath. He could feel the ship swaying beneath him, threatening to knock him off his weak legs. "You're right. I'll deal with the body. I want you to get the crew presentable. We're sharing our galley with Elyia Asier and her crew."

"That's it?" Nanette said dryly. "Get dressed, we have company?"

"They saved our lives. Least we can do is feed them."

"The fact that she's your childhood hero has nothing to do with the decision?"

"Sorry for being grateful," Zayne said wearily. "But I promised to share a supper."

Nanette rolled her eyes. "I'll see what we have in the galley."

Karn's body was lying in a pool of red and black, his arms sprawled and one of his knees bent entirely the wrong way. His face was all but missing, the edges baring the telltale marks of harpy teeth. Only his ears remained, and Zayne noticed they had been opened. The fool had never even drawn a weapon. He pulled a flask from one of his coat pockets and poured the contents into the gaping hole in the front of Karn's head.

The balding man had been born in Lyghton – or maybe it was Caraton; Zayne found he couldn't remember. He was Castilyn born, regardless – and had been a bruiser for some local dust trader. How and why he came to join the Daughters were questions Zayne had never ever thought to ask. He had always thought Karn would be a liability and get them caught or killed when breaking into the Imperial Palace. *Well,* he thought sardonically, *that's one less thing to worry about.*

He poured the last of his flask's contents on the man's clothes before dragging him by the boots to the edge of the deck. He struck a match and dropped it into the hole that had once been Karn's face, kicking the corpse off the deck before flames engulfed him. As he fell, the fire erupted into a powerful blaze that flew to the ground below.

"He died in service to you, Daen," he whispered at the sky. "He may have been a fool, but he served as well as he knew how."

He turned around. "Flea," he ordered, "get these corpses shoved overboard before our guests arrive."

Cassidy groaned. What few parts of her body weren't hurting, she simply couldn't feel. Her breaths were labored in a semiconscious effort to keep breathing at all. Nieves was wrapping a bandage around her chest and back. The sawbones had offhandedly mentioned throwing Cassidy overboard to save on catgut. At the moment, she was almost inclined to agree to it. Just walking from the steps to the storeroom had ben haphazard and clumsy.

"It's going to scar pretty badly," Nieves said. She took a tiny, metal hook and secured the wrapping.

"You think?" Cassidy snapped. That was a mistake. Her chest tightened and ached. "I can handle another scar or two."

"Or six," Nieves retorted. She began to apply a bittersweet smelling poultice to the stitched-up parts of Cassidy's arms. "These should be much less serious," she told her. "Barely noticeable. Unless you decide you want to ride a hydra's back next."

Cassidy laughed, which hurt. "Now that you – ow! – now that you mention it," she said, but she hurt too much to finish the sentence.

Kek entered the room. They had been using the cargo hold. "Damn it, Nieves, you covered her up already!"

"You were too slow," Nieves replied without looking up.

"I'm not the one who stitched me up," Kek whined.

"Listen, you ungrateful shit," Nieves said. She raised her voice only the slightest bit, but it had Kek tense up like she'd thrown something. "Don't belittle that poor girl's efforts just because you missed a chance at seeing a pair of tits."

Kek looked sheepishly out to where Miria was likely standing. Still, he muttered, "Well, it's a very nice pair of tits. Even if they are a bit banged up."

Cassidy scowled. "Speaking on behalf of that 'banged up' pair of tits," she said, "shut up. Especially you, Kek."

"It was a compliment," he said defensively. He stepped out of the way of the door so Lierre and Miria could enter. Lierre had only had a few cuts and grazes, and somehow against all chance, Miria had made off with only a black eye and bruises on her arms. Cassidy would almost think they were the ones with Fae protection.

"Kek, come here so I can hit you," she said, reaching out to grab a hand mirror.

"No, thank you, Miss Durant," he said, planting his feet. "I've been quite battered enough, today, thanks."

"Miria, hit him," Cassidy said.

The princess looked at Kek. "Sorry, Mister Valani," she said. "Orders are orders." She smacked him in the back of the head.

Cassidy started to laugh but she felt like all her stitches were trying to burst, so she stopped and resumed her deep breathing. Lierre and Miria had no such reservations and laughed their hearts out. Kek whined and rubbed his head. Even Hymn seemed to find it funny – if Cassidy was reading the signs right; the light the Fae gave off seemed to shimmer, and she produced a musical chime like tiny bells. Nieves, however, just clenched her jaw and focused on her work.

When the bandaging was done, Cassidy tried to stand. She managed to get to her feet, but her legs betrayed her and buckled. She fell forward and was immediately braced by Nieves and Lierre, with Miria and Kek each poised to offer redundant help. She felt her face flare with indignity when they helped her dress. With an arm around Lierre and another around Nieves, she was able to limp out into the air.

The moons had taken up their traditional places, though only the barest crescent slivers remained of Turye and Meia, and Jiqun was half gone. Asier was sitting on the aftcastle steps, favoring her left arm, when Cassidy saw her. The captain looked at her. "Are you sure you're up to this? You should probably get some rest"

"I'm not staying behind while the rest of you have a good time, if that's what you're asking," Cassidy said. She forced a smile, expecting Asier to return it and praise her tenacity, as was her habit. Instead she cast a nervous glance outside. That put a pit in Cassidy's chest. "Keep your wits," she said to no one in particular. "Hymn, be sure to stay hidden."

"I will unless I am needed," Hymn replied from deep within Cassidy's shirt.

"I need a hat to hide you under," Cassidy decided sourly.

Together, they crossed the gangplank to the *Scorpion*. They were met by a tall, very muscular man with dark skin. His face and arms were covered in shallow cuts, scratches, and bruises. Above the waist, he wore naught but a vest. Cassidy approved.

"Captain Asier," he said in a tone that sounded strained and somewhat rehearsed. "Captain Balthine extends his greetings and asks that you join us for supper. At your leisure, of course." He did not wait for a reply and turned around.

Unlike the *Dreamscape*, the lower deck was reached by way of a staircase, for which Cassidy was entirely grateful. With Lierre's help she made her way down. The *Scorpion*'s galley was twice the size of the *Dreamscape*'s cargo hold – which was originally meant to be a galley itself, though it was only used as such during terrible weather due to Asier's proclivity for hosting supper under the stars – and featured a long table with a dozen seats arranged around it. There were trays of food and bottles of drink lined across the table, and the smell of seared meat and exotic spices filled Cassidy's senses.

Captain Balthine sat at the head of the table across from them, and a thin woman with a decidedly birdlike profile sat to his right with a lute propped against her chair. To his left was an empty seat next to which sat a scrawny, shaggy-haired man with a scraggly beard.

When he saw them enter, Balthine stood, as did the woman. The scraggly man was slow to take the hint, but after Balthine cleared his throat he stood as well. "Captain Asier," he said magnanimously, "and crew. Please be seated." Asier took the seat directly across from the other captain, with Cassidy to her immediate right. Kek took a place across from Cassidy and Nieves beside him. Miria sat to Cassidy's side, and Lierre beside her. Balthine waved for his own crew to be seated – their escort took the seat next to the scrawny fellow – but did not return to his seat. Instead, he walked around the table.

He walked over to Cassidy and placed a hand on the back of her chair. She shifted painfully to look at him. He bore his own injuries from the battle, but he did not appear bothered by them. She noted that he wore his hair long and untied, which would have driven Cassidy mad. "Pardon my boorishness, but did I hear correctly that your name is Cassidy?"

"You did," she said slowly. She eyed him cautiously, though to his credit he pretended not to notice. He held out a hand and flourished it, and when he snapped his fingers there was a rose sitting between them.

"I owe each of you for the lives of my crew," he said, handing her the flower, "but you had the distinction of throwing yourself bodily to save me in the battle. I wish I had more to offer, but alas, a poor mercenary has little to give."

Cassidy accepted the gift and immediately realized it was too heavy. Balthine returned to his seat as she unfurled the petals and extracted a pair of silver coins. She gaped at them, and the flower, and Balthine himself. "This is very generous," she said, "but I can't – I didn't – um . . . thank you."

Balthine smiled – it was something between a smirk and a genuine smile, and Cassidy wasn't sure if it was charming or unnerving. "Before we begin," he said, "proper introductions: this is Nanette Adarin, my First Mate," he said, addressing the woman. "The large fellow who led you down is Jacques Charron, and that disgrace next to him is Flea."

Cassidy found herself nodding automatically to each member of the *Scorpion's* crew. Asier patted her on the shoulder. "This fire-headed girl next to me is my First Mate Cassidy Durant," she said. "Also present are Kekarian Valani, Miria, Nieves Tarhant, and Lierre Myrlin." Greetings were grumbled between both crews. "So this *is* a mercenary ship," Asier added, twirling a fork around her fingers.

"Aye," Balthine replied. "I imagined the crucified rivermaid would have told the tale." He stabbed a piece of hawk meat and slapped it on his plate. The bird was passed around and Asier took a piece.

"That, and the oversized painting of Daen," Asier said. Cassidy gave a start. She hadn't realized that the mural she'd seen on the Scorpion's side was a depiction of a goddess. "Mercenaries and cultists are the only people likely to take on that kind of attention, and you don't have the uniformity of cultists."

Balthine chuckled. "That's for damn sure."

"Correct me if I'm wrong," Asier continued, "But the only band that wears her as an emblem is the Daughters of Daen."

"As far as I know, you're not wrong," Balthine assured her.

Miria turned to Cassidy. "Daughters? But there's only one woman among them," she whispered. She must have been louder than she intended because the *Scorpion*'s crew shared a laugh.

"The name comes from the original members of the band," Nanette explained. "When the Daughters of Daen were founded, every mercenary flying under that name was a woman."

Asier was the one to chime in when the woman took a pause. "But as a band grows in notoriety, they get more people looking to hire. And in order to do the jobs, they need whatever bodies can fly a ship, regardless of what's between their legs."

"That's the long and short of it," Balthine agreed. "Throw in the high casualty rate, and that's how you get a mercenary band that doesn't quite match its name. I'm a bit surprised you worked that out. Most people don't give us a second thought."

"I've had mercenary friends," Asier said. She leaned forward. "And enemies."

Balthine leaned forward, his smile waning, though it did not fade completely from his face. "That sounds ominous." Nanette narrowed her eyes and his men looked ready to rise.

Asier, however, merely shrugged. "I just mean I've seen them from all sides," she said coolly. "I can't see any reason we needn't be friends."

"I'm glad we're in agreement," Balthine said. "Can I offer you some ale? Or perhaps some brandy? Mead? I have some Rivien tea if you'd prefer."

"Brandy for me," Asier replied.

"If I may ask," Balthine said as he passed a bottle around the table, "you flew straight into a harpy swarm when most sailors would put as many miles between us and themselves as possible. Why?"

Asier finished the contents of her mug before pouring more brandy into it. "If my crew were under attack and a ship were passing," she said, "I'd want that ship's help. I could hardly expect that if I won't offer help myself."

The Scorpion's captain seemed to consider that carefully before giving a wry chuckle. "Begging your pardon, I'm not sure you could really expect it anyway. As I said, most sailors would fly away, and you'd be lucky if they prayed you pass without the gods' notice." He took a share of several dishes before passing them around the table. It was a very dull affair with neither spice nor creativity, but it was plentiful, and Cassidy was glad for it. She took a few boiled eggs, a hawk leg, and roasted mushrooms before passing them along.

"While true," Asier said, "if I did not do what I could, I would be contributing to the problem, wouldn't I?"

Balthine smiled into his mug. "I can see how you managed to make yourself a legend," he said.

"No, you can't," she replied, matching his smile. "But I know what you meant."

"More to it than just a noble spirit and an iron spine, then?"

"Much," Asier assured him.

"Why don't you tell me your secret?"

"Maybe one day I'll show you." Asier raised her mug before taking a swig.

As the meal progressed, Kek and the man called Flea swapped brothel stories. Jacques revealed he was the ship's mechanical engineer and began telling Lierre about a time when he had to completely replace an engine after an unfortunate accident with a noble's prized firebird. Balthine made a point to extend conversation to each of his guests, but very rarely did that expand into full discussion. Asier remained civil, but there was a look of distrust in her eye Cassidy had never seen before – and as supper wore on, Cassidy noticed the captain only ate something after watching Balthine eat the same thing first.

"You know, Miss Cassidy," Balthine said, "I'm from Dawnhal as well."

Cassidy looked at the mercenary's hair, which was black as pitch without even the slightest hint of red. "Pigeon shit," she said with a snort.

For the first time since they had joined him, the mercenary wasn't smiling. He didn't seem angry at her denial, but his jovial charms gave way to a pensive gaze. "Oh, I was," he said. "Let me tell you, though, my hair gave me no shortage of grief." He met Cassidy's eye. "I imagine those eyes of yours were much the same."

"A few stones thrown," she replied with a flick of her wrist. In truth, she had been scared to leave her home until she was ten years old, but she didn't think this man she just met needed to know that. "Children are like that."

Balthine made a noise somewhere between a laugh and a sigh. "I suppose so," he said. "Nanette, why don't you pick up that lute of yours?"

"Aye," the woman replied. She sounded bored, but she grabbed her lute and set it on her lap.

The *Scorpion*'s captain set a purse on the table. "I have a little game I want to play," he said as he started to count out coins. "I'll wager three silver falcons *to each of you* that Nanette can play any song you know," he said to the table. Jacques and Flea shared a snicker.

"That's a damn fine wager," Kek said, scratching his chin. "Alright, miss, can you play *Farewell, Midnight Star*?"

Nanette didn't bother to speak before her fingers started dancing along the strings. The notes rang clear and sweet. "*Farewell, my midnight star,*" she sang, and her voice carried with it a longing that made Cassidy tense with its raw emotion. "*Goodnight, my little love. The dawn is come for me, and our dream has come to end. I ask you that you believe we can make another memory.*" She played the song to its entirety, all seven verses and threw in a complicated arpeggio Cassidy had never heard accompany the song but fit. Each note caused Hymn to flutter and warm beneath Cassidy's shirt, and she feared the Fae would expose herself. When Nanette finished, she lowered the lute and stared Kek in the eye. "Maybe you should think of a song not played in every tavern from here to the Reach."

Lierre leaned forward in her seat. "*The Prince of Tinkers*," she suggested.

Nanette adjusted the knobs of her instrument and plucked the strings before beginning. It was a simpler song than the one Kek had suggested, but it was possible Lierre had been counting on its obscurity. Or perhaps she just really wanted to hear the song. Nanette's voice took on a faintly lighter quality to match the song, but Cassidy thought it was laced with boredom. "*Good morning, said the tinker, where might I find a tavern? I've traveled oh, so far and have many a tale to tell.*" As before, the Scorpion's First Mate knew each familiar verse of the story of a prince disguised as a tinker, and added three more Cassidy had never heard, ending the song with the tinker setting fire to the tavern – all to the same lighthearted tune.

"She's good," Lierre whispered to Cassidy.

"Aye, she is," Cassidy agreed.

"*The Queen in the River*," Nieves said immediately. Cassidy wasn't sure if that was brilliant or cheating; the song was outlawed in Castilyn and very seldom reached outside the nation's borders.

However, the birdlike woman did not hesitate to thrum the low strings of her lute, thumping the wooden frame with the flat of her hand after every third chord. She sang in a low, ominous voice about a queen who made a deal with a goddess to kill a rival at the cost of her beauty. At the end, she threw herself in the river below Tal Joyau.

When she finished, Miria cleared her throat. "Do you know the *Flight of the Last Gryphon*?" Cassidy did not, and she wondered if that would win them the wager.

Nanette, however, merely smiled and began to sing a song in an elegant voice about a hunter in the Reach who had been forced to ground and hunted the titular last gryphon. When after years he finally cornered the beast, it flew away, leaving him to die. Cassidy felt tears well up in her eyes from the telling. Hymn was continuing to react to the music, but Cassidy could not be sure what those reactions indicated.

"I've never heard that one before," Balthine said to his first mate.

"It's popular amongst the nobility in Revehaven," Nanette explained. "But every song looks to get free and find new voices."

"How romantic," Asier said. "Can you play the *Tower of Roses*?"

"No," Nanette said, and Cassidy's heart lifted, but then the woman finished by saying, "I can bring the *Tower of Roses* to life."

The *Tower of Roses* was not a quick little ditty. It began with a few minutes of beautiful arpeggios, accompanied by Nanette stamping her foot in time with the music. After a while, Balthine, Jacques, and Flea all began to slam their mugs against the table to the beat of Nanette's boot. The music was rich, and Cassidy could feel Hymn's warmth begin to pulsate beneath her shirt with each note.

When Nanette began to sing, she was accompanied by the crew of the *Scorpion*. "*It started with a Dream we shared*," they sang,

"*Once my life had been enough,*
Duty and pride and friends and love,
I had these and was content.
But on the day I heard her call,
She showed me for what I was meant.
She sat upon the fountain like a queen upon her throne,

Her eyes, they shone with all that man had ever known.
She smiled and beckoned I join her,
And when I did, she bade me look to the water.
In the reflection I saw no skies of blue, nor my face staring back,
In the ripples I saw her against a sunset sky before the Tower,
Just beyond the desert."

Cassidy found herself mouthing along as the song progressed, and she heard Kek and Lierre singing as well. The song was an epic about a man who searched the world over for a tower the color of roses that likely never existed. Everywhere the man searched he found great treasures or wealth or glory, but he ignored it all in search for the tower. Eventually, in his desperation, he fled into the Dreamscape. While the song was being sung, Cassidy believed she could actually see the desperate search and the beauty of the tower beyond the desert.

"You didn't lie," Asier admitted. "I've never heard such a beautiful rendition played on a single lute. Who taught you to play?"

"A sailor in this harbor, a player in that tavern," Nanette said. She caressed her lute lovingly. "I pick something up everywhere I go,"

"And mercenary work provides travel aplenty," Balthine added. He tapped the coins on the table. "So, unless I miss my count, there's still one of you who needs to think up a song." All eyes were on Cassidy. "Unless you want to concede the victory to us," he added.

Cassidy scowled at that. "No, I'll think of something," she promised. But she was struggling. She had never even heard of Miria's song, and the captain picked the most difficult song she'd ever heard. She delayed by shoving a piece of her toast in her mouth and chewed slowly. She thought of every song she'd ever heard in every tavern and every street, from Dawnhal to Majinaar, from Revehaven to the Ruby Cascade, and they all seemed too well known and too simple.

"*The Lights of Tarenvaa,*" she decided. She allowed herself a smile when Nanette drummed her fingers along her lute, but then she started playing the song without error. She felt her heart sink even as Nanette sang a heartwarming tune about the beauty of the strange lights of the northern skies.

When she finished, Balthine whisked his coins back into his purse. "There you have it. If you would be so kind," he said, sending over a bowl.

"Wait," Cassidy said quickly. "You said she could play *any* song we knew. You never said we only got one try."

Balthine pursed his lips. "Well . . . I suppose I didn't. And I do enjoy Nanette's music."

Cassidy took a breath. *"Maids in Velvet."* She had barely finished the title when the musician's fingers began their dancing. She also played *Forgotten Kisses*, *Prince and the Harpy*, *Knife in the Brothel*, and *The First Dawn of the Night* – the latter was a ditty Cassidy had only heard once in an alley, and the singer had been drunk.

Kek leaned over to her. "Cass, you should really just let it go," he said. "We lost fairly. Let's do it with some dignity, at least."

Cassidy slammed her hand on the table, which hurt a lot more than she was ready for. Tears filled her vision and her breathing became strained. A whine tried to escape from her lips, squeaking between her teeth. When she finally composed herself, she said between clenched teeth, "No." But it was becoming more difficult to find a winning song. Every song she could think of – she was certain she would be able to think of more later, which aggravated her – was a common tavern tune. She ground her teeth in thought. She put her hand to her breast, feeling the Fae hidden beneath her shirt. That's when it hit her.

There was really only one way she could win this game.

"Hymn of the Blue Eyes," she said.

Nanette had already prepared to strike a chord, but hesitated. She turned to Balthine. "I've never heard of it," she said.

Kek nearly knocked his own chair over in his hurry to stand. "So, that means we win, right?"

Balthine waved the man down, and Kek sat with a sheepish look on his face.

"Yes, that means you win," he said. "If Miss Durant can sing it for us."

"That wasn't part of the arrangement," Cassidy said weakly.

Balthine shrugged. "I just want proof you didn't just make up a title to win a game."

"Not a very trusting man, are you?" Cassidy joked.

"Occupational hazard," the Scorpion's captain replied. "Nanette, let Cassidy see your lute."

Nanette looked like she was about to spit at Balthine for the suggestion, but she stood and grudgingly walked around the table to hand Cassidy the instrument. "I'm not very good with these," she warned, "and I've been told I'm tuneless."

Kek nodded. "I once heard a cat getting swooped up by a falcon sing better." Cassidy punched him, which hurt her already damaged hand.

"You don't need to bring us to tears," Balthine assured her. "Just prove you played fairly, that's all."

"Alright," Cassidy said, putting fingers to string. She tested the strings to get a feel for their sound. She took a deep breath and felt Hymn's warmth against her. As she started plucking at the strings, she felt that warmth enter her and course through her veins. She began strumming the instrument and found the music was reminding her of the dream she last shared with Hymn – though she felt like she was trying to recall a dream from a year or longer ago, rather than just that morning. Her wounded wrist – and lack of any skill – hindered her, making the song choppy and slow, yet somehow, she was able to recognize the song all the same. After several repeats of the music, she opened her mouth. At first, she hummed wordlessly to stall and think, but she knew it wouldn't last, so she sang whatever words came to mind.

"*She danced like fire in the bright moonlight,*" she sang. She was surprised at how adequate her voice sounded; it was not particularly good, even to her own hearing, but her voice didn't randomly crack like usually happened when she sang.

"*Her eyes of blue saw me true and she danced.*
She took me by the hand and showed me things I never knew.
She showed me a thousand stars and a thousand more,
We walked a thousand roads and walked a thousand shores.
She danced like fire in the bright moonlight.
Everywhere she danced, she kept the sky in her eyes,
Until one day she could dance no more.
When at last she closed those bright blue eyes,
The fire danced in the bright moonlight."

Cassidy noticed Kek staring at her in disbelief. Miria and Lierre applauded. She handed Nanette back the lute and awkwardly hung her head.

Balthine scratched at his stubble. "Well, it was a song," he admitted. He placed his mug over the coins and when he lifted it, they were gone. Kek looked disappointed. "Where did you learn it?"

"The Northern Reach," Cassidy replied. "About three years ago. The singer told me it dated back before people took to the skies."

"I've known people who would pull their own tooth and tell you it was a relic," Balthine said. "Still, that would explain the verse about walking the roads. Very archaic, that." He took a swig of his drink, then poured his mug over and the eighteen silver coins rolled out onto the table.

Miria applauded the display. Kek muttered, "Show off" under his breath. Balthine slid the coins across the table, giving three coins to each member of the *Dreamscape Voyager*. Cassidy flinched in pain when she pocketed her winnings.

Balthine leaned back in his chair. "If you don't mind my asking," he said, "what brought you to the Gulch?"

"Messenger duties," Asier said. Cassidy schooled her face to avoid spoiling the lie. She stuffed a boiled egg in her mouth.

The other captain gave her a knowing smile. "I just hope the messages are worth the risks," he said.

Asier either didn't notice or pretended not to. "Not for me to decide," she said. "And news is only useful for so long."

"No argument there."

"So what brings *you* through here?" Cassidy asked when Asier didn't seem inclined.

"We had a job in Andaerhal," Balthine replied, "and now we're heading to the capital to tell the client it's done."

"Nothing unsavory, I hope," Asier said sharply.

"Nothing much. The truth is, despite the reputation of the Daughters, I personally don't have much of a stomach for violence."

Kek snorted. "You might be in the wrong business, then," he said.

"That has crossed my mind," said Balthine. His eyes were downcast, and he let out a deep sigh. Cassidy found herself fiddling with the flower as she wondered what he was thinking about. The mercenary seemed to break from his pensive reverie. "But I get to meet interesting people and see the world from the comfort of someone else's purse, so it's hardly the worst life."

"That sounds like good toast," Cassidy said. She raised her mug. "To seeing the world."

Balthine smiled, raising his own. "To interesting people." Both crews raised their mugs in agreement.

Vincent E. M. Thorn

It was past midnight when Asier announced that it was time to leave. "We appreciate your hospitality, Captain Balthine," she said, "however, we will need an early start tomorrow, and we aren't out of the Gulch yet."

"Aye, that is true," the *Scorpion*'s captain replied. When Asier rose, so did he. "We have our duties as well. I hope that our courses will meet again, Captain Asier," he added.

Asier gave a strange smile that Cassidy couldn't read. "I'm sure they will," she said.

"Then, maybe next time, I'll be saving you."

Asier chuckled. "We'll see," she said, walking out.

Kek whispered in Cassidy's ear. "Did that seem strange to you?"

"Oh, thank the fucking mists, you noticed too," she said. "She's been acting weird all night." She tried to stand but needed Miria's help to do so. She did not see him cross the table, but Balthine was on her other side to support her. "Hello," she said dumbly.

"My apologies," he said, stepping away. "It just seemed wrong to leave a guest to struggle."

"Nothing to apologize for," Cassidy replied. "You just surprised me. Care to lend me your shoulder?" She tucked the flower between her breasts before throwing her arm around his shoulder. He placed his hand on her hip, and she felt a flutter of warmth that had nothing to do with Hymn. *Get your shit together, Durant,* she thought to herself. They walked together to the gangplank. Asier was standing before her cabin, waiting for the others.

"Miss Cassidy," Balthine said, "I must take my leave. I – thank you, again, for saving my life."

"Had to," said Cassidy. "There is a shortage of handsome men in the world. It would be a shame to lose one like that."

"Oh, I'm sure you get your pick in every port already," he replied.

"I don't suppose you'd be willing to wait a few hours before setting sail, would you?" she asked, feeling bold. "We could find a much more personal means of repayment."

Cassidy couldn't read the look on Balthine's face. "Sorry," he said, all humor drained from his voice. "But we need to be underway immediately. Besides, you look like you'd bleed out if I grabbed you wrong."

Cassidy tried to hide her frown, but she couldn't. "Maybe next time, then," she said with a sigh.

"Your captain seems sure we'll meet again," he reminded her.

"Well," she said, "a smooth voyage to you."

"And to you," Balthine replied. Cassidy gave him a peck on the cheek. Miria and Nieves helped her hobble over the gangplank and once the crew was back home, Jacques and Flea removed it. The sound of the *Scorpion*'s engines clattering and roaring cut through the silence, and Cassidy watched the ship fly away.

When the sound of propellers and engines grew distant, Kek approached Cassidy. "You've never been to the Reach in your life," he said.

"I know I haven't," Cassidy said, staring at the silhouette of the *Scorpion* in the distance. "Your point?"

"He is referring to your claim of hearing that song in the Reach," Hymn said as she flew out from Cassidy's cleavage.

"Oh, right, that," said Cassidy. "I figured the only way we'd win was to make something up."

"I thought that's what you were doing," Kek said, "until you started playing it. Since when do you know a lute from a turnip? And never mind actually *playing* the fucking thing well enough to fake your way through a song."

"It came to me in a dream," Cassidy replied wearily.

"Must have been a hell of a dream," said Kek.

"It certainly was," Cassidy agreed. She yawned. "I'm ready for watch, Captain."

Asier had been watching the *Scorpion* fly away. She turned to Cassidy. "No, you aren't," she replied. "You can't even stand on your own two feet. I'm calling an all-night in, anyway. It'll be a while before another swarm comes to nest here, and you all need your rest."

"Aye, aye, Captain," Cassidy replied.

"And Cassy?"

"Aye?"

"You're in no shape to climb that ladder tonight," said Asier. "You can sleep in my cabin."

"If you say so, Captain," Cassidy replied. Asier took over supporting her, leaving the others to turn in. Asier opened the door and guided Cassidy to her rather massive bed. She helped Cassidy strip down to her small clothes. When she lay on the bed, Cassidy thought she was going to sink into it. Hymn landed next to her.

Asier took to her chair at her desk and lit an oil lamp. She began to write something down in her journal.

"If you'd rather, Captain," Cassidy said, "I can sleep on a cot, or the floor."

"Nonsense," Asier replied without looking up. "I'm not the wounded one. I'll find somewhere else to sleep tonight."

Cassidy wanted to protest, but she was already too comfortable to shift position, much less climb out of the bed. Balthine's rose still rested in her cleavage. She knew she ought to set it somewhere safer before she fell asleep, but she was too weary to move.

"You shouldn't play games if you're unwilling to lose," Asier chided her.

Cassidy felt her face flush. "I'm sorry, Captain."

"'Sorry' doesn't change the matter."

Cassidy watched the captain staring intently at her journal. There was a flicker of discomfort in her eyes. "You didn't trust them," she recalled.

Asier was silent for a moment, and Cassidy was about to repeat herself when she finally answered. "They're mercenaries," she replied. "You can never be too careful with mercenaries." Cassidy supposed that answer made sense. Even still, she couldn't shake the feeling that something was troubling the captain. As if reading her thoughts, Asier said, "Get some sleep, Cassy."

Cassidy wouldn't have been able to defy that order if she tried.

CHAPTER FIFTEEN

Fog obscured the Gulch below, stretching out for many miles, turning the expanse into a featureless, gray glare in the pale sunlight. Zayne looked up at the moons that hung in the morning sky. There were those who said when the moons lingered into the day, it meant the gods were preparing to interfere in someone's affairs. The Iron Priests urged their congregations to take even greater measures to avoid the notice of the gods during such times. Zayne often wondered how different life would be if he had taken that advice.

Manning the helm was Nanette, while Flea and Jacques were scrubbing the blood from the deck. Zayne had taken to swabbing behind them, in part to prevent them from moaning about him not helping, partly to occupy his time, but mostly because the smell of harpy blood was rancid even after it dried. If Karn hadn't gotten himself killed, it would have gotten done that much faster.

"We'll need to replace him," Nanette said when Zayne made it to her station.

"After," he replied. "Not until after."

"How are we supposed to do this job with only four of us?" she demanded.

"Exactly the same way we would if we'd been five."

"So, I'm going to be the only one in the skiff?" asked Nanette.

"No, Flea will be with you, exactly like we planned."

"So it's just you and Jacques?" She sounded angry.

"And if Karn were still alive," said Zayne, "It would have been just me, Jacques, and Karn. Doesn't sound all that better."

"So why didn't you expand the crew?"

Zayne scowled. "I told you twice now," he said. "The more people in on the fucking plan, the more there are to blab about the fucking the plan."

"So you're tipping the scales toward certain death?"

"Nanette, if word of what gets out, we aren't going to die quick." Zayne stopped swabbing and stood to his full height. He wasn't much taller than her, but he did his best to loom over her. He doubted he was doing a convincing job, so he tried not to worry about it. "First they'll drag us to a cell no bigger than the head on

162

this ship. They'll leave us there for a few days to wallow in our own filth and starve a bit. Then, they'll probably break our fingers one at a time until we're ready to talk. Then if we're very, very lucky they'll shoot us once we've told them everything."

Nanette didn't look impressed. "You're Captain," she said firmly. "I accepted that when Salaa died. But as First Mate – and as your friend – I feel obliged to tell you you're making a mistake."

"Everything about this is a mistake," said Zayne. "But it's my job to decide how to mitigate the risk. And when it comes to breaking into the fucking *Imperial Palace*, secrecy is more important than extra fire power."

Nanette's lips grew thin. She turned back to the course she was keeping. "Aye, aye, *Captain*," she said. Zayne returned to swabbing. He wished he could appease her, not just because she was the only friend he had among the Daughters, but because she wasn't entirely wrong. If – *when*, he thought morbidly – the alarm was raised, they would be faced with the entirety of the Imperial Guard, and extra men would fare better than two. But all it would take would be for one man to blab in a tavern or to a whore and they'd be taken in before even reaching the palace. It was a risk Zayne had to take.

"You know she cheated, right?" Nanette asked.

Zayne looked back at his First Mate. "What?"

"The Dawnhal girl. She cheated. She made up that song."

"Oh, that," he said. He thought back. The song hadn't been very good, but she had warned them she was both tuneless and a sub-par lute player. "Maybe," he conceded.

"Definitely," Nanette said firmly.

"The song had to come from somewhere," said Zayne. "And now it's a song you know for next time."

"You just let her get away with it because you thought those weird eyes of hers were pretty," Nanette snapped. "That or her hair reminds you of home."

"No," he said firmly. "If I ever let anything slide – and I didn't – it was because I was grateful to be alive. As should you be."

"Their captain lied, too."

"You don't think she's the real Asier?"

Her lip quirked. "Hadn't given that a thought, actually. But they weren't a messenger crew."

"Aye, that ship's too slow for that line of work," Zayne agreed. "Trade ship, I'd say."

"And that didn't bother you?"

"That she didn't trust us? A little. But it's nothing new."

"Not that, you dunderhead. She was the empress' bodyguard, once, and she was acting suspicious all night."

"You think she was on to us?"

"Possible."

"I think if she had the faintest idea what we were about, the night would have gone very differently."

Nanette rolled her eyes and focused on their course after that. Zayne sighed. From one argument to another. Still, he was grateful the subject of the heist was behind them. He really didn't want to think of that until he had to – every time he did, he imagined torture, flogging, the gallows, and sometimes a firing squad. None of those were very pleasant prospects.

Around midday a storm threatened to roll in. An hour later, it struck. Zayne gave Nanette a reprieve and took the helm. The mountains and other obstructions were sparse and low where they were, so he kept straight on course, fighting only the wind and the rain. The ship rocked and groaned as the storm battered them around, but she held strong. Zayne imagined he heard the rivermaid nailed to the bow screeching, but he reminded himself it was dead, and there was no Siren Song steering him to his death, just the whistling of the wind. Thunder struck close and Zayne felt his hair rise even as the rest of him was knocked aside. As he lost his footing, he pulled the wheel with him and nearly struck a mountain along the *Scorpion*'s starboard side. He pulled the ship back into the open and checked his compass. He veered the ship toward north and held course.

The storm subsided after a few hours. Thunder still rumbled, but it became distant. To the north, the clouds were breaking, and he could see the beach.

He called for Nanette over the pipeline. She took slow, deliberate steps, her arms crossed under her breasts. Her face was schooled, no flicker of emotion showing on her eyes. That was what told him she was still furious. "What do our supplies look like?" he asked.

"Food should last us to Revehaven," answered Nanette, "unless you plan on hosting another feast."

He chose to ignore the barbed comment. "Rationing should be easier with one fewer mouth." The look on Nanette's face and the way her next breath was so deep and slow to cause her chest to swell screamed the fact that he had avoided the hole in the floor only to step on a nail. "So we're fine on food," he said. "What about water, coal, and weapons?"

"After the rains we've been having, we've water enough," she said. "And mead and brandy. Ale is short, though."

"I'd as soon the ship be dry," said Zayne, "but that wouldn't endear me any. Point is, we aren't going to die of thirst anytime soon, correct?"

"No."

"Good. Is there anything we can't reach Revehaven without?"

"No, Captain," Nanette said.

"What does our time look like?"

Nanette looked out to the horizon. "We should reach the sea in an hour's time," she said. "From there, maybe two weeks."

"What if we push the engines?" Zayne said. "No halt, full ahead until we see the city?"

Nanette bit her lip. "If nothing breaks, that estimate might drop from twenty days to fifteen. Maybe sooner, if the winds are favorable and the weather clear."

"Have Jacques do a sweep of all the engines," he ordered. "Once he says it's as safe as it's going to get, I don't want those engines dropping below full speed for the gods themselves until we're ready to make port."

"Aye, aye."

It turned out to be a taller order than he expected. It took three hours of inspection before Jacques was comfortable with running hard, and even then, it was with reservations. "This ship has some years on her," he said, "and if any maintenance has been overlooked, a hard run could be catastrophic." Zayne, however, trusted that Garen – the *Scorpion*'s former engineer – had been diligent enough about maintenance. He didn't bother to say as much, and just ordered Jacques to do it anyway. In order to accommodate the constant running, they needed to alter the watch schedule to ensure either Jacques or Flea was always at the bellows.

The first three days were the most exhausting; Zayne and Nanette attempted to maintain full watches between the two of them, which only served to leave them worn out and starting to sicken. On the fourth day, they took to switching every two hours. There was a false alarm caused by the appearance of a dragon on the horizon, but the creature was heading in a different direction and did not notice the ship.

On the eleventh day, one of the engines blew; it rang out with the thunderous *boom* of a cannon blast and the screeching of grinding metal.

CHAPTER SIXTEEN

Eleven Years Earlier

The docks were clamoring with a myriad of sounds. Vendors shouted to sell their wares. Bells clanged to herald ships arriving and departing. Sailors laughed and joked while merchants demanded to know where their goods were. Airsick passengers graciously set foot on the harbor, some with cheers, others by kissing the ground, while others struck up conversation with the first person they saw. Ship captains yelled at harbormasters, and merchants yelled at ship captains, and strangers yelled at no one in particular. Beggars and whores each clamored for coin in their own distinct ways.

Zayne was aware of it all, but he'd grown used to such things. He focused on his task – he, along with nine other men and two women – were tugging a large rope looped through a pulley in order to unload a massive crate of cargo from the ship. "Careful, lads!" the ship captain told them, "Them's dragon bones!" Zayne rolled his eyes; if they were really dragon bones, they could drop from a thousand feet and they'd be fine. Or the orichalcum inside would, at any rate, and that was the important thing. Still, no one wanted to lose their job calling out a lying sailor, so they set the goods as gingerly as could be managed on the wharf. A crate cracked under the weight of those above it, and Zayne spied root vegetables, which – while still valuable – could never be mistaken for dragon bones, even by the drunkest of idiots.

When the last crate was set, Zayne crossed the docks to the alley where he liked to take his breaks. He sat on a bench, took a swig from his canteen, and let out a tremoring sighed. His arms were burning, but it was a good kind of hurt, he decided. Meryl joined him before too long; she wordlessly plopped down on the barrel next to him. The short-haired girl – red haired like most in Dawnhal – had massively strong arms covered in tattoos – including a new one, Zayne noticed, depicting a rivermaid doing things to a dragon that made no anatomical sense. She pulled a stick of dried meat from her pack and broke off a piece for him.

"Thanks," he replied. "Where's Iden?"

Meryl took a swallow of wine before answering. "Haven't seen him all day."

"Lazy bastard," Zayne muttered. "I got him the damn job! The hammer's going to fall on me if he can't cut it."

"I know, I know," she replied, giving him another slice of jerky. "Maybe if we kick him a good one in the – is that Tam?"

Zayne looked up the alley to see a young city watchman strolling along. Tam was scrawny but tall, with a nose like a rat's, and crooked buck teeth to match. He stopped a few feet away from them and wrung his hands.

"Hey, Meryl, hey Caraden," he greeted with an awkward stoop of a bow. He was sweating and breathing heavy. Zayne nodded. Meryl tossed the boy her canteen. He missed and picked it up off the ground.

"You look like you just saw the Dread Hounds themselves," she said.

Tam swallowed a lump in his throat before taking a drink. After he took a deep breath he finally said, "It's Iden."

Zayne jumped off his crate. "Is he hurt?"

Tam kicked a pebble at his feet. "Not exactly," he said.

"What do you mean, 'not exactly'?" Zayne shouted.

The guardsman's mouth twitched. "If I knew of anything untoward, it would be my responsibility to bring to justice any hypothetical criminal behavior," he said. He sounded like he had been reciting the sentence all day.

Zayne's gut twisted when realized what Tam was on about. "And my father would probably have him hanged," he muttered to Meryl out of the corner of his mouth. "We'll check on him," he said to Tam. He didn't wait to see if Meryl would follow him before he set out, but he was grateful when he heard her just a few steps behind him. Iden didn't live very far from the docks – cutting through a series of alleyways took them straight to his home in about ten minutes.

It was a squat, run-down place situated in the shadow of a tenement building. Zayne tried the door first, but it was locked. He grunted and looked around. There was a beggar fooling with himself on the far end of the street, but otherwise Meryl and Zayne were alone. There was a window a foot or so higher than Zayne's head.

"Give me a boost," he said.

"Why do I have to do it?" she complained. "Every time!"

Zayne pinched her arm. "Because you're stronger than me," he said. She scowled at him, but she cupped her hands and squatted all the same. Zayne had barely set his foot in her palm before she threw him into the air. He barely caught the windowsill. The window was locked as well, so Zayne had to smash it open. He cut his arm on his way in. When he dropped inside, he landed on a small table covered in papers and knickknacks, which collapsed immediately under his weight.

He unlocked the door and Meryl joined him.

"What the fuck happened?" she asked, pointing at the blood trickling down his arm.

"A madman with a knife attacked me," he said. "What do you *think* happened?"

"I didn't call the Ministry of Sarcasm," said Meryl, brandishing her finger like a gun, "and, mists take you, I didn't come here to listen to your shit."

"No," Zayne agreed. "We came to check on Iden. Let's go."

The sitting room was dim and dusty. A faded blanket was draped over a graying couch. One of two armchairs was lying on its side, and the other was tattered and ruined. Iden's bedroom was adjacent to the sitting room, and it was there they found him. He was sitting on his cot, staring at the wall – which was bare – naked from the waist up. He was gaunt in the face, and his usually shaved head was covered in patches of red stubble.

"Iden," Zayne called. His friend didn't turn away from the wall he found so fascinating. "Iden!" When his friend didn't respond, Zayne grabbed him by the shoulder.

"I see her," said Iden. His voice was devoid of any emotion, "She holds it all together. Every star and every moon and the world, and everything."

Zayne forced Iden to face him, though his gaze did not settle on him. "Oh, you stupid fool," he muttered.

"What is it?" Meryl asked, though the tone in her voice suggested she knew exactly what he saw, and she was hoping Zayne would tell her she was wrong.

"It's the Dust," he confirmed as he stared into that idiot gaze. The whites of his eyes were filmed by a milky blue, and his lips were covered in blue cracks. "Hold him down." This time, Meryl did not argue with him. She restrained his arms and held him tight, though he didn't resist or even seem to notice. Zayne sighed. *Why'd you do it?*

he wanted to ask. *They'll hang you if they find out.* He did not want to watch another friend hang, so he did the only thing he could. He forced his fingers down Iden's throat.

Iden immediately bit down hard on Zayne's hand. Zayne yelped in pain but didn't retreat. Instead, he took his free hand and placed one thumb against Iden's eye and applied a light pressure, which caused him to panic and flail and ignore the hand in his mouth even as he tried to scream. Before too long, Iden was vomiting. It was mess of blue with a silt-like texture. When Zayne was satisfied there was nothing left to force out of his stomach, he wiped his hand on the bedspread.

"I'm sorry," he said, though he wasn't sure Iden could hear him, "but we aren't done." He punched him in the mouth. "Ow, damn it! What the fuck are your teeth made of?"

"What was that for?" Meryl demanded.

"He's taken enough it's colored his skin. I'm hoping to hide that with bruises."

"Well, don't punch like that," Meryl said, mollified. "Unless your hands are properly wrapped, you can end up doing real damage to yourself."

"Thanks for that," said Zayne. "Do you think that will be enough to cover the damage?"

Meryl shifted to look at Iden's face from over his shoulder. She sighed. "Unfortunately, no."

Zayne hit the boy again in the mouth, this time with his elbow, which hurt less, though it still stung. He hit him twice more for good measure. He disregarded Meryl's advice and punched him twice in both eyes. "Alright," he said, "if you hadn't seen him, would you be able to tell he was a Duster?"

Meryl looked him over. "Not at first glance," she said. She patted his face affectionately and kissed his forehead, and Zayne looked away uncomfortably.

"Good enough. We need to find a leecher."

Together, they carried him outside, Zayne holding him by the legs and Meryl taking his shoulders. She complained about getting the heavy end. They schlepped down the street, earning a disapproving look from the beggar before turning onto Hangman's Row. They had to sidestep two people shouting at one another over the price of potatoes. Zayne was jostled by inattentive passersby as they worked their way up the street. Once they reached the Row's namesake plaza, they scurried across it quickly as possible. He heard Meryl whisper to Iden about ending up here if he didn't change his ways.

Zayne spotted two members of the City Watch, who spotted him and pretended they hadn't. He started leading them down a nameless alley when Meryl stopped. "Hey, Zee. The leechers work under Tanner's Lane."

"I'd rather not be seen taking him there."

"We're carrying an unconscious boy in the middle of the plaza," Meryl argued. "At half past thirteen on a sunny day," she added. "We've been seen."

Zayne lowered his voice and leaned as close to Meryl as he could. He tried to point at the Watch officers using only his eyes. "My father would love nothing more than to have me locked up. If they see us take him to a leecher, they may find out why. If they see us taking him to a surgeon for his banged-up face, though, that's nothing."

"A surgeon would report you faster than any leecher," Meryl argued.

"Not Roe," Zayne answered.

"You're taking him to that fish-breathed freak?"

"Aye."

"But you said we needed a leecher."

"Aye. And we do. This is a just a detour."

Meryl made a noise somewhere between a sigh and a grunt, but she followed him. The alley led directly into another one from which they emerged on Chemists Lane. The street was nearly as crowded as Hangman's Row, but the pedestrians gave them a wider berth, some going as far as to cross the street entirely.

The doctor's house was a nice enough two-story home at the top of the sloped road. It was a bit humble for a surgeon, but it was far grander than anything around Hangman's Row. Zayne pounded the door and counted to twenty before knocking again. Twice more he knocked, lessening his count each time.

"Maybe he's not home," Meryl noted.

"He's home," Zayne assured her. He raised his hand to knock again when the door swung open. There stood a squat, balding man with horn-rimmed spectacles equipped with extra lenses connected by small mechanical arms.

"Ah, young Mister Caraden," he said. Meryl had not been wrong about his breath. "Good to see you on such a lovely day." He looked down at Zayne's load. "Oh, what's this?"

"Someone who needs help," Zayne said firmly.

"Well, then, do come in," he said, stepping out of their way. Meryl followed Zayne into a sitting room that smelled strangely of what Zayne could only described as scented *cleanliness* and sour medicine. Together they set Iden on a couch. The surgeon offered them tea, which Zayne accepted graciously while Meryl took a sniff and declined. He sat himself in a teal armchair and offered two wooden stools for his guests. "Now, young Mister Caraden, I hope you don't expect me to believe you dragged this young man so far over some bruises."

"No, doctor," Zayne admitted. He glanced at Meryl, who looked like she was ready to start running. He gave a longer look to Iden, who was starting to groan. "He needs his blood cleansed."

Roe began to fiddle with the extra lenses on his spectacles. "A leecher could do the job cheaper than I."

"He's a Duster."

"I noticed." The old man shifted in his chair. "I imagine you want him purged without Judge Caraden finding out."

"Aye."

"You've been working on those docks too long, young man."

"Please, Doctor Roe," Meryl pleaded. "Can you help us?"

"If you can't cleanse him, at least help us get to him to a leecher discreetly."

Roe steepled his fingers. "Unfortunately, I don't currently have any leeches. I can, however, purge his stomach."

"Zayne already did that," Meryl said.

Roe blinked. "With what?"

"His finger."

"Ugh! So repulsive. And inefficient. What is your name young lady?"

"Meryl."

"Your family name?"

"Haven't got one."

"Very well, Miss Meryl." Roe stood and stretched. Zayne could hear his knees and elbows and the gods alone knew what else cracking and creaking like an old ship. "If you would, take the boy into the kitchen and set the stone basin next to the table."

Meryl obeyed wordlessly. She seemed ready to gag over something. In her arms, Iden murmured, "She's so beautiful. Beautiful eyes of gold." Zayne wondered who he was talking about. He was willing to bet Meryl had the same question.

"Mister Caraden, if you would, please get a bottle of Dragon Beard extract from that cabinet, over there."

Zayne rose and found the cabinet filled with dozens of different bottles of varying shapes and sizes and liquid colors. This blue one treated consumption, that green one regulated the bowels, another was made for men who could not stand at attention, and on it went. He would have missed the one he needed entirely – which was written in Rivien instead of Asarian – had it not been for an illustration of a dragon with a beard. He wondered why it would be called that. Dragons didn't have beards; he was pretty sure.

When he reached the kitchen, the doctor was looming over the semi-conscious dockworker groaning on his table. Roe took the bottle from Zayne's hand. He snapped at Iden's ear a couple times before slapping him in the face. When Iden groaned again, Roe upturned the bottle over his mouth. The Duster began to squirm and writhe, but Meryl held him down.

When the bottle was half empty, Roe pulled it away and turned Iden on his side. The Duster looked like he wanted to say something, or weep, or something, but in an instant what little was left in his stomach came out in a blue-green and brown mush. He made a gagging noise before a second wave, this one purely liquid, shot out, sloshing and spilling over the bowl. He dry-heaved a few more times before he started to pant heavily.

"Now about the matter of payment," Roe said calmly.

Zayne opened Iden's eyes and looked at the milky blue where white should have been. "He's still got the Dust in his blood."

"Yes, but as I said, I do not have leeches in my home. I have a cart I use to make deliveries that you can wheel to a leech-craft. But that will cost as well."

Zayne took a deep breath and rubbed his eyes. "Very well. What will it cost?"

"Oh, nothing much," Roe answered. He twiddled with his spectacles. "Just a silver."

Meryl's jaw dropped. "A whole fucking silver?"

"Mind your tongue, young lady, this is a civilized home, not some tavern in a warehouse or whatever. And yes, a silver. Dragon's Beard is not cheap, and neither are secrets in these days." He turned to Zayne. "I also want to see one of those fancy tricks of yours," he added.

Zayne nodded. A silver was a setback – he would need every coin he could scrap to get his family safely out of Dawnhal – but he couldn't leave his friend to die, nor could he leave this debt unpaid. He slipped a hand into his coin purse. Silver falcons were slightly bigger than copper ones. He grabbed one and showed it to Roe. He held both hands out, one with the coin on his palm, the other empty. He closed his empty hand and smacked the back of it with the palm he held the coin in. He opened his fingers and the coin shot in the air as if from his closed hand, landing on the table beside Roe.

The doctor looked at the coin suspiciously, as if checking for forgery. He held it up to the light, adjusted his lenses, and tapped the coin on the table. Finally, he started to laugh. "Very good, Mister Caraden. Very good." He pocketed the coin. "Now, the price for use of my cart is to clean this mess up."

Meryl glared at the old man's back when he walked out of the room. Zayne found a bucket and a water spigot, and Meryl was given some rags. She scrubbed the floor while Zayne cleaned the basin. "To think," she muttered. "We could have been making our wages, today, but you just had to play the hero."

"You can't honestly tell me you'd let him die," Zayne said.

Meryl stopped scrubbing for a second. "Well, no. But . . ." she resumed scrubbing but didn't speak for a moment. Zayne furrowed his brow as he watched her eyes and wondered what she was thinking. Was that sorrow or fear in her eyes, or something different entirely? Finally, she said, "If he'd have just stayed, locked in his room –"

"His eyes are blue! Either he eventually leaves the house and gets caught, or he dies there because he's too addled to climb out of bed."

Meryl looked at the floor. "It's just . . . Zayne, if *we're* caught –"

Zayne slammed his hand on the stone basin. "I don't want to see him hang!"

"Neither do I, but... Zayne, how long do we keep helping him up? When do we decide he made his choice?"

They didn't speak again until the mess was cleaned. Together they carried Iden behind Roe's house, where the old man was standing beside the promised cart. "Set the lad inside and we'll cover him up." Iden took some arranging to fit in the cart without splaying over the sides, and he'd be very sore and stiff when he woke up, but at least he'd be alive. Roe threw a scratchy, linen cover across the cart and bid them farewell.

The cart was heavy, even with each of them pulling one of the handles. They backtracked to the plaza on Hangman's Row and crossed it to Tanner's Lane. Zayne didn't see the same Watchmen he had before, and the ones patrolling now did not seem to take any interest in him or his cart, so he let out a breath. From Tanner's Lane they took a turn into a dark alley and followed the smell of rotting meat.

The leecher's shop was a ramshackle place marked by a little hand-painted sign depicting a leech in a jar. Zayne set the cart by the door. Together he and Meryl picked him out and carried him into the shop. *This is the last time I'm carrying this bastard,* Zayne decided as he kicked the door open. The stench of spoiled and burned meats and plants washed over them immediately, as did the bittersweet smell of incense used in a vain attempt to mask it. Inside were three tables arranged along one of the walls and a dozen chairs along the opposite. Against the back wall was a long counter that separated the customers from the stock and ledgers. There was a bald man lying on one of the tables, covered from head to waist in leeches. The leecher himself was a pock-faced man with greasy red hair, sitting on a stool behind the counter reading a book.

The leech-craft looked up at the sound of the door crashing open and slammed his book. "Why does everyone insist on kicking my door open? You'd think this city was filled with people too stupid to use a door."

"Sorry, sir," Zayne said as he staggered in. "My friend suffered a pretty nasty bite from something a sailor brought in."

The leecher rose and limped toward them. "Yes, yes," he said, taking stock the boy's eyes immediately. "A *very* nasty bite indeed. Damn sailors, always thinking to domesticate the horrors of the ground below. Well, lay him on the table. We'll need to bleed him some; the venom's already spread." Zayne was grateful to set him down, and from the grunt she gave, Meryl was even more grateful.

They sat on the chairs to catch their breaths as they watched the leecher poke holes in Iden's face and arms and chest and stomach before applying leeches to his body. As the disgusting things gorged on his blood, Iden occasionally muttered sleepily about beautiful women or the sky or songs he was hearing.

The leecher returned to his counter and waved Zayne over. "My services aren't free," he told him, "and those kinds of 'bites' are expensive to treat, you understand. A lot of leeches. A certain level of *discretion*. You understand, yes Boy?"

Zayne's mouth twitched to a sneer. "Aye."

"I'm not an unreasonable man," the pockmark faced man said. "Just looking after myself. Fifty copper doves."

"How's about twenty?"

The leecher let out an exaggerated sigh. "Secrets get blown away like parchment in the wind. I need something heavier to keep them in place. I'll accept forty."

"Thirty."

The pockmarked man pursed his lips and seemed to consider. "Thirty-five is a fair rate for the service provided."

Zayne was loath to part with more of his money, but it needed to be done. "Deal." He extracted his purse and counted out the small coins with care. The small satchel was considerably lighter when he was done, which made his stomach churn.

"A pleasure doing business with you, young man. Your friend will be able to walk himself out when this is done. I'm sure you wouldn't want to be seen doing the same." Zayne found himself agreeing, and he stepped out the door. Meryl followed, and together they relished the marginally less awful air of Tanner's Lane. From there they could see the clock tower in the plaza. It was five minutes to four.

"There go the day's wages," Meryl muttered half-heartedly.

"I need to head home," Zayne said. "I'll see you tomorrow."

"Yeah."

They parted ways, with Meryl heading back to the harbor and Zayne going toward high town. When he got home, his family was already eating dinner. His mother offered him a plate, but his father objected. "If the boy can't be here when we sit down to eat, he can do without," he said. Zayne was in no mood to fight so he climbed up to his room and went straight to bed, the weariness in his muscles winning out over the gnawing pain in his stomach.

He woke up to the sound of his door creaking open. Moonlight was pouring into the room and the house was quiet and still. Nanette came in with a small linen bundle. "Zee?" she whispered. "Are you awake?"

"I am now," he replied. "What's wrong?"

The red-haired little girl crept along the floor, stopping each time the floorboards made the slightest squeak. "Father said not to," she said, "but I saved you a couple of mushrooms." She handed him the bundle.

"That's really sweet of you, Nan" he said, ruffling his sister's hair. "Thank you." He opened the bundle to find five truffles the size of his palm inside. He ate each one gladly, and when he was done, he let out a little burp. Nanette giggled, but she stopped when she heard something move behind the walls. Zayne gave her a grin and whispered. "He's a deep sleeper. You'll be fine. I'll see you tomorrow." Nanette nodded and left every bit as cautiously as she had entered.

The next morning, Zayne woke up sore from neck to calves. He pushed himself out of bed. The sun hadn't quite risen, but he could feel the difference between morning dark and night. He checked his watch. It was four thirty. He dressed himself and made his way downstairs.

His father was standing in the dining room, grooming his beard.

"You're up early," Zayne noted. "I didn't think the taverns were open until noon."

"Oh, you think you're so clever, do you Bastard?" Jainin said, not deigning to look at his son. "I'll have you know, I'm up early because there's to be a hanging at dawn."

Zayne tensed a moment but forced himself to relax. "A hanging?"

"Oh, yes," Jainin said. He was smiling. That did nothing to ease Zayne's nerves. "Public endangerment and the use and possession of Fae Dust. I think you know the lad. Iden Barrow."

Zayne's heart plummeted into his stomach. "No," he said. The word came out as a squeak.

"You should pick your friends better," Jainin said, his smile deepening. "But I suppose I can't expect much from you. One of these days, you're going to hang with them." With that, Jainin left, leaving Zayne feeling hollow. He sat down at the table. He wanted to throw something, to break something, but that would do him no good. He found he had no appetite, so he left to go to work. At noon, he went to Hangman's Plaza to see the body. Meryl refused to join him.

As he looked up at the body, all Zayne could see was his own failure. "It's my fault," he muttered to himself.

CHAPTER SEVENTEEN

The wind was quiet as the *Scorpion* sat in the sky. They drifted a little, but not enough to affect their course by any noticeable degree. To be sure, however, Zayne checked his compass repeatedly. He stood with his back to the hull while he watched Jacques fix the mechanisms that had fallen apart in the starboard engine. Flea was holding the hatch open, and it seemed like he was struggling to do so. The engineer grunted as he did something that made a loud scraping noise followed by an equally loud *clang* of metal striking metal. He extracted an iron bar. Zayne recognized the piece; it should have been straight, but something had twisted it and bent it at a sharp angle. He handed it to Zayne.

"Best I can figure," Jacques said, "one of the rivets holding that arm broke and shot off, and the arm fell under this cog here and you have that."

"I trust we have the spare parts we need?"

"Aye," Jacques acknowledged. "But it won't be quick work."

"The gods piss on that," Zayne said.

"I warned you! We shouldn't have push her so hard!"

Zayne bashed the twisted iron in his hand against the bulwark behind him. "We have a job to do! Get the ship back in shape and check the other engines. Make sure this doesn't happen again." He watched the engineer's face darken, and his fists tightened hard enough to crack.

Do it, Charron, Zayne thought. *You may be bigger, but I'm faster and better armed. I'd love to see how defiant you get when you only have one hand.* They met one another's eyes, and Zayne could feel the hatred staring back at him. He was ready to draw.

Good sense overcame anger, however, and Jacques knelt by his tool bag and started working. Zayne had known other captains who would have demanded proper courtesy – an 'Aye, aye, Captain' or the like – but he was just glad to have the giant doing his job. He turned away and made his way to his cabin. Once he was seated at his desk he sighed into his hands.

He wondered if respectable captains had these kinds of problems. Did the crew of the *Dreamscape Voyager* ever think about killing one another? Did Elyia Asier ever take on jobs that made it hard to sleep at night? He leaned back in his chair and stared up at the ceiling.

Elyia Asier had not been what he expected. He had almost expected her to be an arrogant blowhard – with a reputation as large as the Empire itself, it wouldn't be unjustified. What hadn't surprised him, though, was her apparent distrust of his crew – or of him. Mercenaries were notorious for their lack of discipline, and allegations connecting mercenaries to rape and murder weren't uncommon. Stories of pirates pretending to be stranded or endangered only to overtake their would-be rescuers were pretty regular, too. Even still, Asier's hardly masked distrust – maybe even hate – stung him; he had long admired the living legend, and it wasn't his choice to be a mercenary.

His thoughts drifted from Asier to that first mate of hers. *What was her name? Claire? Cassa? No, Cassidy, that was it.* She had been pretty enough, he thought, for a red-haired girl, anyway. Not that he'd ever be able to do anything about it. He unwillingly thought back to when he saw her exposed and bloodied and had to fight the queasiness in his stomach as he forced his thoughts elsewhere. Her singing voice had been awful, he reflected deliberately. Unlike her captain, she didn't seem to have a problem with him – though she treated his little game like a matter of life and death. He wondered if the *Dreamscape's* crew was low on funds – it would explain why she tried so hard. But the others seemed pretty laid back about the whole thing, so he couldn't be sure.

The rest of Asier's crew had seemed friendly as well, but surely they fought; living in confined space did that to people. The question was, did they hate one another as well, or was that just the curse of Zayne's life? He reflected on the first crew of the *Scorpion,* back when Salaa was in charge. He hadn't liked Garen – they had even brawled once, which had led to Zayne lying on the deck with a broken rib – though the man had been good at his job. He hadn't known Tegan very long before he was thrown overboard in a terrible storm that struck during Zayne's first voyage. Sasha Two-Fingers had been decent company, but Zayne wouldn't have gone so far as to call her a friend.

There had been others, of course: some he hated on sight, some he might have called friends, and others he scarcely thought about twice. From the beginning, Nanette had been there, too, and he could not forget Salaa herself. He had owed his life to Salaa, owed everything he had left to Nanette, and despite moments of frustration, he couldn't say he ever hated either of them.

"How would she have handled this?" he asked no one.

It was an hour before Zayne left his quarters. He had been able to hear the *clangs* and *dings* of tools from his cabin, but in the open air it was clearer. He descended to the lower deck and found the engineer absorbed in his work. Flea was still straining to hold the hatch up for him. Zayne took hold of the hatch and motioned for Flea to leave.

Jacques didn't look away from his work. "I won't apologize," he said. "Unless you want to flog me, it won't happen."

"I'm not interested in apologies," Zayne told him. "I want a status report."

"Can't connect the fucking propellers to the fucking pistons so they will *fucking* turn when you heat the *fucking* bellows!"

Daen, give me strength, Zayne prayed silently. "Why not?"

"Hands don't fit in this small space," Jacques replied. "If you let me stop and reassemble the—"

"No."

"With all due respect, Captain, fuck you."

"Shut up, you damn muck-spout and get your hands out of their before you lose a finger." When Jacques obeyed the order and backed away, Zayne peered into the engine. The connecting piece of iron meant to turn the propellers – the replacement piece – was dangling from the pilot's arm. Zayne took the other end and found the appropriate attachment. Jacques' hands may have been too large, but Zayne's fit with room enough to work, and he was able to thread the rivets into place with the practiced dexterity that came from coin and card tricks and – to a lesser extent – pickpocketing.

When the pieces were in their proper places, he struck the rivets with a hammer and tested the strength of the mechanism by bearing down on it. When it did not budge, he stepped away. He wiped the engine muck on his trousers and waited for Jacques to determine if the job was done.

"That should hold," he acknowledged. "I need to check on the rest of the engines before we start again."

Zayne wanted nothing more than to get back on course and to reach Revehaven as soon as possible, but he didn't give the order. Instead, he said. "Do it after you've eaten something. I plan on raiding the larder myself."

"You mean your secret captain's cache isn't good enough?"

Zayne laughed. "Oh, yes, I keep a store of rich food all to myself but still eat the same boiled eggs and mushrooms day in and day out because I like the taste. Or lack thereof, as the case may be." When they reached the galley, however, the last of the mushrooms had already been eaten. The last of the meat had gone half a week before. Zayne helped himself to the eggs, which dried his mouth as he chewed them. He would have thrown Jacques overboard for a potato or turnip in that moment, but there was no helping that. Maybe Nanette had been right about feasting with the crew of the *Dreamscape Voyager*. While that night he had been glad to share his table, he was beginning to regret parting with his stores so readily.

The inspection of the remaining engines took longer than expected, but Jacques wanted to be more thorough. Zayne found no fault in that, though he itched to be moving again. Night had fallen before the engineer declared the *Scorpion* ready to run. Zayne ordered Nanette to resume course and returned to his cabin.

He lay in his bunk and tried to think about what was coming. He fell asleep almost immediately. He dreamed he was on the *Dreamscape Voyager* instead of the *Scorpion*. He was swabbing the deck beneath a gentle sky. The red-haired girl, whose name escaped him, was standing on the aftcastle, watching him. She winked when he looked at her. She was casting two shadows, which Zayne thought strange, but before he could mention it, the blond man – Valani, he remembered – called his name.

"Keep an eye out for that storm," he said. Zayne didn't think there was a cloud in the sky, but he wasn't about to slack off on his first day. He put a spyglass to his eye and a crash of thunder shook the ship beneath his feet. Rain was coming down in sheets and the ship was being thrown about in the fierce gale.

Zayne tried to turn the ship around only to find Captain Asier standing at the helm, her arms crossed. She glared daggers into him. "I suppose we couldn't expect a mercenary to do us any good," she said.

Shame filled him and he tried to speak in his own defense, but words did not come, and he saw the entire Dreamscape crew surrounding him, staring at him, *judging* him. At the heart of his attention, he saw Cassidy – he remembered her name suddenly – looking heartbroken. Lightning flashed and she once more cast two shadows. He felt a cold, stabbing sensation in his chest.

The dream ended abruptly, and though Zayne was aware he had been dreaming, he could not bring himself to wake. *Bad dreams end every time,* he thought to himself as he felt sleep creep over him again, *but when I wake up, that shit is there to stay.* He had another dream after that, but the details were far more fleeting. When he woke again, he remembered that he had been in some amalgamation of his childhood home in Dawnhal and the *Scorpion*, but little else.

Thunder boomed outside and rain was pounding on the ship, so that had not been strictly in his dreams. He forced himself from his bed and took his shift at the helm. The rain did not stop until long after dawn, and even then, the wind was fierce. Once more they kept the *Scorpion* running hard, and even the shortened shift rotations did little to break up the exhaustion or quell Zayne's desire to reach their destination. His was not the only patience being tested, however. Three days after the storm, Jacques broke Flea's nose for drinking the last of the ale. Zayne prayed they would not turn on one another during the job.

When Revehaven finally appeared on the horizon, Zayne almost thought he was dreaming it. Through his spyglass, Zayne inspected the Jade Palace, a massive structure at the peak of the tallest mountain. The central pagoda towered above the world, cleaving the sky with its majesty. He could not quite see them from the distance, but he knew there was no shortage of cannons and other weaponry along the walkways of the towers.

"Daen see us through," he whispered. The city he'd pushed so hard to reach, which spanned the entire mountain range, now loomed before him with a grim foreboding. For a moment his heart was frozen still, and he almost wished he were in the heat of battle against the Siren-kin yet again. That moment passed, but the chill in his chest remained.

"Bring us into the temple district," he ordered. Nanette obeyed, easing the ship's course farther west, toward the last – and shortest – mountain in the range. By the time they encountered the traffic of the city docks, Zayne had been able to smell the fumes of the factories from the next mountain over for some time. They were forced to wait for a free berth, which took three hours. When at last they settled in the port, the harbormaster was quick to approach them. Jacques lowered the gangplank and Zayne descended to meet the man.

The harbormaster was nearly toothless and wore a hat that seemed to cover all his face above his massive nose. "That'll be twenty doves," the man grunted firmly. Zayne didn't try to haggle, and he wasn't even bothered enough to steal his money back from the man. He counted the coins quickly and a few extra for keeping quiet about their arrival. Nanette and Flea made their way down to the harbor. "Jacques keeps watch until seven o'clock," he reminded the skinny man. "Be sure you're back by then." Flea gave a salute and proceeded to walk off. Zayne grabbed him by the collar before he could get far. "And lest you bring the gods upon us, keep your mouth shut."

"Aye, Captain," Flea squeaked before running off.

Nanette sighed as they watched him fall into the crowd. "I suppose you'll be off to the Honeyed Rose, then?" she asked flatly.

"A sailor must keep to tradition," said Zayne.

Nanette sniffed. "Try not to fall in." She began to saunter toward the crowds.

"And where are you going?"

"You have your friends, I have mine."

"As you will. Remember, the alchemist at dawn," Zayne called out. Nanette's only answer was to raise her hand as she vanished into the flurry of people. He took a deep breath and plunged headlong into the mob, walking the opposite direction from Nanette.

Mired with the stench of factory smoke were the rancid odors of human waste. Zayne narrowly avoided walking under someone pouring out a chamber pot. *The charms of the city*, he thought. Adding to the character of the street, a young boy tried to cut his purse. He responded by adjusting the sword on his belt, smacking the boy in the groin with the scabbard.

The Honeyed Rose was one of the richer buildings in the temple district – in fact, after what must have been thirty years of service and the occasional renovation, the three-storied brothel looked like it belonged in the palace district rather than the slums it sat mired in. The proprietor, Madame Talie, had been offered a chance to move the richer parts of town on a few occasions, but purportedly couldn't bear to leave the shabby and grimy neighborhood where she had earned her first coin. Zayne suspected the real reason was more to do with the lower taxes and costs of running an establishment in the city's ass compared to its face.

He walked through the same rose-colored door he had when he had been a boy of seventeen, fresh to the life of a mercenary. Smoke from qalyans and incense hung thick in the air. There was a woman playing *Sonnet of the River Bird* on a zither in a far corner, the music carrying clearly through the room. Men and women alike lounged on couches and the floor or at tables and the bar. Some were even eating, though Zayne could think of better places to eat than a brothel.

Crossing the lobby, Zayne seated himself at the bar and offered a look toward the stairs to the upper floor. He sat there for a few minutes listening to the zither before he was visited by Madame Talie herself. The woman was of an indeterminate age – she couldn't have been very young, given the age of her brothel, yet her long face was smooth but for her laugh lines, and she always dyed her hair in extravagant colors. The last time Zayne had seen her, her hair had been red – not a natural red like the people of Dawnhal, but the pure color of a phoenix – and the time before that it had been colored like gold.

Today, her hair was a bright blue. She wore a voluminous dress of far too many bright colors that made it painful to look at, and her corset was drawn tight in effort to disguise her small breasts. She had the heavy-eyed look of one who was about to take a nap, but that had been true every time Zayne had ever seen her.

"Captain Balthine," she said warmly, "may-hap you've come to take ol' Madame Talie between your sheets this time?" she asked with a wink. "Just because I run this ship don't mean I can't get my hands dirty for the right man."

"Not this time," Zayne said quietly. "I'm here for Ehshaan."

If the proprietor was at all disappointed by his decision, it didn't show on her face. "She's busy with another customer, but if it's a Rivien girl you want, I could–"

"I'll wait."

Talie's lips contorted into a strange, thoughtful sneer. "You haven't forgotten she's one of my best girls, I hope."

Zayne gave a wry chuckle. "If I had, I wouldn't be asking for her, would I?"

"No, I suppose not. Rates haven't changed since you was here last."

Zayne reached into his coin purse and pulled out a pair of gold ravens. "I'll be wanting her until dawn."

Madame Talie gave a faint smile that said she expected nothing less and tucked the coins down her blouse and took to tending to other customers. It was a half hour before she returned to tell him Ehshaan was ready in her room.

Zayne nodded and made his way toward the stairs. Ehshaan's room was on the second floor, the fifth door to the right. He opened the door to find the whore lounging on the massive bed, dressed in red silks that seemed only vaguely reminiscent of actual Rivien styles and a translucent veil of purple across the bottom half of her face. Her black hair was tied in a tight tail that extended from the top of her head to her knees.

"Oh, if it isn't my favorite ship captain!" she said. Her brown eyes seemed to shine.

"I'm sure you say that to everyone," he answered.

"Even if they aren't ship captains at all," Ehshaan agreed. "I had a feeling you'd be back, so I keep a pitcher of water just for you." She waved toward an end table and sure enough, next to a chilled bottle of wine there was water as well.

"How kind," Zayne answered. He poured himself a glass before sitting on the bed. "It's been a while hasn't it?"

Ehshaan stretched. "Has it? Time means so little to me. The brothel is open every day, all twenty-six hours. Sure, I take some days for myself once in a while, but most days are the same from one to the next."

Zayne kicked his boots off and lounged next to her. "Have you considered my offer?"

"Quit this life of boring luxury and become a mercenary?" She gave a laugh. "Not for all the iron in the Empire. I prefer having sex and only occasionally having to stab someone."

Zayne shrugged. "Suit yourself." He finished his glass of water and lay back.

"Ready for the routine?" she asked.

"It is tradition," he said.

Ehshaan began to moan exaggeratedly loud and bounce, causing the brass frame to squeak. She slapped the flat of her hand against the wall, occasionally shouting, 'Oh, Captain!" She knocked a wine glass off the end table, causing it to shatter. The theatrics lasted fifteen minutes – Zayne had been checking his pocket watch periodically during – and when she was done, she fell flat on the bed.

"You know, I think that's more exhausting than actually having sex," she said.

"I'm sorry to hear that," Zayne said wearily.

"Does it really still bother you?"

The question brought Zayne's mind back to his unintended encounter with Cassidy, when she had been exposed and bleeding before him. Even the thought brought memories flooding back to Zayne and his stomach started to churn. He could taste the thickening saliva that preceded bile. He merely nodded, swallowing down the urge to be sick all over the bed.

Ehshaan caressed his stomach. "I'm sorry," she whispered. After a short, yet comfortable silence, she sat up. "Have you tried boys?" she asked.

"Didn't do a thing for me," he replied absently.

The whore slunk back down next to him. "That's a pity," she said.

"You think so?"

"Well, most men go mad after a couple months without."

"Can't miss what you never had." That's what he always told himself, but he was never sure he believed it. He thought maybe rationalizing it out loud might help.

"That's one way to look at it, I guess." Another silence lapsed over them as they lay together, this one lasting several minutes before she asked, "Why do you keep coming back, then?"

It was a fair question, Zayne decided. The first time he had ever come to the Honeyed Rose, it had been at the behest of the late Gen the Iron Belly — so named because he was the only person on the *Scorpion* who could stomach the food he cooked. *The girls here'll make you a man*, he'd promised Zayne, clapping him hard on the back. When asked what sort of women he'd fancied, the young boy who would one day become the *Scorpion*'s captain had whispered, "Rivien women," which had been true enough. And so it was that Gen had had bought him a full night with the young Ehshaan, the Great Wonder of the East. The bed had been somewhat smaller than the one Zayne was currently lying in, he remembered.

That night, Ehshaan was dressed in transparent silks that had left Zayne queasy, and when she had taken off her top, the gory memory that plagued him came rushing to the forefront of his mind and he vomited all over her. The next thing he remembered was that he was crying, telling this stranger, this whore, about what had transpired that day. She had comforted him. She assured him that he did not need to make love to her, that he was no less a man for being unable. But, to avoid shaming him in the eyes of his crew mates, she had taken to rocking the bed and acting out, giving any listening ears a performance. Even years after Gen had stopped taking Zayne to the Honeyed Rose and died, he still carried on the tradition.

"I enjoy your company," he said.

"Aw, thank you." She nuzzled playfully at him. "So, what brings you to the capital, Captain?"

"Can't I just be here to visit my friend?"

Ehshaan giggled. "You can't take a ship and crew across the Empire just for a visit."

"You can," Zayne argued. "Not that it's good for business."

"So, what really brought you back?"

"Delivery. Someone has some expensive cargo."

CHAPTER EIGHTEEN

Eleven Years Earlier

Ships didn't stop for winter, and the docks were as busy as ever. A heavy storm had hit the night before, leaving the docks covered in ice and snow, and the wind was blisteringly sharp. Despite all that, Zayne had managed to sweat through his coat as he helped unload the *Maelstrom Rider*. The crew of the red ship laughed and japed about how everyone else was overreacting, all the while bundling in multiple coats and linens, and at least one of them had re-purposed his turban as a face warmer.

The *Maelstrom* had come from distant Rivien and brought with it dragon-hide leather – the highly durable material used for the balloons of virtually every ship in the sky – as well as exotic spices, and clockwork trinkets, and children's toys, and a whole host of other goods that needed to be sorted. Zayne was part of a team of four lifting a massive crate stuffed full of salted meat – the captain claimed it was aurochs, and Zayne had the sinking suspicion it was really basilisk meat. However, he had no stake in the shipment, so he decided to accept it – though he felt, somehow, he was doing all the work. His foot slipped on their way down the gangplank, and the crate nearly dropped on him. He braced himself, however, and despite falling on his ass he kept the load from crushing his legs. The box was digging into his chilled fingers and his wrist rang out in protest over the sudden change of weight distribution.

"You alright, Caraden?" asked Moch – who was dressed in enough furs to pass as a very small bear.

"Fantastic," Zayne answered between clenched teeth, "now help me lift this fucking thing." He shifted his leg beneath him and tried to stand, only to slip and fall again, this time landing on his knee rather than his backside. He took a deep breath and straightened, and this time the others decided to pull their share of the weight. They reached the level floor of the harbor and Zayne led them staggering toward the pile where they were stashing the other foodstuffs. With the burden gone, Zayne leaned against the stack and took several shuddering breaths. His hands were stinging with cold and his gloves were wet. He took them off to wring them out, but that was of little use.

"You ought to get a pair of dragon-hide gloves," Meryl said. Her face was buried beneath a collection of scarves.

"Dragon-hide is expensive," Zayne said, slapping the gloves together before wringing them again.

"Aye," she agreed, "but winter comes around pretty regular. Seems to me, a pair of gloves that stays dry is worth it."

Zayne looked at her hands. "So, why don't you have a pair?"

"I don't horde money like you do," she said simply.

"Well, if I spent it on luxuries like dragon-hide, I wouldn't be hording it, would I?"

Meryl gave him a suffering smile and shook her head. She checked her pocket watch. "Well, look at that," she said, "I think now's as good a time as any for lunch, don't you think?"

Zayne checked his own – ignoring as best he could how cold the iron was in his damp hand – which read halfway between thirteen and one o'clock. "Yeah, I thought I was hungry," he acknowledged. He slipped his hands back in his gloves and flexed his fingers, as if that would warm them.

Together they walked up the harbor, and Zayne kept an eye out for ships that might take passengers without drawing too much attention. Most of the ships were cargo vessels, and as a rule they seldom carried anything but trade goods. He recognized a few of the ships as regulars along the trade route – he had met the captain of the *Salty Eagle*, the *Queen's Girdle* was a frequently vandalized Castilyn ship that made port in Dawnhal every five months or so, and the blue-painted *Heroine of the North* was a common sight as well – and others, like the *Mist Queen*, the *Countess of Dreams*, and the *Law of Iron*, were less familiar vessels that he would investigate later.

The *twangs* of lute strings rang in the cold air. Along their path, a small crowd had gathered before a black-painted ship with a rather grotesque figurehead. Sitting on a barrel, a girl with richly tanned skin and a hooked nose was playing *Prince and the Harpy*. She sang the raunchy song with a mirthless expression. It was a short ditty about a man who was delirious as a result of Fae Dust when he heard the Siren Song and attempted to seduce a harpy. When the song was over, applause was given and coins found their way into the girl's hat, which sat beside her.

Zayne nudged Meryl, and they worked their way closer as the girl started to play another song he didn't recognize. She sang it entirely in Castilyn, so Zayne hardly understood it, but it was an enjoyable melody, nonetheless. Many in the crowd must have felt differently – understandable with the war in recent memory– for they took the song as a good reason to walk away. Still, when the song was over, those who remained applauded and a fair number shared a coin before departing. Zayne palmed a copper dove as he approached.

"You're really good, Miss." He pretended to sneeze and cast the coin into her hat. If he'd done it right, it would have looked like he'd sneezed the coin out, but the trouble with that trick is how hard it was to tell if he'd done it right.

"Nanette," she said without offering her hand.

"Nanette, huh? My sister's name is Nanette."

"Good for her," the musician said. She returned to her lute, clearly intent to ignore Zayne entirely. He looked to Meryl, who mouthed the word 'bitch' before walking away.

"So, is this your ship?" he asked, waving at the black ship behind her. He realized as he was looking at it from a closer vantage that the thing on the bow was not a figurehead at all, but an actual, crucified rivermaid.

"I'm a crew member of the *Scorpion*, aye."

Zayne turned his head to get another look at this *Scorpion*. Not only was the hull black – save for a white mural he couldn't identify on its flank – but the balloon was dyed that color as well. Nothing was being unloaded from the ship or loaded onto it. There were two men standing on the aftcastle. One of them was speaking to the other, making grand gestures while the other was staring out into the sky beyond. The ship was not massive, but it was still a fair-sized vessel.

"What sort of ship is the *Scorpion*?" he asked.

"An airship."

Zayne furrowed his brow. He opened his mouth, ready to call this girl a bitch, but decided that wouldn't help him get what he needed. Biting back the words fighting to escape, he said, "Does the ship hire out to the public?"

The musician pursed her lips and glared at him. Zayne tried to ignore the fact that she had very pretty eyes. "Come back in an hour," she said. "My captain will be back, and you can waste her time with whatever petty squabble you've got troubling your tiny life. But for now, piss off." Once again Zayne opened his mouth to retort, but he closed it and stamped away. He pushed his way through the crowd, rejoining Meryl at the corner of a warehouse.

"What was that about?" she asked.

"Nothing," Zayne said between clenched teeth. Together they walked toward Rowen's tavern, a little place on the far side of the harbor. The building was smaller than it had any right to be; nine days in ten each week the tavern was overflowing with patrons. Oddly enough, Zayne realized, this was not one of those days. The common room was dark, with only pale sunlight pouring in from the door to break up the gloom. There was a smattering of customers sitting at a few tables, a few hushed conversations, but on the whole, it was uncharacteristically empty. Zayne couldn't say he recognized any of the patrons. There were a few red-haired locals mingled with outsiders – Or maybe not, Zayne considered. My hair's not red, and I was born here. That was rare, though, so chances were good these people actually were traders and visitors – but there was only one party that stood out to Zayne.

Six people, each wearing black coats – though the coats were not uniform in cut or style – sat drinking and laughing as though they were unaware of the bizarrely bleak atmosphere of the tavern. They were four women and two men, not a strand of red hair among them. At a glance, Zayne would have named both men and one of the women as Rivien based on their general complexion and the turbans the men were wearing, and another of the women had the olive-skinned look of Imperial nobility. Given her presence in a tavern on the far edge of the Empire, Zayne figured she was either a bastard or so far down the line of succession she was practically a commoner, both of which were common enough.

He also considered that olive-skin and almond-shaped eyes might just be more common than he'd been led to believe, and maybe the sailors who claimed their appearance came from royal blood were all just full of shit.

The other three he couldn't identify by sight alone.

Diversity alone wouldn't cause the group to stick out – not dockside, at any rate. Perhaps the most attention-grabbing detail about them, in Zayne's eyes, was everyone else in the tavern. They sat in the far back corner, and the few patrons who remained hugged the dockside wall, keeping most of the common room tables between them. That wall was notoriously drafty, and in the dead of winter only the latecomers unlucky enough to get a good table ever sat there. In the summer it was the opposite, but if Zayne's frozen fingers and misty breath were trustworthy, he hadn't fallen asleep and missed seven months during his walk to the tavern.

He and Meryl walked to the bar. The fat and balding Rowen himself was stationed there, as ever, but Zayne couldn't recall the last time he'd seen the barkeep so idle. "Mister Caraden, Miss Meryl," he said amicably, though not enthusiastically. "If you came to get lost in the crowd, you picked the wrong day."

"Good thing I just came for the food, then," he replied. "Maybe I'll actually have time to enjoy it for once."

"We'll take four dozen of those doves I smell cooking," Meryl said, "and a mug of ale for me."

Zayne gave Meryl a look she ignored but dropped it when he felt his stomach growl. "Yeah, that sounds like a fair meal. I'll have some tea, if you'd be so kind."

Rowen snorted at that, as was his custom. "Aye. One of the girls will be with you, so find yourself a table – gods know there's enough today."

"Yeah, about that," Zayne said, dropping his voice. "What's the story with the black coats back there?" Meryl leaned forward as if afraid to miss the answer.

Rowen sneered in their general direction. "Mercenaries. No dove collectors, either. You ever heard of the Daughters of Daen?"

Meryl shook her head, but Zayne had. "They're the ones who forced the Gray Vulture pirates to disband, right?"

Rowen scoffed. "Disband? Aye, they disbanded, alright. After every last ship of theirs was burned to tinder and the severed heads of every third man or woman were dumped on the streets of Skygate. Every second in three was left branded and without hands, while the last third were left without eyes, all in the name of their desert goddess."

Meryl furrowed her brow. "But they were pirates, yeah?" she asked. "Like, 'rape and pillage' pirates?"

"Aye, no disputing that," Rowen agreed. "But you left out 'in the name of their goddess.' Besides, I've heard it said they've done worse to others."

Zayne dared a glance toward the alleged mercenaries. They seemed amiable, at least talking amongst themselves. At least, they seemed no more rowdy or boisterous than any other sailors. *The*

Daughters of Daen, Zayne thought. *Could this be how my prayers are answered?* "You sure they're really god worshipers? Might just be theatrics."

"To act in the name of the gods is terrible, whether you're sincere or not," said Rowen.

Zayne wondered how the man would react if he knew Zayne himself prayed. It was dangerous, he knew, but he also knew he wasn't getting out of town without help. He was ready to leave; he just needed a ship – one whose captain was unlikely to report him to his father – that would take him and his mother and his brother and sister. If these mercenaries were led here by the influence of a goddess, even if that goddess was Daen, he couldn't risk missing the chance he'd asked for. "Yeah," he agreed absently, "you're absolutely right."

"Damn right I'm right," he said. "Now, stop standing around like you're looking for your cocks – no offense, ma'am – and sit down." The old man staggered his way to the back room, and Zayne picked a table about halfway into the room – close enough to hear the mercenaries, far enough to avoid attention, he hoped.

". . . sat and waited for three days for the bastard to return to his ship," said one of the women. "Three days! And when finally he comes, he is drunk and gives me a gormless look like this." Zayne did not see the face the woman made, but it sparked a torrent of laughter. "And then I walked him aboard his ship. And guided him right over the side!" There was more laughter. "He must have fallen two hundred feet before he hit an outcrop of the mountain."

"I am liking that word," said one of the Rivien men after catching his breath. "Gormless," he repeated before chuckling softly.

It was only then that Zayne realized Meryl had been talking to him. "I'm sorry," he said, "what was that?"

Meryl narrowed her gaze at him. "Are you serious?" she said. "I was saying I hope we don't have to unload another fucking freighter today."

Zayne shrugged. "I'd like it if we didn't," he said, "but you know we will."

Meryl groaned but said no more. A waitress who seemed to be turning blue in her low-cut top approached them carrying a large platter of their food. Steam rose from the browned doves and from Zayne's tea. They thanked their server and put their coins on the table. The waitress took them up without comment and walked away, swaying her hips. As he watched her go, Zayne tore into one of the birds.

"She must be new. I don't recognize her," Meryl said with her mouth half-full.

"Me neither," Zayne replied between bites.

"Of course *you* didn't. I bet you didn't even look at her face."

"No, but I have a feeling I'd remember what I saw." Meryl snorted and they ate in relative silence. Zayne fell back into listening to the mercenaries. He listened to them as they swapped stories of distant lands, of jobs, and of killing, but they also talked about protecting people, and yes, on at least one occasion one of the mercenaries had, indeed, taken coin for safe transportation.

As they ate, Meryl occasionally tried to start a conversation, but Zayne only gave distracted acknowledgments, and before long Meryl gave up. When she finished her food, she rose. "We should get back to the docks," she said tersely. "Unless you want to sit here and mope some more."

Zayne looked up. "You go ahead, I'll catch up." She looked like she wanted to argue, but she pushed the chair in and stormed out. Zayne took a deep breath, working up his courage. *It's simple*, he thought to himself, *just go up to them and say, 'Hello, my name is Zayne Caraden, and I would like to hire you.'* So why did it seem so daunting? This was what he'd wanted, what he'd planned for; he'd never get a better chance.

He rose suddenly and crossed the room more quickly than he would have liked. The mercenaries fell quiet and stared at him.

One of the Rivien men was picking at his teeth with a dagger. When he stopped, he spat to the side and asked Zayne, "Are we troubling you, boy?" He managed to make the words sound like an accusation.

"No, no," Zayne said quickly. He formulated his words as best he could. "I would like to hire you."

The Daughters of Daen shared a laugh – for some of them it was a booming, boisterous laugh, while others were merely chuckling. The same man who posed the question to Zayne spoke again. "A young boy like you wishing to hire the Daughters? Did some larger boy steal your woman?" Only the other man laughed this time, though none of the mercenaries were looking at him very seriously. Zayne felt his cheeks flaring with heat.

"I just want safe transport out of the city," Zayne said. "For myself, a woman, and two children."

The man snorted. "Find a passenger ship."

"I need this done secretly."

It was one of the women, the one who had told the story about walking a man off the side of the ship, who replied. "That's always a fun story," she said. There was a glint of interest in her blue eyes. "So, what trouble does a boy find himself in? Debts unpaid?"

"Ancient family curse? Jilted former lover?"

"My reasons –" Zayne started, but the woman slammed her mug on the table.

"If that sentence is some variant of 'my reasons are my own,' this conversation is over, and you can find someone else to haul your sorry ass out of town."

"Salaa is right," said the man. "Bad business to take on people without knowing the details. After all, being confronted with surprises about our charges makes for bad days."

Zayne cleared his throat. His palms were starting to sweat. He realized he had never told anyone, save his mother, what he planned or why. "I want to get myself, my mother, and my brother and sister out of the reach of my father."

"And why would you be wanting that?"

Zayne took a deep breath. He would be ridiculed for this he was sure, but he was in too deep now. "My father is a violent drunk, and a bully besides."

To his great surprise the mercenaries did not laugh. The one named Salaa gave him a sympathetic look, and the Rivien woman nodded as if that made all the sense in the world. The woman who may or may not have been noble blood leaned forward. "Why not hire us to kill him? Job would be done quicker, and you and your family get to stay nice and cozy at home."

Zayne took a step back. "I can't kill my father."

"That's why you'd hire us," she replied, as if explaining to a child.

Zayne hadn't considered the idea before, often as he wished the old man would die. It was tempting. "No," he decided after a moment. "I won't have blood on my hands."

The one called Salaa leaned over to the Rivien man who had not addressed Zayne directly, who whispered in her ear. Salaa nodded and turned to Zayne. "What makes a public ship too noticeable? This father of yours some kind of investigator?"

"Not quite," Zayne said, shifting in his boots. "My father is a city judge. He has lots of people who answer to him. He sometimes has people watching me, too."

Salaa looked at the man who had started the conversation with Zayne. "Go ahead, Kaveth," she said. "You were just saying how much you love easy jobs."

The man scratched at his beard. "Where are you wanting to go?"

"Any other city," Zayne said. "We can start fresh when we get there."

"He's a bold one," said the maybe-noblewoman.

Kaveth made a noise of contemplation before saying, "I'll do it for five silver falcons." Zayne pulled his purse off his belt. He had three silver falcons and a full host of coppers. He set the silver coins on the table and dropped the rest of the purse next to them. Kaveth weighed the purse in his hand. "Not quite enough, boy."

"What if I work the rest of the debt?" Zayne found himself leaning on the table before he realized it. "I can cook, I can swab the decks, I can help move cargo."

Kaveth looked to Salaa who gave a shrug and a smile and rose. "You got a name, kid?"

"Zayne Caraden."

"Well, Mister Caraden," Kaveth said, sweeping the coins and purse off the table, "The *Autumn Raven* sets sail day after tomorrow at noon."

"I'll be there," Zayne promised.

Exhilaration filled him when he clasped hands with Kaveth, who introduced himself formally as Captain Kaveth Darziin of the *Autumn Raven*. Zayne thanked him profusely before taking his leave. He thought about going back to the docks, but realized he no longer needed that job. What he needed was to tell his mother the good news. He could collect the day's wages afterward. He started walking up town toward home, but he soon found himself running. He ran until his lungs burned and continued until his throat felt like it was going to split open, then slowed to a jog.

When finally he reached home, it was a few minutes to three o'clock. He opened the door to find it was dark. The room had a slight odor of refuse, which was unusual. "Mother?" he called. There was no answer. She must have gone out, he decided. Nanette and Cenn liked seeing the vendors with her. Zayne shrugged his coat onto the rack and was about to close the door when he saw something just on the edge of the light. It looked like a small boot sitting just beside the table. "Cenn, leaving your shit in the middle of the floor," he muttered to himself. As he got closer, he realized it wasn't just a boot. Cenn himself was lying in the dark. "Cenn, that's no place for a nap," he said. He knelt and shook his little brother by the shoulder. The boy did not react. Zayne's heartbeat rose and he felt a cold surge through him. "Mother!" he shouted. He grabbed the table to help himself up and felt something sticky there. He jumped to his feet and held his hand toward the light. There was blood on the edge of the table. There was blood in his hands. Tears filled his eyes as he realized what had happened.

"Mother, Cenn's hurt!" he yelled, running deeper into the house. He tripped over something in the dark. He stumbled and hit the wall before looking at what had tripped him. A small girl with orange red hair sat in the dark, her eyes staring unblinkingly at the ceiling, her face bloated. Zayne picked up his little sister and checked for a pulse. He found none. "no, no, no, no, no, No, NO!" he muttered to himself, more quickly and loudly with each iteration until he was all but shouting and crying the words, as if they would make all the wrongness go away.

"Mother!" he shouted yet again as he looked from room to room for her. She wasn't in the larder. She wasn't in her room, nor Zayne's, nor the twins'. He opened the washroom last. Water covered the floor, causing it to gleam in the sunbeam allowed through the small window. Zayne's mother was naked, sprawled on the bathroom floor with one leg still in the tub, covered from neck to waist in wounds that had poured over the floor, with a butcher's knife lodged in her shoulder. Her face was locked in an expression of terror and confusion, and her red hair was sticky with blood that had not yet dried. Zayne fell to his knees and crawled to her, only vaguely aware of how much blood was covering his own body. He sat there staring at her, the blood drying on her naked skin, her wounds exposing bone and muscle and other parts Zayne did not recognize.

Zayne could not help himself; he felt the bile rising for what seemed like his entire life, and he vomited. Three times he brought back chunks of his last meal, and three more times lost whatever fluid and humors were sitting in his stomach. When there was nothing left, he dry-heaved until finally he collapsed, lying under the shadow of his mother, soaked in her blood and his own bile.

There was a crash from somewhere outside the room that seemed like it was a thousand miles away. The entire world felt as unreal as a dream. Maybe it was a few seconds later, or maybe it was a hundred years, when the door to the washroom was kicked open. "You see officers? Is it as I told you? Seize him!" Zayne looked up wearily from his place in the floor. There were three members of the City Watch standing in his house. Behind them stood Jainin Caraden, reeking of ale, and there was murder in his eyes.

CHAPTER NINETEEN

The red dawn had always been a disliked omen among sailors. Zayne wondered if that applied even if one wasn't sailing. The sun was climbing the summit behind the eastern mountain, lightening the gray shadows over the streets. There was a sense of quiet. He drew his coat tighter around himself. The alchemist's shop was not yet open, and the streets were cold.

"The sign on the fucking door says she opens at seven," Nanette griped. "Seventh bell rang half an hour ago!"

Zayne checked his pocket watch. It read five minutes after seven. "Aye," he replied dryly. "A half hour. Definitely."

"Outrageous," Nanette continued. She knocked on the door. "Wake up!" When nothing happened, she pounded harder. "*Wake up!*" She was about to hit the door again when it swung open and a woman so short she didn't reach Nanette's breasts stood staring up at her from half-moon spectacles. Something about her reminded Zayne of Lancen.

"What's with that racket?" The alchemist demanded.

"Racket?" Nanette yelled, "we've been waiting –"

"Please forgive my wife," Zayne said, easing Nanette aside. "She's been very distraught. You see, her father moved in recently, and he's prone to restless nights. We were hoping you might have something to help him sleep."

The alchemist adjusted the spectacles on her nose. "Well, come in then, shop's open."

When the woman ducked back inside, Nanette turned and whispered, "Your wife?" sharply in Zayne's ear.

"That's the story I came up with while you were getting ready to go to war over a short delay."

"That's not —" she began, but Zayne overrode her.

"It's done. Let's go."

Nanette crossed her arms under her breasts and sniffed before following him in.

The dark shop was lit only by the sunlight pouring in from the door and a small, high window. It was a maze of tall shelves and a myriad of smells that fought for the focus of Zayne's nose. One moment he was enjoying the aroma of orange slices, then he walked past a pocket of air that reeked of nepenthe, and then he was smelled what might have been cat piss and onions. He was not pleased by the experience, but he made a point to keep smiling. He was a professional, after all.

The tiny woman sat on her stool behind a counter. "Autumn's Tears should help him sleep like a stone," the alchemist said. She held up a small vial containing a pale orange liquid. "Just a drop of this in his drink and he'll be out before he can snuff a candle."

"Sounds promising," Zayne said, scratching his chin. He eyed Nanette, who took her cue.

"My father doesn't let anyone prepare his drinks," she said. "He always gets his water straight from the spigot."

"She's right," Zayne said, giving an exaggerated sigh. "Do you, perhaps, have any solutions he could breathe in?"

"That's a dangerous thing you ask for, Mister . . ."

"Cevaante," Zayne answered.

"Mister Cevaante. I cannot advise you give your father-in-law any sleeping draught through his *breath*. The dosage needs to be perfect, elsewise he's liable to choke on his own tongue." The alchemist sighed. "May just happen anyway, with the elderly."

"He's also liable to croak tomorrow trying to reach his chamber pot," Zayne argued. Nanette at least had the wherewithal to gasp indignantly. "You're the alchemist, so why not just tell us exactly how much to use, and we'll take care of the rest."

The alchemist adjusted her spectacles. "I cannot in good conscience," she said.

Zayne looked to Nanette. She nodded. It was always good to have second plan. "Wasn't there another potion shop a few streets down the lane?" he asked.

"I think there is," said Nanette. "Madame Bolis, I think the sign read."

The alchemist leaned forward in her seat. "There's no need to trouble yourself to go up the way," she said quickly. "I just remembered; I have what you're looking for. Wait here." She opened a door behind the counter and disappeared behind it. Zayne and Nanette stood waiting, listening to the sound of clattering glass as cases were being moved, and once something hit the floor with a resounding crash. When the old woman finally reappeared, she carried a leather pouch. "Beard of the Sphinx," she declared. She handed Zayne the bag. "Just catch fire to it — a candle or lantern will be plenty — and the fumes will have him asleep in mere moments. Scentless, quick. Beware of the aftertaste, though. Tastes just like — well, never mind that."

Zayne peered in the bag. "Is it really a Sphinx's beard?" It looked like grass.

"Of course not," the alchemist said quickly. "It's just a name. Sphinxes don't even have beards, what is wrong with you? Now, it'll be fifty doves for the bag."

Zayne was about to argue that Sphinxes did, in fact, have beards but a look from Nanette was enough to keep him on track. He supposed that as long as this old woman knew her business, her blatant ignorance in unrelated matters was none of his. "We'll take all you have," he said as conversationally as he could manage, though he was straining.

"All I —"

"Don't worry, we can pay," Zayne assured her. "We just like to be prepared." The alchemist stared at Zayne with her mouth open for a moment before walking into the back room again. This time there was no noise to mark the old woman's progress, yet she took longer than before.

Zayne pointed to his eyes, then the door behind which the alchemist was working. Nanette nodded and fixed her eyes on the spot while Zayne leaped over the counter. The alchemist's coin box was where Zayne had expected to find it, tucked in a corner of the shelf built into the counter. It was unlocked. Zayne examined the contents. The alchemist was fairly well off – given her proximity to the brothel and the docks, Zayne had no questions regarding the nature of her usual patronage – though most of the coins were doves, and she had no iron or even gold at all. "Of course," he said with a scowl. He took a dozen copper coins and pair of silver falcons, wishing he felt safe taking more.

Nanette feigned a sneeze. Zayne slammed the box closed and returned to the other side of the counter. Only a few seconds later the short woman waddled back into the room carrying several drawstring purses.

"This is all the Beard I have," she said breathlessly, climbing back to her seat. "Now, listen, for this is very important! Each of these bags is three full doses. Don't burn more than one dose at a time, lest you —"

"Right, choke on his own tongue," Zayne acknowledged. "Yes, that would be bad."

"Yes. Well," the alchemist set the pouches in a row. "Ten bags should last you a fair while. If you can pay as well as you say. This is no cheap weed your grandfather can grow in his house, after all."

Zayne took a breath. "I understand," he said.

"And since this means I'll need to resupply earlier than I expected, I will need an iron phoenix."

Zayne gasped, but it was Nanette who said, "A whole phoenix?"

"Aye. Your husband said you could pay, but if he was mistaken . . ."

"I wasn't," Zayne said, making a show of reaching into his coin purse. He had a few iron coins at the ready, but he made a show of looking all the same. He didn't pay in raw iron, either, but gathered silvers and gold. With an exaggerated scowl he slammed the small handful of coins onto the counter. "Gods," he said, "all this trouble for a paranoid old man."

"That is my father you're talking about!" Nanette yelled.

The alchemist counted the coins, smiling when she was done.

"It will be well worth your coin," she promised. Zayne merely nodded as he scooped up the satchels – snagging a couple coins back as he swept his hand. The woman didn't seem to notice.

"Come along, Dear," Zayne said quickly. Together they left the shop and its assault on Zayne's sinuses. After the door closed behind them, Zayne spat. "A phoenix's worth, my ass. If we only had coin we came by honestly, we'd be broke because of harlots like her."

Nanette shook her head. "If we only had what we came by honestly, we'd be broke because we'd have no work."

"Point. So, where was the artificer's shop?"

"While I'm sure there's one around here, we'd be better off not seen circling the neighborhood for oddities. There's a good one in the next district."

Zayne looked up at the next mountain on the range and the section of city atop it. "Foot bridge, or barge ride?"

"We can rent a barge. If we walk there and back, we'll have no energy for anything else." They crossed several streets to reach the barge terminal, which was a wide sectioned off area at the edge of the district.

The barges were even busier than the docks, with crowds of people milling to take care of duties that took them to other districts.

The noise of conversations and bells clamoring and station workers calling out commands washed over Zayne as a wave of empty noise. He would have liked to use the skiff from the *Scorpion* and bypass the whole mess, but traffic was regulated, and he couldn't afford to have the skiff identified.

The lines to ticket booths were longer than Zayne would have liked, but he found the shortest one he could and stood with Nanette. Zayne checked his watch every time he felt an hour had passed, only to realize it was always fewer than five minutes. At one point he put the watch to his ear to make sure it was still ticking properly. When at last they reached the booth, Zayne was ready to throw his coins at the head of the man who sold him the tickets. The next barge to the factory district was not to depart until twelve o'clock. Zayne checked his watch as though he hadn't spent the last hour staring at the bloody thing. It was ten-thirty.

With nothing better to do, they found a seat aboard the barge, which was little more than a box full of benches tied to a ship balloon. Zayne offered to play a round of Fortune's Favor. "No thanks," Nanette replied. "You know too many card tricks."

Zayne shrugged and leaned back. They had chosen a seat at the aft of the barge on the starboard side. Through his window, Zayne could see the Jade Palace, though he could hardly make out any details across the distance. Seeing his goal looming over him made Zayne question whether a simple suicide would be better than going through with this suicidal *mission*. He looked toward the ground. It seemed every bit as far away as the palace, and so much easier to reach. Just one step.

He shook the thoughts away and closed his eyes. Nanette must have felt his unease, because she patted him gently on the knee.

The barge filled up slowly until about fifteen minutes were left before departure, when suddenly a whole host of passengers tried to file in all at once. Eventually, the engines started to churn. In the seat across from Zayne, a mother was soothing her fussing child, telling her that flying was nothing to be scared about. Zayne wondered how Nanette – his sister, not his friend – would have handled flying for the first time. And Cenn. He clenched his fist at the thought. They never knew the feeling of the skies, of a trusted ship beneath their feet. Their deaths carried his thoughts, as they always did, to his mother. His stomach churned and he felt the bile threaten to rise.

Nanette grabbed his hand. "Don't sick up on me," she said gently. With a smirk, she added, "it would be poor form for a ship captain to vomit on a little barge like this." Zayne nodded. It was several long moments before he realized he was squeezing her hand. He relaxed his grip, but neither of them let go completely. The barge rode smoothly, but far more slowly than Zayne would have liked. Not that it could have gone any faster with the city regulations being what they were. There was a comfortable silence between them, however, and even surrounded by strangers, Zayne felt more secluded than he had aboard his own ship since it had become *his*.

After the barge came to its stop, they waited until the crowd thinned before disembarking. It was twelve minutes past noon when they stepped into the factory district. The sleepy mornings of the temple district did not exist here, and by the middle of the day business was in full swing. They had to force their way into the crowd and ease themselves along the flow of slow walkers. Zayne followed Nanette's lead along twisting roads and lanes that eventually led them to the shop she had promised.

Above the door was a hand-painted sign depicting a wrench and a clockwork bird, below which was inscribed simply, "Gao's." A bell chimed when Zayne opened the door. The shop smelled of some sort of oily polish. Much like the alchemist's shop, there were arrangements of shelves that created aisles throughout the shop, though unlike the alchemist's shop, they were only chest high and covered with shiny bobbles. The room also had a warmer light to it.

Sitting on a stool behind the counter was a fat man who appeared to be of Imperial noble blood – though from his greasy appearance and threadbare linen clothes that blood must have been distant indeed – with a mustache that drooped far below his chins. He was looking over a clockwork toy of some sort, adjusting the magnifying lenses attached to his spectacles every so often, while a customer looked on. The customer had a fidget to him and a half-hidden sneer on his face, but the artificer gave no notice. After a time he took a fine tool and made an adjustment. When he was done, the customer paid him and left.

"Are you Gao?" Zayne asked.

"Last I checked," the artificer acknowledged. "Need something fixed?"

Zayne stepped up to the counter. "Replaced entirely, actually. I need a new spring loader for one of the harpoon guns on my ship."

"Very vital equipment," said Gao.

"Aye, it is," agreed Zayne. "If you have a replacement for the whole thing, I wouldn't object to paying just a bit more to save myself the installation time, but I definitely need the part if nothing else."

"I'm sure I'll have the equipment you need," the man assured him. "But I'll need the measurements of your ship's gun to get you the right part."

Zayne offered Gao a smile and extracted a sheet of parchment from his coat. "Good thing I came prepared." The artificer looked over Zayne's measurements and assured him he had what he needed. The man provided him with the spring loader, and Zayne worked on getting a few other pieces of equipment he needed for the job. His requests were often prefixed with, "While I'm here . . ." In addition to the spring loader, he procured a set of clamps, a hand vise, forty feet of chains, a dozen razor-wire traps – "For those pesky birds" – and a set of tiny clockwork tools.

"Will that be everything for you, then?" asked Gao.

Zayne nodded. "Aye, I think that'll do quite nicely."

"Then all that's left is the matter of payment."

Zayne reached for his coin purse. "So, what's the damage look like?"

Gao made quite a show of calculating the costs of each item laid out on the counter – he counted on his fingers, he tugged his mustache, and he expelled contemplative groans every so often. Eventually he must have justified the price Zayne assumed he'd already settled on. "It'll be a silver for the lot."

"Steep," said Zayne, "but essentials are called that for a reason."

"Aye, they are that." Gao took Zayne's coin without complaint. The man offered Zayne a large, leather satchel for the goods, which he accepted. He slung the bag over his shoulder and bid the man farewell before stepping out into the crowded streets again.

"Have we forgotten anything?" Nanette asked as they returned to the barge station.

"I hope not," Zayne said simply. "Because we do this tonight."

The return trip to the temple district was just as slow as the ride up, and the wait for the barge itself was longer. When they reached the other side, they walked around where the terminal met the harbor and maneuvered in silence through the jostling crowds until they reached the *Scorpion*.

Flea was sitting on the gangplank talking to Jacques, who was leaning against some crates stacked near the ship. "All aboard," he called as he stormed up the gangplank. Once they were all standing on the deck, he pointed at Flea. "If anyone gets too close, if anyone so much as *looks* at the ship too long, call me over the pipeline."

"Aye, Captain."

"The rest of you, with me; we have a lot to do before nightfall, and little enough daylight left." He led them below the docks into the galley. He swept all the cups and plates still on the table to the floor and spilled the contents of his satchel onto the table. Jacques threw his own bag next to the pile. "You sure you can make what we need?" Zayne asked him.

"Aye," the big man replied, taking the spring loader in hand. From his own bag, he extracted a metal tube and began taking measurements.

Zayne turned to Nanette. "While he's doing that, figure out the best way to turn that sleep draught into a weapon." She nodded and set to measuring out the Sphinx's Beard. Zayne sat down at the head of the table and set his coat on the table in front of him. He started shuffling the contents of his hidden pockets. The deck of cards he traditionally kept in his inner breast pocket would be of no use to him, so he set them aside on the table. The extra coins he had in folds woven within his right sleeve near his lock-picks, however, he left in place. Concealed along the hem of the coat were five folding barber's razors. He slid one into his left sleeve next to his stiletto, leaving the others securely in place.

Satisfied with his coat, he began to clean his pistols. He hoped he would not need even one of them, but he knew if a firefight started, he would have little to no opportunity to reload. With that in mind, he readied six pistols and would carry powder and extra bullets to be safe. When the guns were finished, he tucked two in loops at the small of the back of his coat, one in the inner breast lining, and the rest on his belt straps. His final preparation was to strap a pair of climbing spikes to his vest.

When Jacques and Nanette declared they had completed their tasks, Zayne checked his watch. It was five in the evening. "All rest," he said. "We move out at midnight."

CHAPTER TWENTY

Thunder cracked overhead and the rain poured over them in sheets. Zayne wasn't sure if it was good or ill that a storm had rolled in with no warning just as they were readying the skiff. The small boat moved lazily around the mountains below the city. They kept the engines low, turning them off completely and using a hand-crank to control the propeller when it seemed the storm was beginning to quiet, or when Zayne got a paranoid feeling about being heard – which was more often than was probably reasonable, he admitted to himself. It was slow going, but eventually, they were under the shadow of the Imperial Palace. Zayne peered out and around the balloon. "Well, Jacques," he said, "it's time to see if your device will work like we planned."

"It'll work," Jacques assured him. He held out the tall, pipe-like contraption which had a harpoon blade sticking out of the end. The large man lined it up with a formation of rock just beneath the wall of the palace garden. "Ready, Captain," he said.

Zayne gave a last look for any patrolling ships. "Fire," he said. There was a sharp *clank* followed by the sound of rapidly spooling chain, and after a moment the blade struck the distant rock. Zayne turned to Nanette. "Keep an eye out for the signal. We'll be leaving through –"

"The seventh level of Serenity Tower," Nanette finished for him. "I know."

"Let's go, Jacques," Zayne said. "The longer this takes, the greater the risk of getting caught." He grabbed hold of the pipe connected to the chain. "Do it," he said. Jacques hit a switch and the instant the skiff fell out from under his feet, Zayne thought he was plunging to his death. He and Jacques flew upwards toward the mountainside like a pair of bullets. He made the mistake of looking at the black abyss below at the same moment lightning struck, which illuminated the distant ground below him as well as daylight, if only for a moment. Though he was wearing dragon hide gloves, he suddenly felt his hands were too slick, and the glimpse of what was beneath him made his palms sweat. When Zayne's boots made contact with the rock wall, he thought he was dying.

Zayne waited twenty heartbeats in stillness before he was sure he wasn't dead. A chill coursed through him and he sought a strong foothold before he dared loosen even one hand from the harpoon. He swallowed some spit and tried to fight past the hollow pit in his chest. He took hold of his climbing spikes and slammed them into the rock. "Right," he said breathlessly. "Good work." He climbed. Part of him refused to accept that he was not yet dead. That was foolishness, he knew, yet that rational thought, all thought, seemed distant as he climbed, surrealistic detachment taking over. Lucidity only set in long after he had transitioned from climbing the natural rock formation to the wall made of smooth alabaster. Each swing of the pick made his arms burn; he felt each strike into the stone send tremors down his arm, and with each strike his fingers threatened to betray him. Worse, every strike rang in his ears like a cannon blast, and he feared each progressive step might betray his presence.

The rain helped nothing.

The wall was smooth as glass and the rain made it slick while soaking into his clothes and weighing him down more and more with each passing moment. He climbed blindly, afraid to look at how far he had left to scale, knowing he'd lose heart with each pull if it wasn't the last. *Just one more*, he thought as he struggled for air. *Just one more.* He mouthed the words as his he pulled himself up. *Just one more.* He slammed his pick once, twice, three times to wedge it in and create a strong grip. *Just one more. Just one more. This is the last one. Just one more. Just get this next one. Just one more.*

He swung his pick and found nothing. Dismay and vertigo washed over him as he knew he was destined to plunge until his body cascaded against the rocks below. Instead, however, his arm hooked over the top of the wall. Tears of relief flooded his eyes and obscured his goggles. He pulled himself, fighting the strain in his shoulders. He tried to push up with his feet, but the wall was too slick, and he slipped. He yelped and slammed the pick down on the top of the wall, catching himself. He pulled himself atop the structure and collapsed. His breath was raspy and deep. He tried to control his breathing, to remind himself of the need for secrecy and silence, but his body paid no heed. If he were found now, he couldn't raise so much as a finger to defend himself. He felt like he was dying after all. Yet in the same instant, he felt more alive than he could remember ever feeling. He had taken the first deadly step. He had reached the Jade Palace. Now it was just a matter of getting in and getting out.

Simple, he thought dazedly.

There was a sound somewhere between a squelch and a thud. Zayne let his head roll lazily to the side. Jacques had reached the top as well, and laid face down in the water and alabaster stone. Zayne wasn't sure how long they lay there, soaking in the rain, catching their breaths, gasping like fools. He couldn't even lift his hands to check his watch.

"Fuck," Zayne said when at last he felt like the air was actually reaching his lungs, if only just. "The gods."

It could have been anytime between two minutes and an hour later when Jacques replied, "Aye. Captain."

Zayne drank in what rainwater he could as it fell into his mouth and allowed himself his rest. He eventually felt strength return – slowly, but enough – and he moved to a sitting position. He crawled farther inward so that if he fell off the wall, he would fall into the palace yard. In that moment he decided that, if he should die, he wanted his efforts recognized, if nothing else. What he could make of the garden between flashes of lightning was beautiful. There was a set of marble benches sitting at the end of a paved pathway that wove through well-sculpted hedges. Countless flowers were grown in rows and plots throughout the landscape, and a massive stone tablet stood at the far end commemorating something Zayne couldn't read in the too-brief flashes. There were bronze dragon statues for some reason.

He pushed himself to his feet and helped Jacques do the same. He scanned the palace wall nearest them, with a massive red ironwood door in its heart. "The secret entrance should be about twenty feet to the left of the door," he reminded the big man.

"Aye," Jacques said, "I remember."

Zayne peered into the darkness enveloping the garden. No vines climbed the walls, of course; that would have been too easy. "We jump," Zayne decided bleakly. "Find what looks like the softest grass and remember to roll." They paced the wall – slowly, for they had not forgotten the precarious drop behind them – and searched for a good place to drop. When they finally found what seemed to be their best bet, Jacques jumped down, hitting the ground with a muted *thump*. When he rose and gave a signal, Zayne followed. He had practiced this sort of thing before and knew how to arrange his feet and bend his knees to turn the fall into a roll and mitigate the damage. Nevertheless, when he rolled into the soggy grass, he felt his body jar for moment. He returned to his feet quickly, however, and dashed across the garden.

Zayne counted the steps beyond the door and began to fumble in the dark for the false brick in the wall that would open the passageway promised by the Architect's plans. He found it after a minute and depressed it, wincing at the loud groan that accompanied the descending of the walkway just beside him. The walkway segmented to form a staircase, and Zayne waved Jacques down first before following. There was no light below, but Zayne found the switch to close the passage more easily than the one to open it. In fact, it was an actual switch on the inside. The stairs were no quieter closing than they had been opening, but a blast of thunder rolled overhead, and Zayne prayed that it would cover the sounds of their transgression.

The smell of sulfur struck Zayne before the light of Jacques' match illuminated the small area around them. Aside from the puddle of murky water they had brought in, the catacombs were dry, the air stale and hot. Dust clung to Zayne's glove where he had pulled the switch, and he couldn't wipe it off. Cobwebs and dust were so thick on every surface, Zayne could not be certain of what material the catacombs were built.

They took slow, deliberate steps, acutely aware of each crunch of dust and whatever else lay beneath their feet. They knew the catacombs were fairly thick, but Zayne was paranoid, and he hoped for his own sake Jacques felt the same. "You smell that?" the larger man asked as they walked along.

Zayne turned his nose up. "I smell dust. Mold."

"And shit."

"So?"

Jacques' match burned out and he struck another one, and this time he pulled a candle from his coat and lit it. "So, Captain," he said quietly. "Something needs to be alive to shit. And that's fresh, that is."

"Might be a cat."

"That's no cat shit, Captain."

"How can you –" Zayne shook his head. "Never mind." They were walking through a trove of forgotten lore and artifacts – Zayne accidentally kicked a mold-covered tarp, unveiling a painting marked with a placard that read *Yushiro Yuna, the First Empress of the Asarian Empire.* The woman depicted wore a thick, green-black armor and carried a bizarre sword with a blade that curved slightly and an undefended hilt twice as long as any Zayne had ever seen.

Any of the relics could have seen him rich enough to buy an entire city block in Tal Joyau. "We've been going about this all wrong," he mused. "We should have become burglars."

Jacques merely grunted.

There was a low rumble and a blast of sticky, wet, hot air washed over them in a wave. Their candle was blown out in an instant, leaving them plunged in pure darkness. Zayne shivered despite the heat, his skin feeling like it had been slathered in spittle. "Jacques," he said quietly.

"Aye, Captain?"

Zayne took a breath. He wasn't sure what he was smelling, but it wasn't dust or mold or even shit, though it was equally rancid. "When I say now," he said, "light that candle and we run. Don't look back, run until we hit the staircase. Understood?"

"Aye."

"Now!" Zayne shouted as soon as Jacques uttered his compliance. Zayne did not even wait for Jacques to light the candle – and by the thumping of footsteps behind him, neither did Jacques – and nearly tripped over something metal that crashed behind him with an obnoxious clang. Jacques had the candle lit in mid-stride, and Zayne tossed an ancient suit of armor to the floor as he ran past it. He did not look back as he charged through the dark tunnel. He dared not. Whatever was sharing the catacombs with them was surely just behind them, and he would not afford to slow to look at it. His heart was trying to break free of his chest. Each gasp of breath left him *tasting* the raw stench of the undercroft. There was a loud scraping noise followed by the occasional thump that shook the floor beneath their feet, threatening to topple Zayne in mid-stride.

The staircase came into view. It was a spiraling structure made of stone and narrow enough they would have to climb single file. Zayne bounded as hard as his legs would carry him, and all but leaped to the first step, seeking shelter behind the walls of the upper staircase. Jacques staggered behind him and when they reached the top step, they stopped to catch their breaths and listen. Whatever had been following behind them was silent. The only sounds were their own desperate gasps for air and the blood pounding in Zayne's ears. After a brief respite, they determined they were alone and relaxed.

"The fuck was that?" Jacques asked.

It took a moment for Zayne to find the words – and the breath – to respond. "I have no idea. But it sounded big."

"Did you get a look at it?"

"Fuck no. Do you think anyone heard the noise?"

Jacques seemed to think about it. "If I knew I had a giant . . . *thing* living beneath my house, I'd move the fuck out."

"Maybe. Or maybe they're used to the noise. Used to be I couldn't sleep in the captain's cabin because the wind whistles around the door to the balcony. Now I don't even think about it." Zayne stood back up. "Either way, they probably don't know we're here." He wasn't entire sure he believed that.

There was no door at the top of the step, only a ladder that extended into a seemingly perpetual darkness. There were supposed to be multiple false walls along that climb. If the plans were correct, each hidden door would be marked on this side, so he need only find the one engraved with a gryphon. Zayne beckoned for Jacques to hand him the candle and he began his ascent. Though the ladder was a far easier climb than the wall, the muscles in his back and arms felt like daggers were being wedged into them with each rung, and at least once he thought he was about to fall back and dash his head against the grime-covered stones.

He passed at least three of the secret doors, though the insignia on one had completely worn away and the second one was almost indistinguishable. He was able to recognize a carved sparrow on the third. He wagered he must be at the seventh story by now, but then he saw a hidden entrance marked with an eye and he remembered from the plans he was only on the fourth. He stopped to catch his breath again.

"I'll do it," he muttered to himself, "I'll retire. Repaint the fucking ship. Harvest apples."

Jacques was maybe fifteen feet below him, climbing at a slower rate. "You say something, Captain?"

"Just cursing my life," Zayne replied. He resumed his climb and found the tile marked with the gryphon. He hooked one arm around the ladder and gave the brick a hard shove. There was no yield. Zayne released his hand and was about to push again when he heard the scraping of grinding stone. He had expected the wall baring the mark to open, but instead it was the wall to his left. The newly revealed tunnel was almost perfectly square. It was half his height, so he had to crawl, but it was every bit as wide, so he was not lacking in room as he did so.

He crawled through the seemingly endless tunnel over dust that felt a foot thick. He was vaguely aware that it was starting to cake his wet clothes and groaned. The bricks were arranged so neatly and uniformly that Zayne wasn't entirely convinced he was making any progress. It felt something like a dream in which he was reliving the same moment over and over again. Zayne's shoulders were beginning to ache.

"You see the end, boss?" Jacques whisper was strained and breathless.

"No," Zayne replied. "Not yet." He thought back to the plans. The tunnel did not seem so long in the plans, but he supposed that was always the difference between a map and the world. As he stared into the inky black that lay just beyond the edge of candlelight, he imagined the wall being just beyond it, just another foot. It seemed like it never was, but he thought it with each inch of progress, like he could *will* the end into being. *Almost there*, he told himself, *not much farther now*.

When the light finally reached the wall at the far side of the tunnel, Zayne could scarcely believe it. He pushed himself harder and made it to the end. He turned himself over to look up at the trap door overhead. He handed Jacques the candle and braced himself to push it. With his hands flat on the door, he tried to stand. The door did not budge, and he was left stuck in a squatting position. He relaxed and took a breath, adjusting his hands, trying to find the right spot to leverage. He pushed again to no avail. There must have been something heavy sitting atop the door. "Jacques, help." The large man set his candle down and squeezed in next to Zayne. Their faces were uncomfortably close, and their knees were touching. His breath reeked of garlic and old fish, of all things. "On the count of three, we stand," he ordered, and Jacques nodded. "One. Two. Three!" They both strained to push, and Zayne put all his weight into it. At first there was very little yield, but Jacques grunted and increased the force of his push until eventually the door flew open and whatever had been sitting on top of it made a loud *crash*. Zayne ducked into the tunnel to douse the candle, and they sat in silence, waiting in pitch darkness to see if anyone came to investigate.

Zayne heard his own heart beating as loud as a war drum, and both Jacques' breathing and his own were so loud in his ears he was sure they would be given away. Yet he heard nothing else. No scrambling to investigate, no shuffling of feet, no screams for help. Nothing. Zayne let out a sigh and climbed out of the tunnel. He couldn't see any part of the room in the pitch of dark, save for a brief outline of light around a set of drawn curtains when the lightning outside flashed. Zayne felt his way around the room. There was no space unoccupied by something obstructive and haphazardly set in his way, most of it covered by thick, linen drapes. *Another storage room like in the catacombs,* Zayne decided. He tripped over something that snapped and tore under his weight but caught himself on the wall. He pulled the curtains away, and while it was still dark and stormy out, the occasional flashes of lightning let him map out the room, which he compared as quickly as he could to the plans.

Zayne crossed the room at a slow pace, careful not to make any more noise than he already had done. It took him longer than he would have liked, but he reached the door that led to one of the castle's proper hallways. He knelt and put his eye to the keyhole. There was a light on the other side. Based on the way the light and shadows danced, Zayne figured the corridor beyond was lit by a single torch. Zayne readied the stiletto in his sleeve and tried the door. It was locked. Zayne pulled his lock-picks from one of his sleeves. The lock gave him no difficulty, but the door creaked noisily when he eased it open. He winced.

He turned his ear out and heard a soft whistling accompanied by a low grumble. He crawled out, trying to keep low to the shadows. He realized then the sound he was hearing was snoring. There was only a single guard on patrol in this hall that Zayne could see, and he was leaning against his spear with his eyes closed and his head down. He had a ring of keys hanging from a thong on his belt. Zayne looked to Jacques, who looked at the guard with something that might have been amusement or amazement. Zayne grabbed the keys and cut the thong with his stiletto.

After closing the door, they crouched low and walked slowly down the hallway. The floor was made of marble tiles that formed a mosaic depicting a green phoenix. Zayne recalled from the plans the Architect's Guild had provided that this wing housed the library, and farther down, the offices of the Empress' advisers. They reached the corner and Zayne peered around to ensure there were no guards before they made the turn. There were no doors on this side of the corridor, only a few benches and statues atop tall pedestals – one of a dragon, one of a sphinx, which did indeed have a beard, one a phoenix, and the third was of a massive four-legged beast with enormous claws and teeth that vaguely resembled a cat in much the same way a cobbler's knife vaguely resembled a sword. At the center of the inner wall, framed by the statues of the dragon and the firebird, illuminated only by the light from the storm outside, was a painting of a young girl in a silk dress of lavish design in various shades of green and black and gold. The girl in the portrait wore her hair elaborately, with a collection of golden ornaments hanging from her hairpins. A small plaque beneath the painting, engraved in the exacting Imperial Script read *Princess Yushiro Miriaan.*

Zayne scratched his chin as he looked at the painting. "Does she look familiar to you?" he whispered to Jacques.

The large man crossed his arms and tilted his head in consideration. "Hmm. Maybe if Lucky San still had her nose, she'd look that that."

Zayne narrowed his eyes at the painting while he called up the memory of San Mina. Lucky San, as she was often called, was the captain of the *Knight in Mourning* and one of the Daughters of Daen. She was Imperial blooded, or at least she looked the part and made the claims. She and the princess did share a few facial features, though the presence of a perfectly intact nose was not one of them.

"Yeah," Zayne agreed after a moment. "That must be who I'm thinking about." They were about to continue down the corridor when they heard footsteps. Zayne darted behind the statue of the oversized cat while Jacques hid behind the statue of the phoenix. Zayne reached into his coat for the packets of Sphinx's Beard Nanette had prepared and a match. He waited.

There were two guards walking abreast, speaking to each other in hushed tones. "– makes the best pigeon pie every year for my name day."

"Must be nice," the other guard replied. "All *my* wife does for my name day is roll over and let me stick it in at the end of the night when the kids are finally asleep."

"That doesn't sound so bad."

"Well, no, I guess, but she doesn't make a sound. And I swear, one time, she read a book the whole time."

When the guards drew near, Zayne lit one of the packets and threw it before he risked breathing the smoke himself.

"Why is it every time we talk you gotta turn it into a – what was–" one of them said before the smoke had him face down on the floor.

"He–" the other started, but Jacques was behind him, choking him with one massive arm. The man dropped his spear, forgotten, and made no effort to reach for the pistol at his belt. Zayne watched for what felt like an eternity as the guard struggled. Eventually he stopped his clawing and flailing and kicking and hung limp in Jacques' arms.

"Dead?" Zayne asked.

"No, but I can fix that quick," he replied.

"Don't," Zayne said. "Let's just stash them somewhere they won't be noticed. Back in the storage room." They each took a man and threw him over their shoulders. They backtracked along the corridor, relieved to find the first guard still sleeping at his post. When Zayne reopened the door, however, the man stirred.

"What? Who? What? Who are–" the man sputtered, but Zayne silenced him with a stiletto to the throat. The man continued to sputter, but it became a silent gurgle as blood spattered Zayne's face and hand. Bile rose up in his throat and while he managed to force it back down, he was unable to prevent the spell of gagging that followed. He closed his eyes, shuddering, trying and failing not to inhale the rancid stench of death. He forced himself to carry the dead man on his other shoulder as he entered the room. The blood on his face was hot and thick, trickling down at an obnoxiously slow pace, itching with every inch, and he could almost swear he could feel the man bleeding on him through his coat.

With the light of the torch outside, Zayne could see the room more easily and took large steps over obstacles on his way back toward the tunnel. He dropped the dead man inside first before setting his alive, sleeping captive on top of him. Jacques dropped his more gracelessly. When all three had disappeared into the impenetrable darkness below, Zayne closed the trap door and found what had blocked it before. It was an old, half-empty chest made of mahogany. Zayne dragged it over the trap door and began to fill it with odds and ends he found scattered in the darkness.

"They won't be getting out any time soon," he declared, and they left the room again. Zayne locked the door behind him this time, though it took a few attempts to find the correct key. They rounded the corner again, passing the painting of Lucky San's more attractive double, and stopped at the next corner. Zayne risked a glance. He could see the staircase they needed to reach at the far end, just past the library doors. He couldn't see any guards. He moved as quickly as he could without making too much sound on the marble floor. Jacques was right behind him making more noise than Zayne would have liked. They climbed a flight only to hear approaching footsteps from above and below. Zayne pulled out four more packets of the sleep draught and passed some to Jacques.

Zayne crept up the stairs while Jacques remained poised on the flight. When Zayne saw the first sign of the patrolling guard above, he took a deep breath. He was fortunate that the Sphinx Beard burned quickly enough he could avoid its effects by holding his breath, though it was already starting to give him a headache. He lit the Sphinx Beard in his hand and threw it up at the guard. There was a sound of panicked confusion that gave way to the guards falling, dropping their spears with a clatter. Below, Zayne heard similar sounds followed by a loud crunch as Jacques leaped down the stairs to silence a guard that had not fallen asleep. "Keep it down!" Zayne whispered when he was sure the noise hadn't drawn more attention.

"Sorry, Captain. What do we do with the bodies?"

"Tuck them in the library, somewhere," Zayne sad dismissively. He looked around the landing he had just reached. His target was here, just on the other end of the corridor, behind a massive, red door. Jacques climbed the steps to carry the guard Zayne had rendered unconscious back down to the library below. Zayne listened for more guards. The only sound he could hear was the occasional rumble of thunder outside and the patter of rain against the windows. When Jacques returned, Zayne made his way to the door. All his planning, the preparations, the stress, all of it was for this moment. His heartbeat rapidly. A suicide mission, Dardan had said, yet here he was. He had crossed the Empire for this moment, until all that stood between him and his mission was a door.

He knelt before the door and tried to open it. Unsurprisingly, it was locked, but that didn't distress him. He extracted his lock picks again and went to work. He only had to fiddle with the locks a short time before hearing their satisfying *click*. He pulled it open. It was a heavy door, and it squealed when it opened, but for the first time Zayne wasn't worried about that. He was almost done.

The princess' bedroom was large – larger than both the galley and the captain's cabin on the *Scorpion* combined. There was a large vanity against one wall bedecked with gems and jade with an arrangement of powders and perfumes and other makeup. In the middle of the room beside a massive hearth were a red couch and two armchairs with a table between them. There were a dozen dress forms lined along the window, each bearing an elaborate gown, including the one in the painting they had seen below. At the far corner of the room was a massive canopy bed with velvet curtains draped around it.

Zayne crept slowly to far side of the room, stiletto in hand. Each step felt like an eternity. He felt his heart race, but he wasn't sure why. He had gotten this far; all he had to do was grab and gag the girl and make his escape. The hard part was already done. So why did he feel so uneasy? He put a hand on the curtain. He waited for two heartbeats. He pulled the curtains back.

And the bed was empty.

"What the fuck?" Zayne said, straining not scream the words. He pulled away from the bed. "She's not here." He began to examine the room more carefully.

Jacques scratched his chin. "Think maybe she went to the kitchen?"

"And locked the door?" Zayne retorted. "No. Besides, this isn't the bed of someone out for a snack. It's completely made. Also, what do you smell?"

"Blood," Jacques replied brusquely. "You're covered in it."

"Aye," Zayne replied. "And what don't you smell?"

Jacques stared blankly at him.

"Perfume," Zayne said. "You don't smell perfume, despite the rather large collection of it. You also don't smell a chamber pot."

"Well, it is a princess' room," Jacques said uncertainly.

"I assure you; princesses shit like the rest of us. And even if it was cleaned out in the middle of the night, there would still be a –" he stopped. He heard footsteps, and not a slow ponderous patrol, either. He looked out the door and saw six men with pistols marching down the hall toward them. "Fuck!" he shouted. He gave a glance at the door. How had he missed it? There was a fine-gauge wire tied to the inside of the door. It must have tripped an alarm. He slammed the door shut in time for a volley of gunfire to ring out; each shot hit the door with a mighty *crack*.

"How the fuck did they know we were coming?" Zayne demanded. "And where is that fucking princess?"

Zayne drew one of his pistols and opened the door, taking a blind shot at one of the men in the formation before throwing the spent weapon. Jacques fired as well. One of them hit the mark, blasting chunks of skull and brains across the floor, while the other got another guard in the arm. Gunsmoke filled the hall, and Zayne couldn't make out more than shadows.

He charged at them, hearing another shot, two, three, and he drew his second pistol and fired into the smoke and shadows. He heard a satisfying grunt and threw his pistol at the sound. Between the darkness of the night and the storm and the smokescreen birthed by the firing of guns, Zayne was completely blind. His only comfort was that so were his pursuers. He took the last of the sleeping draught from his pocket and warned Jacques to be ready to run, took a deep breath as he set it all on fire, and dropped it as he broke into a run. He rearmed himself with another pistol in one hand and his stiletto in the other.

He ran clear of the smoke and straight into a terrified and confused guard. He barreled into the man, knocking him to the ground. Zayne scrambled to his feet, ready to fight, but he had run his opponent through with his stiletto accidentally. He couldn't stop himself this time; he vomited on the man as he skulked away.

He reached the stairwell ready to climb when two more guards came down the steps. Zayne fired wide, hitting only the wall behind them. One leveled a pistol at him only for his partner to step in the way as he charged at Zayne with a spear. The spearman's momentum kept him coming, but Zayne sidestepped the weapon and threw his stiletto into shooter's eye. Sickness washed over him but there was nothing left to purge.

Zayne made a hand gesture signaling Jacques to run up the stairs first – Zayne couldn't hear beyond the ringing in his ears now, and he wagered Jacques was more or less the same – and reached into his coat for the wire traps he had purchased. They were small, compact devises, ostensibly little more than balls with spikes on either end. He stuck one end into the wall and pulled the other end, pulling it apart so the spikes were connected only by a thread of razor wire. He planted the second end on the opposite wall of the stair and slightly higher for a diagonal cut. He then proceeded to plant five more along the way every few steps. He knew his pursuers wouldn't be stupid enough to run into the traps more than one – twice if he was lucky – but they'd be slow to follow him if they had to stop to check for more.

He heard a loud crash from the top of the stair and moved to investigate. Jacques had toppled over a statue and was using it for cover while several guards lined up to fire. Zayne positioned himself behind a column and drew his next pistol. He fired at a man who tried to take advantage of Jacques while he reloaded.

The column came under fire, and Zayne tried to count the shots. When they exhausted their fire, he drew his fifth pistol and ran at them headlong. He fired when he was too close to miss, piercing a guard in the lung. He realized then he had left his stiletto in the eye of the last guard he had killed with it, so he hit one of the guardsmen in the head with the butt of his pistol instead. He dropped the gun and reached into his sleeve for the barber's knife. The man he had struck was recovering, so he lodged the blade in his throat.

He did his best to ignore the sickness as he tackled the next guard to the ground. He slammed his knee into the man's groin as they fell to the ground together and plunged his knife into his chest. Zayne rolled off his victim in time to see the last man poised to bring a knife down on him, but he stood frozen in the air after a bloom of red appeared on the chest of his overcoat. He dropped dead and Jacques stood up, holstering his spent pistol.

Zayne pointed at the fork in the corridor leading left. "Serenity Tower is that way," he said. They ran toward the spiral staircase.

Zayne set one foot on the stair and a brick beside his head exploded. He threw himself onto his belly and crawled a up few steps before pushing himself back to his feet. He pulled out another wire trap and stuck it across the width of the stair. A guard rounded the spiral and Zayne braced himself.

There was a pan flash and a loud crack. Zayne left forearm felt like it had been driven through with a white-hot blade. He let out a scream. The guard ran at him, cutting himself on Zayne's wire trap. Zayne felt another wave of sickness pass over him when he watched the man unwittingly slit his own throat with momentum alone.

Zayne didn't remember reaching the first level of the tower, which had a panoramic view of the city and surrounding landscape. Recognition only came to him as he reached the stairs to the next tier. He tried reaching for another wire trap, pushing through the pain of moving his arm, but he couldn't close his hand and was awkwardly padding his pocket. He pushed ahead and caught up with Jacques.

"Nanette and Flea better be there," Jacques said as they climbed.

Zayne merely nodded. His head was swimming. He felt that if he opened his mouth, all that would come out was a scream. The second floor was empty, and the third was occupied by a single, confused guard. Jacques punched him in the face, knocking him flat. Zayne felt a stitch in his side, but he fought through it. The fourth floor was also unoccupied, as were the fifth and sixth, but as Zayne's fatigue began to slow him, he became aware of flickering shadows behind him. *They'll catch us,* he thought dismally. "Dardan was right," he muttered breathlessly. "That bitch."

When they reached the seventh level of the tower, Zayne heard a deafening blast and fell to his knees. "What was that?" he demanded. He turned to see a guard had caught up with them, and the man had a gun leveled at Zayne. *Why isn't he shooting?* he wondered deliriously. He reached for his last pistol, and when he drew it, the weapon and his hand were slick with blood. *Oh,* he realized. *He did.*

Zayne aimed his weapon at the guard, who was busy reloading, then turned it to his side and blasted a hole in one of the windows and struggled to his feet. He staggered over, crawling out into the rain. Walking out on the pagoda, he looked around for the shifts in the shadows just beyond the slanted roof. When he didn't see Nanette, he wondered if she got caught, or shot down, or if he had the wrong floor. Or if she abandoned him.

Don't be stupid, he reprimanded himself. *She'll be here.*

He slipped, sliding across the tiles. There was another gunshot and the tiles just next to his hands exploded. Jacques hit his attacker and jumped out into the storm to join Zayne. He didn't seem to be stopping. *What is he doing?* Zayne wondered, just before the large man tackled him and sent them both careening over the side of the pagoda.

Zayne did not know if he screamed for fear and the realization that he was falling from one of the tallest structures in the world, or if he screamed because he suddenly felt like someone had stabbed him in the ribs, but he screamed. His breath was sucked out of him in that scream and he found himself so frightened and confused that part of his mind deliriously wondered if he would feel it when he hit the rocks.

When he finally stopped falling, he figured he was dead. *You win, Dardan. Daen's Scorpion is dead.* He wasn't sure what to think when he opened his eyes to see the storm. Was that all death was? He stared at Nanette's face for a long time before he realized she was even there, looking down at him. Her mouth was moving quickly, but Zayne didn't catch the words.

"What was that?" he asked.

"I said you were shot three times," Nanette said.

Zayne closed his eyes. "Oh. Where was the third one?" He needn't have asked, for as soon as he had, he felt a sudden tugging pain in his left leg. Someone had put a bundle of cloth in his mouth, but he wasn't sure he had the strength to scream anymore anyway. When Nanette worked to pull the bullet from his ribs, though, he realized screaming was the easiest thing in the world.

CHAPTER TWENTY-ONE

The Dreamscape seemed to stretch out for eternity, with new constellations of stars and moons adorning the sky with each new place the *Dreamscape Voyager* flew over. In the waking world, Cassidy had tried to carry on with her duties in spite of her injuries, only to be stricken by festering that left her feverish and unable to stand. Since being bedridden, Cassidy found herself spending a great deal of time here, accompanied by Hymn, sailing over marvelous lands the likes of which she had never seen. In the waking world, her body was still on the mend, but here she could move as she needed, though she still felt her pain somewhat distantly. She woke up occasionally when nature called or when Nieves came in to change her wrappings or give her food. During the time she lay in bed, her monthly blood came and went, and they still had not arrived in Nasradaan – though Nieves said Cassidy should be walking before they arrived.

Usually, being confined drove her mad, but now she could pass her time in the Dreamscape. Hymn asserted that it wasn't the same as sleeping and that Cassidy was not resting when she visited; Hymn also insisted on saying she was not actually *in* the Dreamscape but was *projecting* herself there, whatever that meant. No matter the reason, she was content to be there, working and sailing like she could not do from the captain's bed. Hymn never gave her directions and always seemed to be looking for something just beyond the horizon.

This day they sailed over a valley of red grass littered with plateaus and silver streams beneath a purple sky. Hymn stood at the bow with her hands folded in front of her lap as the wind tussled gently at her hair. Cassidy left the helm and stood next to her. "Why do we keep coming here?" Cassidy asked.

Hymn gave her a sideways glance. "Would you rather lie in bed?"

"Not at all," said Cassidy. "I just mean, you seem to be looking for something."

Hymn turned her gaze back to the horizon. Her colors shifted from blue to purple. "There is always something to look for," she said absently. "It is best that we keep moving."

"I never suggested stopping."

Hymn took a step from the bow and slowly ran her eyes across Cassidy's body, as if she were sizing her up. As she did so, the color of her eyes and dress returned to their usual blue. "You know a fair bit about running, do you not?"

Cassidy raised her brow. "Running? I did a fair amount as a kid. Not much call for it now, though, living on this boat and all."

Hymn laughed. It was a pure, musical sound. "Oh, Cassandra, I think you are still running."

Cassidy scratched her head. "What?"

The Fae sighed. "Never you mind."

Cassidy peered toward the horizon, trying to figure out what Hymn was seeing there. "So, what *are* you looking for?"

Hymn waved her hand, encompassing the space beyond the ship with her gesture. "Do you recognize this place?"

"It's the Dreamscape, obviously."

"Clearly," the Fae agreed. "But I asked if you recognized this specific place."

"Should I?"

Hymn took a step closer to Cassidy and placed her hand on Cassidy's face. "Look closer."

Cassidy furrowed her brow as she studied ground below. There was a certain familiarity to the slopes of the valley and the way the rivers below winded between the plateaus. She stared at it a long time, but it finally hit her when she blinked. "This is the Black Gulch!"

Hymn nodded. "Yes, though the Fair Folk still remember when this place was called the Autumn Valley."

"But how is it here?" Cassidy asked. "We're in the Dreamscape."

The Faerie grabbed Cassidy's wrist and placed her palm flat against her own. The Fae's fingers were slimmer and longer than Cassidy's and warm to the touch. "Your world and mine are woven together," she said, interlocking their fingers. "The dreams and memories of your world linger here, and across the veil our worlds reflect endlessly much like two mirrors held together." She spread her fingers apart, guiding Cassidy's as well. "Sweeping changes will affect both words, but you can clearly see they are not one and the same."

Cassidy nodded slowly. "So, this is just a... *reflection* of the Black Gulch?"

"Or perhaps your Black Gulch is a reflection of this Autumn Valley," suggested Hymn. "Or perhaps they are both everything the vale ever was and could be." She tightened her grip on Cassidy's fingers. "Follow me." Cassidy didn't feel she had a choice, and with the tug of Hymn's hand she suddenly found herself no longer on the *Dreamscape Voyager*, but on the rock surface of a plateau. She felt unstable, unable to tolerate the steady rock beneath her feet. The sensation passed very quickly, however, and Cassidy let Hymn lead her to the edge.

She had been mistaken. She was not standing on a plateau at all, but rather a flat rock floating above the Black Gulch. She fell to her knees and clutched at the stone beneath her hands. "What is that?" she squeaked.

"This is a platform," Hymn said simply.

Cassidy swept her gaze between the underside of the ridge and the ground to verify what she saw. There was definitely nothing connecting it to the distant ground, and a wave of vertigo came over here. "Daen's–" Cassidy started to say, but a hand clasped over her mouth before the name was fully beyond her lips, the rest of the curse muffled against Hymn's palm.

"You must not speak that name, here," the Fae whispered sharply. "Nor the name of any of your gods. It calls their attention. I understand that in your world you view that as superstition, but as long as you remain here, it is a fact. Do you understand?"

Cassidy nodded and Hymn released her mouth. "Right," Cassidy said. She looked back down. "How is this platform not falling?"

Hymn stood beside Cassidy, peering casually over the ledge. "Should it?"

"There's nothing holding it up," said Cassidy.

"No more than your ship," Hymn replied, hitching a thumb over her shoulder. Cassidy looked up to see the dream version of the *Dreamscape Voyager* floating about twenty feet above the platform. It looked quite impossible there, without a balloon to keep it aloft and instead with a mast and sails flapping gently in the breeze. Yet Cassidy could not deny the familiarity she felt that told her it was the same ship she knew and loved.

"Enough about that, though," Hymn insisted. "We do not have much time before you wake, and I wish to show you something."

Cassidy rose to her feet and Hymn took her hand, leading her across the platform. At the far end was a small set of stairs that led nowhere. The Faerie led her to them, and when Cassidy began to climb the steps, she found herself no longer on the platform, but in front of a massive pyramid-shaped building. She turned around, expecting to see the flat stone she had just stood upon, but instead she found herself standing at the top of a city made of stone. *A ground city*, she realized to her horror. She shook her head, realizing how silly it was to worry about being on the ground when she was already in the Dreamscape. Despite the rationalization, however, she couldn't shake her entire life's understanding of things. It was almost a primal understanding that the ground was bad, and logic wasn't going to change that.

Hymn continued to pull her across a long walkway lined with slim trees adorned with gold and crimson leaves. They crossed a spacious archway into a chamber that dominated the top of the pyramid. Inside was a dais of gold-colored marble with a velvet carpet leading toward a towering throne of gold-trimmed ebony. Seated on the throne was a woman in her middle years, dressed in gold. She had two streaks of black running through her blonde hair on one side of her head. To either side of her were two large men wearing slim and angular armor of black and gold that gave them the appearance of small wasps. At the foot of the dais stood a woman garbed in a rich, purple robe of billowing silk, with black hair that reached her ankles.

Everyone in the room seemed strange to Cassidy, as though she was looking at them through water, seeing them distort and shift slightly before her eyes, and there was a distinct dullness to their colors. Compared to the dais and the throne and indeed everything else in the room, none of the people felt *real*.

The woman in purple approached the dais, and when she reached the first step, the guards tensed, grabbing hold of their weapons. The woman stopped and folded her arms in her sleeves. "And what have I done to earn such fear?" she asked. Her accent was like none Cassidy had ever heard.

The woman on the throne chose not to acknowledge the question, instead asking, "Why have you returned?"

The silk-dressed woman extracted a black, slender box from her sleeve. "There is to be a great war."

Hymn leaned into Cassidy's ear. "This is a lingering memory of the past," she said. "What you see happened long before your kind took to the skies." Cassidy nodded absently as she watched in wonder. "The one on the throne was Queen Acselna, oft styled as the Stone Fist. The one at the foot of the dais is Jysen."

"You speak of Arrelan?" asked the Queen. "I already know they're marching."

The queen's visitor shook her head. "No, whatever your troubles with Arrelan, it is of no interest to me. A time will come when a far greater war will be waged over this land."

"So you've come with vague portents?"

"I have come with a weapon that will turn the tides. If I may step forward?"

The queen's guards looked to her. She nodded to each of them and they relaxed their stance – only slightly – and Jysen began to climb the dais. She presented the box to Queen Acselna. The queen took the case in hand and looked wearily at the guest. "Nothing is free," she said warily. "What do you want?"

"Your third-born child."

The queen stared at her guest for a moment, her brows furrowing and eyes narrowing. The guards braced themselves. Then Acselna started to laugh. The sound echoed in the chamber. She shook in her chair as she laughed and laughed. When finally she took a breath, she leaned forward. "My third? I don't even have a second."

"I know what I ask for," Jysen said smoothly. "If you keep the weapon, you will see me again when I collect."

"Let's see if what you're asking is even worth what you say," said Acselna as she worked the latch on the box.

"Do you honestly doubt my word?" asked Jysen.

The queen opened the box and her eyes widened. Her hand was poised to reach for whatever was inside, but she hesitated, as though afraid to touch it. "This is–"

"Do we have a deal?"

Acselna looked back into the case, then at Jysen. "Very well," she said.

Jysen nodded and made her way back down the steps of the dais. When she was halfway down, she turned back. "Before I go, there is one more thing. You will no doubt be tempted to use that against your rivals in the Autumn Valley, but I advise you, do not. It will be needed in a far greater war to come." The woman resumed her descent and turned her head in Cassidy's direction. Cassidy saw her eyes, then, and realized she was no mere woman; her eyes were inverted, just like Hymn's, with irises of pure white surrounded by deep purple the same shade as her robes, which Cassidy now saw were patterned with stars and swirling clouds. Jysen did not halt, but as she passed, she gave Cassidy a wink before vanishing like a dream. Cassidy looked up at the dais to find it and the throne were empty.

"Could she see us?" asked Cassidy.

Hymn shook her head. "Unlikely," she said disinterestedly. "Let us go, this place has little else of interest." The Fae offered her hand.

Cassidy was about to take it when a thought came to her. "Why did you want to show me that?"

"I thought you might be interested in history."

"This has something to do with what you're looking for here, doesn't it?"

Hymn chuckled softly. "Why are you so certain I am looking for something?"

"Because I haven't heard you say you aren't." Cassidy crossed her arms, eying the Fae carefully. "You can't say you aren't if you are. You're after that weapon Jysen gave the queen, aren't you?"

Hymn frowned. "We do not travel the Dreamscape in search of trinkets, Cassandra. Though, if you must know, yes, I would be interested in knowing where that weapon is today. However, that is not the reason we came."

"Then what are we traveling it for?"

"We travel so that we might elude our pursuers."

Cassidy had expected Hymn to evade the question, so she hadn't been ready for the answer. "Pursuers? Who's after us?"

"I cannot say," the Fae said. She folded her arms and looked out to the Gulch. "I told you our worlds are not wholly separate, and even when you travel in that world you leave traces of yourself in this one. There are those who can follow those traces. It is my hope that by projecting ourselves across the Dreamscape, we can create false trails."

"You seriously have no idea who—"

"*Cassidy,*" a voice called out. Cassidy looked around the room for the source. She felt like an idiot when she realized it was Lierre's voice, calling from back on the ship.

"It seems that it is time for us to return," said Hymn.

Despite having done it several times, Cassidy was still taken aback at how easy it was to wake from her visits to the Dreamscape; it was easier than actually waking up sometimes. She opened her eyes in the waking world to find herself in the captain's cabin. She was glad to be back in the sky where she belonged. Lierre was sitting on a stool beside the bed, holding a bowl of porridge.

"Dream of anymore strange places?" asked the engineer.

"Yeah," Cassidy said, stiffing a yawn. "Hymn showed me an old city in the Black Gulch."

Lierre gave Cassidy a nervous smile before casting a look at Hymn, who was sitting on Cassidy's knee. "Sounds very exciting," she said, rather unconvincingly. She looked at the porridge in her hand as though she had forgotten it. "Oh, Nieves asked me to check to see if you could stand before breakfast."

Cassidy laughed. "I bet her exact words were, 'make her get up and get her own damn breakfast', weren't they?"

Lierre giggled. "You know her well."

Cassidy sighed and threw her legs over the side of the bed, which threw the Faerie off. She felt hot flashes of pain run up her sides as she did so, but she held back a groan. "There," she said. "Not so bad." She rose to her feet. She felt heavy. She tried to shift her weight and her legs gave out. She fell back on the bed and yelped. All the wounds around her body hurt, though the ones around her chest were the worst of it.

"Don't push yourself, Cassy," said Lierre. She scooted her stool closer and helped Cassidy return to a seated position. She handed Cassidy the porridge.

Cassidy ate slowly and found she had to force down every bite. *Gods, I hate this stuff,* she thought.

"We're a few hours from Nasradaan," said Lierre.

"I guess Nieves was wrong, then," replied Cassidy. "She said I'd be walking well before now."

"The wind has been kind, so we're making better time than the captain thought we would."

"That's great. Now if I could get out of this bed, that would be even better."

"I'd hate for you to be stuck in this bed the whole time," Lierre said. "I'll go grab your clothes and see if Nieves can get you anything to help." The engineer left the room, leaving Cassidy alone with Hymn.

"She tolerates me better than Kekarian does," the Fae noted. "With difficulty, however."

"What do you expect?" asked Cassidy. "You're of the Fae, the stuff of nightmares and horror stories. Not to mention, even associating with you is a hanging offense. They have a right to be uncomfortable."

"*They*," Hymn repeated, "but not you?"

Cassidy shrugged. "I made the deal, it's my crime. What happens to me as a result is my own fault. But they didn't ask for this. And I think both of us should consider ourselves lucky that they care about me enough to break the law themselves. I bet damn near anyone else in the world would have turned us in. Or killed us."

Hymn's light turned a pale red for a moment before returning to its usual blue. "That is a fair point."

Lierre returned shortly with Nieves in tow. The engineer was carrying a bundle of clothes while the sawbones was holding a wooden crutch. "Lierre said you were able to stand," said Nieves.

"Briefly."

"Good. I brought you a crutch. It'll help you get around."

Cassidy giggled. "Oh, is that what it's for?"

"Careful," warned Nieves, "or I'll use it to beat your ass, instead."

Cassidy accepted the bundle of clothes from Lierre and started to dress. She was relieved that she didn't need help working the corset, though she needed Lierre to help keep her balance when putting her trousers on. When at last she was dressed, she took the crutch and limped her way to the cabin door. As soon as she opened the door, she felt the rush of fresh air, the sweet smell of the wind after a rainstorm replacing the stifling smell of her own sweat and waste. She had forgotten how bright sunlight could be after however long she had been confined, but she was glad to feel the sun. She squinted as she made her way out. The deck was slick, and a few patches of dark clouds littered the otherwise clear sky. The sight of it put a smile on Cassidy's face. Miria was at the helm, and she finally seemed rather comfortable there.

"Ahoy, Cassy!" Asier's voice rang out from atop the aftcastle. Cassidy looked up and discovered just how stiff her neck was. The captain was sitting cross-legged on the railing, beaming down at Cassidy. "You've been spending entirely too much time confined to a bed, lately."

"Aye," said Cassidy, "I couldn't agree more."

Asier jumped down, landing beside Cassidy with a loud *thump*. "Glad to hear it. Hopefully you'll stop stinking up my cabin. Once you've recovered, you'll need to find a way to repay me for emptying your damn chamber pots. And don't even get me started on the sheets!"

"Hey, that happens to all of us," Cassidy said defensively.

"Except Kek," said Nieves.

"Yes, well," said Asier, "he has his own share of problems, I'm sure."

"Where is he, anyway?" Cassidy asked, giving a sweeping look at the deck. "I'd expected him to be jumping up and down waiting to get to port."

"In his bunk, probably," said Nieves.

Cassidy gave a mock gasp. "Will he be ready for his lady friends?" Lierre burst into laughter and the captain chuckled alongside her, but Nieves merely sniffed.

"Kek will find away, I'm sure."

The lone, mountainous peak of Nasradaan was surrounded by miles upon miles of complex river systems, which shined like sheets of red gold as far as the eye could see when the sun set. As it was now, under the partial cloud coverage, the rivers seemed deeper and mysterious, weaving through the dense forests below. The city itself was barely a speck on the horizon, though Cassidy enjoyed watching their approach. "Miria," she called.

The princess jumped a little. "Yes? Er, aye?"

Cassidy hobbled toward the girl. "Let the ship run free a while. You should enjoy the view." Cassidy led her to the starboard bow. "Let's see, it's around here somewhere," she whispered to herself as she scanned the horizon. "Ah, yes, there!" she pointed at what appeared to be a tall, stone spire in a spot between where a river split in two and reunited with itself. "Check your spyglass." Miria did as she was told, and Cassidy beamed when she heard the girl gasp. She remembered reacting the same way the first time she saw it. "They call it the Nymph's Tower," Cassidy explained, "and, yes, it really is made entirely of water. May I?" she added, holding her hand out. Miria held her gaze on the Tower for a moment before sparing a look to Cassidy and handing her the spyglass. Cassidy felt Hymn shy away from her as she put the iron-rimmed glass to her eye.

The "tower" was an aptly named, ten story spiral of flowing water that did in fact resemble a tower, albeit with no doors or windows. It was comprised of several impossible streams of gravity-defying water that flowed in different directions to form the round column and pointed peak. She handed the glass back to Miria and Hymn returned to her shoulder. "The people of Nasradaan tried to dam the source several times over the years," Cassidy explained, "they got the Iron Veils involved, too. But whatever Fae influence was set there was strong, and nothing could stop the water from rising and flowing."

Nieves snorted. "Since it just sits there looking pretty, they decided it wasn't worth throwing money and priests at it. *Eventually*. It doesn't hurt anyone, except the occasional kids dumb enough to drown in it on a dare."

Traffic picked up as they made their gradual approach to Nasradaan. Kek arrived on the deck with a pair of brandy bottles and suggested a drinking game. Lierre and the captain took up the game while Cassidy and Miria started calling out the names of passing ships. The players took a drink every time a ship had a bird in its name. The first ten minutes went by with the only offenders being the *Fair Falcon*, the *Twin Vultures*, and the *Drunken Crow*. When they were in sight of the pier, however, they passed several more. The last ones they saw before arriving in port were the *Autumn Raven* and the *Frozen Lark*. When Cassidy declared the game was over, Kek gave a celebratory belch and Lierre tried and failed to rival it.

Nasradaan's harbor was a uniformly rusty brown that sat in the shadows of the tiered city. Cassidy took up the helm and found a free berth for the ship. Upon stopping, Nieves showed Miria how to tie the ship down while the captain dealt with the port authority. Cassidy watched from afar as Asier haggled down the docking fees with an old man whose white beard that reached his knees. Eventually the harbormaster gave a defeated sigh and took whatever they had agreed upon.

When Asier returned to the ship, she divvied up their duties. "Lierre and I will deal with the cargo until sundown. Cassy, show Miria the market and get us stocked up. Nieves, you and Kek have leave until sundown, then I want you back for your watch."

"Aye, Captain," replied Kek.

Cassidy watched him take off running into the street. She nudged Miria's shoulder. "Come along, then," she said. The princess nodded and helped Cassidy down the gangplank. When they set foot on the harbor, Cassidy felt the sudden sense of stability affect her balance, and Miria nearly had a misstep beside her. "Already forgot how different a city is beneath you, eh?"

Miria nodded. "I didn't even think about it," she said. "Got so used to the swaying of the ship."

"Wait 'til you feel the ground beneath your feet," Cassidy said. "That's just awful."

Miria looked aghast. "What would we ever need to do that for?"

"Salvage," Cassidy explained. "Sometimes we find fallen ships out there. And dragons and manticores have some valuable innards." She stopped walking when she saw Hymn's flashing light fly by and squeaked in surprise when the Faerie pulled the leather cord from her hair and ducked into it, sitting at Cassidy's neck. Cassidy decided she needed to do something about that. "Before we get the supplies, there's something I need to do. This way."

The streets of Nasradaan were less familiar to Cassidy than some other places they made port, like Revehaven or Melfine, and the streets were narrower and more winding, but it didn't take too terribly long for them to find what Cassidy was looking for. The sign over the door read *Swan Sisters, Hats and Scarves*.

"Is this a . . . hat shop?" Miria asked uncertainly.

"Good eye," said Cassidy. She opened the door. The bell that chimed was far less pure than the sound Hymn occasionally made. *What an odd thing to notice,* she thought. The shop was small and tight, with row upon row of busts, each wearing an elaborate hat and filling the space.

A deathly thin woman – with a white pallor to match – dressed in a pink coat and matching corset greeted them with a tired smile. "Good afternoon, young ladies. Waverly Swan, at your service," she added, extending a dainty hand. Cassidy shook it gingerly, worried she might break it. "What can I help you with today?"

Cassidy scratched at her scalp. "I need a hat," she said simply.

"Of course you do," said Swan, "and you'll find no better in the city, I promise you. But what sort? There are so many to choose from, my dear!" She grabbed a gray hat covered in dark purple plumage from a nearby bust and set it on Cassidy's head. "This one will make those eyes of yours shine!"

Cassidy looked to Miria, who offered her a weak smile. "I'm not sure I need more attention drawn to my eyes, thanks," she said, pulling the hat off.

"Hm, you're right, it's very unnerving," said Swan. Cassidy gave an indignant gasp, but the woman moved on. She took a black, round-top hat with red feathers and a translucent veil on the left side, giving it to Cassidy. "There. Draws attention away from your eyes and would be perfect for either a party or a funeral."

"Um," said Cassidy, turning the hat over in her hands, "while I appreciate utility, I'm looking for something more durable. Something that might last in a storm, perhaps?"

There was a brief flash of disappointment in Swan's face, but it vanished quickly, replaced by a strange gleam in her eye. "Yes, I have just the thing. Wait here, if you will." The shopkeeper made her way farther into the shop, leaving Cassidy and Miria surrounded by the blank-faced busts.

The princess looked uncomfortable, so Cassidy asked, "Are you glad to be off the ship for a bit?"

Miria nodded slowly. "A little. The ship is nice, but . . . ."

Cassidy gave Miria several seconds of silence, giving her the chance to finish her thought on her own. When the girl did not, she leaned in. "But?"

Miria's eyes darted briefly to Cassidy's neck and away. "It can get a little crowded. And Kek doesn't seem to know how to act around me."

Cassidy crossed her arms and leaned against the counter. "I get that. He's usually a bit of a flirt, but given that you... well, considering where you're from, I think he's a bit intimidated. You aren't alone, though. I think he's been avoiding me since he found out about Hymn."

"Avoiding you?" asked the princess. "He seemed fine, back on the ship."

Cassidy shook her head. "It's hard to really avoid someone in a confined space, but... If I ask you a question, will you answer honestly?"

Miria looked nervous. "I'll do my best."

Cassidy held her breath a moment before asking, "Do you distrust me?"

Miria opened her mouth but looked over Cassidy's shoulder. "I think this is a conversation to be had later." Cassidy turned to look, seeing the hat seller carrying a black, flat-topped hat with a wide brim that came to a point in the front and the back, with a single, pure red feather of a phoenix tail tucked into the band. "Try this," offered Swan.

Cassidy took it from her, feeling the durable leather beneath her fingers. Peering closely, she could see scale-patterns and noted that it was as much a dark red as it was black. "This is dragon hide," she noted. She put it on her head and turned to Miria, "What do you think? Be honest."

Miria twisted her lips. "It's a nice hat, but I think maybe your clothes are too light."

"My cousins are a tailor and a corset maker," said Swan. "They have a shop right across the way and can provide you with the finest wardrobe in the city."

Cassidy was tempted to make a comment about the family business but decided not to be rude. "I'll consider giving their shops a look. But I'll take the hat."

Swan smiled. "An excellent choice," she said amicably. "That will be two falcons."

Cassidy didn't let her surprise show. "Even for dragon hide, that seems a tad steep. What say you to a falcon and twenty-five doves?"

Swan's smile didn't so much as flicker away when she answered, "I'd say, I'm sorry you won't be having the hat, then. Two falcons. No less."

Cassidy frowned. "A falcon and fifty doves?"

"Two falcons."

"You know, most shopkeepers barter."

"Most shopkeepers lack the quality of my goods. If you wish to barter, madam, I recommend you go back to the docks. Two falcons."

Cassidy gaped for a moment, then pulled out her purse. "Fine, fine," she said, fishing for a pair of silver coins.

The shopkeeper accepted them graciously, taking a small, hidden purse from her corset, tucking the coins away. "A pleasure doing business. Now, does your little friend see something she likes?"

"No, madam," Mira answered quickly. "We'll be on our way."

Cassidy took up her crutch and tipped her new hat. "Farewell." Swan gave them a half-nod and let them be on their way. Back on the street, Cassidy led Miria toward an alleyway.

"What was that all about?" the princess asked.

"I needed a hat," Cassidy said, ducking between the buildings. They were alone in the shadowed street, and Cassidy whisked her hat off and leaned against the wall. She took a knife from her belt and started worrying at the side of the leather. Dragon hide was tough, however, and she wasn't making as much progress as she hoped.

"What are you doing?" squeaked Miria.

"Giving Hymn a better place to hide," answered Cassidy. She grunted and struggled, but the knife was doing nothing to the leather. "If I can just make a damn hole for her to fly in and out of."

The Fae flew from her hiding place behind Cassidy's hair and into the hat, pulling it right out of Cassidy's grip. The hat flew and landed straight on Cassidy's head. The Fae's voice was muffled but audible as she said, "There is no need. This will serve."

"Oh. Good." Cassidy put her knife away and turned her attention to Miria. "Well, now is 'later'. Do you distrust me?"

Miria seemed to swallow a lump in her throat. "I trust you plenty," she said, "but –" she added, staring at Cassidy's hat.

"But?"

Miria's voice dropped to a whisper. "Can she hear us in there?"

Hymn's voice rang from above Cassidy's head. "It is a hat, not a house. I can hear quite well." Miria looked like she had just swallowed her tongue.

"You say you trust me," Cassidy said. "Why?"

"Asier – the captain – trusts you," said Miria. The princess didn't seem satisfied with her own answer, because she quickly added, "and since we met, you've been kind and helpful, too. It's just –"

Cassidy patted Miria's shoulder. "She scared me too, at first. You said you trust me because the captain does. What do you know about her?"

Miria swallowed whatever lump had returned to her throat, and she let out a long breath. "Growing up, my mother always said if there was one person in the world I could trust, it was Elyia Asier. She always said she was a paragon of justice and heroism. To be honest, she always seemed more like a story, or an aspiration, than a real person. Even knowing one day I'd join her on whatever adventures she embarked, she seemed as mythical as the Twin-Headed Bear of the Reach, or the Fae or –" she stopped, looking again at Cassidy's hat. "Except they are every bit as real as tales would have it, too."

"Yeah," Cassidy agreed. "If it weren't Hymn, you'd probably have seen something else out on the skies. They're real, and never as far as you think."

Miria nodded. "Anyway, what I meant to say was, Asier seems every bit as worthy of trust as my mother said, and she trusts you, and you've given me no reason to question why. But Hymn is –"

Cassidy put her finger on the princess' lip to silence her. "I know what she is. What I've done will see me hanged if word gets out, but I believe she is on our side."

"Our *side?*" asked Miria. "Are we at war or something?"

Cassidy bit her lip. "I don't know," she admitted. "But she means us no harm. She swore to protect me, after all."

Miria pursed her lips and stared at Cassidy for what felt like an eternity. Cassidy could see a strange pain in her eyes, and she wondered, worried, what the girl was thinking. Finally, Miria seemed to relax. "Alright, Miss Durant. I trust you, and if you say Hymn can be trusted, I'll trust her too."

CHAPTER TWENTY-TWO

Nightfall came, and Zayne was no closer to figuring out what had happened back in the palace the night before. His cane clacked against the cobblestones as he made his way through Revehaven's streets, his leg throbbing and burning with each alternate step. Nanette was by his side, helping him balance if he ever seemed to lose his footing. Unlike the palace, the eastern district was alive in the night, with a light in most windows and music ringing out from every tavern. The streets themselves, however, were nearly empty, with most people having found themselves a bed to sleep in or a table to drink at until morning. Hopefully the latter sort were sober enough to answer his questions.

They had spent much of the day hopping from tavern to tavern listening for gossip, occasionally planting the seeds for conversation, but it seemed that the whereabouts of the princess weren't matters of public knowledge or concern. Zayne didn't have any leads, though, so he decided if he didn't learn anything soon, he would have to mount a second break-in. *Only this time*, he thought, *the palace would be under much heavier guard.* The thought was accompanied by the sudden urge to shoot himself in the head, which he pushed aside to focus on finding their next gossip pool. The *Bloodstone and Diamond Crown* was on the next street corner, its sign – a pyrographed plank depicting its namesake and nothing else – illuminated by a gas-lit street lantern.

The inside of the tavern was cleaner than many they had visited that day, with warm colored wallpaper and lamps creating a welcoming environment Zayne had not expected from the name. The establishment was not overly crowded, nor was it abandoned. It would have been perfect for eavesdropping, if nothing else, if it weren't for a group of louts singing old shanties in the corner. There was a harpsichord in the back, but no one was playing it.

They found a table off to one side, away from the singers. It was several minutes before a serving girl came to their table. If Zayne were less weary, he might have been uncomfortable with how much skin the girl was showing. As it was, he just kept his eyes on the table and ordered. Zayne asked for cider while Nanette ordered wine.

They decided to share a plate of boiled eggs and fried wings. As they ate, Zayne did his best to listen to nearby conversations, though the singers were drowning most of it out. People spoke of the foul weather, of fell beasts making their way beyond the Reach or the Gulch, of lost treasures or hidden cities, of gangs and personal debts, but no one spoke of the princess nor of the break in at the palace. It seemed the Imperial Family was doing an expert job of keeping that quiet.

After an hour of unimportant conversations, the third off-key rendition of *Farewell, My Midnight Star*, and an overlarge plate of unseasoned falcon and dry egg, Zayne decided he had enough. It was ready to return to the *Scorpion* to lie down and forget the waking world for a time. And if the gods were good, perhaps he would die in his sleep. He had only just braced his cane, however, when he heard a familiar voice.

"Ah, Captain Balthine!"

Zayne furrowed his brow as he saw the short man waddle into the tavern. Lancen was accompanied by his First Mate, Ander – a larger man than any Zayne had ever known; Lancen only stood as high as the man's waist and was barely wider than his biceps. They attracted a lot of attention. The singers stopped for a measure and conversations halted so everyone could get a look at the unlikely pair who strode into the tavern like they owned it. Zayne cursed, knowing that they would, in turn, draw attention to *him*. "Captain Lancen," Zayne replied warily, rising to his feet.

"Please, please, sit down," said Lancen. "When you sit, I can pretend we are of a height. And it would be a shame to waste all this food." Zayne turned his gaze to Ander, who stared silently back with a sneer, and returned to his seat. "There, that wasn't so hard, was it?" To Zayne's great irritation, Lancen joined him, as did his oversized bodyguard, who shifted the table when he pulled up a chair.

"So, what brings you to the capital?" Zayne asked, crossing his arms.

Uninvited, Lancen started eating from their plate. "Oh, the usual," he said around a mouthful. "Committing high treason, spreading sedition, enjoying the local color. Tell me, Nanette, is Zayne as good a captain as his dear aunt?"

Nanette didn't seem as bothered by Lancen as Zayne was. "We can only hope he's better, all things considered."

"Truer words were never spoken," said Lancen. The serving girl returned. "Wine for myself, your best mead for my friend here. I hear you had a very exciting night, Balthine. So, tell me, why are you still here?"

Zayne scowled. He ripped into a wing to delay answering. He chewed and chewed, thinking about the best way to say what needed saying. When he was ready, he swallowed. "They knew we were coming. They were ready, and – and the prize was missing."

Lancen didn't seem surprised. "Now there's a pity. So, you think this seventeen-year-old girl is just going to show up in a random tavern in the city?"

Zayne scowled. "I wasn't counting on it, but I wouldn't inspect that bird's talons too hard. I was hoping to hear some rumor from the inside."

Lancen dropped a wing bone back on the plate and belched. "Yes," he said, "rumors can be useful. I heard one this afternoon about a pair of thieves who threw themselves off Serenity Tower rather than be captured."

Zayne snorted. "Thieves, huh?"

The waitress brought Lancen and Ander their drinks, which they accepted with gracious nods. "Yes, that is the word making the rounds. I imagine it's less likely to spark a panic than 'assassin.'"

Zayne shrugged. "I suppose it would. Doesn't really help me, though."

"No, I suppose it wouldn't. After all, you already know about it."

"Aye. I don't need fifth hand accounts of what I saw. I need to know how they knew I was coming, and where they are holding her."

Lancen investigated his mug, swirled its contents, and took a long slurp. When he was done, he set the mug down and leaned forward. "What makes you so sure they knew anything?"

Zayne tightened his grip on his cane. "What do you mean 'what makes me sure'?"

"Just what I said. How can you be sure they knew you were coming?"

"The princess was *missing*. And her chambers were rigged with an alarm. What else does that suggest?"

Lancen gave a silent chuckle, and Zayne was ready to strangle the short man, his bodyguard be damned. "Well, I have heard something interesting that might just color your opinion."

"Stop jerking me around, Lancen," Zayne said in a low voice. "What do you know?"

"What do I *know*?" asked Lancen. "Nothing so sure as the sunrise. But what I've *heard* might explain your little incident. And what I've heard is, the princess wasn't in her *room* because she's not even in the *city*."

Zayne blinked. *Not in the city? Then where is she?* "I'm sorry, what?"

Lancen leaned back in his chair. "Oh, yes. It would seem she hasn't been the city for a little over a month."

"And where did you hear this? Why haven't *I* heard this?"

"Oh, Balthine," Lancen said patronizingly. "You can't always expect to get all your answers from one person, unless you know exactly who to get it from. Information-gathering takes time and the patience to put the pieces together. But, when enough courtiers start mentioning things like the princess not attending court or her lessons, or that her handmaidens have all been dismissed until further notice, it starts to create a picture."

"So, that's it?" Zayne asked. "The princess just up and walked out? Decided, 'fuck it, I'm bored,' and took the first ship to anywhere?"

Lancen gave a thoughtful shrug. "Many people dream of doing that very thing. I don't imagine princesses are immune to wanderlust."

"So do these rumors tell us where she ran off *to*?"

The short man gave a sad smile into his cup. "No. But, I could point you in the direction of a man who claims to know."

Zayne straightened in his chair. "And I should trust you?"

Lancen had the nerve to look surprised and offended. "I should certainly hope so! We are on the same side, after all."

"You work for Dardan."

Lancen laughed, looked from Nanette to Ander and back to Zayne. He then leaned in over the table and whispered to Zayne, "So do *you*." Zayne didn't have an answer, but the disgust must have shown on his face, because Lancen said, "Oh, how could I forget. Zayne Balthine is the only man to find himself where he is by circumstance. Truly, his is a uniquely tragic story, and of all mercenaries, only he knows honor and respect. Truly, the rest of us are mere pawns of a gods-worshiping madwoman. Forgive me for —"

"Alright, you made your point!" Heat rose in Zayne's face and he found he was breathing heavily. Ander had not moved, though he seemed tense as a wound spring. "Who is this man?"

"Was that so hard? The man is Malivai Mendrin. He frequents taverns in this part of the city, but he has some relation or another to a courtier."

"So why haven't you found out what he knows?"

"Because *I'm* not looking for the girl. I told you, I'm here to commit treason and the other things. Or to get others to commit treason, at any rate. Besides, I'm sure you're more than capable of convincing him to talk." Lancen took the last egg from the table and popped it in his mouth before downing his wine. He reached into his coin purse and flicked a coin onto the table. "I believe you'll find him in the *Dog's Watch* tonight. It's a nice little place a few streets south of here." With that, he jumped from his chair and waddled out with his giant companion.

When they were gone, Nanette hissed in his ear. "Was that really necessary?"

"Was *what* necessary?" he asked.

"Antagonizing him," she replied brusquely.

"I wasn't –"

Nanette spoke in a slow, deep voice, as though impersonating an idiot. "*I don't trust you. You work for Dardan.*"

Zayne stared at her for a moment, reflecting on the anger in her eyes. For a moment, he was at a loss for what to say. A dozen arguments rose in his head, each one failing to express anything worthwhile "That's a terrible impression," he said at last.

"But not inaccurate."

Zayne glowered at her for a moment. Then he sighed. "Come on, let's go find this 'Mendrin' fellow." Standing sent a jolt of pain that ran from his leg right up his spine, but he managed. He staggered out of the tavern, acutely aware of the whispering he left behind. They headed south as Lancen suggested. Nanette hummed a few notes of *Farewell, My Midnight Star* before cursing the "bastards" back in the *Crown* for getting it stuck in her head.

The *Dog's Watch* was busier than the *Crown* had been, with a harpsichord playing in the back and a pair of billiards tables that had full crowds watching a heated game. They attracted no attention as they walked in. Zayne reached the bar and pulled up a stool. The barkeeper was a barrel-chested man with only the faintest crown of gray hair. He was polishing an already clean glass, eying Zayne while occasionally checking around the tavern. Zayne was sure nothing happened there without his knowing about it.

"Evening," said the barkeeper. "I hope you won't be using those weapons."

"Not if it can be helped," Zayne said.

"See that it can be, then. What can I get you?"

"A tanker of cider for me," Zayne said, placing a few coppers on the table. He flourished his hand and slipped a silver coin between his fingers. "And some information."

The bartender gave a snort that had his mustache quivering. "Alright, what do you need?"

"I was hoping you can point out Malivai Mendrin for me."

The older man sighed. "That's him," he said, pointing to a tall man about Zayne's age or a little younger, with black hair and a strong jaw. He appeared to be flirting with a disinterested looking blonde woman. "If you're going to kill him," he added, setting Zayne's tankard on the bar, "please do it outside." With that, the bartender walked away.

Zayne turned to Nanette. "Work your magic," he said. "I'll find us a better seat." Zayne rose from the chair and walked around looking for a free corner table. The only one available was closer to the harpsichord than he would have liked, but it served. With his back to the wall, he watched Nanette order a drink for their mark and start flirting. The act was usually a slow one, so Zayne surveyed the rest of the *Watch*. One of the windows bore a slightly different stained-glass pattern than the others, he noticed, and many of the chairs and tables around the place were newer than the knife-worn one on which he sat. He assumed a fight had broken out. He drank from his tankard and grimaced. He wouldn't be coming back if he could help it.

It was a few minutes before Nanette brought Mendrin to the table, and when she did, he looked confused. "I'm sorry, Madam, but I'm not sure I –"

"Just sit down and listen to what we have to say," Nanette insisted. He gave incoherent protests as she practically shoved him into a seat, but he didn't fight.

"What is it you want?" he asked suddenly.

"To talk," said Zayne. "What's wrong with talking?"

"Look, I just came here to –"

Zayne shifted in his chair. "I'm sure you came here for a great many things. We won't take too much of your time. We understand you've seen the Princess Miriaan."

Mendrin scratched his scalp. "A few times," he said. "I spend a fair time in court. Lots of people have. Seen her that is."

Zayne sighed and gave Nanette a signal. She pulled the knife to Mendrin's upper thigh. The man froze rigid and let out a tiny *yelp*.

"Let me clarify," said Zayne. "We've been led to believe you know where the princess is."

Mendrin spoke quickly. "Oh, right, the princess! Of course, I should have remembered sooner! She took ship about a month ago. I think the ship was bound for Nasradaan, but I doubt she's still there."

Nanette twisted the blade and Zayne leaned forward. "Why do you doubt that?"

"It wasn't on a passenger ship, and she was dressed like a crew member. I almost didn't recognize her, but her eyes are a pretty distinctive kind of blue, especially for a noble. You never see that, do you?"

"Hiding as a crew member?" Zayne repeated. "Do you remember the ship's name?"

Mendrin swallowed a lump in his throat, and Nanette pressed her knife just a little higher. "The *Dreamscape Voyager*," he said quickly. Zayne's eyes widened in spite of his attempts to control his reaction. He turned to Nanette, whose expression was a mirror of his own. He thought back to the painting of the princess in the palace and realized exactly why it had looked familiar. In that moment, he could almost hear Daen laughing at him.

CHAPTER TWENTY-THREE

Eleven Years Earlier

Three days after being arrested, Zayne had been brought to trial. That trial had been a sham. He had stood in fetters, listening as his own father accused him of beating his brother to death, of strangling his sister, of . . . of . . .. Bile rose in Zayne's stomach just thinking of it, even though his stomach was empty. It had emptied during the trial as they were describing the state of his mother, of the things they said he had done. Someone he had never seen before had had the gall to say the way he broke into tears was proof of his guilt. Compounding his troubles, one of his father's cronies had seen him giving money to mercenaries and twisted the story by saying that the mercenaries had refused to do the job, so he did it himself. The part that left a pit in his chest, though, was that none of his friends had come to help him, to point out the obvious fact that he would never harm his mother or siblings. Zayne had made that argument in his own defense but was cuffed in the ear for speaking.

Somehow, his attempts to hide Iden's Dust usage came into light as well.

He had been declared guilty, sentenced to be hanged at first light the following morning. Zayne had seen the glimmer in his father's eyes when the old man sneered at him, and in that moment, he was certain he understood what really happened.

He was being escorted to the gallows by Tam, who pulled him by the chains that connected his ankles to his wrists. "Tam, you know I didn't do it," he said for what must have been the tenth time. "You know I loved them; I would never!" Tam didn't look at him. He just kept marching, eyes forward, his head never so much as turning. "It was my father! You know what he's like!"

That *did* make Tam stop to look at him, but all Zayne could see in his eyes was disgust. "I thought I knew what *you* were like," he said. "What you did is unforgivable. I hope the gods take notice." Zayne's jaw dropped, and Tam resumed his march, faster than before. He practically dragged Zayne down the street. How could Tam believe Jainin over *him*?

"Tam, you've known me since we were kids!"

Tam pulled Zayne's fetters, nearly knocking him to the ground as he pulled him forward. The watchman opened the door, and Zayne was overcome with the sounds of a hundred voices screaming. He heard several cries of "Murderer!" and "Monster!" and "Coward!" and countless other slanders coming over him in a wave. There were members of the city watch keeping the crowd out of their path, but there were so many protesters that it made Zayne's head spin. He made it several paces before realizing *he* was the one they were shouting at.

He felt his eyes burn as they tried to churn out more tears, but he had run dry. Unable to cry, he convulsed through his forced march. Something struck Zayne, throwing his head to the side and causing his eyes to burn. When he smelled it, he realized he'd been struck by a rotten fruit that had frozen through. Shortly after, a rock pelted him in the shoulder, and another. Tam and the other watchmen pretended not to notice.

Zayne focused on the gallows at the end of the Row in his effort to ignore the crowd that was assaulting him. He found himself wondering which noose they would hang him by, and if he would be alone up there, or if they would find a Duster or a rapist to join him and make a spectacle of it. He wasn't sure which prospect frightened him more. He tried and failed to suppress a shiver that had nothing to do with the winter air or the fact that they had taken his coat from him.

Tam led him up the steps to the gallows and secured Zayne's fetters to the platform, where he would be forced to wait until dawn. He said nothing as he left, leaving Zayne alone as more projectiles were hurled his way. He caught the first stone he saw coming, only to have another one strike his hand. Another hit him right above the eye. Before long, Zayne was huddled down with his face in his knees, trying to protect his head with his chained hands. He looked up at one point and saw Meryl standing at the back of the crowd. Zayne couldn't tell if the look on her face was disgust or shame, but he was struck again before he could figure it out. He was pelted by stones, rotten food, and whatever else the citizens of Dawnhal could find. He wasn't sure how long the initial assault lasted, but after a time the mob grew bored and left to attend their own duties. Every so often some passersby would throw something else at him, but as they day wore on that grew less and less frequent.

By the time the sun began to set, he was left alone but for the watchmen set to keep him from escaping. He wiped at the blood dripping down his swollen face. He bent and picked up a stone someone had thrown. He tightened his grip around it, ignoring the pain flaring across his bruised hand and arm. He half expected his father to visit him, but he knew that was folly. He had a hope that Meryl might have come by, but with each passing hour that hope diminished and soured.

He thought about what must have happened that day. He had been thinking of little else since he first imagined the scenario. In a drunken rage, Jainin must have slammed Cenn's head into the table, killing the poor boy – the thought sent a lurch in Zayne's stomach – and then smothered little Nanette before she could scream for help. Zayne gagged, but continued analyzing it. With two of their children dead, he must have known Zayne's mother would not lie for him. So he . . . so he . . . so he . . .

Zayne's hadn't eaten since the night before, yet still the thought of his mother made him bring *something* up, and whatever it was he spewed was watery and hot and sticky and clung to his lips as it spilled into a murky yellow-red puddle before him. It smelled of disease, and he could not move enough to be rid of it. His breath shook and he was dizzy. He shivered, but despite the cold that left his fingers numb, he felt hot. When the sun fully set and the last sliver of the one remaining moon took it place, he somehow at once felt both the oppressive chill of the air and the strange, sickly heat of his own body.

The guards changed shifts, but none bothered to speak to Zayne. He hadn't escaped, that was all they cared about. He tried to lie down without setting any part of himself in his vomit. When he determined the fetters would not let him recline, he remained sitting and eventually fell asleep.

He dreamed of his mother, his brother, and his sister. They ate together on the deck of a ship, bound for freedom, though Zayne was paranoid every moment of the way. No matter how long or far they sailed, Dawnhal sat in the horizon, unmoving, looming over him. A storm blew in, and snow and ice threatened to tear Zayne apart in the fierce winds. He wondered why he had forgotten his coat in Dawnhal. When the storm finally came to an end, Zayne looked for his family. They were nowhere to be found on the deck, so he went below to the galley. He found Cenn lying face down in his own blood with his brains scattered on the floor. Nanette sat to his side, swollen and purple, her eyes staring up in confused terror. Their mother was against the wall, blood-soaked and naked with knives plunged into every part of her and holding her to the wall, her face trapped forever between fear and heartbreak. He wanted to scream, but he had no voice. He tried to run, but his knees gave way and he collapsed into a heap on the floor. He looked away, but their bodies moved with his vision, forcing him to see their faces.

Something heavy hit the cobblestone street, and Zayne jerked awake. He looked around, confused, and saw the watchmen set to guard him were being dragged away intro the shadows. He blinked, unsure if he was really seeing what he thought he was seeing. A pair of figures dressed in long, black coats emerged from the darkness and approached him.

"Mister Caraden," greeted one of the visitors, as though they were meeting over lunch.

Zayne recognized her voice. "You're one of those mercenaries," he said. "You're Salaa."

The second figure stepped up to him, close enough he could make out her face in the dim moonlight. "That's Captain Balthine, to you."

He blinked at the girl. He knew her as well. "You're the girl from the docks."

"Nanette, yes," the girl replied. The name was like a dagger to his chest.

Zayne looked from one mercenary to the other. "Why are you here?" he asked uncertainly.

Nanette looked to Captain Balthine. "There's gratitude for you," she said.

The captain shrugged. "We're here to rescue you. I thought that was obvious."

"Why?"

"See now," the captain replied, "*that* was ungrateful. Still, if I got pelted by rocks all day, I'd be wary too. But to answer your question, I figured a boy who gives up all his money to ferry his family out of town wouldn't be in any hurry to kill them."

"Not a very good decision," agreed Nanette.

"So," continued Balthine, "I decided, you paid to get out of the city, we're going to get you out of the city."

Zayne frowned at that. "Where is Captain Kaveth?" he asked.

Balthine looked uncomfortable and hesitated before speaking. "When word of your arrest made the rounds, Kaveth set sail early. He took your money and ran, I'm sorry to say."

Zayne's shoulders slumped. "Oh," he said. "You'd think that the man I actually paid would be the one to think about it," he said absently. He added quickly, "Not that I'm ungrateful. This is all just so . . . so . . .."

I know," said Balthine. "Just so you know, I can't take any freeloaders. Mine's not a passenger ship."

"But I don't have any —"

The captain held up a finger. "I don't want for money. But as it happens, you don't have a life here anymore, and I need someone who isn't afraid of hard work. If I set you free, you work for me, got it?"

Zayne looked at Balthine uncertainly. "You mean, become a mercenary?"

"It's hard work," she said, "and it's dangerous. But it's that or die tomorrow."

Zayne looked at the gallows behind him. "You're right," he said. "I'll join you."

"I had a feeling you'd say that." Balthine reached into her pocket and extracted a thin pick, which she used to remove Zayne's fetters. She was quick about it.

Zayne stretched, in part because he could scarcely believe he was really free. He jumped down from the platform to join his rescuers. "Thank you," he said. It wasn't enough, he felt, but there were no other words. They had begun to walk down the Row toward the docks when Zayne made a decision. "Before we go, there's something I need. Back at home."

Nanette turned and pointed a finger in Zayne's chest. "No!" she whispered sharply. "We're not risking our hides for your sentimental —"

"It's not sentiment," said Zayne.

"Do you understand —" she began, but Balthine touched her on the shoulder, shutting her up.

"*I* understand," said the captain. She reached into her coat and extracted a pistol. Zayne's heart froze. After all her effort to save him, surely, she wouldn't shoot him. "You'll need this," she said, turning the grip toward him.

"I – thank you," he said, accepting the weapon. His rescuers exchanged a look before resuming their journey to the docks. He turned east, sticking to the shadows as best he could. The road home was quiet, and every step he took sounded loud in his ears, but he was sure he reached his destination unnoticed. He stood at his front door, remembering the last time he'd stepped through it. That was a nightmare he was still trying to reconcile as real. He moved to the side of the house instead and climbed up a drainpipe that ran next to his parents' bedroom window. The window was shut but not properly latched, so Zayne was able to push it open with ease. The transition from drainpipe to windowsill was not as smooth as he would have liked, and he was worried even his heavy sleeper of a father would wake at the noise. When he climbed in, however, he heard no rustle or panic, so he figured he had worried over nothing.

The room was hot and reeked of ale and sweat and filth. His mother would never have stood for it. In the very dim moonlight, Zayne could see his father lying in his bed, sprawled out as if nothing were amiss. Zayne scowled at the man as he climbed down from the sill. He knocked over a discarded bottle and froze in his tracks, but his father never stirred. Zayne pulled the hammer on the pistol Balthine gave him and made his way to the head of the bed. He slammed his fist in his father's face.

"Wake up!" he shouted. The old man didn't stir. He hit him again, repeating, "Wake up!" Again the old man did nothing. "WAKE UP!" he shouted, slamming the butt of Balthine's pistol into his father's jaw. Jainin's head was knocked aside and a steady stream of vomit poured out of his mouth. It was only then that he realized something he had been missing; his father was a terrible snorer, yet there was no sound. "No," he whispered, his hand shaking. "no, no, no, no, no, No, NO!" he slammed his fist against his father's face again, and again, and again, until his knuckles bled, and his wrist ached. "You killed them! You bastard! I was supposed to kill you, that's how this works! That's how . . ." he fell to his knees. Tears were streaming down his face. "That's how . . . that's how stories go. The hero kills the monster. Not this . . . not this, *you bastard*!" He rose to his feet and punched his father again. "You were supposed to wake up! You were supposed to confess, to beg for mercy!" he shouted louder, slamming the pistol into Jainin's nose. "You were supposed to be alive so I could kill you! You drunken lout, you couldn't even do that right!" Zayne sank to the floor. His breath quivered. He sat there for a moment, unsure of what to do.

Captain Balthine was expecting him.

The thought was as clear as it was sudden. He belonged to the mercenaries now. His life in Dawnhal was over, as sure as if they'd hanged him. All that was left was to rise out of the ashes and start anew.

He rose to his feet and went into the kitchen. He moved past his room without thinking about it. He stopped by the twins' room, however, and half expected to find them snug in their beds, waiting for him to tell them a story when he opened the door. They weren't, of course, so Zayne moved on. Down the stairs, into the kitchen. The last time he had seen the room, he had been dragged through it. He looked at the spot where his little brother had died, the blood-stained floor visible in the moonlight, as if the gods themselves had wanted the memory to remain even in the dark. There were empty bottles of wine and ale strewn about. Zayne ignored the mess as best he could and found a box of matches in a drawer.

He returned up the stairs, into his parents' bedroom and spat on his father's corpse. "I wish you had suffered," he said. He struck a match and set it on the bed. It caught fire quickly. He struck another and dropped it by its side. And another. And another. When he was satisfied with the growing inferno, he took Balthine's pistol and fired it into the brain of Judge Caraden. He climbed out the window and clung to the shadows as he made for the docks. The gunshot had awakened the neighbors, and it wouldn't be long before they noticed the raging fire.

On his way to the docks, he heard screams of panic – an ill-contained fire would be devastating – and saw bucket chains running up the street. He slipped into a nook until they went by. As he passed Hangman's Row, he heard shouts of, "Two dead guards!" "He's escaped!" "Search everywhere!" He darted quickly across the way after the guards moved on.

The *Scorpion* was still in its berth, and Captain Balthine and Nanette were sitting on a pair of crates at the foot of the gangplank when he arrived. The captain rose to her feet. "Well?" she asked.

Zayne nodded and handed the pistol over.

"Keep it," said Balthine. "I've got my own. One last thing before we go aboard. You know you can't be the son of Judge Caraden ever again. He's a wanted man, and I get the feeling his list of charges is about to grow. It just so happens; I always wanted a nephew. So, do you think you can stand to live your life as Zayne Balthine?"

Zayne repeated the name, tasting it in his mouth. "I like it," he said after a moment, then added, "Aunt Salaa."

Captain Balthine smiled. "Now that that's sorted out, all hands on deck. We leave now. Nanette, get this boat moving. Nephew, it's time to introduce you to the crew."

CHAPTER TWENTY-FOUR

Cassidy stood at the top of the gangplank waiting for Kek to return. She was examining her hat under the lamplight. Hymn had suggested Cassidy place the rose Balthine had given her in the band opposite the feather. Hymn's presence seemed to keep the flower alive far beyond its time, and Cassidy found it to be quite lovely. The Fae herself was sitting on Cassidy's shoulder. Together, they were humming the strange song Cassidy had played for Balthine and his crew. Hymn's voice was far superior to Cassidy's, pure while Cassidy was unable to keep the tune right even when she was humming it.

"It is beautiful," Hymn said suddenly. Cassidy looked to where it seemed the Fae was facing. The moons were absent from the sky, but in their place the stars were shining brightly, and far to the west was the red streak of a falling star against the black sky.

"I figured you'd find our sky boring," said Cassidy. "The Dreamscape has so many more stars, and moons, and color."

"It does," Hymn agreed, "but here, there is more focus. In my world, all the stars you see are a set among many sets. Were you to travel for a day in the Dreamscape, you might see a thousand constellations you have never imagined. If you traveled for a day here, however, you would see the exact same stars, but from a completely different perspective."

"That's an interesting way of looking at it," said Cassidy. "We call that one the Masked Falcon," she added after a while, tracing a line of stars in the west with her finger. "Though in Rivien it's called the West Viper."

"I have heard those stars called the Fallen Lady, or the Blue Rose."

Cassidy tilted her head, looking at the arrangement of stars. "Really? I don't see either of those things."

"You are seeing them from the wrong side," explained Hymn. "What about that one?" she flew back and forth in a gesturing fashion toward the north.

"The Firebird," Cassidy said. "The red star in its eye is called the North Ruby."

"There were those who called those stars the Endless Well. They believed the red star to be a fallen god."

"When was this?"

"A long time ago, in a different place," Hymn replied sadly. "*Everything* was different back then. Oh, look, Kekarian has returned." Cassidy turned to look down at the dock, and sure enough Kek was standing there, looking up at her uncomfortably.

"Hey, Cass," he said. "I wasn't expecting you to be here."

Cassidy furrowed her brow. "Why not? I live here too, you know."

Kek looked down, rubbing his neck. "I just figured since you didn't have watch duty, you'd be in town."

"I traded with Miria," Cassidy explained. "We need to talk."

"No good ever followed that sentence," he said. The blond man made a slow climb up the docks. When he was finally aboard the ship, he began to pace. "So, what's the trouble?" he asked.

"Let's start with how you won't make eye-contact with me anymore."

"That's a bit of an exaggeration," Kek said weakly.

"Is it? Are my eyes on your boots, now?"

That did make Kek look her in the eye. "What do you want me to say? That nothing's changed? That I'm glad you invited a *Fae* to bunk with us?"

"I want to know you're still my friend, Kek."

"Of course, but –"

"No!" Cassidy stomped her foot, immediately regretting the tremor of pain that shot through her. Kek made a move to comfort her, but she held up a halting hand. "No. I let Miria slide with a 'but' because I don't have a history with her. But *we* do. If after everything, you can't be around me, you're free to leave, but it would break my heart to see you go."

Cassidy's glare faltered when she saw his eyes shine with tears in the lamplight. "No, no, I don't want to go," he said. "I couldn't live with myself. It's just . . . Cassy, this is a *Fae*! You know, 'the source of all that is wrong with the world' and that mantra."

Hymn's light shifted to an orange-red glow. Cassidy scoffed. "I never took you for a religious sort."

"I'm not, but I've had some history read to me. Tell me you've ever heard one good thing that came from dealing with their kind."

Cassidy looked at Hymn, then back to Kek. "She saved my life." Kek didn't speak after that. He sat down on the gunwale and sighed. Cassidy joined him. "Hymn told me, when you learned about her, you chased her around, demanding to know what she had done."

Kek chuckled weakly. "It was scary. And we'd be lost out here without you."

"You think so?"

"Definitely. If we're stuck in Rivien, who else will order us lunch?"

Cassidy laughed and punched Kek in the shoulder. He joined her in the laughter. After they caught their breaths, Cassidy said, "Miria said you don't know how to act around her."

Kek rubbed his neck. "She makes me nervous."

Cassidy snorted. "You're almost ten years older than her. Wait, you're not fancy on her, are you?"

"What? No! She's too young."

"She's of age," Cassidy offered.

"No," Kek said flatly. "I need a girl with more experience."

"Well, that's what she's out here for."

"Not what – wait, did she say something about me?"

Cassidy snorted. "I thought you weren't interested."

"Well . . . no, no. She's a princess."

"No, she's not," Cassidy said firmly. "She is a member of our crew."

"A member of the crew who happens to be a princess," said Kek.

"You promised not to let that affect how you treat her."

"I know, and I try, it's just . . . Cassy, she's *royalty*. Don't you think that's mad? You share a bunk with the woman who will be collecting our taxes someday! What is she doing here?"

"Adventuring, maybe?" Cassidy suggested with a shrug. "What difference does it make, really? Maybe she's trying to see the Empire from the viewpoint of the people who live in it. Maybe she's in it for the exercise. Maybe she's hoping to find a strong man to warm her bed. What do they call them? 'Contortionists'? No. 'Consorts'? Whatever the reason, she's one of us, and you can't get hung up on it. On the ship, it's awkward, and you can't avoid her forever. And off the ship . . . Kek, she joined us in secret, I don't think she wants it getting out on the streets. And if you're acting weird in public, someone is bound to notice."

Kek nodded. "You're right. You're right. I just . . . it's overwhelming, you know."

"I suppose it is."

They sat in silence for a minute or two. Then Kek said, "Please don't tell Nieves I teared up."

Cassidy smirked. "I don't know, you've got some amends to make."

Kek swallowed a lump in his throat. "What do you have in mind?"

Cassidy's smile deepened, and she leaned in closer to him as seductively as she could manage. She noticed him stealing an eyeful of her cleavage. "I am so glad you asked, because there is one thing I have been wanting to do for months now."

The fighting arena of Nasradaan was not nearly as large or ostentatious as the one in Revehaven, but it still drew crowds. Hundreds of spectators had gathered for the show, nearly filling the theater surrounding the ring. The din was a low rumble as the warm-up bouts were being settled. At the moment, a bald woman wearing naught but baggy trousers and a corset was fighting a large, muzzled falcon. Seven rows up, Cassidy was sitting between Kek and Lierre.

"Thank you," she whispered to Kek.

The blond man whispered back, "I still can't believe I thought you were talking about sex."

Cassidy shrugged. "Aye, I have no idea where you got a silly idea like that."

A little louder, he asked, "Did you place any bets?"

"No, I didn't recognize anyone. Lierre put some money on 'Lucky San' though."

"My money is on 'Iron Foot' Emilia."

Nieves, who was sitting to Kek's left, gave a snort. "Why do you hate money so much, Kek?"

"Do you know something I don't?"

"Lots of things. Why did you bet on Emilia?"

"Well, the odds seemed safe, and with a name like Iron Foot –"

Nieves shook her head. "*Nyuran's milk*," she muttered, "you're hopeless. Listen to some gossip once in a while. Lucky San isn't affiliated with the Guild."

Kek blinked. "So? Sounds like all the more reason not to bet on her."

Nieves shook her head. "No, you dunderhead, she was hired specifically for this fight."

Kek blinked. "And that affects tonight's bout . . . how, exactly?"

"Kek," Nieves said patiently, "what were the odds on Iron Foot?"

"About thirty to one," the blond man answered offhandedly.

Kek didn't seem to get Nieves' point, but Cassidy did. "I'm going to go place a bet," she said. "I'll be back as soon as I can." She rose and made her way past Lierre and the row of strangers.

Outside the fighting theater itself was an enclosure filled with merchants selling their wares – most of it was either foodstuffs or trinkets promising good fortune or the like. One man offered to sell her a necklace of teeth salvaged from the arena floor. Cassidy politely declined. She did buy a satchel of fried mushrooms, however. There was a long queue for the betting window, so Cassidy had to look for the end.

She considered giving up on taking a bet and returning to her seat with the others when she heard someone whispering nearby. "I'm sure the captain can handle it," said a woman with a thick Rivien accent.

It was a man who replied. "I don't care, the Guild's not paying us to take chances. I got money riding on this."

Cassidy turned her head to see a pair of black coats ducking a flight of stairs that led to the fighter's den. "That sounds illegal. Do you think we should follow them?" she whispered to Hymn.

The Fae replied disinterestedly from within Cassidy's hat. "I would not say we should, but it must be more interesting than standing in this line."

Cassidy looked around to see if anyone was looking in her direction before following the dark coats. "Can you even see in that thing?"

"I have an intuitive sense of my surroundings," the Fae replied. "Be quiet, your voice carries down here."

The fighter's den was dimly lit and smelled of incense and coal tar. There were wooden chairs scattered about, and the far wall was dedicated to lifting weights and canvas sandbags, though no one was using them. There were voices coming from around a corner, and Cassidy could see a changing screen separating the common room from what she figured was a sawbones station.

The coated figures Cassidy had followed were standing over a refreshment table, speaking in hushed tones. She hid behind a support column and listened. "The guild lady said Emilia drinks the mead, right?" asked the man.

"No, you idiot, she drinks tea."

"You sure about that?"

"Damn sure. Now, quick, before they come out!"

The man pulled something from his coat and dropped it in a pot of steeping tea and the two of them ran back up the stairs.

"Poisoners!" Cassidy gasped.

"It appears to be," Hymn agreed. "It would seem they have no faith in this 'Lucky San' of theirs."

"Sounds like it," Cassidy agreed. She made her way around the pillar and was about to cross over to the table when someone walked out from the dividing screen and marched straight to the table. It was a muscular woman with short, black hair, wearing loose trousers, a corset, and fingerless gloves. She poured herself a cup of tea and Cassidy shouted, "Wait!"

The fighter froze with the cup to her lips, her eyes locked on Cassidy. There was a brief moment of confused silence before she gave an exasperated sigh. "Listen, sweetheart, this room's for fighters only. If you want an autograph, wait outside after the fight." She was about to take a sip when Cassidy ran up to her and slapped the cup out of her hands. In the second before the fighter's fist met Cassidy's nose, when time seemed to dilate before her eyes, she realized she should have planned better. There was a resounding *crack* and Cassidy hit the floor.

"Alright, you dumb bitch! I tried being nice, but I guess you'll have to be the warm-up before my fight."

Cassidy tried to speak, but all that came out were groans. The only actual word she managed was "poison."

A look that might have been confusion or horror made its way to the fighter's face. "What?" she asked.

"They . . . poison . . . you."

"Pissing blight!" The fighter helped Cassidy to her feet and set her on a chair. She set Cassidy's nose right with a *crack*. "Tell me true," she said. "What do you know?" After Cassidy's head stopped throbbing and she could breathe again, she told the fighter about following the suspicious figures in black coats and what she had seen.

"You're Iron Foot Emilia, aren't you?" she asked after a moment.

"The one and only," confirmed the fighter. "You said one of them mentioned a 'guild lady'?"

"Aye," replied Cassidy.

"That bitch. When I refused to throw tonight's fight, she replaced my opponent with some mercenary. I thought that would be the end of it."

Cassidy snorted, which hurt. "Looks like they had other plans."

"Yeah, it does, doesn't it?" Emilia smiled at Cassidy. "Well, I guess I owe you my life."

"Well, I don't have much use for all that. But, how's about after you beat this Lucky San, you buy me and my crew some drinks?"

Emilia gave a giggle that Cassidy felt befitting of such a muscular figure. "And if she beats me?"

"Then you'll need someone to drink with."

"Alright then. What's your name?"

"Cassidy. Cassidy Durant."

"Alright, Miss Durant. Meet me at the *Bottomless Well*, on Crows' Road... let's say three hours after the fight."

Cassidy smiled. "I'll see you there." She made her way back up to the theater and to her seat between Kek and Lierre.

"What took you so long?" Kek asked.

Lierre looked over at her. "And what happened to your face?"

"I was making friends," said Cassidy.

Nieves chortled. "You make friends everywhere you go, then."

"Hey, I got us drinks with Iron Foot after the match."

Kek raised his eyebrow. "You went to bet on her opponent."

"Didn't quite get that far," said Cassidy. "I'll explain later."

It was several minutes before the main event started. Below, a reed of a man with a thin, drooping mustache stepped out into the ring, wearing an oversized blue robe. "Ladies and gentlemen!" his voiced echoed across the arena. "We have a special show for you tonight! In the west gate, hailing from the Shattered City of southern Castilyn! She is the reigning champion of the Nasradaan Imperial Arena! You know her, you love her! Iron Foot Emilia!" A cheer erupted from the audience, and when she saw her, Cassidy stood up and cheered Emilia. "In the east gate, hailing from parts unknown! She has wrestled with rivermaids and the great bears of the land below! Lucky San Mina!" The roar that followed was smaller, but still loud. The woman who stepped out to oppose Emilia was tall and muscular, with waist-length hair tied in a tail, dressed in a shirt with no sleeves. Cassidy couldn't be sure from where she sat, but something seemed off about her face. She had a white and black tattoo or set of tattoos Cassidy couldn't quite make out extending from her wrists to her back. "Ladies, take your places!"

Lucky San and Emilia crossed the arena, standing three feet apart. Emilia held her fists up at the ready while San kept her hands open, palms down.

The proprietor pulled a gong from his voluminous sleeve and struck it. It rang loudly and clearly, and Emilia opened with the same swift punch that had laid Cassidy on her ass. San, however, took half a step back and slapped Emilia's fist away with a dismissive air. Emilia struck again and again, driving San back several paces, but never once did any of Iron Foot's attacks make contact. Cassidy leaned forward in her seat. She thought the fight would be over when Emilia landed a kick to San's face that knocked her off her feet. However, as soon as the tattooed woman's back hit the floor, she threw herself back to her feet and slammed the ball of her palm into Emilia's temple and kicked her on the other side.

There was a sudden hush when Emilia's head struck the floor. Cassidy sat gaping. A pair of sawboneses rushed into the arena and checked on Emilia. After a moment, one of them made a gesture that made Cassidy let out a sigh of relief. She had survived. The announcer stepped forward and took Lucky San's hand, raising it up. "The winner!"

CHAPTER TWENTY-FIVE

Smoke drifted from Cassidy's lips as she stared at the sunset. The *Bottomless Well* was packed – it was apparently *the* tavern to visit after a fight. Cassidy and crew had been lucky enough to arrive just as a group was leaving, so they had a table toward the middle of the common room. Asier had elected not to join them, as she didn't trust the harbormaster or the dock workers to guard their ship the way she trusted Revehaven's port authority. The captain had, however, encouraged them to have a good time.

"You sure she's coming?" Nieves asked for the third time.

"Yeah, she said she'd meet us here three hours after the fight," Cassidy said. "She should be about any minute."

"She did get hit really hard in the head," Kek reminded them. "Maybe she forgot."

"Or maybe she's still down," offered Nieves.

"Now that's a bleak thought," said Kek. "Say, Cassy, you never did say how you arranged the whole mess."

"I saved her life from a poisoner," said Cassidy. She took another drag of her cigarette and looked back out the window, this time hoping to see the fighter walking up the street.

"Pigeon shit," Kek replied.

"She is not lying," Hymn replied from under Cassidy's hat.

"There, that settles it," said Cassidy. She looked back to the table, noticing Miria looking uncomfortably at her. "Something wrong?"

Miria flushed and looked down at the table. "I was just wondering... if I could try one of your cigarettes," she said.

"Of course you can, you silly girl," said Cassidy. She slid the box of cigarettes across the table along with a match.

Kek gave a questioning look at the exchange, but he didn't say anything about it. Instead, he said, "Why would someone want to poison her?"

Nieves hit the table hard with a coin. "This is why, you idiot," she said. She offered Miria a sympathetic glance when she started coughing.

"But why bother? Lucky San had her dead to rights without it."

"One of the poisoners said they didn't want to risk it," said Cassidy. "By the sound of it, they work for the same company Lucky San worked for, so they had a personal stake as well as a professional one."

The tavern door opened, and Cassidy saw Emilia walk in, wearing a burgundy dress and overcoat instead of her fighting gear. There was a general cheer from patrons who recognized her, and Cassidy waved her over to their table. She looked terrible, with fat bruises covering both sides of her face, and there was a slight sway to her step. Still, she smiled at Cassidy and took a seat next to Miria who was finally catching her breath.

"Emilia!" Cassidy said cheerfully, "I'm glad to see you made it. This is my crew. Kek, Lierre, Nieves, and Miria." At each introduction, the fighter gave a smile and a nod.

A barmaid – a mere slip of a girl – came by and took their order. Emilia bought the first round of drinks and a fried falcon that turned out to be one of the beasts fought in the arena. She also bought the second round, and the third. Nieves, however, bought the fourth, paid out of the fat purse she won from the arena.

"You know," Emilia said between drinks, "normally I'd be insulted you bet against me, but I think that nose-less bitch knocked it out of me."

Nieves shrugged. "It bought us these drinks," she said.

Emilia grinned, revealing a missing tooth. "Can't argue with that." She took a long swig. "Defeat never tasted quite so good."

"I'll drink to that," said Cassidy, raising her mug.

"To sweet defeat," Emilia declared, repeating the gesture in turn. Cassidy's crew cheered in agreement and raised their mugs, except for Miria who lifted hers and let out a resounding belch and slumped forward in her chair.

"I think you had enough, pr– kid," said Kek, reaching for Miria's drink.

"No," said Miria, pulling her mug away, spilling some on her shirt. "I'm fine. And I'm not a kid! I'll have you know I'm six – no, I'm *seven*teen years old, I'll have you know. And I'm fine," she repeated. She gazed into her cup and said, "Put more of the stuff . . . in the thing . . . more stuff goes in." She rested her head on the table.

Cassidy ruffled the girl's hair. "I guess we should get her back to the ship." A little louder, she said, "You're going to learn about hangovers."

Emilia rose at the same time as Cassidy. "Wait," she said, reaching into her corset. She extracted a small object on a leather cord. She held it out for Cassidy to see. "I want you to have this. For saving my life." Cassidy took the thing from her uncertainly. It seemed to be a wolf's face carved from stone. "If you ever need a favor, show this token to anyone from the Fighter's Guild. It won't matter what city; they'll answer the call."

Cassidy wasn't sure what to say. She couldn't think of any favor she would ever need from the Fighter's Guild, but she knew it wasn't an empty gesture to dismiss, either. They stood there for a few moments before Cassidy untied the cord and retied it around her neck. "Thank you," she said finally.

"No. Thank *you*."

Cassidy helped Mira to her feet, all the while listening to the girl's complaints that they didn't have to leave, and that she could walk herself. Two blocks away from the docks, however, Miria's mantra of 'I can walk on my own' became 'hurry up, I need to piss.' Still, the walk served the girl well, and once they came in sight of the *Dreamscape*, Miria was able to hobble on her own toward it.

Behind her, Kek and Nieves were arguing. "It was a slip of the tongue," said Kek.

"Exactly the kind of slip of the tongue we don't need," said Nieves.

"Oh, come on!" Kek shouted. "You think just because I say the word 'princess' people are —"

Nieves slapped her hand over Kek's mouth. "If they know what she looks like and start thinking about it, they just might. So keep your beak closed or I'll muzzle you." Kek slouched and they returned to the ship. Asier was sitting on the gunwale, reading a news sheet.

"Ahoy, Captain," Cassidy called.

"Ahoy, Cassy," replied the captain, folding the sheet. "Miria was in too much of a hurry to talk to me. Did you have a good time?"

"Aye, Captain," said Lierre.

"Iron Foot is pretty, when you get past the bruises," Kek said, as though that answered the question.

Nieves sneered. "You think everyone with a pair of tits is pretty," she said.

Kek made his way toward the ladder. "Not true. Remember the girl we bought the seats from?" Nieves and Kek descended below, the rest of their argument fading.

When they were alone, Cassidy asked Asier, "Did anyone try to steal the ship while we were gone?"

The captain tapped her sword on the deck. "I could never be so lucky."

"What were you reading? Anything interesting happen?"

"A man in town claims to have found a dog that can speak Rivien. There is going to be a play mocking the former Lord Minister of Nasradaan, who was found drowned in a bathtub of wine with a lady of the evening. There was a fire in Andaerhal a few weeks ago. And there have been claims of dragon sightings less than ten miles from the city. None of that is what I was looking for, though. I was looking for any news regarding the Daughters of Daen."

Cassidy raised an eyebrow. "Oh? And did you find any?"

"Just one mention, offhanded," Asier unfolded the sheet and pointed at a small block of text toward the bottom.

There were three survivors recovered from the wreckage. The captain of the ship attributed the destruction of the ship to 'Daen's Scorpion', a mercenary of some repute. The captain was later revealed to be Jaes Tunbae, the pirate responsible for attacks on trade ship between Melfine, Nasradaan, and Cielhal. Next to it was an illustration of a bearded man with terrible teeth cowering from a scorpion.

"Sounds like a wasted evening," said Cassidy.

Asier shrugged. "Not really. The story about the talking dog was entertaining. It had two pictures."

"I think you'd have had more fun drinking with us. Or are you fancy on Captain Balthine?"

Asier sneered for a moment but covered it with a snort. "He's not my type. You know me better than that. Besides, you're the one wearing his rose on your hat."

"Of course. You may not realize it, but he is a rather handsome man."

Asier laughed, though it sounded forced. "I may not be interested, but I'm not blind, either. I can see a man's appeal, even if it doesn't do a thing for me."

"So, what *were* you looking for?"

Asier sighed and tucked the news sheet under her arm. "Do you know the religious significance of scorpions?"

Cassidy scratched her head. "I haven't set foot in a sanctum since I was ten," she replied, "but I know they're associated with the desert, along with Daen."

"Aye. It's said that what's now the Grand Desert was once a thriving land, rich and bountiful. Before the Ascension, Daen called upon the animals of the meadows and forests of the land to help her slay her enemies and remake the world in her image. All refused, save one."

"A scorpion," Cassidy answered, remembering the tale.

"Aye," said Asier, "a scorpion. And so it was that scorpions became the vanguard of evil."

"Since when do you take stock in religion, Captain?"

Asier snorted. "It's all stories, and stories are important. But, you're right, we weren't talking about that. We're talking about a very real man they call 'Daen's Scorpion'. How do you suppose a man earns that moniker?"

"Well, it's the name of his ship, obviously," said Cassidy.

"Sure, but people don't call me the 'Dreamscape Voyager', do they?"

"Um . . . actually–" Cassidy lifted her hat, letting Hymn's light shine out from it.

Asier stared blankly at the Fae for a moment before shaking her head. "Fair play. But, no, my point is, a name like that leaves its mark, and I don't doubt there's blood behind him."

Cassidy crossed her arms. "Captain, you've been weird about that ship since we saved them. What's going on?"

Asier met Cassidy's gaze, and Cassidy couldn't help but notice a sense of pain beneath an otherwise placid mask. "The Daughters of Daen aren't just a mercenary band with a religious name, Cassy. They were founded by a gods-worshiper. And Daen's Scorpion is a name with a long, bloody history."

A chill shot down Cassidy's spine. She tugged her jacket tight around herself. "Still, the sky's a big place," she said. "We'll probably never see them again."

Asier smiled faintly. "We'll see." She patted Cassidy on the shoulder. "We leave for Melfine at dawn. You have the next watch."

"Aye, Captain." Cassidy watched Asier saunter to her cabin and saw a slight stiffness in the way of her usual swagger. "Hymn," she said when Asier closed the door behind her, "you can catch a lie. Was the captain being honest?"

"I think you know the answer to that Cassandra," the Fae replied. "She spoke no lies, but she is hiding something."

Hearing it confirmed hurt Cassidy. "Aye," she said. "I *did* know. I was just hoping I was wrong. What could be so bad she'd hide it from me?"

CHAPTER TWENTY-SIX

Nine Years Earlier

Colors swirled, accompanied by black spots in Zayne's vision. He tried to shake his head but that hurt far too much. Laughter echoed in his ears, and it had a surreal quality, like he was hearing it from underwater.

"I think you knocked his brains loose," Nanette called over the noise, and there was more laughter.

Zayne grunted and picked up his training sword from the deck. He took his stance and glared through the blur at Gen. The bearded man gave his blade a flourish and beckoned Zayne toward himself. "You don't know when to quit, do you, boy?"

"Never have," said Zayne, a moment after he lunged at Gen with his practice blade poised. Gen swatted the tip of the blade away as he had done before, but Zayne stepped with it, evading the strike to the head that had knocked him flat. He brought his sword down on the older man's outstretched arm, the unsharpened edge striking his wrist with a deafening *crack*. For good measure, he slammed his fist and the sword's pommel into Gen's jaw. The older man didn't fall, but he did stagger back a step.

"Ah, that was a damn good blow," he said. "Maybe one day you'll be as good as your auntie."

"Don't tease the boy, Gen," said Salaa. "He's doing just fine."

"I meant no insult, Captain," the bearded man said. "I only —"

"I know damn well what you meant. Alright, you scallywags, the fun's over. Today is a big day, and I'll not tolerate laziness. Anyone who makes me look bad today will be hanged just beneath the rivermaid, do I make myself clear?" There was a scattered chorus of 'Aye, Captain' from the crew as they dispersed to carry out their duties. Salaa stepped up to Zayne and offered him her canteen. "You're getting better," she said.

"Thank you, Auntie," he said before taking a swig.

"How's your head feeling?"

"It stings, but the dizziness has already gone."

Salaa took her canteen back and nodded. "Good. You'll need to keep your wits about you."

"You're still not going to tell me, are you?"

"No. You need to face it raw. I can tell you it's a deeply religious experience, and terrifying for it."

Zayne snorted. "Will it hurt? Can you tell me that, at least?"

"Aye. It will. It will hurt a lot."

Zayne stared out at the landscape. Fog flowed like a network of rivers between the autumn-colored trees. Without the excitement and laughter over a fight, the *Scorpion* had fallen silent but for the clamoring of the engines. "How long do we have?" he asked.

"It won't be long, now," promised Salaa.

She wasn't wrong. Zayne counted fewer than fifteen minutes before they saw another ship drifting through the gloom. It was a larger ship than the *Scorpion*, painted the same black with an identical mural of the Desert Goddess along its flank. But while the *Scorpion* proudly displayed the corpse of a rivermaid along its prow, the *Martyr's Demise* put it to shame with the corpse of a mighty dragon nailed and fastened across its bow.

"I'm warning you now," Salaa whispered, "Dardan isn't a woman to cross. No matter what you may feel or think, keep that in mind. You'll want to run. You'll want to fight. Don't. Do you understand me, boy?"

Zayne didn't, but all the same he said, "Aye, Captain," because it was easier than admitting he couldn't imagine what could be so scary.

The two ships eased side by side to one another and the engines died, creating as true a silence as Zayne had ever heard. Gen and Sasha laid down the gangplank and Salaa ushered Zayne and Nanette across it before following suit.

Aside from the three of them, the *Martyr's* deck was occupied entirely by a dozen hooded figures in featureless, black robes surrounding a thirteenth figure covered in a black shroud. The cowled figure was carrying a lantern with fogged glass and a peculiar flame inside.

"Captain Balthine. I can see the journey in their eyes. You have kept them from me." The woman in the middle of the formation spoke with a deep, sultry voice that somehow brought a snake to Zayne's mind. *That's ridiculous,* he thought, *a snake wouldn't have such a musical voice.* Despite that, he couldn't shake the feeling. He also couldn't help but wonder how she saw anything in their eyes when her face, and indeed everything as far down as her waist, was entirely covered by the shroud.

"We have been busy, Captain Dardan," Salaa replied. "But we are here now, and the deed will be done."

"It shall indeed," replied Dardan. "Balthine the Younger. Adarin." Zayne came to attention and his heart grew chilled. He couldn't imagine Nanette having a different reply. "Today is the day you truly join the ranks of the Daughters of Daen. Salaa, they shall return to you when they bear the Mark."

Salaa placed her fist over her heart and bowed. "Of course, Captain Dardan." Without another word, Salaa returned to the *Scorpion* and had the gangplank removed. In that moment, Zayne was sure he felt what a rat must feel within the talons of a falcon.

The *Martyr's Demise* descended, but Zayne could see no one releasing the air from the balloon. Before long, trees with leaves of orange and red were towering above the ship, surrounding them. Zayne wondered how much practice it took for them to descend so perfectly, never once catching on a tree limb. When the ship touched the forest floor, Zayne felt a jolt of panic course through his body. It was not a crash, he knew, but there was something unnatural about a ship touching the ground.

All Dardan's hooded crew members laid a large plank that reached from the deck to the ground below. One then gestured toward it as if to say, 'after you.' Zayne looked to Nanette, who looked as uncertain as he felt. He nodded and stepped off the ship first.

The forest floor was like nothing he had ever felt. His boots sank into the dirt, which was softer than any rug he'd ever stepped on. It was almost spongy. The stability was also an overwhelming sensation. He always thought cities felt sturdy and stable, but that was nothing next to this bizarre immobility. He kept trying to sway with the breeze to compensate for movement that wasn't there and found himself sickened as well as off balance. When Nanette took her place by his side, she seemed just as thrown by the experience.

Dardan descended the ramp alone. She seemed unperturbed by the solid ground beneath her feet. "We are two leagues away from the place the ritual will begin," she said. She held the lantern in front of herself and began to march into the fog, clearly not hindered by the cover of the shroud that by rights should have left her blind.

Zayne glanced at Nanette and whispered, "What the fuck is a 'league'?"

"It's a measure of distance," Dardan replied offhandedly, and Zayne shivered. When the mercenary leader refused to say anything more, Zayne grumbled and pulled his coat tightly around himself. He hadn't expected it to be so blasted cold. As they walked, Zayne couldn't help but wonder how Dardan was guiding them so confidently. Even without the shroud draped over her, her lantern did nothing to illuminate whatever path they walked; the flame illuminated no more than a foot in any direction of Dardan before giving way to a glare as the fog merely reflected their light back at them. Still, Dardan strode confidently and never once suffered a misstep, while Zayne had stumbled into two holes and once tripped over a tree root.

There were whispers in the wood. Zayne could see nothing beyond the trees and the gray, but he could hear. One moment he would rationalize that he was hearing animals breathing and calling in between the trees, the next he would hear a clear word or his name and suddenly he was fighting off chills that sank into his very depths.

There was something oppressive in the air, and he wasn't entirely sure it was just the forest. Even looking at Dardan's back gave Zayne hackles, and he wanted to run, or to fight, but he knew that would be hopeless. Without Dardan, he and Nanette would be trapped in this forest, lost until something came upon them. So he followed, even though he didn't trust the woman for an instant. When Zayne let his eyes wander, he could still see Dardan out of the corner of his eye, and thought he saw something in her shadow. He saw silhouettes moving on the edges of the fog and unsheathed his sword. "They'll not impede us," Dardan said without turning from the path. Zayne wasn't reassured and kept his weapon in hand.

His legs were aching as he trod the uneven ground. Sweat dripped down his face and his clothes clung to his body in spite of the chill. For over an hour Zayne could see no change in their surroundings as they walked between the gray trees with their blood-colored leaves in the endless expanse of fog.

Then in one moment they passed the final tree and emerged into a large clearing. There was nothing, no foliage, no leaves, nothing within the hundred-foot ring of trees but cold, rocky ground. Dardan led them to the center of the clearing and took something from beneath her shroud and set it on the ground. Zayne took a step closer and realized it was a human skull.

She then took a water skin and upended it over the skull. Instead of water, however, a fine, blue sand that shimmered like sapphires despite the dull light of the fog poured from the spout and flowed into the empty eyes and mouth of the bone face.

Zayne's eyes widened in realization. "Myt Dust," he whispered. It was the sand of the Dreamscape and one of the deadliest and most potent drugs in the world. He had never seen so much before, and he knew there were people out there who would tear their own eyes out for the smallest taste of it. "We're not going to take it, are we?" The last thing he wanted was to become dependent on the stuff. He'd seen where that road ended.

"Take it?" Dardan asked. She chuckled. "No, Balthine the Younger, you're not going to take it. The Dust has a far more worthwhile use." She began to pour more of the dust in a circle and drew a glyph with it. When the last of the sand had been placed, Dardan waved them over. Zayne felt Nanette touch his arm as they walked together. Every instinct was telling Zayne to run away in that moment. To run away and hide. To put this madness behind him. To die clean. But he remembered Salaa's words back on the ship. *Don't*, he repeated to himself. *Don't*.

When he and Nanette were standing on the edge of the Dust circle, Zayne allowed himself a good look at the pattern. It seemed to be a pointed crook with three overlapping crescents at its core. Something about the sight made Zayne's eyes water and his stomach churn, so he looked away.

Dardan loomed over Zayne and Nanette, her features even now obscured from them, leaving them faced with a featureless mask of cloth that somehow left Zayne completely unnerved. She set the lantern on the ground and snatched at Zayne's hand. Somehow, she managed to grab both his wrist and Nanette's, despite her hand not being large enough to completely wrap around them, and Zayne felt immobilized. His legs were burning, not just from the forced march but from the desire to run. His hand felt cold. The cloaked woman took a knife from her shroud and in a blur, it swiped between Zayne's and Nanette's arms. Blood poured from the mirrored wounds along their forearms, trickling down and dripping to the ground. Then a few drops of blood touched the sands, and Zayne could no longer hear his breath, or the breeze, or any rustling in the woods. It was pure silence.

That silence lasted the span of half a heartbeat.

The tumultuous roar of an explosion came alive as the earth beneath his feet churned and a great blast of wind accompanied dark purple light that enveloped him. He heard the cackling of an inferno in a tempest, hurricane winds drumming across his ears, and a screech of something in pain behind it all. He felt the power of the explosion pushing him away while another, unseen force pulled at him to keep him in place. He felt as though the warring energies were tearing him apart.

He opened his mouth to scream but the air was sucked out of his lungs and his chest burned. The purple light began to swirl around him with shades of blue and red, creating distorted images. A shadow swam between the trees in the distance, screeching and howling like a nightmare made manifest. Before him stood a creature with half the face of a beautiful woman and half the face of a hideous beast with scales that were partially torn away to expose bones that were not quite human in shape, and horns like a ram. When he saw the creature's mismatched eyes – one was stark white surrounded by a deep, bloody red sclera, the other was an empty black well – Zayne identified it as Dardan's face.

There was a figure looming in Dardan's shadow. It appeared to be skeletal in form, but Zayne couldn't make out the details. It whispered softly, "You belong to Daen, now," while *almost* simultaneously, Dardan was repeating the words louder. The wind and light became a vortex of bizarrely colored flames that burned at Zayne's skin. A thousand miles away he heard Nanette let out a scream. Even more distantly he was aware that some of the screams were his own.

He saw shapes in the fires, painting pictures that moved and changed, searing his mind. In those flames he saw his father hit him, again and again. He saw his father hit his mother and far worse, again and again and again. He saw Meryl standing there watching his trial with gross indifference. He saw her looking at him before the gallows, and when she turned his back on him, she *smiled*. He saw Tam sell Iden the Myt Dust that nearly killed him. He saw Iden hang for it. He saw a drinking Jainin strike Cenn across the jaw so hard his head struck the table. He saw little Nanette open her mouth to scream only for their father's massive hands to squeeze her throat until she grew purple and stopped struggling. He saw his mother try to escape her brutish husband only for him to plunge a knife into her quivering, naked flesh time and time again. He saw the old man drink himself to death. He saw himself burning the old man's body.

Then he saw the flames take the shape of those dead. He saw his friend Iden, with a noose around his neck. He saw his little brother with his skull fractured, blood and brain matter dripping from it. He saw his little sister, with her face swollen and bloated from suffocation. He saw his mother, bleeding from wounds Zayne couldn't bring himself to count. And above it all, he saw his father, not shaped in the flames, for he *was* the fire. All of them stared, judging him. He heard them whisper and shout overtop one another, *"This was your fault."*

Dardan whispered now in his ear, and Zayne could hear that other voice whispering in hers only half a heartbeat ahead of her. "Your freedom has been no boon. What have you wrought with it but failure? Trust in Daen. You need no will but hers."

Zayne tried to speak, to deny, but only succeeded in biting his tongue. He remembered the prayers he whispered at night, and on days when the moons sat in the sky. He had prayed for the death of his father. Daen had delivered. He had prayed to leave Dawnhal. Daen had delivered. What small part of him could think beyond the searing pain he felt encompassing every part of his body realized it was too late to deny Daen now.

Then the experience ended.

There was no fading, no gradual dissipation of fire and screams and visions. One second Zayne was in the midst of a nightmare of flames and noise and pain, and suddenly he wasn't. He was on his knees, sweat and blood dripping from his face onto the grass beneath his feet. His skin was throbbing in pain. His ears were ringing like a struck bell. He was breathing heavily as though he had been held underwater. For a minute his mind didn't register that the nightmare was over. Another minute afterward, he realized that the grass beneath his hand wasn't burning, but he refused to believe it. *This isn't real,* he thought, *everything is fire. I'm not safe. I'll never be safe.* His arms, which were the only things keeping his face off the ground, were shaking, and if he tried to move in any way, he would lose what little strength was holding him up.

The part of his mind that struggled to keep him grounded, that stayed aware of the world even under stress, was puzzling over the grass he was clutching beneath his hands. That hadn't been there before, had it? He found he didn't care, shouldn't care, but couldn't stop noticing it anyway. Then he noticed something on his arm. It was a white scar, bizarrely shaped. The scar resembled a crooked staff with spiked ends and three crescent moons nested inside one another within the crook. *Daen's Glyph,* he recalled from his studies as a child. He had seen the mark on some of the *Scorpion's* crew a time or two and had taken them for tattoos. As he stared at it, Zayne was almost sure he could see a shadow moving *inside* the mark.

You're mine, a feminine voice whispered from nowhere.

Zayne had almost forgotten Dardan until he saw her boots, and subsequently the rest of her, standing in front of him. A rebellious instinct sparked inside him when he saw her outstretched hand emerging from beneath her dark shroud, and it gave him a strength he didn't know he possessed. He would *not* show weakness to her, he decided. He somehow forced himself to his feet, despite every muscle in his body feeling like jelly. When he remembered Nanette, who was also on her knees beside him, he stooped back down and, fighting the weakness that permeated his body, helped her to stand as well.

He narrowed his gaze, intent on meeting the place where Dardan's eyes should be. He didn't know if her eyes were truly as monstrous as what he saw. He had no idea if what he saw held any truth at all, or if it was just a drug-induced hallucination. As far as he was concerned, it didn't matter. He was certain, though, that Dardan was a monster, whether she resembled one or not. He didn't know what made him so certain, but there was no doubt in his mind.

"The ritual is complete," Dardan intoned. "You are now a brother and sister of the Sisterhood. You are Daughters of Daen, sworn in blood in the name of Daen."

Zayne didn't trust himself to speak, so he nodded. He faintly heard Nanette give some sort of acknowledgment, but he paid it no heed. *I can't fight you today,* he thought at Dardan, *but one day, I'll slay you like the monster you are.* As if in answer, Zayne heard laughter in his head. It sounded almost like Dardan.

CHAPTER TWENTY-SEVEN

The morning was off to a terrible start. Zayne's arms shook as he supported himself over the washbasin. He had awakened in a cold sweat, dizzy and nauseous. The scar he had acquired during his initiation was itching incessantly. He was panting. His heart was pounding as though he'd been in ten fights. He felt like he was on fire. He hadn't slept much since they had left Revehaven. Between his night terrors and the feeling that what happened at the palace wasn't the worst thing he'd face on this mad errand, he found he couldn't stand to close his eyes if it could be helped.

"Pull yourself together, Balthine," he said slowly to the reflection in the water. He cupped a small pool of water in his hands and splashed his face in it. In his mind, he was repeating what he had to do. *Get to Nasradaan*, he recited, *find out where they went next. Follow. If they're gone, find out where they went. Find them. Take the girl.* It sounded so simple, until that last step. He was confident in his skills as a duelist – and his handling of the Falcons had given a slight boost to his ego – but he didn't think he was good enough to face Elyia Asier, and damn anyone who said her prime was years ago. He could see it in her eyes, in the contours of her figure, she had not been idle since the war ended. For this plan to work, he would need to resort to trickery. He would only get one bluff, though, and his best shot was to bet on the hope Asier had no idea who the girl was. *And while I'm at it, I might as well bet on the sun rising in the west. Asier worked for the Empress for years.* He needed to think of a better plan. The only fight he felt he had any hope of winning was ship-to-ship – the *Scorpion* was larger and far better armed than the *Dreamscape Voyager* – but that would put the princess' life at risk.

He realized he had been tracing the scar on his arm – Daen's wretched glyph – and forced himself to stop. *It's not what you wanted,* he reminded himself, *but it's what you've got.* He comforted himself with the idea that he might never encounter the *Dreamscape Voyager* or her crew. The skies of the Empire were vast, and it was easy for one ship to get lost in them – and if they should ever leave the borders in any direction, there was even more vastness in which to become lost. Zayne could spend the rest of his life searching aimlessly after the rumors of Elyia Asier. He smiled at the thought. He could just sail on, using his mission as an excuse.

That was an idea. He could go to port and claim he'd heard they traveled anywhere else in the Empire. Or out of it. They could sail to the Reach, as far from the troubles of the world as they could, all on behalf of a fool's mission. Then he considered the promise he made to himself, his promise to kill Dardan if the chance ever presented itself, and hesitated. He shook the thought from his mind. Dardan would never be undefended in his presence. It was a fool's dream. Better to sail, to try and fly out of her grasp. He threw on a dark red shirt and black waistcoat. Then he tied his gun-belts and sword-belt around his waist. His watch wasn't for another hour, but he was restless.

He picked up his coat only to decide he didn't want to deal with the added weight of all his hidden tools and weapons. He hung it back on his chair and stepped outside. The sky was clear and bright; it was a perfect contrast to Zayne's mood. He sneered and made his way around the deck. Flea was looking out to the horizon, looking for anything amiss and occasionally correcting the course. The scrawny bastard couldn't navigate to save his beard, but at least he could manage to keep the bow pointed in the right direction, if given a landmark as a guide. Zayne left him to it and took the stairs to the lower deck. Jacques was manning the bellows. He was wearing a scowl, and Zayne wasn't sure if it was aimed at him or the world in general. For a moment he wondered why he cared, but soon after he decided he didn't, and he moved on to the galley.

He made his way to the larder and took stock. They had resupplied before leaving Revehaven, and Zayne hadn't wanted to risk the stocks running low again, so they had overstocked. He stared blankly at the barrels, biding his time to forestall making decisions. Eventually he reached in one and grabbed a mushroom. He ate it on his way out the opposite door from the one he'd entered. In the tight corridor at the aft end of the ship, he knocked on the door to his left.

"Enter," Nanette called. Zayne took a breath before complying. Her cabin smelled of paint, as it always did. Nanette had her back to the far wall so the sunlight peeking through her window would strike the canvas before her. She didn't look up from her work when she asked, "What can I do for you, Captain?"

He didn't answer right away. "What are you working on, this time?"

"A memory," she answered vaguely.

"May I?"

"Please yourself."

Zayne stepped around the easel and took in Nanette's latest work. Zayne recognized the two prominent figures in the foreground crossing blades in a market street. Even though they were incomplete, he recognized the arches, the cobblestones, the vendor stalls of that city in southern Castilyn. He recognized the face of his 'aunt' and that of a man she had scorned in the moments before his guts spilled onto the walkway. He even remembered some of the onlookers, though not with nearly so much detail as Nanette clearly had. Were it just for the shape, it would be awe inspiring. But the colors were all wrong; the fairer-skinned people were portrayed as somewhat jaundiced while the darker ones were as likely to be purple as brown, the shadows were green, and the stonework was burnt orange where it should have been sand-colored. He didn't say any of that, though. Nanette couldn't see more than a few colors – it was a strange condition Zayne never fully understood – and that was a source of great frustration for her. In one of her more vulnerable moments, when the moons had taken a certain turn and she drank more than usual, she had thrown a canvas at him and demanded to know why the gods gave her the rare gift of perfect pitch but denied her the basic ability to see color properly, declaring she had no real love for music.

"You know, sometimes I find myself forgetting her face," said Zayne as he stared at the off-color representation of Salaa. He took a seat on a spare stool beside Nanette. "When I look back, it's so easy to forget how bright her eyes were. I remember her voice like I heard it only an hour ago – strong, fierce, stern – but every time I think on her face, I can't recall how full of life she always seemed to be."

"Probably because you could never relate," Nanette replied as she added more paint – red this time – to the walls. "If you're not angry, you're melancholy. Salaa saw this ship as freedom. You treat it like shackles."

Zayne was about to agree with her when he remembered something. "That wasn't always true."

Nanette stopped painting for a moment. "No, I suppose not. That day in the forest . . ." her mouth snapped shut and she stared intently at the painting, as if she were looking for something hidden beneath its depths. "No, let's not go back there."

"I couldn't agree more," replied Zayne. He focused on the painting. "So, what made that memory worth committing to canvas?"

Nanette chewed at her cheeks. It seemed like she wasn't going to answer. However, when Zayne opened his mouth to change the subject, she said, "It was the last time I saw you happy."

Zayne blinked in surprise. "Was it?"

Nanette nodded and tapped a figure on the far side of the street, behind Salaa's shoulder. He hardly recognized himself so young – though that may have just been the yellow skin and green hair. He saw excitement in the boy's eyes, though he questioned the honesty in Nanette's memory. Though he remembered the duel and had watched it with bated breath as his aunt and captain danced around the arrogant duelist, he couldn't remember *smiling*. Then again, he also couldn't remember what the duel had been about, either. What he did remember, though, was that the next time they had set sail, it was to Dardan.

After the silence between them grew uncomfortable, Nanette asked, "So, why did you come down?"

Zayne wondered the same thing. "I just wanted to talk," he said. "I couldn't sleep."

"The nightmares?"

"Those don't help. Between that and the hunt, I feel like every time I close my eyes I'm falling out of the sky."

Nanette looked at him. "You seem even more on edge than when you were breaking into the palace," she said.

"That was just a heist. The most dangerous we'd ever gone through, but still just a heist. This is . . . so much more."

"We're chasing after a cargo ship."

"A cargo ship captained by the woman who ended the war. A living legend."

Nanette hit him with her brush, splattering red paint on his shirt. "Zayne, you were taught to fight by Daen's Scorpion. Shit, you *are* Daen's Scorpion, now. It wasn't all that long ago you killed seven Emerald Falcons. Does Elyia Asier's legend really scare you so much?"

"Honestly? It terrifies me." What he didn't mention was that he not only feared Asier's prowess, but he also had no desire to fight her because of what she represented. She was a hero.

278

The look on Nanette's face was hard to read, but Zayne expected her to start yelling, to call him an idiot or a coward, to hit him again. Instead, she placed her hand on his arm and sighed. "It's still a ways to Nasradaan," she said softly. "From there we'll have to pick up the trail and catch up. You'll think of something, I know. We've got time."

"Yeah," he said. "It'll be a while before we need to worry about any sort of confrontation."

There was a loud cry as Flea yelled over the pipeline. *"Captain! You'll want to come up here! The* Dreamscape Voyager *is in sight."*

CHAPTER TWENTY-EIGHT

"You're shitting me," exclaimed Cassidy.

Asier shook her head and offered Cassidy a grin. "Not at all," she said. "It's not something I *enjoyed*, but sometimes it's the only way, and that day it was."

Miria tilted her head. "Forgive the impertinence, but how is breaking your wrist in any way helpful?"

Asier snorted. "I think you're the only one on this ship who knows what impertinence *means*, my dear. No sense asking for forgiveness for it."

Cassidy felt herself blush at having her ignorance laid out. "You're avoiding the question," she said. "Why was breaking your own hand the thing to do?"

They had to wait for the captain to stop laughing to get their answer. "The thing about a well-made knot is, they don't get loose just from squirming, and your wrists and hands don't tend to change, either. So, when your hands are bound," she turned her chair around and put her hands together behind it to demonstrate, "you'll usually be in a position like this. Sometimes, a captor is pretty bad with knots and you *can* get out by twisting and squirming. But when they know their trade, you'll get nowhere. I'd recommend you try to get something sharp and cut the ropes, but that's not always an option either. I really don't recommend breaking your own bones if you can find *any* other way. That shit hurts. But when you get right down to it, nothing good can come of staying captive. When you break your wrist, the bones are in a less rigid formation and you can squeeze one hand out, and then freeing the other is no trouble."

Cassidy winced at the idea, but Miria seemed more intrigued than uncomfortable. "How do you do it?"

"Planning to get kidnapped?" mocked Asier.

"No one ever plans for such things," retorted the princess.

"You'd be surprised," replied the captain. "No matter. It's pretty simple. When your hands are bound, you have a pretty limited range of moment. You'll need to push past it. Cassy, hold my wrists in place." Cassidy obeyed. The captain's wrists were small enough that Cassidy could easily envelop them tightly in her hands. "What you do is lift one arm as high as you can manage, like so. Then, twist and add pressure, then you'll do this," she said, and she began to press on her left hand with her right. "And if you aren't holding anything back, you break something and slip out. Word of warning, that won't be easy, either, and will hurt every step of the way."

Cassidy released Asier's hands and allowed herself another wince. Her own wrist was aching in sympathy. She rubbed at Hymn's brand and the surrounding scars.

"What happened next?" asked Miria.

"I found a –"

"Captain!" shouted Kek from the deck below.

Asier leaned over the edge of the aftcastle. "What's wrong, Kek?"

"Ship approaching fast," he said. "It looks like the *Scorpion*." He took another look through his spyglass. "Sorry, Captain, I should have said, 'it *is* the *Scorpion*'!"

"What?!" the captain shouted before muttering something. Cassidy only caught the words 'too soon' and 'more time.' "Kek, run down, wake Nieves and tell her to grab the blades. And send Lierre, too. Cassy, Miria, ready some pistols from the storeroom. Two per person."

Miria and Kek raced to obey, but Cassidy stayed to ask, "What's wrong, Captain?"

"I'm just being careful," said Asier.

Cassidy folded her arms. "Do you really expect me to believe that?"

The next moment struck Cassidy like a thunder crack. Asier slammed her fist against the railing and pinned Cassidy with an icy glare. "I *expect* you to follow orders, Sailor. Now *go!*"

Cassidy's body was already obeying long before her mind could take in what was happening. Her chest was cold with fear and she found herself passing Miria through the doors to the storage room. She loaded two pistols and strapped them to her shirt with a belt and loaded two more. Miria matched her step for step until they had enough.

"You can stop," said Cassidy. "The captain keeps hers on her at all times. Let's go." Lierre was already topside and Nieves was climbing up the ladder with Kek behind her. Cassidy passed around the pistols and took a sword from Nieves, all the while eying Asier, who was watching the black ship approach with a silent intensity.

There was anger in her eyes, softened somewhat around the edges, though Cassidy wasn't sure why.

The *Scorpion*'s approach was fast — as Cassidy watched, she was certain the *Dreamscape* wouldn't be able to outrun it — but she had a lot of sky to cross before it reached them, so the crew stood watching apprehensively as she approached.

Is this a coincidence? Cassidy wondered. She tried to imagine the *Scorpion* had simply run a course that just so happened to cross theirs. She tried to imagine Balthine was just looking to see friendly faces where he could find them. She found Asier's paranoia rubbing off on her, however, and she couldn't hold the image for long.

"Be ready for anything," she whispered to Hymn.

"That was my intent," came the Fae's voice from beneath her hat.

When the *Scorpion* was close enough Cassidy could make out the face of the rivermaid nailed to the bow, the ship began to slow and change course, coming to a nearly perfect stop when it ran alongside the *Dreamscape Voyager*. Captain Balthine stood across from them on the edge of his ship, his arms folded in front of him and a solemn expression on his face. He had tied his hair back, Cassidy noticed, as she unwittingly recalled how he looked with his raven locks flowing in the wind amidst gun smoke and harpy blood. She felt Hymn tap on her the head and returned to the moment.

Balthine swept his gaze across the crew, briefly making eye contact with Cassidy before moving on. "This isn't as warm a greeting as our last," he said, just loud enough to be heard.

"Different circumstances," replied Asier. Her voice was like ice. "A ship in peril isn't the same as a ship running at full speed toward us."

"Especially a ship with this one's reputation, I'm sure," the other ship's captain replied with a sigh. Flea and Jacques dropped a gangplank and Balthine crossed over.

Asier took a heavy step forward and Balthine stopped, though he didn't step back. Cassidy would have stepped back. "I never gave you permission to board my ship," she said sternly.

Cassidy watched Balthine's chest heave as he took a deep breath. "I'm afraid circumstances forbid I ask. You see, I'm here on matters of Court." Cassidy tensed at the statement.

Asier took another step toward Balthine. "Court?" she demanded. "What business could you have with the Court?"

The *Scorpion's* captain sighed again. "I've come on behalf of the Empress." He pointed at Miria without looking at her. "She wants her daughter back." Kek swore under his breath while Lierre and Nieves shared a gasp and Cassidy took a step that placed her front of Miria.

Asier didn't move. "No, you haven't, and no, she doesn't."

Balthine sighed yet again and shrugged. "I didn't think that would work," he said heavily, "but I had to try. Please understand, I respect and admire you and your crew, but there are bigger things at work. Please, hand over the princess. I really don't want to hurt any of you, but I will if I must." As if to punctuate his sentence, Jacques, Flea, and Nanette all drew and leveled pistols at the *Dreamscape* crew.

Asier was a blur as she closed the last three steps to Balthine. Cassidy blinked and nearly missed her steal a pistol from the opposing captain's belt and press it to the underside of his chin. When she pulled back the hammer, it rang out in the relative silence. "Tell them to drop their weapons," she said slowly. Balthine tilted his head back slightly and gave his crew a wave. There was a moment of hesitation and shared glances, but the *Scorpion's* crew eventually lowered their weapons.

"You seem to have forgotten who you're dealing with," Asier said, taking half a step closer so their faces were less than a hands-breadth apart. Cassidy couldn't see either of their expressions, but she could see Asier's shoulders rise and fall with her breathing. Balthine, in contrast, was still as stone. "Let me remind you; I am Captain Elyia Asier. One click of my tongue could have the Empress herself on her knees. When you were still clutching at your mother's apron strings, I was facing down *gods*. You earned your name burning a few battered pirates, but I earned mine by stopping the pursuit of the Dread Hounds. In my time, I've made deals with the Fae and come out on top each time – a feat few can claim – and with a good crew behind me, I've killed dragons with the same ease you've killed men." She shoved the pistol hard into Balthine's throat, twisting the barrel, rubbing it into his skin. "Threaten me, or my crew again, and you'll wish I'd killed you today. Now, *get off my ship.*"

Zayne's heart was pounding like a dozen drums and sweat was beading on his forehead. He stared into the amber eyes of Asier. He was so close he could count the spots on her sun-kissed skin. He knew she meant every word – even if he didn't know her history, there was no hesitation in her voice. His life was only a twitch of her finger from being snuffed out like a candle. *And no one would mourn me,* he thought somberly. So it was that he surprised himself when his voice didn't break, or shake, or in any way reflect the fear that was tugging at his heartstrings. It was calm. "Of course, Captain Asier," he said, taking one long step backward after another. He didn't lower his hands until both of his feet were firmly planted within the bounds of the *Scorpion,* and he never turned his gaze away from Asier. *She already hated me,* he thought, *and I just burned any chance I could have had to change her mind.* That shouldn't have mattered, he knew, but it hurt to think about all the same.

"Nanette," he said, loud enough Asier could hear, "set our course for Dardan. It seems the princess is out of our reach." *I mean it as a peace offering,* he thought, *but I can see from that glare she thinks it's another threat.* As the *Scorpion*'s engines began to roar and the ship rose and pulled away from the *Dreamscape Voyager,* he finally tore his gaze away from Asier and turned toward the girl from Dawnhal. *We come from the same place,* he imagined telling her, *but it seems our destinies couldn't be more different.* He wondered what would have been if he had never met the Daughters of Daen, if the captain he had booked passage with had been the legendary Elyia Asier. Would she have seen his plight and spirited him away from his execution? Or would he have been hanged for the murders he never committed. He looked back at Asier as they drifted apart and wondered what it would be like to see respect instead of contempt in the depths of those eyes. In the moment before the ships grew too far apart, Asier threw Zayne's pistol at him. He caught it with his off hand, grateful he didn't fumble it. She never broke her stare, so he watched her until she disappeared from view and the *Dreamscape Voyager* was a distant shape that faded away.

He turned to return to his cabin, but Nanette stood in his way. "So that's it?" she demanded. "We're really just going to fly away? I thought you were going to order us to start blasting them before we got out of cannon range."

Zayne's shoulder's slumped. "If we turned this into a battle of ships, they would still never surrender. They'd fight to the last woman – and I will remind you, one of those women is the princess. So it would all be for nothing."

Nanette's mouth worked silently for a moment before she found the words she seemed to be looking for. "So you're just going to give up?"

"Miss Adarin," he said wearily, "I may not love my life, but I'm in no real hurry to end it, either."

"So you're trading one death sentence for another? Dardan will kill you for this, and she probably won't be pardoning the rest of us, either." Jacques and Flea each gave a grunt of agreement.

"I'll deal with Dardan," Zayne said flatly.

"Like you handled Asier back there?"

Zayne felt a wave of anger rush through him. He shouted, "Asier is a warrior and a hero. I'm not afraid of Dardan." The lie tasted like oil in his mouth, but his course was set. Still, he could hear Dardan's laughter, and that of whatever monster lurked in her shadow, chasing him through the years.

Jacques spat. "Well, you can count me out. Flea, turn this ship around. We're getting that girl. I'm the captain now."

"Jacques," Nanette started, but Zayne cut her off.

"Care to fight for that title?"

Jacques didn't speak a response. Instead, he drew his pistol, but Zayne still had his own in hand. His shot cracked like thunder and Jacques yelped as his own weapon backfired and flew out of his hand in the same moment. Before the larger man had time to take stock of whether or not he was injured, Zayne pulled his sword from his belt, still in its scabbard, and struck the broad side of it across Jacques' face, knocking him aside. Blood and a trio of teeth spilled from his mouth when the engineer hit the deck. As he tried to push himself up, Zayne slammed the scabbard's point into his fingers. There was a faint *crack*.

"Flea, I suggest you step away from the helm." He knelt to Jacques, grinding the scabbard into his wounded hand as he did so. "Will there be any more talk of mutiny, Jacques?" Zayne stared into Jacques' eyes and saw his own anger reflected. A sneer formed along the other mercenary's face. "Well?"

Jacques' mouth twisted and twitched, and Zayne saw the beginning syllables of a dozen curses form on his lips. What he said, however, was "No."

Zayne pressed down on his weapon. "No, what?"

There was a longer pause. "No, Captain."

"Good." Zayne stood and returned his sword to his belt. "Next time," he said, "you'll be thrown overboard in pieces. Now, clean this mess up." He turned to Nanette. "Set course for the Dragon's Nest." *It's time I slayed a monster.*

TWENTY-NINE

It wasn't until the *Scorpion* was completely out of sight that Asier finally turned away from the gunwale. Cassidy watched her, unsure of how she should react to everything that had happened. She raised her hand to touch the captain's shoulder but stopped when Asier stomped past her. "Put us back on course, Cassidy," she said firmly. Before Cassidy could confirm the order, Asier stepped into her cabin and slammed the door.

Cassidy looked from Kek to Nieves to Lierre, each of whom looked as confused or nervous as Cassidy felt. She turned to Miria next. The girl was still staring in the direction the *Scorpion* had flown. She was fidgeting with her fingers.

"Are you okay?" Cassidy asked.

Miria pulled her eyes away from the empty sky and focused on Cassidy. "Yes," she said. "I mean, 'aye.' I'll be fine, I'm just . . . Cassidy, how did he know?"

"I don't know."

Miria's eyes widened. "The only people who are supposed to know I'm on this ship are my mother and Captain Asier! He shouldn't know!"

Cassidy wrapped her arms around the girl. She was shaking. "He can't hurt you," she promised, stroking her back gently. "The captain will see to it. As long as she's here, no one can hurt us." The princess nodded into Cassidy's shoulder and Cassidy pulled away. "You can take the rest of your watch off," she said. "I won't mind."

Miria shook her head. "No, I'll be alright. But thank you, Cassidy."

Kek threw an arm around Cassidy's shoulders. "If you've got extra time off that needs to be taken, I would gladly take that particular bullet for the good of the crew."

Cassidy snickered. "Ain't he just a big damned hero?"

A small chuckle cracked Miria's crestfallen mask, and she said, "Yes – er, aye – he is, Ma'am. So selfless in the face of adversity."

"What ever would we do without you, Kek?" Cassidy added. "Fortunately, we don't need you to sacrifice your precious work time. Keep on the lookout while I fix our course."

"Aye, aye, Miss Durant."

With naught but ocean as far as the eye could see in any direction, Cassidy checked her compass and corrected course accordingly, so the ship was heading north. She decided to run at full speed for a time to make up for the delay. She removed her hat and let Hymn float freely by her side. Nieves had returned to her bunk and Lierre to the bellows. Kek and Miria were focused on any other surprises the horizon might have to offer, so Cassidy was alone with the Fae. Or, at least as alone as anyone could be on the deck of a ship. "I guess the captain was right about Balthine," she said conversationally.

"I am not so sure," said Hymn.

Cassidy cocked an eyebrow. "Oh? Why's that? He threatened us."

Hymn's light shimmered in a way Cassidy interpreted as a shaking of her head. "He did. However, he was not eager to carry out the threats and did not double-cross the trust of the Dreamscape Voyager, despite the fact that the weapons of the *Scorpion* are larger and more numerous than those of this ship."

Cassidy hadn't considered that. "Huh," she said. "Why do you suppose that is?"

"Did you see his eyes?" asked the Fae.

"No. Didn't think to look, why?"

"I suspect that if you had, you would have seen conflict. I believe he was sincere in his desire to avoid confrontation."

Cassidy mulled that thought over, all the while staring at the glistening sun reflecting on the water ahead. "That could just mean he was afraid, couldn't it?"

Hymn's light briefly flashed red but quickly returned to its usual blue. "It is possible," she said tightly.

"What's wrong?"

"If you do not wish to listen to me, why speak?"

"Hymn, I'm listening," she said, "I just have a different opinion."

"You have a belief and are ignoring evidence that speaks against it."

Cassidy didn't have a response to that. She decided to change the subject. "Say, how old are you, anyway?"

"Why does *that* matter?"

Cassidy shrugged. "Just a curiosity. You know a lot about what happened before the Ascension, and I know the Fae can live for a long time, so I'm curious."

"I was there when the first dawn broke across this world. I doubt you could grasp how long ago that was, much less how much longer I have been."

"I'm not stupid, you know," Cassidy said bitterly.

"I never said you were," Hymn replied dismissively. "It is not a question of your intelligence; it is a question of your experience and your perspective." The Fae stopped floating beside Cassidy and took to standing atop one of the spokes of the wheel in front of her. "You speak sometimes to the Dreamscape Voyager about a war that ended when you were a child."

"The war with Castilyn, aye," said Cassidy.

"To you, that war seems like a long time ago, yet when weighed against the course of history, barely any time as past."

"I . . . guess," Cassidy conceded.

"Even if you only compare it to the history of your Empire, this war between the Jade and the Ruby thrones was nothing. If I have kept track correctly, the first Empress of Asaria united your sky cities nearly four thousand years ago, yes?"

"Three thousand, eight hundred, thirty-seven, aye."

"And yet a war that started twenty-one years ago and ended eighteen years ago – a span of time in which you yourself were alive – seems distant to you. With this in mind, how could you hope to understand the scales which the lives of my kind are measured?"

Cassidy rubbed her temples. "That . . . I hadn't considered it that way," she said. "What do you do for all those years?"

"I do not understand the question," said Hymn.

"If the Fae live so long, what do you do with all that time?"

"We live," Hymn said simple. "So long as we can."

"Yeah, but . . ." Cassidy tried to order her thoughts. "People – that is, human people – don't live long, so we try to make the most of the time we have."

"Not all of them."

"Granted," Cassidy conceded, "but what I mean is, what motivation do the Fae have to take part in things? I mean, you'll outlive anyone – any person, I mean, human – you'll ever meet, so why get involved?"

"Our reasons are as varied as yours are," said the Fae. "I know a fair course of your history. I know your people – at least on a cultural level – see mine as unequivocally evil. It is how your stories and your history paint us. But in truth, we are each individuals, much like humans. True, our priorities are different than yours, and our experiences shape us differently than yours ever will, but there is disagreement between us, dissension, and from our differences breed culture and factions.

"There are those who seek only their own entertainment, choosing to live as tricksters. There are those who prey on your kind, as you believe we all do. There are those who are curious to see how life outside the Dreamscape will unfold. Some are drawn to grand causes, and others who wish only for solitude. But for all that, there are universal truths, things that will stir us. The turnings of the moons, the shedding of blood, powerful emotions, beauty of art and music and nature. All these and more attract us, though how we act upon them is up to the individual. Ultimately, there is too much in life to simply pass it by, no matter how long one lives, regardless of what one lives for."

Cassidy guided the ship gently along as she absorbed what the Fae said. Even after dealing directly with Hymn for some time, the idea of humanizing the Fae as whole was a foreign one to her. Despite what Hymn said, despite what she had *done*, Cassidy still had a hard time picturing the Fae as more than shadows lurking in wait. *That's silly, though,* she thought, looking at Hymn. *She's been my friend, and it would be foolish to think she's unique. Besides, the Fae cannot tell lies, so she must mean it.*

"So what about you?"

The Fae's light flickered, and Cassidy thought she might have turned red for an instant. "What *about* me?"

"Which of those things motivates you?"

Hymn was quiet, hovering in place. Unable to see her expression, Cassidy didn't know if she was thinking or ignoring her.

Cassidy had given up on getting an answer when Hymn said, "There was a time when I believed in grand causes."

Cassidy imagined Hymn uplifting ragtag bands of heroes to fight evil and right injustices, like a wise mentor in an old storybook. It was silly. She pictured the Fae in her full size, speaking before empresses or queens of the distant past, as the Fae in the Black Gulch had done. She figured it must have been a noble life. "So what changed?"

"The world," said Hymn. "Or perhaps I was the one that changed, and I simply couldn't reconcile with it."

Cassidy had no answer for that. The next few hours passed in relative silence. As the sun began to set, Nieves took Kek's place at watch, and two hours later Asier emerged from her cabin to dismiss Cassidy and Miria. Cassidy thought she looked more composed, but there was still a shadow hanging over her.

"Is everything alright, Captain?" she asked after Asier took up the helm. Asier didn't answer, so Cassidy repeated the question.

"What? Oh, yes, just . . . I wasn't expecting today. Run along, Cassy. You need your rest."

Cassidy hesitated before saying, "Aye, aye, Captain." Before Cassidy descended the ladder, she offered one last look as Asier, who was staring out ahead of them, yet her gaze seemed to be elsewhere.

"Something's wrong," she whispered to Hymn as she climbed down.

"What do you suppose it is?"

"I don't know. It's something to do with the mercenaries."

"You figured that out, did you?"

Cassidy ignored the barbed comment. She entered her shared cabin and climbed into her bunk. She stared at the ceiling until her eyes grew heavy, and the last thing she saw before sleep overtook her was Asier clashing blades with Balthine.

CHAPTER THIRTY

The desert expanse stretched out around them. It was late autumn everywhere else in the Empire, but it was eternally summer in the Great Desert. Even under the shade of his ship's balloon with a breeze crossing through, it was still hotter Zayne could comfortably tolerate. From his place at the bow, he could see a pillar of black smoke and falling ash and stirred dust blotted the landscape in the distance.

"It looks like we missed the dragons." said Nanette.

"Good," replied Zayne. "Seeing that once was enough.'"

"You'll get no argument from me," said Nanette. She looked through her spyglass to the nest. "Are you sure this is a good idea?"

Zayne didn't answer immediately. "Yes," he lied.

"But Dardan —"

"Dardan is just one woman," said Zayne.

"So is Elyia Asier."

It's not the same thing, he wanted to say, but that wasn't explanation enough, he knew. "Dardan isn't a fighter," he said.

"She won't be alone," said Nanette.

"Likely true."

"And unlike the crew of the *Dreamscape*, these are killers, not cargo pushers."

"Nanette."

"What?"

"Do you trust me?" They turned to face each other, and Zayne looked into her dark eyes. Had they always seemed so deep? Those eyes seemed to be searching for something in his. There was a weight to her gaze.

"Yes," she said at last, and they broke their stare. They watched together as the Nest grew nearer. Before too long, they could make out the well of ships that made it up. Their numbers were slightly diminished, but Zayne could already see ships incoming from the west and the south to replace those that were missing. As they drew nearer, one ship with a flowing Imperial banner draped over either side broke away from the formation and set course toward them.

"Slow approach," ordered Zayne, and Nanette stepped away to return to the helm. As the other ship closed in, he recognized the exacting Imperial script emblazoned on the side in gold paint. The *Justice* slowed its approach and drifted casually in the *Scorpion*'s path. Nanette turned hard to starboard, and the two ships met side by side little over a dozen feet apart. When the ships came to a relative stop, Zayne called over, "Captain Hawkwind."

"So you remember me, mercenary," replied the Imperial officer. "I'm flattered." She *sounded* disgusted. "What brings you back to the nest?"

"I've come, once again, to meet my employer," said Zayne. "I fear she has an unhealthy obsession with this place."

Zayne could see Hawkwind glance up at the top level of the formation. "We are coming aboard."

"Of course you are."

A gangplank was put down between the two ships, and Hawkwind and two burly soldiers – one a bald woman and the other a man with a scraggly beard and hat – accompanied her. The soldiers began what presumably passed for an inspection while Hawkwind herself seemed to be sizing Zayne up. "That must be a heavy coat," she observed. "It hardly moves in the wind."

Zayne shrugged. "It helps build muscle."

"It must be hot."

"Well, it was almost winter where I was just yesterday. Besides, I feel naked without it."

"I imagine a gun or two makes a man feel big," Hawkwind said.

"It distracts from certain inadequacies," Zayne agreed absently. *She's stalling,* he thought. *She wants something.*

"As long as you don't use them on my people, I don't much care what you carry," she said.

Ha! If you'd found what we smuggled in last time, you wouldn't say that. Instead, he said, "I came here to see my boss. *You* flew to *us,* remember."

"Yes, your employer," Hawkwind said slowly. *Here it comes,* Zayne thought. "She has been here for months now. Do you know why?"

"I think she has an unhealthy obsession with gunpowder and loud explosions."

"Don't screw with me, mercenary."

Zayne furrowed his brow. "I wasn't. I don't know what she sticks around for," he lied. "I try to avoid talking to her when I can."

Hawkwind nodded. "Aye, from what I've seen – never mind."

Hawkwind's inspectors returned to the deck far more quickly than they had the last time Zayne had come to the nest. "All's clear, Ma'am," reported the bearded one.

Hawkwind nodded and turned to Zayne. "You'll find the *Martyr's Demise* where you found it last." She sent her cronies over the gap first, and when she started across, she turned back to face Zayne. "And Captain Balthine." She paused, and there was something in her expression Zayne couldn't quite make out. It might have been either confusion or discomfort. "Be careful."

That wasn't what I was expecting, he thought. He stood there a moment, watching as the *Justice* departed. "Well you heard her. Top ring of the formation." The *Scorpion* began to rise. Zayne stared at the fleet and spotted the *Martyr's Demise* rather easily. He stared at it for most of the approach and realized as they drew close enough to make out the dragon fixed to the bow that he had been subconsciously rubbing the scar on his arm. He tried to break his attention away from it, to focus on the people manning the nest, but he found he couldn't. He was too close.

"Too late to turn back, now," Nanette said, mirroring Zayne's thoughts exactly.

"Aye." The silence they felt was weighed down by dread. He suddenly felt as though there were a million things he forgot to do, though he couldn't imagine why. "If the situation falls ground-ward . . ." he began, "I just want you to know . . ." *What? What is there to say?* "No, everything will be fine," he decided.

"And if it wasn't going to be?" Nanette asked. "What then?"

"Forget it," said Zayne. "Just sentiment. Who has time for that?"

"We've got a minute or two for it."

Zayne snorted. "I guess we do. Alright. I just wanted you to know I was always grateful that you saved me, back then. And that you're the best friend I ever had. And . . ."

Nanette waited only a few seconds before asking, "And what?"

Several thoughts crossed Zayne's mind, each with a different way to fill the silence. He weighed the notion that whatever words he chose could be his last to her. Finally, he decided to say, "When we first met, I thought you were a complete bitch. I'm glad I was wrong."

He turned back to see Nanette's face trapped between laughter and outrage. She quickly schooled her features, however, and replied,

"It's okay. Back then, I thought you were a total git. I'm glad I was only half right."

They shared a laugh that came to an abrupt halt when they fell in the shadow of the *Martyr's Demise*. Their ascent continued until they were level with the vile ship, and they slowly drifted into place beside it. Dardan was in her customary place, seated beneath her shroud in the center of her ship's deck. Behind her were two thin women dressed all in black with translucent veils, standing at parade rest with curved swords at their hips. Set apart from them, Nyrien stood with her arms crossed, staring scornfully at the *Scorpion*. To Zayne's great surprise, Lucky San was standing on the deck as well. She seemed to have been reporting to Dardan when she noticed the mercenary leader's attention turn to Zayne.

Flea and Nanette moved to put down the gangplank, but Dardan's bodyguards laid their own down first. Zayne made a show of adjusting the lapels of his coat to cover his checking of the stilettos hidden in both sleeves. He crossed the gangplank. San's presence could be a problem – Zayne wasn't afraid of Nyrien or Dardan's bodyguards, and he was confident he could handle San on her own, but together the odds were poor – and there was no turning back.

"Captain Balthine," Dardan greeted him coldly. "I do not see the princess in your custody."

Zayne took a deep breath and counted to three. "There has been a complication. It would seem the princess is out of reach."

Nyrien snorted. "Took one look at the palace and pissed yourself, eh, Balthine?"

"Not at all," said Zayne, with a great deal calmer than he felt. He wanted to scream and rage and rave, but he needed to get close enough to Dardan to strike. That took a certain level of calm and tact. "In fact, if you did more than stand around using your tongue to polish Captain Dardan's boots, you might hear tales of a rather successful break in."

Dardan cut in. "But not so successful you actually took the girl."

Zayne bit his cheek and took a few casual steps toward Lucky San. "No. It's rather difficult to capture someone who isn't home. Lucky San, it's good to see *you*. Jacques and I found a painting of the princess in the palace, and as it happens, she looks almost exactly like you."

"You don't say," San replied dryly.

"The princess has a bit more nose, though."

At the reference to her missing appendage, her scrunched face twitched in a way that resembled a skull. "Not much of a passing resemblance, then, is it?"

"So where *is* our princess, Zayne?"

Zayne placed himself, with as casual a grace he could muster, roughly between San and Dardan. "That's the trouble," he said. "She's taken on with Elyia Asier."

Nyrien scoffed. "So, you know where she is. Go get the bitch."

"Do you know who Elyia Asier *is?*" Zayne asked.

"Old news," Nyrien said spitefully.

Dardan laughed. "It would seem Balthine is as sentimental as his aunt. He can't touch the girl because he has a hero."

Zayne felt heat rise in his face. "Pigeon shit," he retorted. "I can't touch the girl because Asier is a better fighter. Dardan, I've done a lot of things some would deem suicidal for this band. I've faced pirates, Falcons, and dragons; I've hunted horses for their horns, I've broken into the fucking Imperial Palace, and I smuggled thirty *barrels* of Myt Dust and the seed of the World Tree across the Empire. I did all of that because I knew I could. But I'm not stupid. If you think I'll fight Elyia Asier for you, you're sadly mistaken."

Nyrien and San stared at Zayne in stunned silence, and even Dardan's bodyguards looked uncomfortable. Dardan herself drummed her fingers against her lantern. As she did so, the flame behind the smoked glass flickered a different color. The sight left Zayne nauseous.

"Are you saying," Dardan asked when the silence stretched to its breaking point, "that you fear a glorified bodyguard more than you fear *me?*"

Zayne felt his heart constrict as he considered the question. When he looked upon Dardan's shroud, he remembered what he saw beneath it that day so many years ago. He was sure it was still there, lurking in her shadow. She was evil, and the cause of more than a few of Zayne's nightmares. *So why did I run from Asier to charge straight here?* What was Asier next to the nightmare? Then, Zayne came to a conclusion.

She is a better life.

Zayne drew himself straight. "Yes."

He barely saw Dardan rise from her seat and clear the distance between them. She wrapped a slender-fingered hand across his throat and dragged him across the deck. He flailed haphazardly as she squeezed the breath from him. It defied all reason; she was shorter than him, thinner than him. And yet, she held him by the throat with one hand and moved him with no signs of exertion.

Zayne thrashed his feet trying to gain leverage to stand or break free, gripping at Dardan's thin hands with both of his own, but her grip was like iron. When she stopped dragging him, she hoisted him, and he found himself hanging over the vast expanse. He stared where he estimated Dardan's eyes were. She held him at full arm's reach. *Impossible,* he thought again. Yet, there he was.

Between the moments when his vision was clouded with black spots, Zayne thought he could see the scowl marking Dardan's face behind her cowl. "Do you wish to rethink your answer, Captain Balthine?"

This looks like the best chance I'll ever get, he thought as he stared into that black shape. He stopped trying to break her grip and flicked one arm, catching one of the stilettos in his hand. With an instinct honed by years of practice, he drove one dagger into Dardan's forearm and twisted it and dragged it around to come as close to severing the arm as he could. He braced himself for the fall.

But he didn't fall.

Blood, hot and sticky and red, spurted from the wound, but Dardan's grip never wavered. Despite heavily mutilation, she didn't even flinch. Her head turned as she examined the knife sticking in her arm. Then she turned back to Zayne.

"What was your plan, Balthine?" with her free hand, she punched him hard in the side, hard enough Zayne would have sworn she was wearing iron knuckles had he not seen her bare hand fly. He grunted and spat blood in a single breath. Distantly, he thought he heard Nanette gasp. He had forgotten the *Scorpion* had not departed. He shook his other hand and grasped the other stiletto. He tried to drive it into Dardan's face, but with the hand she had used to punch him she took hold of his wrist and twisted it until he dropped the weapon down into the Nest.

Zayne wondered what any of the ships below would make of the sight. Then he realized they might go unnoticed, for each ship was concerned with its own recovery and the next day's dragon awakening. It was a strange notion, that he might die surrounded by people yet without witnesses.

He thought that Dardan's grip was shaking, that she was weakening and would let him go. It was only when his hands spasmed that it was his own body, starved for air. Dardan remained still and in control. "Let me tell you a secret, Balthine. There are no heroes. Asier can't save you from your destiny; she's enslaved to her own. And while you can dream and pray and swear your secret oaths at night, you'll never kill me, any more than you could kill your father. You think me the monster you slay at the end, but this isn't a bedtime story. And before this is done, you'll see yourself every bit as monstrous as I."

Zayne found he couldn't struggle any more. His heart was pounding desperately in his chest and his blood was going cold. He panicked. He couldn't breathe and he no longer had the strength to fight or try. He was going to suffocate. Some detached, possibly delirious part of his mind reflected that this must have been what his sister went through in the end. Black spots flickered like insects across his vision until he could only see a tiny patch of the world, and that was made blurry by tears.

Then he found himself seizing a lungful of air. Another. A newer panic swept through him when he thought his body had forgotten how to breathe properly. He was sprawled on the deck of the *Martyr's Demise* and Dardan had returned to her seat. He tried to stand but his limbs wouldn't heed him at first, and there was a flaring pain beneath his ribs. His breathing was still off-rhythm when it deteriorated into a fit of violent coughing that ended with another splotch of blood splattering onto the deck.

"You will bring the princess to me," said Dardan. Her tone brokered no argument.

He *wanted* to argue all the same. He wanted to fight, until his dying breath if need be. He wanted to tell her to do it herself. He wanted to draw one of the pistols strapped to his coat and put it in her brain. He wanted to die clean.

He pushed himself to his feet, bursting with righteous fury.

But amidst that rage, fear bubbled up from his depths, permeating him. He clutched his wounded ribs, and instead of making his valiant declaration, he said, "If Asier kills me, I can't bring the princess."

Dardan made an unsettling noise that Zayne eventually realized was laughter. She reached under her shroud and extracted an odd bundle wrapped in black cloth. "Take this," she said. Zayne reluctantly staggered toward her and accepted the gift. Whatever was beneath the cloth was hard and smooth. It was warm to the touch and pulsed against Zayne's hand. It made him nauseous.

"Is this –?"

"If you use that, even Asier will be unable to kill you," Dardan said simply.

Zayne wondered at the implications before strapping the thing to his belt. He tried to push them out of his mind. "It will take some time. I have no leads on their destination."

"Oh, poor, simple fool," Dardan cooed. "I *do*. So long as Asier seeks to control her own destiny, I know where you will meet her."

"I'm not sure I want to know what you mean by that," Zayne said wearily.

Dardan seemed to ignore the comment. "Take the *Scorpion* to Justiciar Lake. There you will wait, and when the first snow falls, the *Dreamscape Voyager* will come to you."

CHAPTER THIRTY-ONE

It was a cold and gray dawn when Cassidy's watch ended. She let out a yawn and watched her breath drift away in the mist. The cold had struck a week or so after their run-in with the *Scorpion* and hadn't let up since. Miria had awakened early and made breakfast – slightly burned omelets and hot cider – so when Lierre came to relieve her and Kek, Cassidy made her way to the storage room with Hymn on her shoulder instead of climbing down the frosted ladder. The princess was sitting at the table they had laid out – with winter on its way, they started sharing their meals there instead of outside – staring blankly at a steaming cup in her hands. She was dressed in a fur-lined coat and corset much like Cassidy's, but she also had a blanket wrapped around her arms.

Cassidy joined her at the table. "Is something wrong?" When Miria didn't answer, she added, "This is the kind of day you should be curled up in bed until we pull you kicking and screaming into the cold. Instead, you get up an hour before your watch make everyone breakfast." She grabbed a plate and omelet that looked more brown than black and started eating. "Not that I'm ungrateful," she clarified after washing down the foul taste after a few bites with a mouthful of cider.

Miria gave her a faint smile. "I'm okay," she said quietly. "I just couldn't sleep."

"If you need another blanket, you can take one from the storeroom."

"No, it's not that. I just had a nightmare is all."

Cassidy patted Miria's arm sympathetically. "Monsters in the privy kind of nightmare, or forget your trousers before heading into the market?"

Miria giggled. "Neither," she said. "It's not important. Just a bad dream, is all."

"Well, if you ever want to talk about it, my bunk is right across from yours." She forced herself to eat at least half of the rest of her omelet and drank two cups of cider to get the taste out of her mouth. "But for now, my watch is over, and yours is about to start."

Miria nodded and moved out to the deck. Cassidy stayed behind for a minute. Hymn moved to the table. "You have a question," the Fae noticed.

"How can you tell?"

"You knit your brows when you cannot decide whether or not to ask what is on your mind," said Hymn. "Well, go on. If we are to stay here until you ask your question, ask it. Otherwise, you should get some sleep."

Cassidy made a conscious effort to relax her eyebrows. "I was just wondering why iron hurts the Fae."

Hymn stared blankly at Cassidy for a moment. "Why does fire hurt humans?"

"Um . . . because it's hot and it burns."

Hymn nodded. "There you have it. Cold iron burns us. There is nothing else to it."

Cassidy wasn't sure why, but she felt disappointed. She had expected there to be some kind of origin myth behind it. "So, if touched one of my iron coins, you'd get blisters or something?"

"No. If I was very quick about it, the best I could hope for would be my hand catching fire."

"Oh. Shit."

"It would not be pleasant."

"Aye, it doesn't sound like it would be," Cassidy agreed. "You want some of my omelet?"

"Cassandra, not even *you* want to eat that."

Cassidy dropped her head sheepishly. "I just feel bad, because she did try."

"If you are very lucky," said Hymn, "empathy will be the only bad feeling you have."

Cassidy gave a look to what was left of her breakfast. She didn't want to insult Miria's work, but the only thing she could find to say was, "That sounds a bit harsh, doesn't it?"

Hymn offered a shrug and floated back to Cassidy's shoulder. "No matter. Let us be on our way." Cassidy agreed and made her way to the deck. While the storeroom hadn't been warm by any means, it hadn't been open to the wind, either. A chill cut through her coat and corset. She tucked her hands under her armpits and shivered. Kek seemed to have already answered the warm call of bed. Lierre was comically flapping her arms to keep her blood flowing while Miria swept the landscape with her spyglass.

301

"Three hours until Nieves' watch," said Lierre, seemingly to herself. "Three hours."

"What's so special about Nieves starting her watch?" Miria asked as she crossed the ship to look out the other side.

"I get to sit next to the burning coal in the engine compartment," Lierre explained. "*Fuck*, I hate these Imperial winters!"

"I seem to recall Naariem got pretty cold this time of year," said Cassidy. "Besides, we aren't even into winter yet, and you know it."

"*Fuck*," Lierre repeated miserably.

Cassidy shook her head and made her way down below. "At least you have daylight," she added before making her way down the ladder. "Kek and I had to deal with the cold *and* the dark." She didn't wait for any response on Lierre's part – the iron rungs were freezing her through her gloves, and she was eager to make it back to her bunk." She heard the captain's cabin door open and close above, but she was not about to climb back up. She gave the harpoon gun a playful pat as she passed and marched up to her cabin.

Nieves' entire body was wrapped snugly in her blankets, and Cassidy envied her snoring. She stripped off her coat reluctantly as the cold air nipped at her skin like daggers. Her corset went next, followed by her boots. When she finally removed her shirt and trousers, she practically leaped up to her bunk and pulled her blankets tightly around herself, relishing the itchy wool as it trapped what little body heat there was to keep. She considered slipping into the Dreamscape – it was so easy for her now she almost did it by instinct – but the weariness that sank over her made her think better of it. There was no rest in the Dreamscape, as Hymn was always eager to remind her. So instead, when she closed her eyes she merely lay there and waited for sleep to take over. It wasn't a very long wait.

Though she dreamed, when she woke up the details were foggy. She was sure it likely involved Asier and Balthine – she had dreamed of them most nights since their encounter with the *Scorpion*. She let out a groan and turned over. Nieves was gone from her bunk, so it was at least eight o'clock. Stifling a yawn, she curled up tighter and nestled into her bunk. "Hymn, what time is it?"

The bright, blue light of the Fae briefly shone against Cassidy's eyelids. "You should get up and check your own watch, if it is so important to you."

Cassidy didn't even open her eyes. "Sorry, forget I asked. Why are you such a bitch, sometimes?"

The Fae didn't seem to deem that worthy of a response, and before long Cassidy forgot she had even asked the question. She drifted to sleep again, only to be awakened by her own snoring and took to staring at the ceiling. "Do you ever sleep?" she asked.

"Everyone sleeps, Cassandra."

"But I never see you sleep."

"Everyone sleeps," the Fae said again. "When and how are different matters. I have slept enough for the time being."

"If you say so," said Cassidy. "I could use another five minutes. Or an hour, or however long until the –" her sentence was interrupted by the sound of the lunch bell. ". . . *shit*." Reluctantly, she sat up, pulled away from the comforting embrace of her blankets, and jumped down from the bunk. She dressed quickly and ran out the door. Lierre, true to her word, was sitting in the engine compartment, warming her hands in front of the fire. "Ahoy, Lierre. Going to come eat with the rest of us?"

"I'm thinking about it," the engineer said, "but I just got warm."

Cassidy laughed. "Come on, it's not that bad anymore. Let's get you some lunch, you'll feel much better."

When they climbed up, Asier was alone on the deck. "Hurry up, ladies," she said, "before it gets cold." Cassidy nodded and hurried into the storeroom. The smell of cooked meat and steamed vegetables struck her. Kek was already fixing what Cassidy thought looked like his second plate when she sat down with Lierre only a step behind her. She scooped up a ladle of mushrooms and onions and a slab of a falcon's breast. "This your handiwork, Nieves?" she asked.

"With some help from Miria, aye," said Nieves. Cassidy hesitated for a moment. Then she decided it couldn't be worse than breakfast and ate. The food had flavor, which had been woefully absent from breakfast, and Cassidy was on her second plate before Asier finally took her seat.

"We just crossed the Guine River," the Captain reported. "Melfine will be in sight shortly, and we should dock within the next couple hours."

"Is it true what they say about Melfine?" asked Miria.

"You mean that it's the home of perverts and degenerates?" Cassidy volunteered. "No, Kek is just a special case."

"Hey!" Kek protested, "I am not a degenerate! If anything, I have been told I'm quite a chivalrous pervert."

"Only by people who don't know you better," said Lierre.

Miria cleared her throat. "I, um, actually meant regarding its size, considering that the entire city is airborne."

"Aye, it is," Kek boasted, "and far more beautiful than the tales would have you think, for words cannot do justice to the city's craftsmanship and engineering."

"The foundation of the city is made up of several retired warships," Cassidy explained when Kek stopped for breath. "The architecture is based on the work of shipwrights as well as salvaged and re-purposed vessels. The minister's home and office are located in an old naval ship, and former passenger ships serve as everything from inns to tenement homes."

"So there's really not just an oversized caravan?" Miria asked.

"No," Kek said proudly. "In fact, it's not only the only airborne city in the world, it's larger than Dawnhal or Bajin's Landing. You'll find nothing like it in the Empire, Rivien, or Castilyn."

"Why is that?"

"It's expensive," said Nieves. "Back when Melfine was being constructed, there was talk about making it the new standard – it sounds nice in theory; not needing to restrict expansion based on the size of any foundation, and with absolutely nothing connecting it to the ground there's even less risk of Fae influence than in a standard city. But it requires more maintenance than the suspension anchors of other cities, and just keeping it over Evere Lake is a full-time job."

"Honestly," said Asier, "if Melfine weren't in such an important location, it would have failed long ago. But, there's nowhere else to build a city for a thousand miles in any direction, so Melfine makes for a rather important port for ships to resupply and trade."

"I can't wait to see it," Miria said wistfully.

"Well, once you finish eating, you can grab a spyglass and keep an eye out for it," the captain said. "It's really quite a sight." The princess took that as a suggestion to hurry up and wolfed down what was on her plate before running outside.

Cassidy giggled. "She's so excitable."

"I remember you acting just like that," said Asier.

"Maybe a little."

"No, not a little. You hung over the bow with that spyglass pressed firmly to your eye until we were right upon the city."

Cassidy felt herself blush. "Oh, right."

Kek snorted. "That must have been quite a sight."

"Oh, please," said Cassidy, "you nearly pissed yourself when you first saw the Nymph's Tower."

Nieves chuckled. "Really?"

"N-no, of course not," sputtered Kek. "Cassy, where do you get off, telling them things like that?"

Cassidy stood up. "Aye, the truth is an ugly beast. I'm going to go make sure Miria doesn't fall overboard." She set her plate aside to be washed later – she was on scullery duty that night, she remembered – and stepped out into the cool air. The princess wasn't hanging over the bow, but she was standing as far forward as she could, checking her spyglass every few seconds. "Spotted the city?" Cassidy asked as she approached.

"Not yet," said Miria.

"Well, I wouldn't worry too much." Cassidy sat herself on the gunwale and Hymn set herself beside her. "You'll see it before long."

"Say, Cassidy?"

"Aye?"

"Are we mercenaries?"

Cassidy looked at the horizon as she pondered the question. "I don't think so. Why?"

Miria put the spyglass back to her eye. "I'm just a bit confused," she said. "I mean, Captain Asier hates mercenaries, yes?"

"It sure seems that way," Cassidy agreed. "Of course, given our last run-in with Daen's Scorpion I think she has a right to be angry."

"Certainly – I mean, 'aye' – but it seems deeper than that. I haven't been with her long, so I may just be over-analyzing, but she always seems calm and in control, ready with a kind word of encouragement."

"Except when the subject of the *Scorpion* and mercenaries comes up," Cassidy finished for her.

"Exactly," said the princess. "I tried asking her about how that man knew who I was, and she suddenly got cold and distant. She gave me one-word answers to everything after that for the rest of my watch."

"How does all this lead you to ask if *we're* mercenaries?"

"Just a line of thinking. I mean, we don't have an employer. We go where the captain decides, and the captain decides based on where we get the most money to go, right? Isn't that what mercenaries do?"

"Is this bothering you?" Cassidy asked uncertainly. "This life?"

"What? Oh, no, no, no. I love it out here. I'm just wondering . . . Captain Asier seems to really hate them, but . . . aren't we doing exactly the same thing?"

Cassidy bit her lip and thought it over. "Have a seat," she said, patting the gunwale. Miria obeyed, and Cassidy continued to look at the sky. She saw a trio of ships in the distance diverging, which told her they were close. *What is a mercenary?* she thought. She wondered what Captain Balthine did from day to day. She considered the stories of mercenaries she'd heard of, and what Asier said about Balthine, about Daen's Scorpion. It couldn't *all* be true, could it? "I think," she said after a while, "the thing that separates us from mercenaries is that a mercenary will do *anything* for money. They may carry cargo or passengers one day, defend a caravan, or fight and kill the next. We just have one job we stick to. We carry cargo. If we have to fight, it's in self-defense. That's all we've ever done. So, no, I wouldn't say we're very mercenary at all."

Miria nodded slowly. "So you think it's more about what they do than the freedom to do it?"

"Hey, you're the educated one," Cassidy said, nudging the girl with her elbow. "I don't even know what 'impertinence' means, remember?"

The princess giggled. "You're right," she said. "Why am I asking you?"

"Fuck if I know."

Miria put the spyglass back to her eye. "I see it!" she squeaked. Cassidy rose to her feet and looked ahead. Without her spyglass, Melfine was just a black blot in the sky, but it was a distinctive black blot to be sure. Miria stared through the spyglass for a while, making the occasional noise of awe.

Cassidy smiled at her. "Wait 'til you see it up close."

"There's so many balloons," the Princess said absently. "I recognize some of the coat of arms on them."

"A lot of the city's development and structural support depends on donations as well as taxes," Cassidy explained. "And a lot of rich folk like to be seen helping. So they paint their banners on the balloons, because they think it looks good. Honestly, I think some of them are tacky. Who wants their family to be represented by bees?"

"House Mendrin," the princess replied instantly.

"You're shitting me," said Cassidy.

"Not at all."

"Huh." Cassidy reseated herself on the other side of the bow and peered out. As they neared the city, Cassidy was able to separate the balloons from the structures they were holding up. As they sailed on, Cassidy pointed out the endless line of propellers cycling along the bottom of the city. "They have hundreds on each side of the city, active at all hours of the day, to keep the city from drifting away. In case of an emergency, there is also a set of anchors they can drop into the lake below.

"It's beautiful," Miria said. She hadn't taken the spyglass away from her face since she'd spotted the city.

"Admiring my city without me?" Kek called from behind them. He was accompanied by Nieves and Lierre. Captain Asier remained at the helm. When the captain saw her looking, she gave her a smile before focusing on flying.

"Figured you were busy emptying our larder," Cassidy replied.

"Now that's unfair," said Kek. "You and I both know you eat twice as much as I do!"

Cassidy gave a sarcastic gasp. "Are you calling me fat?"

"In this area, at least," Kek said, gesturing around her chest.

"You know you love it."

"I would if you let me."

"I believe you can find plenty of ports to dock in without sullying mine."

It was Kek's turn to act indignant. "'Sullying'? Cassy, I'll have you know I'm a proper gentleman."

Nieves snorted. "And I'm the queen of Rivien."

Miria raised an eyebrow. "But Rivien doesn't even have – oh, never mind." She returned to casting her gaze on the city. Ships pulled from her harbor and scattered to the winds, and they were drawing near enough that Cassidy could identify some of them.

"Hey, Miria," she said, "let's play a game."

The princess faced her. "A game?"

"Aye, a game." She pointed at a ship passing them a fair distance off the port side. "What's that ship's name, and what's its story?"

Miria looked through the spyglass. "It's called the *Ivory Sparrow*," she said. "But I don't know anything about it."

Cassidy sighed. "Kek, show her how it's done."

Kek took the spyglass from Miria, who gave a small squeak of protest. "The *Ivory Sparrow* is smuggling contraband medicine," he declared. "The captain's sister has fallen ill with consumption, but since Red Tac doesn't grow in Castilyn and trade taxes are so high, she has to smuggle it in fish barrels."

Miria stared at the passing ship, gaping like a fish. "How can you –" she began, but Cassidy interrupted.

"Lierre, what about that one, heading east?"

Kek passed the spyglass to the engineer, who read out, "The *Lonesome Star*." She paused longer than Kek had, but when she started, she kept a steady pace. "The captain was a hero in the war, but in peace time he couldn't reconcile with what he saw. He had himself declared killed in action and stole his own ship, painting it and giving it a new name. Now he travels the Empire to make amends."

Cassidy pretended to wipe a tear from her eye. "That was beautiful, Lierre."

Miria squinted at the ship before it faded from view. "How do you know –?"

"Nieves," Cassidy said, trying and failing to withhold a giggle when Miria looked angry at being interrupted again, "what about the red one that's just making harbor?"

The sawbones took the glass from Lierre and set her gaze straight ahead, "The *Lost Compass*," she read. "This is her maiden voyage. She was commissioned as a wedding gift for the captain's husband-to-be, but he had an affair, so she took to the skies without him. She plans to sail into every port and indulge in every vice until the heartache stops."

Cassidy clutched at her chest. "Ah, it's so tragic!"

"How do you *know* all this?" Miria said. It was nearly a shout.

"We're making it up," said Kek.

Miria blinked. "You . . . you're making it up?"

"Sure," said Cassidy. "Every ship out there has a story."

"And while most of those stories are probably boring," came Asier's voice, "some of them are bound to be tragic or romantic, and filled with regret or glory." She seated herself on the gunwale next to Cassidy. "But, there's no way to really know someone else's story, what they go through, unless they tell you. So, sometimes we look at the ships as they pass and try to imagine." Cassidy couldn't help but smile. To her it was just a fun way to pass the time, but Asier made the game seem somewhat romantic.

The sun was low on the horizon when they finally reached the city, which gave the sky a golden hue and the city that stretched before them appeared to be a shimmering red. They spent half an hour waiting for the dock workers, operating in small, personal skiffs, to direct them to an open berth. When at last they docked, Cassidy joined the captain to show the port authority their permits, papers, and trade manifests. The captain said it was important Cassidy do it with her so she would be ready to do it herself one day, but she had been saying the same thing for nearly ten years. When everything was in order, Asier declared that they would send for the cargo's recipients in the morning.

Nieves fixed the crew's supper – a spicy concoction that utilized what was left of the falcon meat and the remaining onions and mushrooms – before the captain declared it would be an all-night in. "Don't give me that look, Valani," she said when Kek's shoulders slumped. "Once the cargo is dealt with and our ship resupplied, you'll have plenty of shore leave." It was well past dark before the crew turned in. They continued telling stories about the other ships in the harbor – Miria's were awkward and full of long pauses, and ultimately, they never went anywhere, but Cassidy couldn't fault her for trying. The princess was the first to turn in, followed by Nieves and Lierre. Kek lasted a little longer, but in the end, it was just Cassidy, Hymn, and the captain – and the Fae was sitting quietly on Cassidy's lap, possibly pretending to sleep.

"I love this crew," Asier announced when the two of them had lapsed into a comfortable silence.

"Getting sentimental on me, Captain?"

Asier shrugged. "At my age, you get to be."

"You're not that old."

"Maybe, maybe not. Still, nothing wrong with a bit of sentiment now and then, is there?"

Cassidy smiled. "I guess not. Coming into Melfine, I was thinking about when we first met Kek."

Asier laughed. "I remember you insisting we didn't need, oh, what did you call him? 'That relentless flirt'?"

"Something like that."

"So, ten years later, what do you think now?"

Cassidy smirked. "I've never met a more relentless flirt."

Asier nudged her. "But?"

"But I wouldn't have anyone else watching my back."

"I'm glad to hear it. Out in those skies, nothing is more important than friends you can count on."

"I guess we should count ourselves lucky," said Cassidy, "because I trust all of them with my life." She looked down at the Fae on her lap and gave her a gentle nudge with her fingertip. "That includes you, you know?" Hymn merely made a noise that might have been a snort.

"You'll make a good captain someday," Asier said.

"Maybe" said Cassidy softly.

Asier cocked an eyebrow. "You don't sound too happy to hear that. I seem to recall you once telling me you wanted to captain your own ship."

"Once. But, honestly, I can't see myself ever leaving this crew, and I couldn't just steal them from you."

Asier chortled. "That *would* be most ungrateful of you. Still. I won't be able to captain the *Dreamscape* forever."

"Sure," said Cassidy, "but you're not *that* much older than me."

"Over ten years."

"By the time you retire, I won't be too long behind you."

Asier just smiled and shook her head. "Well, regardless of what happens, just know, you've got the makings of greatness in you, Cassy."

Cassidy blushed and turned her head. "Thank you, Captain."

CHAPTER THIRTY-TWO

It was clear that Dardan trusted Zayne as little as he trusted her. When the shrouded zealot sent the *Scorpion* on what her captain was calling 'the last mission' – at least to himself – she had added two new faces to the crew. Kales was a pudgy, blond boy who couldn't have been more than sixteen. Tana was a muscular young woman with intricate tattoos woven along her arms and hands. The newcomers were only recently branded, and ostensibly were to replace Karn and pad their numbers for when they confronted Asier, but Zayne was sure they were sent to keep an eye on them. He stood at the aftcastle, watching them carry out the watch he'd assigned. He expected they'd be obedient until the moment he slipped and betrayed Dardan's orders.

The boy didn't worry him much – he didn't seem particularly good at anything, but he lacked the exaggerated clumsiness that often came from feigning stupidity and ineptitude. That probably meant his mediocrity was genuine. Or he was a good actor. The thought made Zayne reconsider his position. The woman, on the other hand, was definitely a threat. She had a grace about her that spoke of skill and confidence. She had the body of a fighter and a dangerous gleam in her eyes. He needed to test her.

"Kales," he called out.

The fat boy came to attention. "Captain?"

"There is a crow's nest on top of the balloon," said Zayne. "Take whatever eggs the fucking bird left behind and boil them. Scatter the nest."

"And if the crow's still there?"

"Kill it and cook it," said Zayne. Kales saluted. He moved with more speed than Zayne expected. Not much more, but more. "Tana."

The woman's reaction was more casual than Kales' had been. "Aye, Captain?" Her accent was distinctly from the southern-most province of Castilyn – there was a noticeable lilt to her speech that spoke of wealth and taste.

"How good are you with a blade?"

Tana patted the sword hanging on her hip. "I've dueled a time or two, and I'm still here to tell it."

Zayne had expected nothing less. "Go down to the storeroom and get the practice swords. We need to get ready." He focused on her expression after giving the order, expecting either amusement or annoyance to show on her features. Instead, she looked mildly surprised. She disappeared below deck. As Zayne waited, he heard the crack of a pistol above. Shortly after, there was a loud *squawk*. When Tana returned, he took one of the practice blades and crossed the deck. "En garde," he said, readying the weapon.

Tana hesitated, waiting for Zayne to make the opening attack. He feinted left before attacking her right. He watched her eyes as she calculated before blocking. He attacked again. She parried. She lunged, he parried. As they engaged in a waltz of swords, Zayne kept his eyes on hers. They were a deep blue, they were dark. Those eyes hinted at meticulous thought, of careful planning. Zayne decided he'd had enough. He locked blades with his opponent. She met his gaze, then yelped in surprise when he hooked his leg around hers and pulled her off her feet.

Zayne placed the tip of the practice weapon against Tana's chest. "You were holding back."

Tana smiled up at him. "So were you, captain."

He snorted and stepped away from her. "So I was. Did Dardan tell you what we're after?"

She picked herself up from the deck and brushed herself off. "Some girl."

"Aye. Some girl. As it happens, this girl is under the employ of one of the greatest fighters in the Empire. Does the name Elyia Asier mean anything to you?"

There was a flicker of what looked like surprise and something else in Tana's eyes. Was that anger or fear?

"We're going after *her*?"

"So you're familiar with her reputation?"

"Of course I am." Tana spat. "Castilyn is stuck paying tithes to Asaria because of that bitch."

Zayne narrowed his eyes. "There's more to it than that, isn't there?"

"What's it to you?"

Zayne shrugged. "Honestly? Nothing. But now you know the score. So pick up that damn sword and take this sparring seriously."

Tana poised herself. "You plan to beat Asier in a duel?"

"If I can keep her crew isolated," said Zayne. He had worked out the plan in his head. He didn't like it one bit, but that seemed to be the standard for this job. "Ship-to-ship risks killing the girl," he explained. "The only way I see this working is to lock down the crew, and . . ." he hesitated. He swallowed something in his throat. "And kill Asier. Then, while the crew is demoralized, we take the girl."

"Sounds like you've got it all worked out," said Tana.

"If I can kill Asier."

"And if you can't?"

Zayne didn't think before saying, "Then I die and it's someone else's problem." *That sounds very tempting,* he told himself. It would save Asier and her crew – though he knew it was arrogant to think so, Zayne was certain that if Asier could kill him the rest of the crew would be easily dealt with – and he would be out of Dardan's reach. *But Nanette would die, too,* he realized. He couldn't allow that. He couldn't allow his actions to jeopardize her safety. "Enough talk," he said. "Come at me."

Tana attacked faster than she had in the first bout, and there was considerably less thought and more instinct in her form. But Zayne could tell she was still holding back. *She doesn't want you to know what she can do,* a voice in the back of his mind told him. *She wants the element of surprise when she betrays you. Or when you betray her, as the case may be.* Zayne deliberately left himself open for an attack on one side to see if Tana was even trying to win. When she didn't take the invitation, he parried three more attacks before punching her in the face with his free hand.

"Stop playing!" he ordered. "You won't catch me off guard later by pretending to be weak now."

Tana blinked, rubbing her cheek. "What? Captain, I'm sorry, but I know a lot of captains don't like the idea of their subordinates being better fighters than themselves."

"Pigeon shit," said Zayne. "Dardan sent you so you could kill me if I slip, didn't she?"

"What?" she repeated, "No, she –"

"Don't bother," said Zayne. "I'll not fall for it, I'm no fool. Now, give it your all. If you don't, I'll throw you overboard."

The next bout was much more intense. Tana was a natural. Their weapons clanged against one another repeatedly and Zayne fell into the motions. There was no question in Zayne's mind that she had come from either a noble or wealthy background. She was good. But as he stared into her eyes, he felt something was missing. She was no Elyia Asier. There was a passion to her, and an anger, but they seemed distant.

Zayne struck a blow to Tana's ribs. "Dead. Again." She came at him again. The next bout was longer, ending with Zayne's sword pressed to Tana's collarbone and hers in his ribs. "Better. Again." They clashed and fought, and Zayne ended the bout by striking Tana in the head. "Dead."

He was about to call for another bout when Jacques stepped on the deck. "What's all the noise up here?" he asked.

"Sparring," Zayne replied. "Join us."

"Alright," said Tana, "I can handle both of you."

In spite of himself, Zayne laughed. "You misunderstand. Jacques is on your side."

"This should be easy."

Jacques cracked his neck. "Maybe," he said uncertainly. Zayne had to hold back another laugh at the way Tana's confidence melted off her face. Jacques grabbed a practice sword and joined Tana.

Zayne gave the order to begin and his opponents slowly circled him. He frowned when they flanked him. He realized, if he was remembering correctly, the *Dreamscape Voyager*'s deck was roughly a span narrower. The helm of the *Dreamscape* was also closer to the middle of the deck, unlike the *Scorpion* where it was toward the bow. He couldn't risk getting too comfortable with the space he had on his own ship.

Tana struck at Zayne's left. He took a casual step back and flicked at her weapon with his own, carelessly deflecting her blow. Jacques went for an overhand strike which Zayne rolled forward to avoid. Tana swung at him while he was still low to the deck, but she misjudged his speed and her stroke fell short. Zayne came to his feet and his sword's dull tip met Tana's thigh. He blocked a particularly heavy attack from Jacques – he'd meant it to be a parry, but the engineer put all his weight into it and Zayne couldn't redirect him – while taking a step to the side. With a flourish, he slashed along Jacques' back.

"Again," he commanded. There were three more bouts. The second went similarly to the first. In the next, Zayne was struck in the jaw by a vindictive Jacques. In the last, Zayne redirected Tana's sword into Jacques' stomach. They stopped when Zayne spotted Justiciar Lake ahead, and the city of Sanarhal behind it. He noticed

Kales heading below deck with the carcass of a mother crow slung over his shoulder. "Kales," he called.

The boy froze. "Aye, Captain?"

"I want a report of our stores within the hour."

"But what about cooking this thing?" asked Kales. "And boiling the eggs?"

"Supplies come first," said Zayne. The boy nodded and ran to the galley. Nanette gave the boy a curious look when she climbed up to the deck but said nothing to him.

"We're stopping in the city?" she asked.

"Of course," said Zayne. "If Dardan's right –" that sentence made him shiver "– we have until the first snow. I don't fancy sitting over the lake freezing our asses off for what could be a month. I want to resupply, at the very least."

Nanette nodded. "Shall I bring us in, Captain?"

"Please do. I have preparations to get to." With that, he made his way into his cabin. His coat was lying on his desk where he'd left it when he started his watch. He had been about to sew a thin chain mesh along the inner lining. He had left out a few patches meant to cover the back. He sat down to resume the work. He knew from his dealings with the Priests of the Iron Veil that this would be no protection against being shot – in fact he knew it would probably result in *more* shrapnel filling his body – but then again, the only protection for *that* was simply not to be shot at all.

Zayne took needle and thread and was ready to weave the metal into his coat when he heard a chime, like a bell. He looked up. He searched for anything out of place. Then he remembered it. The noise came again, and Zayne opened one of the secret compartments in his desk. The sound was coming from Dardan's mysterious weapon, still wrapped in a black cloth. *Leave it alone,* he told himself. *No good can come from this.* He took the bundle from the compartment and set it down on the desk.

It had fallen silent, but when he held the thing in his hand, it was hot to the touch despite the cool cloth shrouding it. Whatever it was, it was smooth and cylindrical. He was tempted to unwrap it – in fact the desire to know what it was burned at him – but the feeling of dread such thoughts gave him stayed his hand.

Throw it overboard, he thought, feeling a frantic sense of panic. *It is evil. I need to throw it away. Just stand up, open the balcony door, and cast whatever it is into the lake. Do it, damn you!*

But no matter how desperately he thought out the steps, he could not bring himself to follow through. He rubbed his thumb along against the surface of cloth. *Even Asier will be unable to kill you,* Dardan had said. The words repeated in his mind and he nearly unveiled the mystery right then. He stopped, however, when he felt a strange chill penetrating him through the warmth. *It's evil.* He pushed the thing away from himself — but he didn't put it back in the secret compartment. He left it sitting there on the edge of his desk. He tried to work on his coat, but he found he couldn't focus. He took the lengths of iron mesh and draped them over the weapon and went out to the balcony to vomit.

CHAPTER THIRTY-THREE

Fog obscured the streets. It was slowing Cassidy's work considerably. She had missed two turns because she couldn't read the street signs. All around her she could hear footsteps against the groaning, wooden streets that held the city together. She heard merchants loudly hocking their wares. She took her map from the messenger bag she was carrying and backtracked with one eye on it. It was the last stop before she was free to enjoy her leave, so she wanted to get there quickly. Admiralty Street ran along the northern side of an old, three-deck warship that served as city's center of government. She let herself be stopped by a vendor selling mushrooms stuffed with basilisk meat. She bought two and ate them as she made her way down the street.

"It is quite busy here," Hymn observed. Amidst the crowds of people milling in the fog, no one seemed to notice or hear the voice coming from beneath Cassidy's hat.

Cassidy put her hand against her lips to mask the fact that she was talking – chances were no one would notice her, but she didn't want to take chances. "Why wouldn't it be?"

"Fog like this often keeps people inside," the Fae said.

"Where's that happen?"

"Places I've been, before we met. I suppose you would not recognize them."

Cassidy took a bite of her mushroom before answering. "I've been around the Empire," she said, "and to a few parts of Castilyn – Rivien, too, but it's usually too dry there – and I've never known a little fog to keep folks from working. Trade needs doing, and there's always work to be done somewhere."

"That is one attitude to take, I suppose. If you are not concerned about what is lurking there."

As the street meandered away from the old warship, smaller vessels capped with multiple cabins lined the way. She passed three before she finally spotted one with a hand-painted sign written in all three languages that read *Caster's Alchemical Wonders*. On the door was a smaller sign that said, *All sales final. No bartering, coins only.*

There was a bell that chimed dully when Cassidy stepped inside. An old man with a hook nose and a pair of horn-rimmed spectacles sat behind the counter. He gave her a glance before returning his attention to the gentleman wearing a bowler hat in front of him.

"Apply it to the inflamed area thrice daily," the old man was saying. "The swelling should go down in a week, and the rash sometime after that."

Cassidy saw the younger man's face turn red as a beet. "Ahem," he said. "Yes, well. Good day." He took a small satchel and tucked it in the pocket of his overcoat before making his way out.

As he passed Cassidy, she said, "Harpy itch, huh? A friend of mine caught that once. Unpleasant." The man stopped for a moment and stared at her, as if surprised she had seen him. Then he turned his nose up and scoffed, slamming the door behind him as he made his way outside.

The old man snorted before throwing his head back in laughter. "He stuck his hand in the fire, but don't want to admit he got burned."

"He stuck something somewhere, alright," said Cassidy. "Are you Alistair Caster?"

"I am, I am," said the shopkeeper. "How can I help you, young lady?"

Cassidy took a note from her bag. "A shipment of supplies from Nasradaan is waiting for you at the docks. If you can't collect them in person, just have your runner show this to my captain. Details for the payment are on there."

The man took the note and looked over it before nodding. "The *Dreamscape Voyager*. That must make you Cassandra Durant."

Cassidy felt Hymn become still in her hat. She imagined the Fae crouching as if ready to pounce. She would have laughed if she weren't feeling a tinge of paranoia herself. "I actually answer to 'Cassidy'," she said slowly. "Have we met?"

"No, no," said Caster. "But a friend of yours said to expect you. She said you could find her in the Sanctum on Star Fall Way. Can't remember the name, I'm afraid."

Cassidy furrowed her brow. "Did this 'friend' say anything else?"

"Just that she was looking forward to seeing you again." Caster shrugged. "Asked that I pass the message along."

"I see," said Cassidy. "Well, thank you, sir." Caster gave her a small wave, which she returned as she walked out the door. When she was back on the street, she asked Hymn, "That was weird, right?"

"It is not for me to know how your friends arrange messages. In fact, I did not think you had friends, aside from your crew."

"Oh, there's people all over who might call me a friend," said Cassidy. She started walking and chewed on her lips. "But I don't know how anyone would know where I'd be stopping. Something's wrong"

"Do you suspect a trap?"

Cassidy frowned. "Like, the Daughters of Daen?"

"Possibly. You have not mentioned any other enemies."

"I've brawled a time or two," said Cassidy, "and dueled, as well. But I can't imagine thinking of anyone I've ever known as an *enemy*."

"Even the mercenary?"

"Captain Balthine?" Cassidy thought back to when he had demanded Miria come with him. It still made her angry – Miria was her friend, and a member of her crew, her family, and he had tried to take her away. And he had terrified the poor girl. But she couldn't shake the thought of what Hymn had said after the fact. *He didn't want to do it*, she thought. But, during what little time Cassidy had spent in his presence, he had seemed in control, strong. Who could make someone like him do something he didn't want to do?

She shook her head. She didn't really know him.

"Maybe, maybe not," she said after a while. "But how would he have known we were here?"

"Well, whether or not it is the mercenary," said Hymn, "someone knew you would be here."

"Maybe. So, what do you think? Is this a trap?"

Hymn hesitated. "It would be best if you do not risk finding – you are walking there now."

"You're damn right I am."

"Why?"

"Because if someone knows where I'll be before I do, I can't rightly avoid them, can I?"

"I believe your logic is flawed."

Cassidy quickened her pace. The fog was beginning to dissipate but hadn't completely lifted when she finally reached Star Fall Way. It was a street of boxy shops that stretched onto the northern edge of the city. The sanctum was easy enough to find. While most everything on Melfine was built from wood with only a decorative amount of iron involved, the Sanctum was built entirely of the stuff. It stood nearly two stories tall, as well, towering over its neighbors.

There were no windows in the structure, so as to deny the gods any chance of spying upon the hopes of humanity, lest they twist and pervert their wishes. Or so it was said.

"Cassandra, it would be better if you did not go," Hymn said when Cassidy was fewer than twenty paces to the door.

"I'll be fine. I've got you, remember."

"I would be of no help to you," said Hymn. "I cannot cross the threshold."

Cassidy looked at the entrance, and at the decorative engraving featuring a glyph for the word 'Wall'. Or maybe it meant 'Door'. She couldn't remember. "But you wouldn't be touching it. You'd be safe in my hat."

"The fact remains, I cannot cross," said Hymn. "Let us turn back."

"I need to know who wanted me here," said Cassidy. She glanced around for onlookers. The only person she saw was a middle-aged woman carrying a basket of goods. Once the woman turned a corner, she took her hat off, allowing Hymn to fly free of it.

"I cannot protect you if I am not with you," said Hymn. "My oath is —'

"To do what is within your power to protect me," said Cassidy. "So, it stands to reason, if you can't follow me, the only way to protect me is to keep watch."

"You expect me to keep watch on a building with no windows?"

"It'll be simple! I go in, and if I don't come out in a reasonable amount of time, you go tell the captain where I am."

"And how would you define 'a reasonable amount of time', Cassandra?"

"I don't know. Half an hour, maybe?'

Hymn fidgeted uncomfortably. "I cannot stop you, much as I wish to."

"I appreciate your concern," said Cassidy. "Just hide out until I get back."

The door of the Sanctum screeched loudly as metal ground against metal. A blast of warm air rushed out to meet her. It smelled of stale incense. It was gloomy inside, with the only source of light emanating from candles arranged every few feet in sets of three. The door swung shut behind Cassidy as she stepped into the main room. A tremor of discomfort rose in her stomach. A sudden thought occurred to her. *What if they know about Hymn? What if this was just a trick to separate us?* She would be executed if that were the case. She

320

had to force herself to keep her breath level when all she wanted to do was panic. *Don't be stupid, Cass,* she told herself. *The only ones who know are you and the crew.* The priests couldn't know.

But if that were true, why *was* she here? She shivered despite the warmth of the room. *Stay calm,* she thought.

Once her eyes adjusted to the gloom, she spotted two figures garbed in meshes of iron links sitting on small benches in contemplative silence with their heads bowed. There were three rows of those benches. Behind them sat a bookshelf that spanned the wall, which caught Cassidy's attention due to the presence of a small hand mirror that was reflecting candlelight directly into her eyes.

Cassidy took a step toward the priests and they immediately turned to look at her, then to each other. One of them nodded to the other, who got to his feet and disappeared through a door in the back of the room. The remaining priest rose to her feet and approached Cassidy. She stared at her from above a veil of iron links that covered her face from nose to chin and beneath a matching cowl.

"We meet again, Cassandra," she said. "Thank you for coming."

Cassidy took a step back. She remembered that voice, and the thick Rivien accent it wore. "Madame Venitha!" she exclaimed.

"It's 'Sister' Venitha, now." The priestess put her hand to her forehead in mock despair. "Alas, I could do no good to the people as a fortuneteller, for you see, my dear, no one took my warnings seriously. It was a game to them, and so they ignored the portents I gave them."

Cassidy raised an eyebrow. "So you joined the priesthood."

"But of course," said Sister Venitha. "When a man asks a priest a question, he is more inclined to accept her answer than he would a fortuneteller."

"It seems like such an ironic change in vocation," said Cassidy, though she was beginning to see how Venitha's chain-link veil framed her eyes in much the same way the thin silks had in Revehaven.

The priest chuckled. "Less than you might think, my child. All that has changed is that I am now heeded for my wisdom instead of dismissed as a joke. That, and my wardrobe is heavier."

Cassidy considered that for a moment. She remembered how dismissive she herself had been the first time she encountered the fortuneteller. "I guess I could see why you'd want a change. What brings you to Melfine?"

"I'm needed here," she said. "I can do more good here than I could in Revehaven, at the moment."

"I see. So, how –"

Venitha smirked. "How did I know you were coming? Oh, child, I know a great many things. You probably want to know why I asked you here."

"Almost as much as I want to know how you knew I was coming."

"Oh, I wouldn't worry about that. Come along." She led Cassidy to the benches where she had been sitting. When Cassidy simply stood there, the priestess said, "Sit, sit!"

Cassidy obeyed reluctantly, eying the former fortuneteller as she sat across from her on another bench. "The Fae make dangerous bedfellows, you know," Venitha said without preamble. A chill ran through Cassidy, and she was unable to stop from shivering. *Of course she knows,* Cassidy remembered. *She knew then.*

"So are you going to arrest me?" she asked. Her voice cracked, and while she had wanted to sound defiant, she sounded as afraid as she felt. "Or are you just going to throw me in a box and torture me?"

The older woman shook her head. "You misunderstand me, child," she said, patting Cassidy's hand. Her touch was cold but comforting all the same. "It is true my brothers and sisters of the Iron Veil do not usually admit it, and fewer still in the world remember it, but there are greater evils than the Fair Folk."

"Greater evils?" asked Cassidy.

"The gods for a start," said Venitha, "and more." Then she laughed. "You travel with a Fae by your side, so surely you believe there to be good in them."

Cassidy was taken aback. "You're a priestess!" she exclaimed. "You're supposed to –"

"I am supposed to protect my charges from the evils of gods and the Fair Folk and whatever else would threaten them. And so I am. Trust a Fae's word to the letter but know that there is always meaning in what remains unsaid."

Cassidy chewed her lip. "Is that all you came to tell me? That the Fae lie by omission?"

"No, that's not all. But it's good to remember." The priestess laughed again. "It's easy to be dismissive when you hear the stories.

It's so easy to hear the tale of maidens seeking love, or heroes looking for adventure, and call them fools when they let themselves be caught in the web. But when you share warmth on a cold night or see wonders the like of which you've never felt before . . . when you feel the call of friendship, it's so easy to trust, for few people ever see themselves in those stories."

Cassidy wrapped her arms around herself. Had the room always been so cold? "I still don't understand," she said. "Why are we having this conversation? You're an Iron Veil, what I've... what you're implying I've done is the highest crime."

From behind her veil of tiny chain-links, Cassidy could see Venitha smile. "And should any of my brothers and sisters of the Veil hear of it, it will surely be devastating for you. But I didn't put on this mail and travel halfway across the Empire to have you dragged away to Castilyn to rot. There is so much potential in you, and though you've never given yourself the chance, one day you will truly shine.

"There are greater evils than the Fair Folk," she repeated. "Evils the likes of which the world has forgotten. It is not your own destiny that will lead you to them, but it will be for you to answer for what comes."

"And what comes?"

Venitha's eyes met Cassidy's, and Cassidy felt like she could drown in their dark depths. Then she shrugged and the illusion was shattered. "If I told you, you'd think I were mad."

Cassidy stared dumbstruck for a moment. Then she rose to her feet. "Oh, no. You do not get to play a game like that. You've said this much, don't jerk me around! What is coming?"

Venitha rose to her feet as well, and though she was shorter than Cassidy, she had a presence to her that made Cassidy step back. "I meant what I said. You would not believe me. And ultimately, that's not the important thing. What *is* important is that when the darkness starts to fall, when it seems there's no reason left to carry on . . .." she leaned close to Cassidy, and Cassidy could feel the warmth coming from her lips as she whispered, "You are not alone."

Cassidy stared at Venitha. "I thought you were done playing fortuneteller, but you're still spewing vague portents. Unless you tell me plainly what you mean, I'm leaving." The priestess merely looked up at her, and Cassidy turned. She left the room unimpeded.

As she closed the door behind her, Venitha said, "Until next time."

CHAPTER THIRTY-FOUR

Zayne thumbed his nose as he looked at his cards. It was a false tell that always had people thinking he had something and was trying to signal his partner. For her part, Nanette looked lazily at what was in her hand. To Zayne's left was a bruiser who called himself Tag, and to his right was a thin woman named Setrah. The two of them kept making eye contact with one another, trying to use their eyebrows to communicate something profound. Maybe it was working, but from where he sat, they looked silly.

The tavern door opened slowly, like someone was trying to go unnoticed. Zayne had intentionally positioned himself so he could see everyone who came in. What he hadn't expected was for Kales to slink in. The boy looked around at the clientele – most were large, threatening men and women, and those who weren't were in the company of those who were – and seemed to be as nervous as he was out of place. The *Tarnished Silver* was not a tavern for the faint of heart.

Zayne tried to ignore the boy and put two silver falcons in the pile. Nanette matched the bet, and after much eyebrow wiggling, their opponents did the same. "Show me the cards," he said. He glanced at Kales again and realized he was heading straight for them. *What now?* He wondered bitterly. Tag laid down his cards first – the Blind Man, the Four of Cups, the Five of Cups, and the Six of Cups. "I expected better. Kales, what do you want?"

The boy tried to duck behind Nanette upon being addressed but must have quickly realized the folly of trying. He removed his hat from his head and began to worry it between his hands. "I was just wondering, Captain, if perhaps . . ."

Zayne raised an eyebrow. "Well, speak up." Nanette laid down her cards, revealing the Chains, the Moon, the Two of Rings and the Two of Staves. "A twin and a secret," he declared dryly. "Now, Kales," he added sternly.

"I was just wondering if perhaps, Sir, we might purchase some spices, Sir." Tag snorted.

"Spices?" said Zayne. "You look about ready to piss yourself in fright. Over spice?" Setrah played her hand. It was a good hand; the

Ace of Swords, the Ace of Rings, the Ace of Cups, and the Two of Swords. Zayne's hand was better though. "What's so important about spice?" he asked, laying his cards flat on the table. The Baphomet, the Burned Man, Judgment, and Death. His eyes lingered on the Death, portrayed by a woman in a wispy white cloak surrounded by black space, and a face shrouded in shadow.

"It's just that, the food on the ship is so bland, I was hoping I might be able to –"

Setrah slammed her hands on the table. "You cheated!"

Zayne sighed. "You lost. Be graceful about it."

"I'll show you graceful! Tag!"

Both of Zayne's opponents rose to their feet and fists flew at Zayne's face from both sides. He leaned back in his chair and hooked his foot under the table. Nanette pushed herself away just before Zayne flipped it over, distracting his attackers and sending their coins and drinks in the air. He caught his fall with his hands, sprung to his feet, and drew two of his pistols. The weapons gave Setrah pause, but Tag hefted a chair. Zayne was prepared to pull the trigger on his weapon, but the burly man came to a sudden halt when Nanette placed a dagger to the side of his neck.

"Now," Zayne said as forcefully as he could, "you are going to pick up the coins you made me drop and put them in a bag for me to collect. And my cards, too. And then you are going to leave. If either of you does something funny, your partner is going to see what your brains look like." They were quick to obey, though gathering all the coins and cards took them some time. While they did so, Zayne surveyed the tavern. He saw a few greedy eyes wander toward his scattered winnings, but few if any of them seemed at all interested in getting involved with the spectacle. When Tag put the new purse of coins on the floor, Zayne waved him on with one of his weapons, and he and the woman broke into a run to get out of the tavern.

Zayne holstered his guns and grabbed the coin purse. "The food is food," he said to Kales, as though nothing had happened. He looked at the boy, who was shaking in his boots and looked like he'd been shot at. "Oh, relax, will you?" He looked like he was trying to obey, so Zayne let it go. "Anyway, my only concern when food is concerned is that we don't starve or fall ill. Flavor is a frivolous expense."

"Frivolous?" the boy asked, and it seemed he had forgotten some of his fear. "Sir, to deny flavor is to deny life itself!"

Zayne looked at Nanette, who shrugged. "Odd thing to be passionate about," he muttered, mostly to himself. A little louder, he said, "When Dardan sent you, did she give you coin? Or did you have any before?"

For a moment it seemed like Kales didn't understand the question. Then he shook his head. "No, Captain."

"I see." Zayne snorted. "I'm going to tell you the same thing I told Jacques, Flea, and Karn."

"Who's Karn?"

Zayne ignored the question. "If you want anything that isn't vital for either our survival or our jobs, you pay for it out of your own shares. When this job is over, you'll get a cut to do with as you please. Until them, learn to eat because you have to, not because you want to."

Zayne couldn't tell if Kales looked more like he was about to cry or fight him, but he did neither, instead standing up straight and nodding. "Aye, Captain." *Where did Dardan find this one?* He didn't strike Zayne as mercenary material.

Kales walked briskly out of the tavern, leaving Zayne and Nanette to deal with the strange looks from the nearby patrons. Zayne reached into his sleeve and extracted a silver, tossing it to the grizzled bartender on the way out. The older man caught the coin with a casual gesture. "For the damages," Zayne told him. When they were outside, he turned to Nanette. "Did he really say what I think he said about flavor?"

"Loudly," said Nanette.

"I don't understand."

"Well, he certainly didn't get that fat from abstaining."

"True."

From atop a sloped street, Zayne could see the *Scorpion* floating in the harbor. It wouldn't be long before he took her out on what could be her last voyage. She was twenty years old and had seen four captains, the ends of the world, and more blood than any man in the Empire. She had survived dragon fire, harpies, manticores, pirates, and so much more. While he knew its history was sordid – and he himself had contributed to it – it still seemed wrong to condemn it. *Even Asier will be unable to kill you.* The words felt like oil drizzling down the sides of Zayne's brain. He tried to suppress a shiver.

He looked at Nanette, who was taking in the same view. Was she picturing the same doom? Was she picturing success? Was she even thinking about tomorrow at all? Zayne couldn't be sure, but he knew he couldn't bear to cause her death, should things go badly with taking the princess. *If I use the thing Dardan gave me,* he thought, then quashed that line of thinking. *No, I'll do this without it. I'll face Asier alone, and should I die, that will be the end of it.* It was a foolish hope, though; without him to keep his crew in line, Jacques would likely attack. That would result in the death of the princess, and their efforts would be wasted. And of course Nanette would be at risk. If he had at least the stomach to see for himself what Dardan's gift actually was, maybe he could plan around it. But he trusted his instincts. No good could come of whatever it was. He had his suspicions, of course, but they were so absurd he couldn't bring himself to really consider them.

Are these really my only choices? He asked himself. *Use the weapon, or risk Nanette?* He let his gaze wander along the street until his eyes settled on an inn. That was the answer he needed. "Nanette," he said calmly.

"Aye?"

"I need you to stay in the city," he said calmly as he could manage.

Nanette responded almost exactly how he'd imagined. "What?" she shouted in his ear. "Whatever for?"

Zayne turned to face her and found he hadn't been ready to face the anger in her eyes. "This job could see us all killed," he said, "I need you here to . . ." *Damn it, Balthine!* He thought, mentally scrambling for an excuse. "To report on the death of the *Scorpion*, should she not return to harbor."

Nanette stood with her mouth open for a while, and Zayne was about to try saying something reassuring when she hit him in the jaw. His head whipped hard to the side and he bit his cheek.

"That's the biggest pile of pigeon shit I've ever heard! Maybe your ego was too big to notice this, but *every time* that ship set sail could have been the last. But now that we're faced with your childhood hero, suddenly things are too difficult? She's a woman with a crew of *five* people under her! We've killed pirates, and these are cargo pushers. We've killed harpies, and these are cargo pushers. We've killed dragons, and *these are fucking cargo pushers!* Get it through your fucking skull, will you?"

Zayne was ready to rebuff her when she gently put her hand on his arm. Her expression softened, and her eyes glistened, just a little. "And we're a team," she said gently. "Through thick and thin, from that day you first set foot on the *Scorpion*, we've been together, and we'll keep it that way until the end."

Zayne felt tears welling in his eyes. He choked down his emotions and smiled. "You're right," he said. "We're a team. You know you're the best friend I've ever had, right?"

Nanette nodded. "I know. Now, let's head back and set sail."

As soon as Nanette turned her back on him, Zayne struck her in the neck with the edge of his hand. She went limp immediately and he had to move fast to catch her in his arms before she hit the street. "I'm so sorry," he whispered in her ear. He cradled her in his arms and listened for her breathing. Once he was satisfied, he carried her to the inn he'd spotted. On her own, Nanette wasn't terribly heavy, but the gear Zayne kept concealed in his coat added up and he had barely covered a dozen feet when he broke into a sweat. His legs were burning by the time he was able to read the faded words *The Treasured Memory* painted over the inn's door. He kicked the door open and immediately felt the eyes of several unsuspecting patrons. He ignored the gawks and approached the innkeeper, a middle-aged woman who sat behind a counter and had the decency to pretend she wasn't staring.

"My wife had a fainting spell," he explained before the innkeeper could ask. "So I figured now was as good a time as any to look for lodgings. One room, please."

"Thirty coppers if you're okay with a small room. Forty if you want the large one."

"We'll take the large room. If you'll let me take her to bed, I'll pay."

The innkeeper looked ready to protest, then looked at Nanette. "Alright, but if you're trying to stiff me, I can have the Watch here in mere moments."

She led him to a room upstairs, which was bigger than his cabin on the *Scorpion*. He set Nanette on the bed and reached into his purse, extracting a silver coin and pressed it into the older woman's palm. "I'd appreciate that no one disturbs her."

The woman looked at the coin in her hand as if surprised to find it there. Then she nodded. "Of course, sir." She handed Zayne two keys and departed. He set one key on the end table beside Nanette and put his coin purse beside them.

"I'll do my best to come back," he swore. She didn't stir, and he left the room. He locked the door behind himself and slid the key under the door so Nanette would have them both. He wouldn't need them where he was going.

"Leaving so soon, sir?" asked the innkeeper.

Zayne nodded. "My wife needs rest, and there's still the day's errands to run. Thank you." He closed the door to the inn behind him and set out. The journey back to the dock was a long one, filled with contemplation. If he came back, Nanette would probably never forgive him. If he didn't, she would *definitely* never forgive him. He shook his head. He would worry about that later. He needed to focus on getting the princess.

When he finally returned to the *Scorpion*, Kales was sitting on the gangplank talking to Flea. "Is everyone aboard?" he asked.

"Everyone except Nanette," said Flea.

"Good. We leave now."

Flea blinked and stared incredulously at him. "Um, Captain, I just said Nanette —"

"I heard you," said Zayne. "She's working on the next step of the plan." It was easier to lie to Flea than it had been to lie to Nanette.

"Ah," Flea said uncertainly. "Aye, aye, Captain." He shoved Kales onto the ship and Zayne stepped aboard. It was only a minute before he heard the *Scorpion*'s engines roar to life, and Zayne took his place at the helm. He offered a last look at Sanarhal, toward where he had abandoned his best friend. *No*, he corrected himself. *Not abandoned. She's safe as I can be sure of.* He hesitated only a moment longer before adjusting the ship's telegraph, launching the *Scorpion*, and preparing for battle.

CHAPTER THIRTY-FIVE

Cassidy's arms were burning by the time she loaded the last crate of the cargo off the *Dreamscape* and onto the waiting rickshaw at the bottom of the gangplank. She set the load down with a grunt and the cart groaned under the strain. Despite the cold, her shirt was soaked with sweat and clung to her skin.

"And that's the last of it," she said between gasps.

Mister Caster smiled at her. "Hard to believe flasks can get so heavy, isn't it?"

"I'm used to it," Cassidy insisted. She leaned against the rickshaw. She then cast a glance at Kek, who had stopped to sit down on the dock a few feet away. "Have to be with this lazy bag of bones," she added.

Kek didn't stand up, but he did put his fists on his hips all the same. "Hey, I did an even share!"

"An even share?" Cassidy repeated. "You wouldn't recognize an even share if I dropped it on you!"

"Now, now, children," said the old man. "No need to drop anything on anyone. Thank you both for your help. If anyone here was slouching, it was that damn grandson of mine!" he added, directing his voice toward the front of the rickshaw. A timid looking boy peered around the side of the wagon before ducking back in front of it. "Ah, he'll get plenty of work in on the way to the shop. Say, Miss, did you ever meet that friend of yours?"

"Aye, I did." She wasn't sure what else to add to that, so she left it alone.

"I hope it wasn't any trouble. In any event, I must be off. Fair voyage to you." The alchemist tipped his hat and he departed, his timid grandson carrying their goods into the city with wheels so squeaky Cassidy could hear them after they were lost in the crowd.

"Well, come on," she said to Kek. She reached a hand down, and he took it graciously. When she hoisted him to his feet, she caught a whiff of him. "You smell like old eggs."

"I think you're smelling yourself, love."

"I swear, I'd hit you if my arms weren't so tired."

"You'd still smell like eggs."

Cassidy hit his shoulder with her own as they made their way aboard the *Dreamscape*. "That's everything, Captain," she called when they reached the top. Asier didn't reply. The captain was sitting on the gunwale atop the aftcastle, a lit cigarette in hand. She was staring out at the sunset. "Captain?" Cassidy climbed up the steps to the aftcastle. Asier heard her approach and finally faced her.

"Cassidy," she said, a clear tone of surprise in her voice. "What did you say?"

"I said all the cargo was delivered."

"Oh," said Asier. She took a drag of her cigarette. "Good."

"Since when do you smoke?"

"I decided I needed a new hobby." She moved as if to smoke again, then made a noise of disgust. "You know what? Forget it. I don't know how you can enjoy these things." She handed the half-used cigarette to Cassidy.

"They smell like my ma, before she took ill," said Cassidy. She sat down next to Asier. She looked up her. "So, what's bothering you?"

"Nothing."

"Captain," Cassidy began, but Asier shook her head.

"Don't worry about it, Cassy," she said wearily. "Just send word we're ready to take on new cargo."

Cassidy hoisted herself up. "Aye, Captain. Just tell me our itinerary, and I'll send the word." When Asier didn't reply, Cassidy asked, "Captain? Where are we going?" As soon as Cassidy say Asier's jaw tighten, she regretted saying anything.

The captain didn't look at her. "I don't know, Cassidy," she said coldly. "Never mind it. I'm going to turn in." Cassidy watched her walk away. She walked past Kek on the way down to the deck and didn't reply to his greeting. She entered her cabin and slammed the door.

They stood there watching Asier's cabin door for a minute, as though Asier was going to march back out and explain herself. When it became clear nothing of the sort was going to happen, Kek finished climbing the steps.

"What's got the captain worked up, lately?"

Cassidy sat down on the gunwale. "I don't know. You know, she just got mad at me for asking where we're setting sail next."

"How many times did you ask?"

"Once!"

"What were you thinking, Cassidy?"

"Please, no sarcasm right now."

"Alright, sorry, Cass." He sat down beside her.

Cassidy raised her hat to let Hymn fly free, then lowered it. The Fae sat on Cassidy's knee as she finished the captain's cigarette. The sky had grown dark before she dashed the last ashes overboard. "It involves the mercenaries," she said after a while.

"What does?"

"Whatever the captain's thinking about. It involves the *Scorpion*'s crew."

Kek leaned back, holding tight to the gunwale and staring toward the horizon. "She handled them pretty well. You really think she's worried about them?"

"Miria told me there were only two people who were supposed to know who she was," said Cassidy. "The captain and the empress. It shook Miria pretty badly. It might be the captain's shaken up by it too."

Kek let out a long hum, making a big show about thinking. "Why do you think they want her, anyway?"

Cassidy snorted. "Why would they want the *princess*? The *heir to the Empire*? Kek, the ransom could buy you a seat on the Rivien Trade Council, even if you can't speak more than ten words in Rivien – maybe even two seats."

"Yeah," Kek said slowly, "that would be a lot of coin. Gotta say, 'Prince Kekarian' sounds grand." He paused. "Though, it's a terrible idea."

"Oh?"

"Yeah, think about it. You'd have to collect the ransom, yeah?"

"Obviously."

"Well, if I were the empress –"

Cassidy snorted.

"You're picturing me in a dress, aren't you?"

"A silk one, yeah. Bedecked in jade, and your face is painted white and red."

"Nyuran take you," Kek said, clearly struggling to keep a straight face. "Anyway, if I were the – if I were in charge of the largest navy in the world, it would be pretty easy to catch whoever goes to collect the money, get them talking, get the princess, and bring in or kill anyone involved. Too much risk. If I were after a ransom, I'd go for someone from a well-off but less important family. Like you, maybe."

"My pa is Captain of the Dawnhal City Watch," argued Cassidy, "he's got enough people and pull to do the same thing you suggested."

"Sure, but he's no empress."

"True."

"I agree with Valani," Hymn declared suddenly. "I do not believe money is why the Scorpion wants the girl."

"Since when did you grow an opinion?" Kek asked the Fae.

"Kek, don't be rude!"

"Cassidy, it's a –"

"I know what *she* is, Kek."

Kek hesitated. "I'm sorry, Fae –" Cassidy glowered at him and he finished by saying, "Hymn."

"I shall not punish you, human Kekarian."

Cassidy snorted again, and when Kek gave her a look somewhere between confusion and annoyance, she laughed harder. "Ah, sorry. Now, Hymn, why do you think Kek is right?"

"It is as he suggests, monetary gain is not worth the risks." The Fae's light turned a deep, burnished red, for just a moment. "And there is power in royal blood. It is why royal families tend to exist at all."

Cassidy looked to Kek, who merely looked blankly back, so she turned back to Hymn. "What kind of power?"

"Terrible power," Hymn replied. "I do not know who employed these mercenaries, nor what it is they intend to do, but I can assure you that no good can come from it."

"Well, we won't let that happen," said Cassidy.

"If future attempts at taking her are as halfhearted as the last, you will have no trouble."

"You know, a little optimism would be nice."

"What do you want from me, Cassandra? I cannot lie and tell you all will be well."

Kek leaned forward. "I have a question for you," he said to the Fae.

"Of course you do," the Fae said sardonically.

"So I know the Fae can't lie. That's one of the only things all the stories agree on. So when a Fae makes a promise, they have to keep it, right?"

"That is the entire basis of my relationship with Cassandra, yes," said Hymn. "I hope that was not the extent of your question, because if it was, it was a foolish one."

"No, no," said Kek, "that was called set up, you stupid lantern. No, my question is, what happens if you make two promises that conflict? Like, what if you promised to protect Cassidy, but you also promised to protect, say, Miria, but for some reason you couldn't do both?"

"I suspect that would be a terrible situation," said Hymn. "And a foolish one. That is one reason you will seldom hear so binding a promise as the one I pledged to Cassandra. When one is bound to their words, they tend to be sparing with them."

"Why can't Fae lie, anyway?" Kek asked.

"For the same reason you cannot see the inside of your own head," Hymn said dismissively. "It cannot be done. My kind cannot deny the nature of the world, or of ourselves."

"Huh," said Kek. "Must be difficult."

"No more than speaking your native tongue," said Hymn.

"Kek just can't imagine what he'd do if he couldn't lie to women," Cassidy said teasingly.

"Hey, I am a perfect gentleman!"

"You once told a girl the burn scar on your leg was from rescuing orphans from a fire."

"One time! And I was seventeen! When am I going to hear the end of that?"

"What are you guys talking about?" asked Lierre. The engineer climbed the steps to join them.

"Kek's inability to impress women without lying," said Cassidy.

"How did we start talking about this?" asked Kek. He then quickly added, "And that's not even true!"

Lierre snorted.

"Hey!"

"Well, if you're done tormenting the boy, supper's ready," said Lierre.

Cassidy stood and helped Kek to his feet. "I'll fetch the captain," she said. After they descended the stairs together, she waited until the others made their way into the storeroom before knocking on the door to the captain's cabin. She counted to ten before knocking again. She counted five before the door opened slowly. The room beyond was dark, so Cassidy couldn't see beyond Asier standing in the doorway.

The captain's eyes were red and swollen and her hair was disheveled. She seemed to be breathing harder than usual. "Cassy," she said quietly. "I'm sorry about earlier."

"It's okay, Captain," Cassidy said automatically. "Did I wake you?"

"No," said Asier. "Let me guess? Supper?"

"Aye, Captain."

"I'll be right there. Go ahead and get started, I need to take care of something first."

"Aye, Captain," Cassidy repeated. As Asier started to close the door, she said, "Wait, Captain!" Asier held the door open a crack. "If there's anything you need . . . you can always tell me."

Asier gave her a faint smile. "I know, Cassy. I'll tell you everything when it's time." She closed the door and Cassidy stared absently at it for a moment.

"That was . . ."

"Cryptic?" suggested Hymn.

"I was going to say strange, but aye, cryptic works." The Fae followed her into the storeroom. The others were seated at the table, which bore a pile of huge fish Cassidy didn't recognize. As she drew near, Cassidy was struck by the aroma of rich peppers and exotic spices. She took as deep a breath as she could, savoring the scent. "You went all out, huh, Nieves?"

Nieves shook her head. "Actually, Miria bought it and did most of the work."

"Uh, oh," said Kek.

"At least I didn't set it on fire," said Miria.

"Oh, come on!" Kek exclaimed, "You weren't even there for that! You don't get to take those jabs!"

Cassidy took a seat between Kek and Miria. "Captain says she'll join us, and to get started without her."

Nieves took it upon herself to divvy up the portions. Cassidy took up her fork and chanced the first bite. Unlike breakfast, there was an actual flavor to it. Out of the corner of her eye, she saw Kek wait for her to continue before starting.

"This is actually good!" Kek announced with his mouth full.

"Your confidence is inspiring," said Miria.

"Hey, don't take it personally," said Kek, "but those omelets had me shitting a dozen odd colors."

Lierre sneered. "Ugh, I'm eating, Kek! I don't want to hear things like that!"

"I'm eating too," said Kek. "I'm not uncomfortable."

"Because you're the one talking about it, you pigeon!"

Kek rose abruptly to his feet, slamming his hands on the table, spilling the juices from his plate onto the table. Miria gasped. "You want to take this outside, Myrlin?"

"No, I want to eat my meal in peace."

"Oh." Kek sat back down. "Alright, then."

"Do you like it?" Miria asked.

Cassidy wiped her mouth on her sleeve. She let out a loud belch at the same time she said, "Aye."

Miria gave her a strange look. "Good, good," she said, giving one last raised eyebrow at Cassidy's sleeve before looking around the table. "Kek? Lierre?"

"It's quite good," said Lierre.

"Mph, mph, mph," said Kek, spraying some food onto Cassidy's sleeve and face.

She slapped his arm. "You can like things without spitting them on me!"

"Sorry, Cass."

As the meal continued, Cassidy kept eying the door, waiting for the captain. Kek finished eating first and let out a belch.

"Kek!" snapped Lierre. "That's disgust —" she let out a longer, deeper one and pretended to be embarrassed. Miria laughed from behind her hands.

Cassidy finished her food and pushed her plate away. There was a funny aftertaste on her tongue, but she resisted the urge to make a face where Miria could see, so she buried her face in a mug of mead and let her tongue sit in it for a few moments before swallowing. It wasn't much longer before everyone seated had eaten their fill, yet their captain still hadn't joined them. The others picked up their plates, clearly ready to depart, but the idea of leaving before the captain joined them seemed wrong to Cassidy. "Who's up for a game?" she asked.

"What did you have in mind?" asked Kek.

"How about Twisted Virtue?" Cassidy suggested.

Kek looked to Nieves, who shrugged, then to Lierre, and finally to Cassidy. "Aye, I'm game."

"I'll play," said Miria, "but you'll have to teach me."

"As long as it's a fun game," said Lierre. "No coins or chores on the line, please."

Nieves sat back down. "You got the cards?"

"There's probably a deck in here, somewhere," said Cassidy. She got to her feet and started looking through the few boxes and trunks that actually belonged to the *Dreamscape* and her crew. While she searched, moving containers and rummaging through them, she heard Kek explaining the rules of the game to Miria. She eventually found an old set of cards buried beneath a pair of old coats bearing the colors of the Imperial Navy. The wood-grained backs were stamped with illustrations of rivermaids encircling a dragon with a head on both ends. "There we are," she announced. She shuffled the deck somewhat gracelessly as she returned to the table.

"May I make a suggestion?" asked Kek.

"We're not taking our clothes off," Nieves answered immediately.

"I wasn't going to ask that," said Kek.

From her perch on Cassidy's shoulder, Hymn announced, "He lies."

Kek's face flushed red. "Well, it wasn't going to be the *first* thing I suggested."

"What else could you want?" asked Lierre.

"I was going to ask if I could shuffle the cards."

"No, you cheat," said Nieves.

"Oh, and Cassidy doesn't?"

Lierre patted Cassidy's arm. "Our dear Cassy is too obvious to get away with it."

"Thanks, I'm glad you trust me so much," Cassidy muttered as she straightened the deck. She dealt around the table, giving each player three cards before setting down the remainders. She picked up her hand and looked at it.

A ticklish tinge rushed down Cassidy's spine when she felt Hymn's breath in her ear as the Fae whispered, "That is quite a terrible hand." Cassidy did her best not to show, but the Fae was right. The Burning Man, Judgment, and the Burden – the latter had green lip paint staining the card, which depicted a naked woman dragging a massive chain up a mountain. In most games, having three face cards from the start would be a boon, but in Twisted Virtue, they were practically worthless. She wondered at the lip mark on the card. "Kek, are these your cards?" she asked.

"Never seen them before in my life," said the blond man. "Why?"

"Looks like someone kissed this card. Thought it might have been a trophy or something."

"Nah, if I had anything like that, I'd keep it in my cabin."

"Strange," said Cassidy. "So, who wants to make the first move?"

Cassidy was the first to lose the first game, followed shortly by Miria. In the end, despite his protests, Kek won out. They played three games after that, with Miria winning the second and Lierre the third, and Kek once again winning the last.

When all the cards were back in the deck, Nieves let out a yawn. "That's enough for me, thanks," she announced.

"Oh, don't be like that," said Kek, "I'm sure you'll do better next time."

"It's not about that," said the sawbones. "I was up all day, and I can barely keep my eyes open."

Cassidy checked her pocket watch, surprised to see that two hours had passed since they sat down to eat supper, and still there was no sign of Asier.

"I'm going to turn in, too," said Miria.

"That sounds like a good idea," added Lierre.

Kek watched as the others left. "Well, I guess that's the end of the games," he said.

"Aye," Cassidy agreed. "I'm going to make sure the captain gets some supper," she announced. She started to pile up a share of the leftovers onto a plate.

"Is she alright?"

Cassidy opened her mouth, wanting to say "aye," but instead the words out of her mouth were, "I don't know."

"Do you want me to try to talk to her?"

She hesitated. "No," she said, "I'll do it."

"If you're sure."

"I'm not, but thanks, Kek."

"Alright, well, let me know how she is, okay?"

"Of course." Cassidy wrapped the captain's plate in a dry linen and rose. They walked out to the deck together and Cassidy took a moment to look up at the sky. Only a few, sparse clouds hovered in the great expanse, giving her a mostly unobstructed view of the stars. She wondered if she would see the same ones in the Dreamscape, and if she would recognize them if she did. The air was prickling through her coat, which was still partially damp from her earlier excursions. In contrast, the plate in her hands was somewhat warm against her fingers. "Goodnight, Kek," she said gently.

"Goodnight, Cassy."

Cassidy watched Kek as he made his way down to the lower deck. When he was gone, she counted to ten and turned toward the captain's cabin. She raised a hand to knock only to lower it again to get a better grip on the covered plate in her hand. Would the captain be angry if she bothered her again? And what was keeping her cooped up in her cabin? She raised her hand again and hesitated again, only for Hymn to tap a foot impatiently on her shoulder. She rapped gently on the door. She heard a creak and footsteps from within almost immediately. After a few moments, the door creaked open.

"Cassy, what's the —" she looked at the plate in Cassidy's hand. An expression Cassidy could only describe as distraught crossed her face. "I'm sorry," she said, "I forgot all about it."

"Is everything alright, Captain?" Cassidy asked, and she immediately wanted to kick herself. *No, you idiot,* she chided internally, *clearly everything is* not *alright. You should have asked, "what's wrong?"*

"Aye," Asier said easily. "Just distracted with a book I bought in the market, is all."

Cassidy struggled to act like she believed the lie. It was difficult, and her voice broke when she asked, "Is that so?"

"Aye," Asier repeated. "It's the story of a . . . well, honestly, I'm not quite sure what it's about yet, but it seems exciting so far."

Cassidy bit her tongue before she said something rude. When she organized her thoughts, she said, "I see. May I come in?"

Asier looked surprised Cassidy would even ask. "What? Oh, aye, yes, come in, by all means." She opened the door wider, letting Cassidy inside. The captain's cabin was dark — lit only by a single lantern at the captain's writing desk on the forward, port-side corner of the cabin. Cassidy noticed the only book on the desk was Asier's journal, and Cassidy doubted very much that she was distracted by *that.*

"Where would you like your supper, Captain?"

"Hm? Oh, just set it on the table," she said, waving at the table offhandedly bolted down in the middle of the cabin.

Cassidy obeyed and stood beside Asier, who had taken a seat on her bed. "Captain?"

"Aye?"

"What's wrong?"

"Nothing's wrong –" Asier began, but Cassidy's face must have shown just how she felt about being lied to. "Alright," she said with a sigh. "I'm worried."

"With all due respect, Captain," said Cassidy, "that's pretty damn obvious. This is about the *Scorpion*'s crew, isn't it?"

"What gave it away?"

"Well, you didn't start acting weird until we ran into them."

Asier took a deep breath. Then she scooted over and patted the space next to her. "Have a seat, Cassy." Cassidy obeyed. Even after sleeping in it when she was wounded, she couldn't get used to how much softer it was than her own bunk. She and the others had bought the damn thing as a name-day gift for Asier years before, but she had never thought to wonder if the captain preferred the stiff cot she had had previously.

"There comes a point in every woman's life," Asier said wearily, "when she does something she regrets." Cassidy wasn't sure what to say to that, so she decided it was better not to say anything. It was tempting to ask something, however, watching Asier's mouth open and close in silence for a while. Finally, she continued. "Eighteen or so years ago, I left Shahira's – sorry, *the Empress'* service. That was a difficult choice."

"So why'd you do it?"

Asier snorted. "A few reasons. You see, Cassy, I – well, I went to war for her. I was her bodyguard and her champion, but what she needed was an admiral. I'd have done anything for her, or so I told myself, so as much as it pained me, and as much as I worried it was the wrong thing, I took command of the *Jade Phoenix*. And in the span of two years I forced the Queen of Castilyn to bend the knee to the Empress of Asaria. War over. Parades in every city. A street named in my honor. When I came back to Revehaven, Shahira had a newborn child.

"She asked me, Shahira did, to watch over her, to teacher her, to help raise her. To stay by her side." Asier gave a bitter laugh. "I was angry. I shouted at her, 'If you wanted me by your side,' I said, 'you'd never have sent me away!' I turned my back on my – my *Empress*," she finished, though there was a slight tremor in her voice. She stopped, and Cassidy put her hand on her shoulder, hoping the captain would appreciate the gesture. Asier took it as a sign to continue. "That wasn't the only reason I left that day," she said. Her eyes darted toward the lantern then back down. "That's a story for another time," she decided. "So, I spent a few years adrift, working for the chance to keep moving. I worked in the scullery of one ship, swabbed the deck of the next. I stopped thinking about where I was bound, until... a little more than ten years ago I found myself back in Revehaven.

"As soon as I set foot on the docks, I was looking for the next ship out. I couldn't stand to be in the shadows of the palace, of the memories there. Well, Shahira found me before I could find passage elsewhere. She summoned me to the palace. I thought she wanted me to answer for my desertion.

"Instead, she wanted to apologize, to tell me . . . well, that's private," Asier said. "Anyway, that was when I met Miria. Sweet little Miria. After spending an evening in her company, I felt a pang of regret I can still remember so clearly. I looked at her and saw she could have been my – my ward."

Asier took a breath. "I won't bore you with the details," she continued, "but eventually Shahira allowed me to leave with my own ship, on the condition that when she came of age, Miria would come into my care to learn of the world."

Cassidy looked up at Asier. Though it was dark, Cassidy was sure her eyes were glistening with tears. "Is that it? Do you regret taking the ship?"

Asier shook her head. "No," she said. "Without it, I'd never have met you, or Kek, Lierre, and Nieves. All of you are . . . precious to me."

Now it was Cassidy's eyes that were wet and blurry, and her chest was warm with emotion. "You mean a lot to us, too, you know," she said. "So, what's the problem?"

Asier was quiet. "I'm sure Miria told you that only Shahira and I knew Miria was coming with me, aye?"

"Aye," Cassidy agreed.

"Well, the Daughters of Daen found out, somehow. So as we travel, I'm sick with worrying how they know. Are there traitors in Shahira's court? Was she herself hurt? I've quite a few regrets, Cassidy – that's what tends to happen when you make decisions – and right now I'm regretting being unable to protect them both."

Cassidy found herself hugging her captain. "If the Empress were harmed, or in danger, we'd hear about it," Cassidy assured her. "And Miria's with us – she's one of us. Ain't a soul gonna take her."

Asier returned Cassidy's hug and patted her on the back. "Thanks, Cassy."

"Only thing to do is to keep moving."

The captain pulled away from Cassidy and wiped her eyes. "Aye. You're absolutely right. First thing tomorrow, I want you to pick our destination."

"*Me?*"

"Who better?" asked Asier. "You'll need to learn to make these decisions sooner or later."

Cassidy pursed her lips. "The best trade from Melfine goes north and east," Cassidy decided. "With winter underway, food and furs will be in high demand farther north . . . Sanarhal," she decided.

The smile Asier gave her was strange and lethargic, but she sounded like her usual self when she said, "It's settled. First thing tomorrow, put the word out that the *Dreamscape Voyager* is bound for Sanarhal, and we're taking cargo. Until then, get some rest. That's an order."

Cassidy rose to her feet. "Aye, aye, Captain," she said with a salute. She looked back several times at Asier on her way out, but the captain merely smiled that same strange smile at her until the door closed behind her.

When she reached the ladder, Hymn spoke in her ear. "She was honest when she was telling you how important you and this crew are to her," the Fae said.

Cassidy began her descent and looked at the Fae curiously. "I know," she said. "Believe it or not, after a while people get pretty attached to each other."

The Fae bristled. "You miss my point. No matter. Get your rest, Cassandra."

Cassidy sniffed and made her way to her cabin. "I'm not sure I'll ever understand you," she said to the Faerie.

"Who can say what will be tomorrow?"

Cassidy had nothing to say to that, so she shrugged and entered her cabin. She stripped lazily and climbed into bed. She should have been pleased with how her talk with Asier had gone – she was sure of it. Instead, she was unsettled. Was it something Hymn said? Or was it something the captain herself said? Answers didn't come to her before sleep did. As she followed Hymn into the Dreamscape, she felt a burst of recognition about *something*, but in an instant, it was gone, forgotten in the way dreams often are. What wasn't forgotten, however, was the way it made her heart feel cold with dread.

CHAPTER THIRTY-SIX

Beneath a starry sky of gold and amber mixed with clouds of purple, Cassidy guided the Dreamscape counterpart of the *Dreamscape Voyager* over a valley of silvery grass. Hymn stood silently at the bow and stared at the horizon as was her custom. Cassidy enjoyed a warm, gentle breeze that smelled of honeysuckles, far removed from the bitter chill in the waking world. As she looked around at the beauty of the Dreamscape, she wondered why she was ever afraid of it.

It's a world of evil, a voice in her head reminded her. She snorted at the thought. How could something so splendid be so evil? *You've only met Hymn,* she reminded herself. For the first time in a while, Cassidy wondered about what enemies Hymn might have. *She was desperate to strike a deal with me.* She looked at the Fae, staring out into distance. *What is she looking for?*

Her thoughts were disrupted by a sudden crack of thunder. Cassidy looked around only to see nothing amiss, but Hymn was suddenly at Cassidy's side. "Do not speak to me, do not *look* at me, until she has gone."

Cassidy was about to ask who *she* was, but when she turned, she saw a woman she had never seen before on the deck. She had bronze skin, ankle-length gold-blonde hair, and wore a dress as black as night. The stranger was pacing along the length of the bow, seemingly oblivious to Cassidy or Hymn. She passed within a hands-breadth of Hymn, who was standing still as a statue with her hands clasped together over her chest. The colors of her dress seemed thinner than usual.

Cassidy curiously watched the woman circuit the ship before she found the trespasser more annoying than interesting. "Who are you?"

The woman stopped pacing and turned to Cassidy. A jolt shot through her heart when she saw the woman's eyes were inverted, with pure white irises surrounded by inky blackness. She instinctively reached for a sword she could not have brought into the dream, yet when her fingers closed, she held the hilt of a weapon. She drew it, holding the point less than a foot from the stranger's chest. Steam rose from the tip of the iron blade. The mysterious Fae didn't seem to notice or care, and all she asked was, "How come you to travel the Mythscape?"

Cassidy furrowed her brow. "The *Myth*scape? You mean the Dreamscape?"

The invader flicked her wrist dismissively. "These are two names for the same thing. How did you come to be here?"

"You're on my ship," said Cassidy. "I think that entitles me to ask the questions."

The Fae looked at the ship beneath her feet, as if seeing it for the first time. "Ah, this is the *Dreamscape Voyager*." She took a deep breath through her nose, which struck Cassidy as more theatrical than practical. "I knew smelled the mark of the deceiver."

"*Who are you?*" Cassidy repeated, moving half a step closer, bringing the blade closer to the Fae. The steam seemed to rise faster the closer the weapon was to the Fae.

The golden-haired Fae acknowledged Cassidy's weapon for the first time, though it was only to look dismissively down at it. In that same moment, Cassidy noticed she had mistaken the Fae's eyes and dress as black when they seemed to be a shifting gradient of dark purple. Just like Hymn's dress, this Fae's clothing also appeared to be a window into some foreign sky.

"I am called Djian," she answered.

"Why are you on my ship?"

Djian's laugh was musical, but it sent a chill down Cassidy's spine. "This is not your ship, nor should you be here." Cassidy waved her sword as threateningly as she could manage, but the Fae looked down on the gesture contemptuously. "If you wish to threaten, you should bring the real thing. The deceiver plays a dangerous game. You would do well not to put your trust in her hands."

Cassidy gave a mock laugh. "But I should trust you because . . . you said so?"

"Would that it could be so simple," said Djian. "Heed my words. Whatever she promised you is not worth the price you will have to pay."

Cassidy scowled. "I'll decide for myself what's worth what, thank you."

"If you will not trust my words," said the Fae, "perhaps you will trust your eyes."

Cassidy was drowning. She didn't know how, or why, but she was no longer on the deck of the *Dreamscape Voyager*. She was thrashing and kicking just beneath the surface of water colder than ice. Her lungs burned and the rest of her body was stung by the sudden cold that was like a million tiny knives poking at her bones. She couldn't swim, and with every thrash she felt herself being pulled deeper by the ferocious current. Her thoughts took the form of panicked screams for air.

Her vision was obscured by black spots and blurs, but beyond them she could see a red-orange light above the surface and an enormous black shadow at its heart, growing larger by the second. Whatever the shape was, it struck the water with a rumbling boom and soon reached Cassidy, enveloping her, putting an end to her attempts to reach the surface as it pressed her down. Whatever the shape was, Cassidy realized it was on fire, even in the water. The coldness she felt was swiftly replaced with unbearable heat, the likes of which she had never felt before. Her skin was boiling, and blisters were rising in that cruel darkness.

Cassidy lost sight of the surface. There was only the darkness, the weight, and the desperate need for air. She struggled to pull away from the burning weight, but she soon felt rock and sand at her back and the weight began to crush her. Her lungful of old air was forced out of her and water rushed in to fill the void it had left behind.

She screamed.

She was back on the *Dreamscape Voyager*, still in the Dreamscape. When she fell to her knees, she expected water to pour out of her mouth, but it was dry. She took a deep breath to compensate for the pain of suffocation, but she was not in pain, as though she had never been drowning. The only source of the wetness was the flood of tears in her eyes.

Djian stood a foot away from her. The Fae's bizarre eyes were cold. "A taste of the horror that lies along the path set before you."

Cassidy caught her breath and glowered at the intruder. Djian's hand darted at her, snatching her by the wrist. Realization dawned on her; Cassidy knew her scar was *Hymn's* mark, and if Hymn was hiding from Djian, Cassidy was oath-bound to keep her from seeing it.

Before Djian had a chance to raise Cassidy's sleeve and see the brand, the sailor took her sword again and leveled it at Djian's throat. Despite the Fae's earlier statement, she stopped moving completely when the steam began to rise in waves from the iron weapon. The Fae released Cassidy's arm and stepped away.

"It's not too late," Djian said when she reached the edge of the deck. "Set a new course. No good can come from following whatever path she set your master down." She stepped off the ship and vanished in the air. Cassidy pushed herself up to just one knee, but she couldn't find the strength to go much further.

Hymn finally moved from her frozen stance and placed her hand on Cassidy's. "Are you hurt?" she asked.

Cassidy considered the question for a long minute. "No," she decided. "Just shaken. Who was that?"

"Djian," said Hymn. "She is no friend of mine."

"Can't imagine why," Cassidy said sarcastically. "Ugh, my head feels like a bell at midday. Why did she call you 'the deceiver'?"

"I do not think she knows I was ever here," Hymn replied. "There are old influences here, and the Dreamscape Voyager was set on her path before you were born. Regardless, nothing good could have happed if her attention had fallen on me." She paused, then in a bizarre mockery of affection, she smoothed the sleeves of Cassidy's shirt. "You need real rest," she said in a voice approaching tenderness. She looked away for a moment and added, "Thank you."

Cassidy furrowed her brow. "For what?"

Hymn bit her lip, then shook her head. "Let us leave this place." Cassidy was too tired to argue. The next thing she knew, she was back in her cabin aboard the real *Dreamscape Voyager* in a place between sleep and wakefulness. When she closed her eyes fully, she was reminded of the darkness and the water, and her heart skipped. But sleep broke through her terror. She dreamed, but by the morning she couldn't remember the details. It had been a nightmare; she remembered that much. It had involved the crew, and that something had seemed very important.

CHAPTER THIRTY-SEVEN

"I'll need you to put that in writing," Cassidy said to a middle-aged man in a brown bowler hat and mottled coat that may have matched once. "Preferably with a notary seal."

"Why?" the man demanded indignantly.

Cassidy sighed. "Because if the recipient doesn't pay his share," she recited dryly, "I need to prove to a magistrate that we had this discussion and that you only paid part of the fee."

"This is pigeon shit!" the man complained. He spat to one side.

"Unless you're planning to rip us off, I don't see how this is a problem."

The man clenched his jaw tightly, his blue-gray eyes aiming daggers at her. Cassidy snorted and put her hands on her hips. "The way I see it, you have three options: put your promise writing, pay us in full, or buy your own boat and deliver your fucking parcel in person." The man brandished his finger like a gun, opened his mouth and closed it again. Then he closed both hands into fists and stamped his foot before walking away. Once she was sure the prospective customer was out of earshot, she let out a groan and said, "Fucking idiot."

"*What do you mean my word's not good enough?*" came Nieves' voice from the ship, mocking the customer's accent. "*I don't want to pay full price!*"

"Ugh," said Cassidy, feigning a headache by grasping her head. "Please don't. I don't think I can handle another one right now."

Nieves let out a wry chuckle. "They are the worst, though, aren't they?"

"They're up there, aye," Cassidy agreed. She climbed up the gangplank and sat on the gunwale next to Nieves.

"You feeling alright?" the sawbones asked.

"Aye," said Cassidy. She rubbed her eyes before burying them in her palms. "Didn't get a lot of sleep. Bad dreams."

"Dreams, or *dreams*?" Nieves asked.

Cassidy looked up wearily. "A bit of both," she confessed.

"I'm not going to pretend I'm an expert," Nieves began.

"That's exactly what someone says before they pretend to be an expert."

She leaned in close to Cassidy, her next words were whispered. "I don't believe it's safe for you to see so much of the Dreamscape. It's the place of the gods and the Fae. No matter how much you trust Hymn, it's still the realm of evil."

Cassidy snorted. "When did you get so pious?"

Nieves narrowed her eyes. "Cassy, you brought a Fae on this boat, and while she hasn't driven us all mad yet, that doesn't mean the next thing you meet will be as generous."

Her words made Cassidy think of Djian, and of how she thought she was drowning. She shivered. "I'm sorry," said Cassidy. "Consider your point made."

Nieves raised an eyebrow. "Just like that?"

When Cassidy closed her eyes, she saw Djian staring at her. She felt the image was clearer than a memory had a right to be. When she opened them, she said, "Aye. Just like that." It was easy enough to say; Hymn and Cassidy had already agreed not to enter the Dreamscape for a while, lest they attract Djian's attention. The Fae had refused to tell Cassidy anything more about her, or even how she hid from her, leaving Cassidy with nothing to tell the others. *What would I tell them, anyway?* she wondered. *'I ran into a Fae that left Hymn scared shitless'? That would go well.*

Cassidy checked her pocket watch. It was five minutes to thirteen. She was anxious to get back to the sky, though the desire was mixed with an anxiety she couldn't place. She checked her watch again thirty seconds later.

"Is your shift on backwards or something?" Nieves asked. "Calm down."

"Just want to set sail," said Cassidy.

"Why? Something special in Sanarhal?"

Cassidy blew her cheeks out. "I don't know," she said. "Things have been weird since . . . well, before we got here. Maybe I just want to get away, find the normal, you know?"

Nieves shook her head. "I'm not sure if you noticed, but things have been weird since the day you got that," she said, pointing at Cassidy's forearm. Cassidy instinctively touched Hymn's mark.

"I think we can get used to all that."

"Cassidy, listen to me!" Nieves snapped, "We all get it; you trust Hymn. And you know what? Maybe you're right to. But the rest of us can't see what you see when you dream. We don't know what she whispers in your ear when the rest of us are asleep. We don't *know!* What if the next time you go to sleep, you don't wake up? I know you think she's your friend, Cassy, and I know you want to stand up for her when the rest of us worry, but you've…." She looked around to make sure no one was nearby. "You've bargained with the Fae, Cassy! That's maybe two steps below calling the gods on your head. Whether or not she can be trusted isn't really the point here.

"I know why you did it," she added more gently, taking one of Cassidy's hands. "Shit, if I understand what you said correctly, I'm not even sure I'd have had a clear enough head to barter like you did." She squeezed Cassidy's hand tightly, and Cassidy returned the gesture. "But please, don't take offense when we watch or worry. It's not a question of trust, Cass. I'd fly into the Dreamscape myself for you, if it came to that, and I know the others would, and you know it, too."

Cassidy smiled. "Thanks, Nieves."

Twenty minutes passed and the man in the brown bowler had returned, holding a sheet of parchment in one hand with a parcel tucked under the opposite arm. Cassidy marched down the gangplank to meet him. He gave her the parchment without a word. Cassidy nodded when she read the brief contract and saw the seal of the port authority stamped at the bottom.

"That wasn't so hard, was it?" asked Cassidy.

The man was red as a beet. Through clenched teeth, he said, "No, Ma'am."

Cassidy pretended not to notice his attitude. "Well, everything seems to be in order, Mr. Alde. Six silvers, and you can put it out of your mind." He grumbled something that might have been insulting if it had been coherent. He all but slammed the coins into Cassidy's hand before giving the parcel up and storming away. She resisted the urge to throw the parcel into the lake below, but professionalism won over petty revenge. She climbed back up the gangplank and entered the storeroom.

Kek was there, sorting and strapping down the cargo. "Got more for me, Cass?"

"Not much," she said, "just a box."

"Can you update the manifest?" Kek asked as he lifted a crate on top of one marginally bigger. "It's on the table."

"Gods be damned, Kek," Cassidy said with a smirk, "making me work while you slack off!"

"Oh, fuck you!"

"Now that's not very nice." She added the parcel along with the names of its client and the recipient to the manifest. "This is a pretty good haul," she said.

"Not bad," Kek agreed. "Speaking of good, Captain's mood seems better."

"I guess she just needed someone to talk to."

"I never saw her like that before," Kek said. He grabbed a stool and sat with his back to the table. "Remember when we were boarded by pirates?"

Cassidy pulled up a seat next to him. "How could I forget? That was the first time I ever got shot. That shit hurt. I've still got the scar."

"I know, I've seen it. My point was, Captain didn't bat an eye when the anchors struck us. Her voice didn't crack when she told them to turn back, and her hand didn't shake when she fired the first shot."

"She's always been brave," Cassidy agreed. "I wish I knew how she does it. I've never been able to keep a brave face in a fight."

"I don't think the face you're making matters so much," said Kek. "You've never been one to hide in your cabin and wait for the danger to pass."

"That's an option?"

"Not a favorable one, but there are people out there who do it."

"Shit, I've been doing this all wrong," said Cassidy. "Maybe next time, *you* look a dragon in the mouth, I'll hide under my blanket."

"Piss off; if it comes to that, I'm joining you." They shared a laugh at that.

The storeroom door opened. Asier was standing in the portal, a smile on her face. "If you two are done kissing in here," she said, "we're about to set sail."

"Kissing?" Cassidy protested, "His lips are too thin to enjoy."

Kek recoiled as if he'd been struck. "Oh? Well, your hair is oily."

"Ooh, scathing. Come on, Kek, let's say goodbye to your home."

"Ah, but what a beautiful home it is."

Out on the deck, Asier was standing by the helm while Miria and Nieves stood at the bow, talking about something Cassidy couldn't hear. Lierre was likely down in the engine compartment readying for launch. Cassidy joined the captain, who offered her the wheel. "Take us out, Miss Durant."

"Aye, aye, Captain," she replied. She opened the pipeline and called down to Lierre. "Engines ready?"

"Aye," came Lierre's reply from the copper pipe. "Ready whenever you are."

Cassidy pulled the lever on the telegraph down to full reverse. The engines came roaring to life, disrupting the relative quiet that had settled on the *Dreamscape*. After a few moments, the ship began to push away from the dock and Cassidy turned the wheel hard, putting Melfine at her back. Kek ran up to the top of the aftcastle and looked back at his childhood home while Cassidy gradually adjusted the telegraph until the ship was running at full speed ahead. As they gained speed, the wind picked up, and Cassidy felt like it was cutting at her face. She put her goggles to her eyes when she found she could no longer take the windblast, and she wished she had a scarf. In front of her, she saw Miria shivering and putting her back to the wind, her goggles sitting forgotten around her neck until she spotted Cassidy wearing hers. Kek didn't climb down from the aftcastle until Melfine was out of sight. When he did, he joined Cassidy and Asier.

"It never gets old, does it?" Asier said over the roar of the engines.

"Never," Cassidy agreed.

"There's no better life to be had," said Kek.

"Right you are," Asier said, barely audible over the engines.

The first three days were uneventful, and on the fourth the only excitement came when a lone phoenix struck the ship and started a blaze that Cassidy had to put out. It took the next three days of regular scrubbing to get the black marks out of the wood. The skies wavered between days of being completely overcast and days when the sun broke through the clouds in golden beams. Every so often Asier would order Cassidy to bring them up over the clouds, just for the sake of the view, only to bring them back down when the cold was too much.

On the tenth day out, as evening was drawing near, Cassidy and Kek were keeping watch. Cassidy had upturned a bucket to use as a chair while Kek sat on the gunwale. Meia and Tureye were partially visible above the horizon, blanketed in the gently reddening sky above. She was beginning to look for patterns on their faces when she came to a sudden realization.

"I'm so bored!"

Kek turned to face her. "Should I sing a little song? Maybe dance a jig?"

"I said I was bored," said Cassidy, "not suicidal."

"My singing is better than yours."

"That is not an achievement," Hymn declared. Cassidy looked around for the Fae, finding her floating leisurely around the helm.

Kek let out a short laugh. "Even your faerie admits your singing is terrible!"

Cassidy felt her face flush. "Oh, just shut up, will you?"

"What's the matter, Cassy?" asked Kek. "You can dish it out, but you can't swallow your fair share?"

Cassidy scowled and adjusted her bucket, sitting back down as forcefully as she could, staring at the sky. "Just one goose," she muttered. "Just give me *something* to shoot." Cassidy wasn't so lucky, unfortunately, and the next few hours passed slowly. When the sun had nearly set and cast black shadows along the ground, Asier emerged from the storeroom – which was strange because Cassidy didn't see her enter it in the first place.

"All's well out here, I trust?"

"Aye, Captain," said Cassidy.

"I don't know," said Kek, "I think Cassidy is trying to provoke geese into attacking us."

"Really?" asked the captain. "I hope you're planning to give them honorable deaths."

Cassidy snorted. "Geese are a dishonorable breed of bird, Captain."

"If you say so. In any event, it's time for supper. Call the others."

"Aye, aye, Captain," said Cassidy. She made her way to the pipeline. First, she brought the ship to halt, then she opened the copper pipe and repeated the captain's message. Miria was the first onto the deck, with Lierre shortly behind. Nieves climbed up a couple minutes later with her short hair a mess and her shirt only half tucked in.

"You're a real mess," Kek told her.

"Still look better than you," said Nieves. "So, what are we having, Captain?"

"You'll see," Asier answered coyly. She opened the door to the storeroom and stood aside for the crew. "After you."

Once again, Miria was first, though Nieves cut just ahead of Lierre. Kek looked at Cassidy and they raced to the doorway, and Cassidy beat him in only to run into Lierre, who was just standing in the way. "Ow! What the fuck, Lierre?"

"Sorry," said Lierre, "I was just admiring."

"Admiring what?" Cassidy asked, though once the engineer moved out of the way, Cassidy saw what had captivated her attention.

Asier had already taken the liberty of loading everyone's plates, and what Cassidy saw made her mouth water. In addition to the standard fare of scrambled eggs and baked potatoes, everyone was given an entire apple and the meat that served as the core of the meal was neither fish nor fowl. Though Cassidy couldn't tell on sight what it actually *was*, the aroma of seared meat was powerful. As she made her way to the table, she looked back at Asier, who smiled back at her.

"Nyuran's milk," Kek said as he sat down. "What's the occasion?"

Asier seated herself at the head of the table. "Do I need an occasion?"

Cassidy swallowed a mouthful of saliva before answering. "Most people wait for one before spending . . . however much *this* must have cost."

Asier chuckled. "Well, today's nothing special," she said. "I just felt you all deserved it. Something to warm the spirits before winter hits. Now, all of you, stop staring at me and eat!"

Cassidy wasn't sure where to begin. Miria didn't share her problem and started immediately with the meat. She made a rather undignified noise Cassidy had never associated with food before announcing, "It's real unicorn!"

"You're shitting me!" Cassidy exclaimed before quickly cutting a piece. When she tasted it, the sudden burst of savory mixed with a strange sweetness sent a shiver across her skin. It was a concentrated effort on her part not to repeat the noise Miria had made. Cassidy had only had unicorn one other time in her life, but it wasn't a taste easily forgotten or mistaken. She looked at how large a slab she had been given, then noticed the rest of the crew were given comparable portions. *The meat alone must have cost a fucking fortune,* she thought.

"I can't believe you really did this," Kek said with his mouth full. Cassidy chose to save the rarer foods for last and partook of the eggs first. Even those the captain had spiced with rare herbs.

"Why not?" Asier asked with mock indignation.

"Because this is just *so much*," Kek explained. "You've really out-done yourself"

"You're all worth it," said Asier. "You're a damn fine crew."

Cassidy swallowed the last of her eggs and smiled at Asier. "Only because we have such a great captain."

"That's kind of you," Asier said quietly.

"She's only saying it 'cause it's true," said Lierre.

Miria raised her cup. "To the captain," she declared.

Cassidy repeated the gesture, as did everyone except Asier herself. "To the captain!" Cassidy drank down her mead.

The meal was the best Cassidy could remember ever having, even if she felt bloated by the end of it. She leaned back in her chair and let out a low groan while holding her stomach. "That was so good," she said.

"Aye," agreed Kek, mirroring Cassidy's pose. Nieves looked ready to fall asleep where she sat, and Miria was snoring gently. Asier was the only one who didn't seem defeated by the meal.

"I'm glad you enjoyed it," she said. "I'm glad we could share this."

"We should do it again," said Lierre.

"That would be wonderful," said Asier. "I don't say this enough, but the years as your captain have been the best in my life."

A dumb smile found its way onto Cassidy's face. She refilled her mug and raised it. "To the next ten years," she declared.

Nieves nudged Miria and everyone raised their cups and repeated, "To the next ten years!" All except Asier, who instead said, "To everything that lies ahead."

CHAPTER THIRTY-EIGHT

The moment Zayne opened his eyes, he knew the day had come. Maybe it was in how the cold woke him up like dozens of needles being driven in his naked flesh. Maybe it was how the brand on his arm was itching incessantly. Maybe it was how the burden of dread he had felt every day since he had first come face to face with Dardan was oppressively heavy on his heart. Whatever the reason, he knew it was time. He forced himself to sit up in his bed and throw his feet over the side. With the slightest flex of his shoulders a crackling ran through his spine.

He put his feet on the cold floorboards and asked himself, *Is it worth it? Is it right?* He was sure the answer to each question was 'no,' but still he forced himself to stand. Every muscle in his body seemed to be working against him, and it took a concentrated effort not to fall back into sleep.

He found a clean shirt draped over the chair at his desk. It was white as winter snow. Blood would show on it. *There's blood a plenty,* a voice in his head chided him. *Surely you can stomach seeing it in your clothes.* He threw it on and buttoned it up. He tried to imagine a different life, one in which he still had a mother, a brother, and a sister, one where he was dressing, not to kill, but to make a good impression.

He thought about the twins. They would have been seventeen, or close to it. That thought put a cold pit in his gut. His fingers stopped for a moment when he realized he couldn't imagine his siblings as adults. Not Cenn, who Zayne could hoist with one hand and who enjoyed being tossed in the air. Not Nanette, who always begged for a second bedtime story only to fall asleep before it was done. No, they were trapped in his memory like a painting. As ever, such thoughts led to the memory of his mother and he forced his eyes open, so he could focus on what was real. *I'm not there anymore,* he told himself. *There is no blood on this floor.*

He finished buttoning his shirt and threw a black vest over it. He put on a pair of trousers and found his sword belt. He held it up and looked at the two pistols secured beneath the sword, which would sit at the small of his back. *Too much weight,* he decided, *the ones in my*

356

coat will have to do. He undid the clasp holding the weapons, and they tumbled onto his bed.

He slung the belt around his waist and found himself regretting the choice. He reached down to pick the pistols back up when his eye caught the iron chainmesh draped over Dardan's mysterious weapon. *Now's the time to see what it is,* he told himself. At the same time, he felt his hackles rise. Every instinct told him once more to throw the thing into the lake below. He stepped over to the cloth-wrapped object and ran a finger under the seam. It was cold, yet Zayne felt as though he was burned and withdrew his hand.

Even Asier will be unable to kill you, Dardan's voice repeated.

He sneered but found himself putting the strange bundle in the now-vacated holster on his belt. He checked to make sure it was tight and secure before moving on.

He put on his socks and boots, tucking and checking the latter for his hidden knives. Of course they hadn't gone anywhere, but it was still comforting to feel them. He took a thin strip of leather and tied his hair back. He drummed his fingers along the falcon decorating the pommel of his sword. Was something missing? What would happen if he forgot something now? Could he find himself one tool short of victory, or would his extended arsenal slow him down? The questions were like sparrows pecking at his brain.

At last he grabbed his coat, feeling the weight of its hidden contents like an old friend, but also as a newly realized burden. He put it on and stepped out into the blistering cold that was the sky over a freezing lake. Zayne had known what to expect, but really seeing it curdled his blood. Snow was falling. Asier was fast approaching.

The night before, Asier had ordered an all-night in, saying that she wanted everyone alert and ready come the morning. As Cassidy stood shivering under a gray sky, she found she couldn't understand why. The skies had been clear of dangers. Still, Cassidy wasn't one to argue with the captain's orders. So it was that, aside from Lierre who was below manning the bellows, the crew was all on the deck keeping watch, redundant as it seemed. She stood on the aftcastle with Kek, leaning on the gunwale, listening to him tell of his time with a girl in Melfine.

". . . so I told her," Kek was saying, "I'd rather charge headlong into the mouth of a Dread Hound."

Cassidy rolled her eyes. "I don't think you said that at all."

"Well, no," Kek admitted. "But I thought it the entire time."

"I'm sure it was really hard for you to –" she stopped when she saw something out of the corner of her eye.

"Ship approaching, Captain," called Nieves. Asier broke away from the helm and took Nieves' spyglass from her.

Cassidy put her own to her eye and looked at the ship. She gasped. A black hull painted with a white mural of Daen and the rotting corpse of a rivermaid nailed to the bow filled her vision. "It's the *Scorpion,*" she whispered to Kek.

"How the –?" he began, but Asier cut him off.

"Everyone be ready for orders," she commanded. She took two pistols from her belt.

Cassidy and Kek looked to one another, then to the cannon sitting on the aftcastle not even two feet away. "Should I use the cannon, Captain?"

"No, Mr. Valani," Asier said, "we'd be out-gunned. They want Miria alive, so they won't risk blowing us up – unless we open fire first."

Cassidy put her hand on her pistol and took a breath before taking it from the holster. Kek's first question burned in her mind. *How?* She wondered at it, but she could think of no justifiable answer. The black ship loomed over them, matching their speed with little effort. Asier slammed the *Dreamscape Voyager's* telegraph to a halt and the *Scorpion* began to circle them. Then, the engines stopped thrumming and the ship settled above them on the port side. It descended gently until its deck was level with the *Dreamscape's* aftcastle. Captain Balthine stood overlooking them, flanked on either side by his crew, which included two new faces. Balthine's hands were empty, his thumbs tucked under his belt, while the rest of his crew had pistols drawn with intent. Cassidy found herself staring down the barrel held by the muscular engineer, Mr. Charron.

"I didn't want it to come to this, Asier," Balthine called, "but circumstance has forced my hand."

"You've got a lot of nerve," Asier replied, "when I get my hands on you –"

Balthine held up his hands. "You'll have your chance in a moment," he promised. "But first my crew is going to make sure yours don't interfere."

Cassidy furrowed her brow. "Interfere?" she repeated.

Zayne looked over in her direction. "That's right. Asier, call that engineer of yours up."

"Lierre was lost in a storm," Asier lied easily.

Zayne looked to Mr. Charron. "Jacques," he said loudly, "If Captain Asier doesn't comply before I count to ten, shoot the redhead." Cassidy held her breath. *This can't be happening*, she thought. "One."

"Alright!" Asier shouted. She grabbed the pipeline. "Lierre," she said angrily. "I need all hands on deck."

"Unarmed," Balthine specified. Charron checked the sights on his weapon in a showy fashion.

"Unarmed," Asier repeated, resignation heavy in her voice. One of the unfamiliar faces from the *Scorpion*, a portly boy, jumped down to the *Dreamscape* with a surprising grace but unsurprising *thunk* as Lierre climbed up the ladder. He grabbed the engineer by the arm and held his weapon to her neck.

Charron leaped over to the *Dreamscape's* aftcastle, his pistol trained on Cassidy the entire time. "Drop it," he ordered, eying Cassidy's weapon. She slowly opened her fingers, dropping the pistol with a thud. The other unfamiliar face, a lithe woman, landed beside Charron, her job apparently to threaten Kek. "Hands on the rail, both of you." Cassidy and Kek obeyed, overlooking the main deck, where the scrawny man who went by Flea and the fat boy had Nieves and Lierre at the bow while Asier stood, weapons still in hand but impotently at her side, with Miria backed to the gunwale behind her.

Cassidy's heart was pounding in her chest. How could this be happening?

Zayne leaped down, landing in a crouched position. When he rose, he was standing face-to-face with Asier. The contempt in her amber eyes still stung him, even though this time he proved that hate was completely valid. "One last chance," he pleaded. "Hand the princess over and no one has to get hurt."

"No one except Miria, you mean," the other captain said with a sneer.

"I won't harm her," Zayne promised.

"On that we can agree," said Asier. "I'll never give you a chance."

Zayne took a deep breath. *You've come too far,* he said to himself. *You've stacked the deck; you can't let her call your bluff.* "You've left me no choice," he said. "Let's settle this with minimal bloodshed. You and me."

Asier's laughter was short and caustic. "You expect me to believe that when you die, your crew will just let us all go?"

Zayne shrugged. "Maybe. I can't say. I had them give their word, maybe we'll see what that's worth."

Asier spat in his face. He recoiled. Spittle landed in his eye. He wiped his face clean with the swipe of a gloved hand. He sneered and took a step around her. Asier countered by stepping backward and to the side, keeping herself between him and the princess. He faced down her scowl, his stomach churning. His breathing was heavy and rapid, and they hadn't even begun their battle. He shrugged out of his coat, which hit the deck with several *clangs* and *thuds*. He drew his sword, leveling it with Asier's center. "En garde," he whispered. Asier's face never changed as she threw her pistols to the deck at her sides and drew her sword and extracted a stiletto from her coat with the other hand. Unlike Zayne's, there was nothing ceremonious about Asier's blades. They were utterly average, save for a few scratches and notches that marked them as well used. "First blood?" he offered. He wondered if she could catch the sincerity in his tone.

"Death," answered Asier. She lunged.

Zayne took a slight step to the side and slapped the tip of her sword with his own. He ducked under a stab from her stiletto and pulled the knife from his left boot. Rising, he parried the next strike. Another. His retreat was one step at a time. As he moved around the deck, he pecked at her.

Swish, clang, swish, swish, clang, clang, swish.

Asier's blade grazed his forehead, just above his left eye. Blood trickled slowly down his face. It was an irritating itch he couldn't afford to scratch. He pressed the attack, putting Asier on the retreat.

Swish, swish, clang. Swish, swish, clang. Clang, clang, swish. Clang, clang, clang.

He pressed his weight into an assault, locking swords. He backhanded her with his knife hand and cut her cheek. The world slowed. The edge of his weapon tore her face, and he was back in the washroom of his family home, gaze locked on his mother's lifeless eyes.

Far away, he heard a gasp, which brought him back into the moment. There was bile burning in his throat. He swallowed it.

Asier pressed the attack. They locked swords again. Asier wound a punch with the hand holding the stiletto. He slammed her fist with his own. Pain flared, accompanied by a tremendous *crack*. He and Asier both dropped their knives.

Zayne flexed his hand to determine he hadn't broken anything. Asier did the same, but she flinched. Her knucklebone was split, her skin torn.

Rather than retreat or try to recover, she thrashed like a cornered animal. Zayne swung his sword with both hands to overpower her, but she dropped and slid along the deck. She kicked his feet. He fell. He braced himself, springing off his hands. Asier's blade grazed his back as he returned to his feet. The tip of Asier's sword pierced the floorboard where Zayne had been. Zayne swung at his opponent, who rolled behind her trapped weapon and ducked low. A tremor ran through his arm as he struck the blade. Asier kicked him squarely in the ribs before drawing the sword from the deck.

He gasped and recoiled. She stabbed blindly, grazing his arm. She stabbed again and he flowed like water around the blade. He slammed his knee into her stomach. The gasp she let out was a pathetic noise and involuntarily he wondered if his mother had sounded like that. That moment of hesitation gave Asier the chance to back away and heave in a deep breath. He tried to strike before she was recovered, but she caught his blade with her own and forced it aside before slamming her forehead into his nose. He backed away and with his thumb and forefinger he forced his nose back into place with an agonizing *crunch*. He barely parried the next few strikes. With each attack, she seemed less and less elegant, driven by fury and aggression rather than finesse. Zayne hooked his ankle around hers and pulled it out from under her.

Asier flailed, but she managed a one-handed handspring – she gave an agonized screech as she did so – and kicked him in the jaw. He bit his tongue. When she returned to her feet, she crouched low and swiped at his leg with a kick. He stepped over it. She lunged up and slammed her knee into his core. He fell to his knees and gasped for air.

There's only one trick left in your bag, a voice in his mind told him, followed shortly by Dardan's voice whispering, *Even Asier will be unable to kill you.* He spit the blood from his mouth. The world seemed to slow as Asier prepared the coup de grâce. He did the only thing he could think to do. He rolled out of the way of her attack and reached his coat, unclasping one of the hidden holsters. Asier turned on him.

He rose to his feet and fired his pistol, the shot cracking through the silence like a thunder strike. In a plume of blood and smoke, Asier stopped coming at him, a bloom of red spreading across her blouse. Her sword tumbled from twitching fingers. She collapsed to her knees, then onto her back. Blood flowed around her, forming a puddle of red. Once again Zayne was taken back to the horrendous sight of his mother's death, and this time he could not stop himself. He staggered to the gunwale and spewed over the edge.

It couldn't be. Cassidy stared in abject terror. Asier couldn't be . . . no, she was Elyia Asier, she was invincible. She was Cassidy's captain. She couldn't be beat. She couldn't *die*. Her whole body trembled as she stared at the captain bleeding on the deck. *No,* she thought, *this can't be. No, no, no,* "NO!" she screamed at the top of her lungs.

She felt a surge of energy that sent a tremor through her and she whirled around, grabbing Charron's pistol which had been aimed at her back the entire time. She pulled the weapon aside and ignited it. The pan exploded as the entire barrel ignited. The woman threatening Kek screamed as her hand exploded in a shower of blood and bone, her own pistol flying overboard.

Cassidy drew deeper on the Fae's power and screamed again, this time wordless and primal as she leaped down to the deck. She drew her sword and charged at Balthine.

Zayne was wiping his mouth of the bile when he saw something moving out of the corner of his eye. His ears were still ringing so he hadn't heard the approaching attacker until she was upon him. He raised his sword, hoping to parry whatever attack was coming.

It was the girl from Dawnhal. She grabbed one of Asier's discarded pistols. She practically punched him with it as she fired. His fingers sprang open as the bullet bit into his arm, and his sword dropped overboard. He barely managed to curse before she was already on top of him. He parried a blow with his spent pistol, but she was too fast for him to keep up with. She drove her blade into his stomach. He felt the iron tear through his inside and emerge from the small of his back. In a distant part of his mind, one that continued to think through the agonizing pain, he thought of the mysterious weapon he'd kept there, strapped in a holster. Even now, he couldn't be sure if he had made the right choice by refusing to use it.

Even more distantly he was aware the sky had gone dark. But at the forefront of his mind, he was focused on the sword in his stomach. He swung his uninjured arm, attempting to bash his pistol into the girl's head when a hand caught it. It wasn't Durant's hand. It wasn't even Asier's. Slender fingers the color of pearls in the moonlight ensnared the barrel and completely stopped his momentum.

Behind Durant stood a tall woman with hair the color of night that seemed to flow as though underwater, dressed in brilliant blue. He looked the woman in the eyes – irises of purest white with sclera of shimmering blue. Zayne blinked. *No,* he realized dumbly, *how could I have thought that was blue?* The strange woman's eyes and dress were deep scarlet, and surely had always been.

He felt a wave of static ripple across his mind. "You!" he declared in a voice he hardly recognized as his own. Before he could connect the word to any thought in his mind, the mystery woman's hand burst into flames – unnatural flames the same pure red as her eyes and dress. The fire spread rapidly along the length of his pistol as though it were coated in oil. His hand burned. The sword in his stomach was withdrawn and he felt a second wind come over him, only for the blade to be driven into his throat. Fire – naturally colored fire, he noticed absently – enveloped the sword.

Is this really it? he wondered. The thought flittered across his mind like a dream and gave him some relief. After fighting between fear and longing for death, now that it was upon him, it didn't seem at all real.

No, said a voice, not unlike his own. The voice was calm. *There is still work undone. You have promises to keep.*

Durant withdrew her sword again and kicked him squarely in the chest, sending him toppling over the gunwale. He flipped a time or two before his body leveled out. He was plummeting toward a starry sky that was slowly giving way to a cloudy afternoon. Why was he falling up? He realized it was the lake when he saw himself – wreathed in flames, blood trailing in streams behind him– in the image. He struck it flat, sending a shock through his body that felt like it broke every bone. He heard the sizzling of boiling water and extinguishing fires. He sank beneath the surface, feeling it freeze him to his core until he couldn't feel anything anymore. He sank into the darkness of the lake.

CHAPTER THIRTY-NINE

Cassidy clutched Asier's hand as Nieves tried to remove the shrapnel in her chest. Kek knelt beside her, putting pressure on the wound. Lierre held the captain's other hand and Miria took it upon herself to wring a rag of water into her mouth when she needed it. The captain's breath was labored. She looked up at Cassidy with eyes that brimmed with tears. "Is everyone okay?" she asked.

Cassidy looked around to the others. "Aye," she managed, though her voice broke and she had to wipe away her tears. "Aye, Captain," she managed. She clutched Asier's hand tighter.

"And the boarders?"

"Dead," said Cassidy. "All of them." She wasn't sure about the details – she was so fixated on Balthine that she never saw how the crew dealt with their would-be captors.

"You did me proud," Asier said with a weak smile. "I love you. All of you."

"Captain, don't sound so glum, you're gonna be alright," said Kek, though his voice was breaking every bit as bad as Cassidy's, "we'll stay in Sanarhal until you get better."

"We'll get the best surgeons," Nieves added as she worked.

Asier chuckled, which sent a wince and a tremor across her body. Cassidy gripped her hand tighter. "I expect the lies from Kek," she said. "But Nieves, you know this it for me."

"No!" Cassidy screeched. "You can't! You'll get better," her tears had her convulsing instead of breathing for the span of several heartbeats. "You're – *hic* – you're –*hic*"

"Shh, shh, shh," Asier cooed gently. The hand Cassidy was holding was weak but Asier brought it to Cassidy's face, brushing her tears gently. "I know I don't stand a chance. Never known anyone… to walk away from this. And I know I don't have much time. I want –" she winced. "I want a few private words, with all of you. Nieves, please, stop wasting your efforts." The sawbones looked helplessly at the captain, then the others, and slowly backed away.

Cassidy retreated while the captain whispered something to Miria and put her hand on Nieves' shoulder – before that moment she hadn't been aware of how bloody they both were.

Nieves said quietly, "I failed her."

"Me too," said Cassidy. They hugged. Tears streamed down Cassidy's face, which she buried in Nieves' shoulder. "If I had acted before he got the drop on her this –" she broke down into sobs, her lips unable to form the words. She let out a ragged scream. Nieves' tears were quieter, but not silent.

There was a pat on Cassidy's shoulder. She broke her embrace to see Miria. "Nieves, she wants you next." Cassidy watched as Nieves knelt by the captain and saw the captain's pained expression as she whispered in her ear. She thought about asking what she told Miria, but she couldn't speak. Lierre was next, then Kek. Anguish filled the whole of Cassidy's being as she watched and waited. Hymn appeared by her side, a wisp of smoke rising from her light. She hovered there a moment, then landed on Cassidy's chest. Cassidy could feel the Fae's tiny arms stretch out, and she realized Hymn was hugging her. She gently placed a hand over the Fae's back.

When Kek stood, he looked to Cassidy, nodded, then stepped away from the captain apprehensively. Each step toward Asier felt like a mile. When she knelt beside her, Asier strained to push herself up. Cassidy propped the captain's head on her leg and leaned down.

"You've grown," the captain said weakly. "You're not that little girl running from home anymore."

"I had you," said Cassidy. Tears fell from her face, dripping on the captain's bloody cheek. "You can't die now, we need you."

"No," Asier breathed, "*they* need *you*." Cassidy opened her mouth but was again unable to speak as a new wave of crying began. "You'll be a better captain than I ever was," the captain continued. "I love you, Cassy."

"I love you too, Captain."

"I'm not captain of anything, anymore. Call . . . me . . . Elyia."

"Elyia," Cassidy repeated weakly. After so long, her first name sounded foreign on her tongue; it felt almost like calling her mother 'Cassandra.' "Please, I'm not strong enough."

"You're stronger . . . than I ever was," Asier gasped. "Get the others."

Cassidy nodded. "Everyone, Captain wants a word." The others were quick to regroup.

Asier looked around the circle. "Thank you," she said, "all of you . . . for making . . . my life . . . so wonderful. I am so sorry." She closed her eyes. She relaxed, and for a moment, Cassidy convinced herself the captain needed a rest.

Cassidy stayed there with Asier's head on her lap for several moments. A thousand thoughts rushed through her head like a fire, so many thoughts that, ultimately, she was unable to consider any of them. She stared at the captain's face, the dying smile tattered with blood, and let out one more anguished cry.

She set her captain's head down gently before getting to her feet. She made her way to the helm, not really thinking of the steps she took.

"Cassidy?" asked Kek, "What are you doing?" Cassidy didn't answer. Instead, she turned the engines on and turned the ship, guiding it around the *Scorpion* until the black ship was on their starboard side. Then she sat down on the rotary gun and started turning its crank as fast as she could. Her turns were clumsy and weak, so the gun only fired in short bursts, but each shot hit something on the *Scorpion*. She turned the crank again, and again, the bullets ringing loud and hard.

When her arm got tired, she felt a hand on hers. It was Kek's. He closed his hand around hers and they turned the crank together. Smoke rose from the gun and bullets thundered as they tore through the *Scorpion*'s hull. Before Cassidy knew it, Lierre, Nieves, and Miria were all beside her. Nieves helped steady her aim, Lierre and Miria each put a supporting hand on her shoulders and watched.

At some point they hit the igniter of the *Scorpion*'s balloon, which broke off and caught fire to the ship. They fired several rounds into the balloon, which endured a great deal being made of dragon hide, but eventually they worried a hole in one of the seams. They continued to shoot until the rotary gun ran out of ammunition. They watched as the ship burned, falling slowly into the lake below. Cassidy rose to her feet and spotted something else on the deck. She crossed the ship and examined Balthine's coat. It was heavier than she expected. When she picked it up, a deck of cards spilled out. She turned the coat over in her hands, quickly discovering the weight came from a host of weapons and other oddities, like coins and cravats, hidden throughout. Cassidy remembered the way he had presented her with a rose filled with silver coins. She closed her fists around the coat.

"She was right about you all along," she said. She ground her teeth in remembrance of how she had once thought fondly of the mercenary. She reached up to her hat and found the rose, preserved by Fae influence, and crushed it into the coat before throwing both into the lake.

Cassidy stood with her crew as they watched the wreckage of the *Scorpion* fall into the lake. The embers still glowed for a time as the ship sunk far below the depths. For good measure, Cassidy spat down at the water – her spit was red as her hands. "Good riddance," she muttered.

"What now, Captain?" asked Kek.

It was several seconds before Cassidy realized the question was aimed at her. *I'm the captain, now?* The thought gave her shivers. "We continue to Sanarhal," Cassidy said quietly. "We need to arrange a funeral for the captain – for Elyia. And we still have cargo."

"I'll bring us in," said Kek.

"I'll make sure . . . *Elyia* is presentable," Nieves said quietly. "Cass – Captain, would you like to help me pick out some clothes for her?"

Cassidy nodded. "Aye," she said wearily. She turned to look at the deck. There was so much blood. "I should really clean this –" she began, but Miria interrupted her.

"I'll take care of it, Captain," said the princess.

"I'll help," Lierre added.

"That's not fair to –" Cassidy said, but Lierre stopped her.

"You're the captain, Captain," she said.

Cassidy couldn't be the captain. She wanted to slap her; instead, tears welled in her eyes and Lierre held her tight. "You worry about making sure we do right by her," she said, "we're here to do right by you."

"Thank you," she said, looking to her crew. *Her crew.* "All of you."

CHAPTER FORTY

From the moment the crew had arrived in Sanarhal, things only became more difficult. Docking fees had apparently gone up an entire falcon since the last time they had made port in the city. Cassidy had intended to arrange for Asier's funeral rites as soon as she had arrived, but first she was directed to the Ministry of Imperial Affairs, who directed her to the Census Office to report her captain's death and to check to see if a will existed to prove or disprove Cassidy's legal right to call herself Captain of the *Dreamscape Voyager*.

She sat on a tiny bench that left her ass numb after five minutes, watching as a woman of noble blood – who must have been a thousand years old, based on all the lines on her gaunt face – looked through a book larger than her person. Cassidy was convinced the day's events were a bad dream brought on by a particularly long watch and a meal that wasn't sitting right. Any minute she would wake up for supper with Asier and the others.

The nightmare didn't seem to be ending, however. After several long minutes of watching the woman turn numerous pages filled with tiny script, the woman finally said, "Aha!" and tapped on a section of the ledger. "Elyia Asier, born on the second day of the Lotus Month, in the year Three Thousand, Eight Hundred and Five, Imperial Standard?"

"Yes," Cassidy said exasperatedly. She had told the woman when she started, and again after the woman had flipped through half the book. The woman nodded and peered at the script; then, deciding her eyes weren't quite good enough, put a pair of spectacles to her face that suddenly made her eyes look abnormally large and gave her the general appearance of a frog.

"It says here in the event of her death, her ship, the *Dreamscape Voyager*, and all her possessions be bequeathed to her First Mate, Cassandra Durant IV."

"Yes," said Cassidy, "that's me."

"It goes on to say that in the event that Cassandra Durant IV is unable or unwilling to accept this inheritance –"

"But I am," Cassidy protested, "that's why I'm here!"

The bureaucrat did not heed her, "– the first registered member of the *Dreamscape Voyager's* crew manifest instead inherits."

"That's all well and good," she said, "but I am here, so –"

"Furthermore," the woman continued, "in the event the ship and or the possessions of Elyia Asier are unable to be bequeathed –"

"But it is," Cassidy said, "it's how I got here!"

"– then a payment is to be made in the amount of the ship's value, which the Imperial Logistical Offices has determined to be one thousand iron phoenixes."

"Again, I have the ship in – wait, it's worth a thousand phoenixes?"

"Yes, it says right here." Cassidy stood up and looked where the woman indicated, and sure enough, the stamp of the Imperial Logistical Office was right next to the amount.

"Huh." She sat back down on the uncomfortable bench. She watched as the bureaucrat began to write something on a piece of parchment then took a stamp and pressed a seal into it.

"In order to legally claim ownership of your inheritance, you need to take this writ to the Imperial Registry Office – it's the room six doors down the hall to the left."

Cassidy accepted the writ as graciously as she could in her condition. She could barely remember the walk when she reached the registry. When she opened the door, there was a queue of people in front of her, so after presenting her name to a bored-looking attendant at a desk, she took a seat on a bench that was somehow less comfortable than the one in the other chamber. She sat there staring at the writ in her hand before exhaustion set in. When she closed her eyes, she was back on the *Dreamscape,* sword in hand, the blade of her weapon lodged in Balthine's abdomen.

How could you? she wanted to scream. She saw the fear in his eyes. She pulled the blade out. *Captain* . . .. She shoved the blade into the mercenary's throat and kicked him in the chest. She fell forward with him.

Her eyes snapped open and she found she had nearly fallen off the bench. She took a steadying breath and sat back. She checked her pocket watch repeatedly. It was twenty minutes before her name was called. A slender man in a long, green tunic, with a mustache that drooped from the corner of his lips down to his shoulders, led her into a cube of an office to discuss her case. At least the chair she was directed to sit in was cushioned, but not nearly so well as the one on the opposite side of the mahogany desk before her. After a long-winded reading of various inheritance laws, she had to sign three documents verifying her identity and three more to finalize her ownership of the *Dreamscape* and its contents.

"... and then, of course there's the matter of the Inheritance Tax," the government official continued, stroking his mustache with needle-thin fingers.

"An inheritance tax?" Cassidy asked, unable to keep the misery from cracking her voice.

"I'm afraid so," the man said, not so unsympathetically. "Fifteen percent of the total estimated value of your inheritance."

"But the *Dreamscape* –" Cassidy began.

"I'm aware of its worth." The man held up a hand to indicate silence and rose from his desk. He made a show of poking his head out of the office and looking around. Then he returned to his desk and said, "technically, we are required to tally and tax *every* part of the late Elyia Asier's estate, since she explicitly bequeathed you with her *every* living possession, but I don't want to dedicate the manpower to rummaging through the affairs of a dead woman, and you doubtless have enough on your plate. I cannot reduce the tax on the ship – its value is clearly stated in other documents – but if I write that your benefactor parted with no other personal possessions . . ."

Even in a devastated and distracted state as she was, Cassidy had the wherewithal to know when someone was sticking his neck out for her. Her eyes widened and watered with tears she thought she'd already spent. "Thank you," she whispered.

"Thank me for nothing," the Ministry worker said, then he added in a calm tone that suggested he did her no favors. "You have two years to pay the tax, otherwise your ship will be repossessed. You can do so at any Ministry Office in the Empire. You are dismissed."

Cassidy didn't remember leaving the building and coasting along the streets. She was only aware enough of her surroundings to avoid walking into the occasional rickshaw or other pedestrians. *Two years*, she thought. It didn't sound so bad. Asier had a healthy pile of coins in her quarters. Once her funeral was dealt with, and their cargo unloaded, she would see what she had to work with.

She found a Sanctum near the docks, and they agreed to provide a pyre and hold a service, though they demanded two gold ravens for it, and would not be bartered down. She paid and arranged a time that night for the service to be held. It would be shortly after dark.

Cassidy nodded and told the priests she would see them that night. As she left, she thought briefly of Madame – or Sister, or whatever she really was – Venitha, and how she was nothing like the Iron Veils in Sanarhal. Or like any other practitioners of piety Cassidy had ever met for that matter. Despite that, she had seemed so much more comfortable in her iron vestments than the life-long priests.

She returned to the *Dreamscape* to find Kek seeing off some of the cargo while Lierre and Miria were still scrubbing the blood from the decks. Cassidy was sure they'd have to repaint the whole deck to have any chance of hiding the splotch where their captain had breathed her last.

"Captain," Kek said by way of greeting, a fist over his chest in proper salute.

The gesture and the title sent a wave of anguish through Cassidy's heart. She tried to let it pass with a shiver and said, "The funeral is at seven o'clock tonight. The Iron Veils will come with a pyre." She sighed. "I still can't believe this is real," she said quietly. "I keep expecting any minute I'll wake up and she'll tease me for sleeping in."

Kek clasped her shoulder. "I know," he said gently. "This morning came so quick, I just . . . I don't understand, Cassy – Captain."

"'Cassy' is fine," she said gently. "I'm going to help them scrub up," she said. "I need to keep my hands busy." She went into the storeroom and found a bucket, a rag, and a brush. She was about to fill the bucket from one of the rain barrels when she discovered the water was a thin, reddish color. "What the –" she started to ask.

"When I stopped the mercenary from striking you, I was burning," Hymn. "I had to dowse the fires in water. Do not drink from this barrel."

"Great," Cassidy said absently. She popped a cork from the side and let the water flow out over the side of the ship to the ground far below. "Are the other two clean?"

"To the best of my knowledge."

As she dipped the bucket into one of the clean barrels she asked, "Does it hurt?"

"Yes," the Fae said simply.

"How bad is it?"

The Fae hesitated. "I will heal. I was not holding it long, and the water helped."

"But how bad?"

"Do not fret over me, Cassandra." Hymn said. She flew into Cassidy's hat without another word. Miria and Lierre were scrubbing hard where Asier fell, so Cassidy found another bloody patch to clean. She knelt on the port side of the ship, a few feet away from the steps leading to the aftcastle. The spot where she had killed Zayne Balthine. There was far less blood than where Asier had fallen, of course, but there was still so much. There were ashes, too. She had used her connection to Hymn to set him on fire. *He deserved it,* she told herself, but it was still a heavy thought.

She knelt on all fours and took to scrubbing. As she pressed the brush into the bloodstains, she thought about the moment when she plunged her sword into Balthine's belly. She had killed people before – mostly self-defense, and there was one time she had dueled with a woman for reasons she had been too drunk to later remember – but she had never felt what she had with Zayne. It was a raw feeling. She felt it in her gut, in her heart; he didn't just need to die, and it wasn't about survival. She had *wanted* him to die. She had wanted him to *suffer.* She knew why, of course, and she didn't regret doing it, exactly. That scared her. What did that make her?

She scrubbed and she scrubbed, thinking over that moment. The sight of her captain falling like she did, the ringing in the air after the shot that took her . . . the raw fury that pushed her to risk her life and everyone else's – *Oh, gods,* she thought. She hadn't considered until just then that she had put the others at risk.

Her thoughts came to an abrupt halt when, as she moved just slightly to keep working, something dug into the palm of her right hand. She let out a little yelp and set herself on her knees.

"Are you okay?" Lierre asked.

"I'm fine," Cassidy replied. "Just found a little surprise is all." She looked at her hand and found a thick piece of glass embedded in her palm. She pulled it out gingerly, trying not to break it off in her skin, and looked at it while pressing the wet rag into her wounded hand. The glass had an iridescent tinge to it.

"That is ironglass," Hymn said in surprise, ducking back out of Cassidy's hat. "I did not expect to see it in this world."

"Ironglass?" Cassidy asked, turning the thing over in her hand "Feels like regular glass to me."

"It is an alchemical substance created by combining orichalcum, iron, and a long list of other minor components," said Hymn. "It was oft used to hide, entrap, or safely carry powerful forces, like artifacts and other things that can influence the world around them, usually from the Dreamscape." Cassidy weighed the piece in her hand. It didn't feel any heavier than real glass.

"Why are you so surprised to see it?" asked Miria. Cassidy almost jumped in surprise to see the princess had crawled her way over to join in the conversation. Lierre and Kek wandered over as well.

"In addition to the fact that I was under the impression that gale-rot does not exist here," Hymn said, "there is the high value your people place on cold iron. If I am not mistaken, due to your fear of my kind, you only make steel for the massive enterprises that require it, such as the support structures of your cities."

"That sounds about right," said Lierre.

"And orichalcum grows only in the bones of dragons. You use it as jewelry, correct?"

"Well, rich people do," corrected Cassidy.

"My point is, I did not think it could, or even would, be made here anymore."

"So, where did this piece come from?" asked Kek.

Cassidy thought about the small armory and collection of novelties she had seen in Balthine's coat before she had thrown it overboard in her fury. "The mercenaries probably had it. Balthine seemed to be the kind of person who carried everything with him. Maybe he came across it and kept it as an oddity." She checked her hand, which was still bleeding, and put pressure on it.

"You should have Nieves stitch that up," Kek suggested.

"Aye," Cassidy agreed.

"I'll get her, Captain."

Cassidy still felt weird hearing that directed at her. Instead of saying so, however, she just said, "Thank you, Kek."

Night came faster than Cassidy was ready for it. Six Iron Veil priests arrived on the docks, four of whom were carrying a tall casket. The precession was followed by a fairly large crowd in mourning white. Several carried paper lanterns. The priests climbed aboard the *Dreamscape Voyager*, and Cassidy moved to greet them.

The woman who appeared to be the head priestess of the congregation offered her a gentle bow. "I am sorry for your loss, Captain Durant."

Cassidy nodded graciously. Then she nodded to the crowd. "Who are they?"

The priestess turned to look at the crowd. "Sympathizers and well-wishers," she said. "Some who recognized the name of a fallen legend, others who know loss and wish to provide comfort when they can."

"That's very generous," Cassidy said quietly.

"Take us to her," the priestess requested. Cassidy nodded and led the priestesses into Asier's quarters. Asier lay in her bed, fully dressed in a purple coat, with a black corset trimmed with red over a white shirt, with black trousers and boots that reached her thighs. It had been her favorite ensemble. Her hands were held together over the hilt of her sword which lay along the length of her body. Her long, black hair was loose as was traditional for Imperial funerals. Cassidy helped the priests lift Asier off the bed and outside, where the casket was waiting. They lowered her in, and the priests began to chant.

The chant was an old dialect of the Asarian language Cassidy could scarcely make out, but she remembered asking an old woman at her mother's funeral what the chant meant. It was a request made to the winds that the gods not see her soul before it became one with the fires and was beyond their clutches. A white skiff carrying three oil lanterns flew around the *Dreamscape* from the city. Its flier was another Iron Veil who brought the skiff to a halt alongside the Dreamscape. They loaded the casket onto the skiff and pushed it off. It was Elyia Asier's final voyage. In moments, one of the lanterns ruptured, catching fire to the skiff, which drifted listlessly toward the lake. The same lake into which her killer had fallen.

The paper lanterns the onlookers had been holding were thrown into the air over the docks. There were others Cassidy had not seen on other ships in the harbor, thrown from decks and atop balloons. Before Cassidy knew what was happening, the night was full of hundreds of paper lanterns sent off for Elyia Asier.

Kek nudged Cassidy and handed her a lantern. She nodded her thanks and threw it up into the sky as she watched as the skiff carry away her captain. The realization that she would never see her again struck her hard in that moment. She would never hear her laughter again. She knew she was being watched, however, and kept her head high as she watched the pyre burn. After several respectful minutes, she retreated into Asier's cabin and out to the balcony in the aft of the ship. Finally alone, she fell to her knees and cried until the flames of the pyre reached the lake below and stopped burning.

That was it. Elyia Asier was gone from the world, and the world was a lesser place for it.

CHAPTER FORTY-ONE

After the funeral, when Cassidy had finally cleaned herself up enough to be seen, Kek declared it time they all go to a tavern. No one argued. They went to a local favorite of his, the *Lotus Princess*. It wasn't the *Dog's Watch* – it was cleaner, for one thing, and there was a lot of red in the decor – but if it got her drunk tonight, Cassidy could forgive it that. They found a table toward the back of the room and sat in sullen silence until a man of noble blood in a red vest came to take their order. Cassidy thought he was cute – even if he had the same mustache as the bureaucrat from that afternoon – but she felt guilty at the slightest positive thought that intruded on her mourning.

Miria ordered grape brandy – that had always been Asier's favorite, Cassidy knew – Kek and Nieves ordered ale, and Lierre wanted wine. Cassidy, however, felt her thoughts were too heavy, and asked, "What's the strongest thing you have?"

"Phoenix wine," the waiter replied.

"I'll need the biggest jug you've got."

The crew fell back into mournful silence. *She would have liked it here,* Cassidy thought bitterly. *Damn you, Zayne Balthine. I hope Daen heard you invoking her name. I hope she saw you die. I hope she's torturing you right now.* Her anger must have shown on her face, because Kek touched her shoulder and gave her a concerned look. "I'm okay," she said. "Just thinking, that's all."

Their waiter dutifully brought their drinks and departed, clearly reading from their expressions this wasn't a social drink. The crew stared at their cups for a moment. After a minute of uncertain silence, Cassidy said, "To Captain Elyia Asier," and raised her cup.

"To Captain Elyia Asier," the others repeated.

Cassidy downed the first cup of the phoenix wine in one shot, and she could feel it burn its way down her throat, then up through her nose, then spread everywhere else for good measure. It didn't so much *taste* as it *felt*. She poured a second cup and downed that as well, then a third. She filled it a fourth time but left it. She was hesitant to say what she felt she needed to stay. She took a deep breath, powered through her reservations, and said, "I understand if you want to go home. I won't force you to go anywhere with me. I can take you to

Revehaven," she said to Miria, then to Kek and Nieves, "to Melfine," and to Lierre, "to Castilyn. Or, anywhere else you want to go." The others exchanged looks and Cassidy felt the hollow space in her chest get deeper.

Kek was the first to answer her declaration. "Are you out of your fucking mind?"

Cassidy blinked. "What?"

"We're with you to the bitter end," Nieves said fiercely.

"After everything we've been through," said Lierre, "you actually think we'd leave you *now?*"

"You're our captain!" Miria said, slapping a fist on the table for emphasis.

Tears burned at Cassidy's eyes and she buried her face in her hands. Kek put a hand on her shoulder again. "The *Dreamscape* is our home, Captain. We lost Asier," his voice broke a little, "but we didn't lose you, and you didn't lose us."

Cassidy wiped her face and looked around at her crew. She smiled in spite of her sorrows. Then she frowned when she remembered why Miria was with them to begin with. "But your mother —" she began.

Miria waved that off. "Piss on that," she said. "She wanted me to grow and learn, and I'm going to do just that. I'm not going to run crying to her at the first sign of hardship. You know, she always wanted Elyia to raise me like a daughter," she said with a snort. "Well, you've treated me like a sister, so that should be good enough for her. And if it's not? Fuck her, I'm with you anyway."

Kek moved to peer into Miria's cup. "How are you already that drunk?"

Miria blushed. "I'm not," she protested, "I've just been thinking a lot about this today."

"And it's been a long day," Nieves added, mirroring Cassidy's thoughts.

"Still, Miria's going to get us all charged with high treason," Kek muttered into his cup. Nieves nudged him with her elbow. Cassidy laughed, though it died quickly.

The waiter came by with a fresh round of drinks and a several large plates of fried falcon, spiced eggs, and potato salad. "We didn't order this," Cassidy said, regarding the food with confusion.

"No ma'am," he replied. "They did," he indicated, nodding his head toward the back of the tavern. A tall man in a white mourner's tunic tipped a hat he wasn't wearing at her. She waved back at him and he turned his attention to his own party, all of whom were dressed for mourning.

Cassidy's mood elevated somewhat. She decided maybe, just maybe, she shouldn't drown herself in spicy wine she couldn't even taste. "When you bring our next round, I'll take some mead," she said.

"Of course," said the waiter. "You may be interested to know, that party over there," he indicated a group in the opposite direction from the ones who paid for their food, "have paid for your next round." Cassidy turned around to look, feeling her crew mates looking as well, to find there were more mourners. She raised a cup to them, and they did the same.

"It was easy to forget just how famous she was, sometimes," Kek said in wonder.

"I've seen funerals for nobility that had fewer mourners," said Miria. "There were so many lanterns."

"The lake outshone the sky," Lierre concluded.

"Aye," said Cassidy. "It really did."

As the night wore on, more and more patrons bought their drinks, and they recounted stories of their legendary captain. As Kek retold the story of how the *Dreamscape* was boarded by pirates, he highlighted Asier's bravery, even going as far as to undercut his own to do so. Lierre told of how she met Asier – a pickpocket had stolen her purse with Asier as witness, and the captain had chased the offender through the streets of Naariem until she overtook him and forced him to return the stolen money before turning him in to the city watch. Nieves recounted a story of a time a man had insulted her honor and Asier stepped in to duel him and his three friends who had laughed. Unlike Kek, Nieves was not exaggerating when she told of how the captain utterly humiliated them, leaving all three them bloodied and bruised and without trousers in the middle of the street.

Cassidy took a deep drink to empty her mug before she spoke. "The day I met the captain was the luckiest day of my life," she said. "I was ready to take any ship on the harbor. I just needed to get the fuck out of Dawnhal. Too many memories after my ma died. I didn't care where I went, who it was with, or what we did when we got there. So when I got to the harbor and the first ship, I saw was the *Dreamscape Voyager*, I met the captain and asked if she needed a deck hand. Imagine my surprise to learn this mad woman claiming to be Elyia Asier had traveled across the skies of the Empire in this ship *alone*. So of course she needed a deck hand. She promised me a healthy cut, adventure, and good lodgings in exchange for work, and we set out that afternoon. It was exhausting work, manning that ship just the two of us. I don't know how she did it alone.

"Well, one day that seemed as normal as any other, we find a fucking *manticore* stowing away on the aftcastle!" The others were leaning in close as if in anticipation, though the only one who hadn't heard the story before was Miria, "she didn't think anything of charging up to it. When it tried to gore her with its horns, she grabbed hold of them and *flipped* onto the fucking thing's back before stabbing it in the brain." She put her mug back to her lips, forgetting it was empty, and said, "It won't be the same without her."

"No," Kek agreed. "But we'll pull through. It's what she would want."

"Aye," said Cassidy. "You're right." When the next round of drinks came around, she raised her mug. "Here's to us," she said.

"And facing the future together," Kek concluded.

"To us!" the others cheered.

CHAPTER FORTY-TWO

Despite agreeing earlier to avoid the Dreamscape, Cassidy found herself sitting with Hymn on the dream world's twin of the *Dreamscape Voyager*. The ship was not currently in the sky but in the water just off the shore. The rainbow-patterned light of wisps encircled the lake. She looked over at Hymn, who was nursing her hand. Now that Cassidy could see the Fae in her full size, she saw the wound the Fae had suffered protecting her. Her right hand from fingertips to wrist was splotched with black and red blisters, and it seemed she was unable to flex or close her fingers at all.

"How did it happen?" Cassidy asked.

"I stopped the mercenary from striking you in the head," Hymn said flatly, dipping her hand into the water. She let out a slight hiss and Cassidy saw what appeared to be blood flowing from her wounded hand. It made the Fae look vulnerable and almost – *almost*—human. "His weapon was iron."

"I *meant*, how were you able to be full sized to stop him in the first place?"

Hymn winced as she twitched a finger beneath the surface of the water. "Sometimes the veil between this world and yours is thinner in some places than others. It is not uncommon, though it tends to be in places that attract my kind – forests, usually. Where the veil is thin, I can come into my full strength and I am as you see me now."

"But why did it happen then?"

Hymn pulled her hand out of the water and sat silently for a few moments, trying to twitch her fingers. Every time she did so, she made a pained face. She stuck her hand back in the water and said, "It is *possible* it was because of the bloodshed," said Hymn. "That draws the power of the Fair Folk well enough, especially in conjunction with fear and rage."

Cassidy considered that for a moment. She turned her attention back to the strange lights of the wisps circling farther across the lake. "What are they doing?"

"I do not know." Hymn said quietly. "It is not impossible that someone is mourning the loss of the Dreamscape Voyager, as you are."

"You mean the captain?"

Hymn nodded. "Did she ever tell you about Lucandri?"

"No."

"Lucandri was... one of my kind," said Hymn. "He was vile. Above all things, he favored trickery and wonton cruelty. In particular, he enjoyed using one to beget the other. It is said by those who listen for such things that he made a deal with the Dreamscape Voyager long ago. As a consequence, many people died. The Dreamscape Voyager was outraged and tore him asunder."

"Your people are mourning the captain for killing one of their own?"

"*Might* be," Hymn corrected. "I cannot risk investigating to be sure. Besides: Zayne Balthine was one of yours – you even called the same mountain home, if I understand correctly. And yet you killed him because he was your enemy. It is the same. There are those who condemned Lucandri, and so laud the Dreamscape Voyager."

"You keep calling her that," said Cassidy. "Why? Is it because of the ship?"

"No," said Hymn. "She gave her ship that name because that is what she was called. As a child, she traveled the Dreamscape, and as a woman grown, she took a ship through it. As I understand, she rather liked the epitaph."

"Wait, she *physically* took a ship through it?"

"Yes," said Hymn. "It is not a thing I recommend trying," she added.

"How did she do it?"

"She found a place where the veil between worlds was thin enough that she could easily pass through it. I believe it was a crash landing, not a deliberate choice on her part."

Cassidy whistled. "I wonder what that must have been like," she said.

"I am sure it was a worthy experience," Hymn said vaguely. The Fae rose to her feet and stared again at her wounded hand with a scowl. "We should leave," she said. "I fear we have lingered too long, and you have much to do."

"You're right," Cassidy agreed. She closed her eyes, and when she opened them again, she was lying in Asier's bed staring up at Asier's cabin ceiling. *No,* she corrected herself, unable to hold back the pang of sadness that came with the thought; *it's my bed now, and my ceiling.* Despite everything, she felt like an intruder in the space, so she dressed quickly and was out the door in a hurry. As she made her way out the door, Hymn took refuge under her hat. Kek and Miria were unloading more of the cargo they had brought to Sanarhal, while Nieves was waiting on the deck for her.

"Good morning, Captain," Nieves said amiably.

"You seem to be in a good mood," Cassidy said.

"I got my first good night's sleep in years since I didn't have to listen to you snoring."

Cassidy reacted as though she had been punched in the chest. "That's so mean! And here I spent all night lamenting how much I'd miss *your* snoring."

"Pigeon shit, Captain."

Cassidy noticed how easy it was for Nieves to call her that. She tried to pass off her wince as a pain in her wrist. "We should get going," she said.

"Aye, aye," said Nieves, and they departed into the city together, leaving the others to finish with the cargo.

The last time Asier's crew had come to Sanarhal, it was during a New Year celebration. The city had been colorful then and a joy to behold. But now Cassidy walked through streets where the snow was the color of ash, and she found she couldn't hold a smile for very long. She gave Nieves a sidelong glance and thought she looked like she was holding together better than Cassidy. *Then again,* Cassidy thought, *she's always had a quiet energy to her. Maybe that makes it easier to hide.*

"What do you think, Captain?" Nieves asked abruptly when they came to a fork in the road. "Medical supplies or weapons first?"

Cassidy was about to ask why it mattered what was done first before she remembered the price she would have to pay for the *Dreamscape.* They had a fair amount of coin, at the moment, but that wouldn't last. They would need supplies, and those would bleed them dry if they weren't careful. They needed catgut, coal tar, poppy milk, and basilisk venom. They also needed new harpoons, gunpowder, cannon balls, and bullets to replace the ones Cassidy carelessly fired into the *Scorpion* in her fit of rage. Lacking any of the latter could cost them their lives in a critical moment. *But lacking the former will cost us our lives if it comes to that,* she thought.

"Let's go to the apothecary," she said. "Priorities." They took the path to their left which led to a shop called *Wyn's Remedies and Tonics,* where Nieves purchased her surgical supplies whenever they came to Sanarhal.

Mr. Wyn's shop was austere, gray, and poorly lit, but clean. There were several cabinets of carefully organized bottles with their labels prominently displayed, promising everything from curing lung rot to increased sexual prowess. The man himself stat stooped on a stool inside, wearing a gray patchwork overcoat. He was on the brink of being called elderly, and the hair that poked out of his misshapen hat was a black that clearly came out of a bottle. He gave them a half-hearted attempt at a smile that came off as a sneer and showcased the fact that he was missing almost every other tooth.

"Miss Tarhant," he said in a low voice. "You've brought your new captain, today, I see."

Nieves narrowed her eyes and said, "Word sure gets around quickly."

"What's a poor community to do but gossip?" asked Mr. Wyn. "Especially when the subject of gossip is such a *hero*."

Cassidy tensed at the insult in his tone, but she didn't say anything. She looked around the shop, content to let Nieves take care of business.

"We need some supplies," said Nieves. She pulled a list of what they needed, accompanied by the quantities, from her coat.

Mr. Wyn took the list from her and muttered the items out loud as he read them. "Fine, fine," he said. He licked his teeth, and folded Nieves' list before handing it back to her. "Ten ravens."

What?" Nieves shouted, echoing Cassidy's thoughts. "That's more than ten times what you've charged that stuff!"

"Aye, it is," Mr. Wyn agreed. "Times change."

"This is outrageous!"

"No, 'outrageous' is what your bitch of a former captain made me pay for her silence."

Cassidy felt a rush of heat course through her body. "How *dare* you!" she demanded. "How dare you insult her? I should call you out right now and have your brains splattered through the streets for that!" She was breathing heavily. She didn't realize until afterward that she had taken her pistol into her hand.

Mr. Wyn didn't look impressed. "The only thing threats will convince me to do is *raise* my prices." He turned back to Nieves. "Fact o' the matter is, Miss Tarhant, that I undercut my prices for your crew because Elyia Asier was a contemptuous, blackmailing *whore*! Well, no more! You can buy from me, or you can buy from my competitors, and I know *exactly* what each of them charge for what you want."

Cassidy ground her teeth together, struggling against the desire to shoot something to shut him up. Nieves touched her arm. "Let's go, Captain," she said, "we'll find a better store." Cassidy let herself be escorted out.

When they were a block away, Cassidy shouted, "That rat-faced little bastard! Did you hear what he said?"

"Aye, I did," Nieves said calmly. "Ignore him; he's not worth our time. I think there's another apothecary just around the bend."

The next apothecary was kinder, though he charged slightly more than Mr. Wyn. The next charged double that. They searched for an hour before finding another shop, only to discover the shopkeeper – a young woman affecting a terrible Castilyn accent that fooled no one – was selling 'secret remedies' that smelled like piss and ink and nothing they actually wanted. After that, they asked around – twice being redirected to Mr. Wyn's establishment – before learning that there was at one shop in town they hadn't yet visited.

It was a long walk up town, and along the way, a woman slammed into Cassidy, nearly knocking her over. Already in a foul mood, Cassidy was ready to curse at the woman when she noticed something familiar about her. The woman ducked into a nearby inn called the *Treasured Memory* before Cassidy could get a good look at her. "Did you see that?" she asked Nieves.

Nieves, who had kept walking during the entire exchange, turned back. "See what?"

"I thought I saw . . ." she began, then she shook her head. "Never mind, I guess I'm just fixating on things."

The shop they found was a tiny place. Like Wyn's store, Mrs. Toff's shop was full of cabinets showcasing her goods, but *un*like Wyn's, *Mrs. Toff's Miraculous Emporium* was not built for them, so Cassidy and Nieves had to stand single file lest they knock into the damn things.

Mrs. Toff herself was a short, old lady who carried the bittersweet smell of poppy milk about her and seemed about to doze off at any moment. She looked at Nieves' list for a long minute before handing it back. "This won't be a problem. For such large quantities, that will be ten ravens."

Cassidy was tempted to jump at the woman and strangle her, but she took a deep, shuddering breath. "I don't suppose we could work out an agreement to lower the price?" she asked when she trusted her voice. When the old woman didn't respond, she added, "perhaps my crew could deliver an order out of the city? Or we could promise to spread the word that you're the best apothecary in town?"

Mrs. Toff tapped her lip with a gnarled finger for a moment. "Tempting," she said, "but I'm afraid I just can't afford to do that. These aren't things you'll find in an average garden. At ten ravens, I'm barely making a profit as it is."

Cassidy took another calming breath. Her knees were sore from the walk, and her eyes were starting to grow heavy, and they still hadn't finished their first errand. "Fine," she said, "ten ravens it is." She tried to mitigate the pain all their efforts put on her mind by telling herself, *At least she was polite*, but it did no good. It felt like they were being robbed, yet after visiting multiple stores with the same result, a part of her mind – a treasonous part of her mind that made her angry with its very presence – wondered if maybe Wyn hadn't been lying. Had they really been living off prices set by blackmail?

She tried to put the question out of her mind – it was ridiculous to think that Asier would have *needed* to resort to such underhanded methods, never mind that she wouldn't have – and focused on walking back to the *Dreamscape Voyager*. She would have Kek buy the weaponry tomorrow – she was surprised to realize how casually that decision came to her; she was supposed to relay orders, not make them. She was too tired, and her head was spinning.

She had thought with a little frugality a hundred and fifty iron marks wouldn't be impossible, but after the waste that was her day, she wasn't so sure. If they were so starkly under-paying for medicine, what other sudden surprises were they going to find? Under Asier's command, Cassidy had never worried about money. Now the dread of it was crushing her. On an intellectual level, Cassidy knew the deadline provided a realistic time frame for planning ahead. In her heart, however, she felt it looming over her.

She reached the *Dreamscape Voyager* before she even realized she had reached the harbor. Kek greeted her, and she answered vaguely. She stood standing on the dock for a few minutes, unsure of what she was doing. Eventually, she entered Asier's cabin, closed the door behind herself, sat at the table in the heart of the room, and started planning their next three destinations. Asier wouldn't let a little thing like tax take this ship away from her. She wouldn't fold and weep over a little hardship.

So neither would Cassidy.

CHAPTER FORTY-THREE

In the six months following Asier's death, Cassidy found the trade business had become much harder. She had never been aware just how influential the captain's name had been. Word of the Legendary Admiral's murder – as well as elaborate tales of the death of Daen's Scorpion – preceded them at every port, and while there were some curious to see the woman who sank the *Scorpion*, they received less business. At their third harbor since Sanarhal, Kek took it upon himself to find out why, and confirmed what Cassidy had started to suspect – the name of Elyia Asier instilled a sense confidence in the crew, and also presented a chance to see the hero of the Empire herself. Against that, 'Cassidy Durant' was just one more sailor amongst hundreds vying for business, one with no significant accomplishments save perhaps killing one somewhat-notorious mercenary. Hearing the truth of it had hurt. In spite of that, however, she kept her head up and took what patronage she could.

Spring had not yet given way to summer, and the weather was still weaving between days of frost and heat. On the day the *Dreamscape Voyager* made port in Andaerhal, the weather was just warm enough that Cassidy didn't need her coat. The sun shone brightly between light cloud coverage and a local smokestack, leaving the *Dreamscape* bathed in the light as it arrived in the harbor.

"Kek," she called out.

"Aye, Captain?" the blond man replied from the aftcastle.

"You've got the ship while I'm gone. Miria and I are going to send word to our various customers."

"That's a real fancy way of telling me I'm stuck on cargo duty," said Kek.

"Don't sound so glum," said Cassidy. "You've got Lierre and Nieves helping you." Kek muttered something under his breath, but Cassidy wasn't in the mood to confront him. Instead, she ordered Miria to follow her and descended the gangplank into the city. When the princess caught up with her, she asked, "What's the first address on the list?"

"Stone Well Street," Miria read as they walked, "Mrs. Song, a toymaker."

Cassidy nodded, leading her charge into a crowded street. "Do you remember which way that is?"

Miria didn't reply at first. "North and east," she called over the crowd after a moment.

Cassidy nodded and led the girl along a north-bound street. When they broke away from the thickest part of the crowd, she steered Miria ahead of her and said, "In three blocks, there will be a tight alley between a tavern and a barber's shop – don't ask me the name of the tavern, it's changed every time I've come this way – cutting through there will save us about an hour." When they reached the turning point, Cassidy had to point it out to Miria – which was understandable, as the alley in question was not only narrow but sat an odd angle that wasn't clearly visible from their approach.

They emerged in a market district and made their way through another back street when they were stopped by three men in black uniforms with jade-colored sashes across their breasts. *Royal guards?* Cassidy realized with surprise. Their apparent leader was a stern-faced man whose beard was starting to gray. "Cassidy Durant?" he asked in a tone that suggested he knew the answer. He patted the pommel of his sword for good measure.

"Aye, that's me," she said, her eyes flickering briefly to the man's sword hanging from his hip. "What's your interest?"

"By order of the Empress, Princess Yushiro Miriaan is to return to the capital in our custody."

Miria stepped in front of Cassidy and squared her shoulders. "Prove you are who you say you are," she demanded.

"We have the password; amber peonies."

A memory flashed in Cassidy's mind, of two Royal Guardsmen in Revehaven, asking Asier to come with them. They had said that phrase, which Cassidy remembered finding strange at the time.

"They're imposters!" Miria snapped, drawing her pistol.

Cassidy followed the girl's lead and drew her pistol and blade simultaneously. The alleged Royal Guard flinched. Rather than the quick rattle of iron of opponents meeting a challenge, she heard a slow, patronizing applause. With her pistol still trained at the man with the graying beard, she slowly turned her head to track the sound. Emerging from a shadowy alcove stood two men, one the most giant of men Cassidy had ever seen, the other the shortest. It was the short man who clapped.

"You're quick on the draw, your highness," he said. "I thought surely it would take closer scrutiny to see through these disguises. It would seem my coin was poorly spent. What do you think, Ander?"

"Very poorly," the giant agreed.

The tiny man nodded. "Still, they did what they got us through the port authority, so I can't complain too much."

"Who the fuck are you?" Cassidy demanded, giving a forceful wave of her pistol at the imposter in front of her.

"Who am I?" he repeated. He made a show of looking thoughtful. "Well, I suppose you could call me an interested man. You're the one who killed Zayne Balthine, yes?"

Cassidy felt a queasy mix of heat and coldness flood in her chest at the memory. "What of it?" she demanded.

"Not much of a denial," he said. "Then again, I can't blame you; he was a very rude man, truly. Always looking down on other people – and no that wasn't a height joke."

"I'm losing my patience," Cassidy warned, and she curled her finger ever so slightly tighter around the trigger of her pistol.

"Ah, of course, introductions. I am Captain Corin Lancen." He then gestured toward his hulking friend, "And this is my little brother and first mate, Ander." The giant made a flippant gesture of acknowledgment. "As to why we're here, well . . ." he scratched is cheek as if embarrassed. "You see, while Balthine wasn't what I call a *friend*, we within the Daughters of Daen –"

Cassidy had heard enough, and anger flooded her chest. The memory of Balthine demanding Miria and killing Asier flooded her vision like tears. She pulled the trigger, blasting the fake guardsman in the chest before breaking into a run at the Lancen brothers. She would not let those mercenaries take another person from her. Her sword was poised as she ran to skewer the shorter of the two in the throat, but the large man stepped in the way with a speed Cassidy would never had thought possible for someone of his stature. Before she could change tactics, he swung a massive fist through the space between them.

Cassidy's ears rang as the world slowed down, the moment crystallizing itself in time. The air was sucked from her lungs. She felt her feet were no longer on the street. She was partially aware that she was trying, and failing, to scream. Her momentum was being completely reversed. She saw spittle and blood hovering in the air just in front of her face and it took what felt like an eerily long time for her to realize it was her own.

Time snapped back into its proper rhythm abruptly and Cassidy flew several feet backward before crashing, bouncing once, and skidding along the alley and landing in a pile of refuse. She tried to groan, but all that came out was a raspy gasp, and she was struggling to breathe. She clutched and grasped at the cobblestones beneath her feet but was unable to make any progress toward standing. She lifted her head and saw the monstrosity that had knocked her down had thrown Miria over his shoulder like a sack of potatoes. His smaller brother and the surviving guardsman impersonator followed in his wake as they vanished.

"Cassandra!" Hymn called, her voice obscured by a fog in Cassidy's mind, as though she were resting her head in a bucket of water. "Hold very still, you have multiple broken ribs."

Cassidy forced herself to seize a breath. It was the most painful thing she had ever done. "Find . . . Miria . . ." she demanded, trying to push herself up. She slipped and her face crashed into the ground.

"Cassandra, I am sworn to protect –"

"The only way . . . I will be safe . . . is if I get back to the . . . *Dreamscape*, right?"

"You could also find a local healer," Hymn suggested.

"The only way . . . you can stop me . . . from chasing those bastards . . . is if . . . you do it."

"Cassandra, that is –"

"That is the only way you protect me," Cassidy said firmly, rising to her feet. Her stomach and chest felt as though she were driving sharp knives as far into them as physically possible, but she fought through it, drawing on her strange connection to Hymn more by instinct than understanding. "Either you track them down and report where they go while I get to safety, or I go after them and you break your oath."

The Fae hovered for a moment. She was so still, so silent, that Cassidy worried something in her brain might have broken. But eventually, she chimed like a bell and sped off in a blur. She called back, "I will return for you." Cassidy took a step only for her ribs to send tremors of agony through every fiber of her being – *too far*, she realized. Bile rose up in her throat. She might have hurled, but she was afraid at how much that would hurt, too. *Smaller steps. Small step.*

She limped back through the alley that led into the market district, where she promptly collapsed.

She heard screams, but they were even more distant than Hymn's words had been. She closed her eyes with her face pressed into the street. *Is this what the captain felt?* she wondered as the pain started to go numb. She thought of Miria, held at the mercy of those bastards. *I can't . . . I can't save you. I'm not the captain Elyia was . . . .*

The thought was cut short when a fresh bout of pain surged through her body, and she realized she was staring up at the sky. She felt another wave of sickness, but it hurt too much to give in to it. Her head rolled slightly, and she realized she was being dragged in a rickshaw.

"Easy, there, Cassandra," a familiar voice said through the fog.

Cassidy closed her eyes and tried to place the voice. Her first thought was her mother. But that was impossible. Was it Asier? No, she was gone, too. Hymn must have come back. But it wasn't the Fae blocking the sun and staring down on her.

"Sister Venitha?" she asked groggily. "How – *ah!* – how did you find me? Why are you here?"

"It's just Miss Venitha, now," the woman explained. "I found you when you fell into my stall. I sell vegetables, now; there was no profit in the priesthood."

Cassidy felt there should have been something odd about her explanation, but amidst all the pain and confusion, she could only agree with the logic of it. She felt every bump in the road as the former priestess pushed her on. Constant waves of pain shuddered through her body, as though someone were tugging at her insides with pliers. She cried out only for her breathing to be cut short again. She was acutely aware of blood drying on her face.

"This is where I leave you," said Venitha, "but unless you do something stupid, we will meet again." Cassidy didn't – couldn't – respond. She lay there staring at the sky from within the rickshaw.

Kek's voice rang out, the first clear voice she had heard since the pain set in. "Cassy! Lierre, get Nieves, *now,* Cassy's hurt bad!" The rickshaw was on the move again.

The next thing Cassidy knew, Nieves was hovering over her, her hands hidden beyond Cassidy's line of sight, which was locked upwards. The sawbones said something about her corset keeping her bones rightly aligned, but beyond that she might as well have been speaking Rivien for all Cassidy understood her.

Then Kek asked something simple and coherent. "What happened?"

"They took her," Cassidy said. "The Daughters . . . Took Miria. Sent Hymn . . . to find out where."

As if her name had been a summons, a blue light found its way into Cassidy's vision. "The princess has been taken aboard a ship called the *Second Chance*. They have set sail, heading south."

"Kek," Cassidy ordered, "get us . . ."

"On it, Captain," Kek replied. "Those sons of whores are going to learn they fucked with the wrong crew."

"Damn right," Nieves agreed. "We'll chase them down to the ends of the world if need be." She whispered to Cassidy, "Have no fear of that, Captain. I'll get you poppy milk for the voyage."

Cassidy tried to shake her head but failed. Before she knew what was happening, Nieves had a saucer to her lips and she drank, and sleep overtook her.

CHAPTER FORTY-FOUR

When Cassidy woke up, she felt the ship moving beneath her. She heard the engines roaring, telling her they were running hard. She tried to push herself up only for a jolt of pain to course through her body. She let out a yelp and stared helplessly at the ceiling.

"Cassandra," came Hymn's voice from somewhere nearby, "your crew wishes you to know they have found the *Second Chance* and have been pursuing it. Kekarian also wanted me to inform you they would run them down in a 'few minutes,' but that was twelve hours ago, and the mercenary ship has not slowed since they realized your crew were attempting to catch up to them."

"So they know," Cassidy said wearily. Her head was still a little foggy from the poppy milk – or maybe it was just exhaustion – but she was coming around. "How far behind are we?"

"This ship is close enough to follow, but not close enough to attack. However, consider also *they* cannot attack *you.*"

Cassidy groaned. "Sorry, Hymn, but I'm in no mood for platitudes. We have to get Miria back." The Fae said nothing to that. Cassidy tried again to rise, only for the sharp pain to sap the strength from her. She swore and closed her eyes. She considered slipping into the Dreamscape, but when she did, she felt something different. It felt like an open door in the walls of her mind, like a patch of cool air on a hot day. She reached for it like it was a thought just out of mind, and she felt a rush of coldness course through her body.

"Cassandra, you should not –" Hymn said.

Cassidy ignored the warning and pushed herself out of the bed. It wasn't painless, but it wasn't agonizing, either. It felt more like her bones were bruised rather than broken. She took a breath as deep as she could manage, though it was laced with tremors. There was a pressure on her head from holding the strange power, so she released it. The numbness vanished and all the pain hit her all at once like a massive hammer. As she fell, she seized the power again and caught herself.

"Is this," she asked, "what I did when I fought Miria?"

"Yes," Hymn replied. "As well as when you killed Zayne Balthine."

"How long can I hold this?"

"As long as you can focus. But Cassandra, you are not healed yet. You should not be walking."

"I have to," Cassidy replied. She found her clothes and dressed, wincing in pain when she tightened her corset. She stepped onto the deck to see Nieves at the helm, staring intently ahead. "Nieves, what's the situation?"

Nieves turned to face her, confusion fighting worry for dominance on her face. "Captain? You shouldn't be up."

"I'm going to be until Miria's back where she belongs," said Cassidy. "Where are those bastards?"

"Dead ahead," Nieves said. "Heading due south. They haven't changed course since they left Andaerhal."

"Where the fuck are they going?" Cassidy wondered. "The only thing south is the Great Desert."

"Probably hoping to lose us," said Nieves.

Cassidy shook her head. "No, if they wanted to lose us, they could fly up in the clouds. They're in a hurry, but I don't think we're why."

"What makes you think that?"

"Chalk it up to a feeling." Cassidy took Nieves' spyglass and held it to her eye. The *Second Chance* resembled the *Scorpion* in many ways – both were of Imperial make with the hull painted black with a stark white portrait of the goddess Daen decorating the starboard side.

"Where are you going?" she whispered at the fleeing vessel.

"Captain?" Kek called down from the aftcastle. "You should be in bed."

"Everyone keeps telling me that," snapped Cassidy, "but you call me the captain, so I'm here to be your damn captain. How long have we been flying?"

"Two days," said Kek. "Captain, your nose is bleeding."

Cassidy wiped her face on her sleeve, and sure enough, when she drew her arm back there was blood along the length of it. "Thanks," she replied before turning her attention to the fleeing ship. She could see the desert on the horizon. *Are they running to Cielhal?* she wondered. The desert grew closer and closer until it was finally upon them and then around them, but the *Second Chance* kept the same distance.

Cassidy fought through the pressure in her head. The pain in her body scratched at the wall of Fae power she was building. *Keep focused,* she thought. She formed a mental image of blue light filling the space between her ribs like water, stopping them from collapsing. She didn't know if that was how Hymn's gift actually worked, but it left her with a cool sensation in her gut all the same.

The sun was low when Cassidy saw something looming on the horizon. In the dim red and purple glow of dusk it was a black pillar. As it drew nearer, she watched the silhouette of the *Second Chance* charge straight toward it. "The Dragon's Nest," Cassidy whispered aloud. She turned to Nieves and said louder, "they're going to the Dragon's Nest."

"I see it," Nieves replied.

A chill settled in Cassidy's chest, and she asked, "We're not going to let that stop us, are we?"

"Never," Nieves replied firmly.

"Damn right," said Cassidy, borrowing from Nieves' confidence. *We're coming, Miria,* she thought, *they can't run forever.*

Before long, they were able to see the shadows of the fleet that encircled the nest. Under other circumstances, Cassidy might have been awestruck by the sight, but now all she could think of was rescuing Miria and bringing down the *Second Chance.*

A ship broke away from the fleet and moved on an intercept course with the *Second Chance. Good,* Cassidy thought. The other ship stopped briefly, and the *Dreamscape Voyager* cleared a fair distance, but soon the mercenaries continued on their way and the other ship turned to intercept *them.*

"Orders, Captain?" Nieves asked.

Cassidy bit her lip. They couldn't afford to stop and lose their mark now, but an Imperial Warship could blast them out of the sky, cutting their rescue short. *What would the captain do?* she wondered. "She wouldn't second guess herself," Cassidy whispered to herself. Louder, she called to Nieves, "Full speed ahead. Don't stop for anything. Nothing is more important than catching them."

"Aye, Captain."

The Imperial ship closed in quickly and turned their broadside to the *Dreamscape* to encourage them to come to a halt. Cassidy read the gilded word *Justice* painted across the side in Imperial script. "Turn fifteen degrees to starboard," Cassidy ordered. She then opened the pipeline. "Brace for impact!" The *Dreamscape Voyager* struck the bow of the *Justice,* sending a tremor through the ship. Cassidy was thrown off balance and for a moment her focus on containing the Fae power slipped, opening the door to agony. She quickly seized it back and caught herself on the gunwale as the port side of the *Dreamscape* scraped along the bow of the other ship.

Once they were clear of the one-ship blockade, Lierre called over the pipeline. "That was a little too close for comfort, Captain," she said.

"We aren't done yet," Cassidy replied.

"They're following us," Kek replied, "and I don't think they're happy."

"Keep flying," Cassidy said to Nieves.

The Imperial vessel caught up to them faster than Cassidy expected and made contact, the *Dreamscape* pressed against the much larger *Justice*. Standing on the deck of the other ship, bedecked in medals and sashes, stood a woman about Kek's height. "Bring your ship to a halt or we'll blow it out of the sky!" she demanded.

Cassidy pointed at the *Second Chance*, which was ascending the Nest. "They are mercenaries who have captured the princess. *Princess Yushiro Miriaan!*"

As soon as the words left Cassidy's mouth, they sounded crazy. Who would ever believe *that* claim? Still, the *Justice's* captain didn't scoff or roll her eyes as they sped across the desert. Instead she looked thoughtful. Then a distasteful look spread across her face as though Cassidy had confirmed something she didn't want to think about. "Let them go," she ordered to her crew. "We need to confront the *Martyr's Demise. Now!*" She gave Cassidy a glower and a nod before the *Justice* broke off and the Dreamscape was free to pursue.

As they began their climb, there was a brief tremor of *cold* in the air, and when Cassidy looked, Hymn was standing on the deck in her full-sized form. Her dress was red, like rubies in the light of dusk. Her eyes were wide with what looked like terror.

"No, no, no, no!" the Fae muttered to herself. She then turned to Cassidy. "Cassandra, we must turn back," she said, and there was a frantic edge in her voice Cassidy had never heard.

"We can't," Cassidy said firmly, "Miria is still in danger."

"There is an evil ahead that you cannot comprehend. We *must* turn around. We must *flee.*"

Cassidy wanted to shout, but she knew Hymn wouldn't be swayed by her feelings, so she had to think her reply through carefully. "If we turn around, will this evil go away?"

Hymn didn't speak.

"If we turn around, they get Miria. You said there's power in royal blood? Well, it sounds to me, 'evil' is the last thing we want to have that."

"Yes, it would be terrible, but Cassandra –"

"Stop worrying," Cassidy replied. "I'm sworn to protect you, remember?" Again, Hymn was quiet, but rather than fearful, or frustrated, she looked surprised. Her eyes relaxed just a little and her colors faded back into their usual blue. She nodded and turned to face what was to come.

"Um, Cass? Why is Hymn suddenly a beautiful woman?'

"Eyes on the target, Valani," Cassidy ordered.

"Aye, Captain," Kek replied.

His question wasn't entirely lost on Cassidy. "You said this form comes from being close to the Dreamscape," she said. "What can we expect?"

Hymn considered. "Have you ever heard of the concept of 'hell'?"

"No," Cassidy replied. "Should I?"

"You will experience it soon enough."

Cassidy put the spyglass to her eye and watched as the *Second Chance* made contact with another black-hulled ship that had a white dragon mounted to the front. The people milling between the decks were little more than specks against the sky, but she was certain she was seeing a trade. "Miria's being brought to another ship," she reported. "I can't make out the name but –"

Boom.

A growing pillar of smoke and maroon light erupted from the heart of the Dragon's Nest into the sky. The explosion trembled outward, proceeded by roaring winds. A vicious sandstorm came to life without warning. The *Dreamscape Voyager* recoiled and rocked as though struck hard by an object. The storm hit a moment later, and Cassidy put her goggles over her eyes just before receiving a face full of sand. Even numbed by the Fae power, she felt as though she were being pricked by a thousand needles. The sun was blotted out by the smoke.

The unnatural light of the Nest expanded outwards, bathing the *Dreamscape Voyager* in deep red stripped of shadow. The storm grew more intense. The scorching desert heat vanished, replaced by sudden, impossible coldness. Several floorboards began to crack as the temperature dropped and ice formed along the deck. There was a strange sound overhead. Cassidy looked to find not a balloon, but a mast and sails flapping in the wind. *We're in the Dreamscape,* she thought. How was that possible?

White flashes flickered in Cassidy's vision. All around them, balloons melted away to be replaced by old fashioned rigs and masts and sails. Several vessels in the formation caught fire, seemingly at random. Cassidy's stomach turned when she witnessed people flailing around on fire. She watched in horror as the deck of the Justice became a blazing inferno. Someone tried to throw a bucket of water to douse the conflagration, only for a block of ice to fall out and shatter on the deck. Two people flailed in a panic as fire engulfed them. One leapt to his death, while the other collapsed on the gunwale and died.

The winds buffeted the *Dreamscape Voyager*, and she was forced along a course that had her circling the Nest.

Boom.

A loud shriek filled the air. *No,* Cassidy realized, *several.* It was a chorus of screams.

Boom.

The Nest exploded. Rocks and liquid fire spiraled through the air in the eldritch light. The screeching grew louder. Dragons swarmed from the broken plateau like frenzied insects. Some of the creatures were too small to escape the pull of the storm and were dragged through the air along the same spiraling course as the debris and ships.

Something heavy struck the underside of the *Dreamscape*, throwing Cassidy off balance. She pulled herself to her feet and looked out at what it might have been.

They had been struck by a *tree.*

An enormous tree grew out of the Nest, emerging ominously from the smokestack. A scarlet dragon ascended from molten rock only to be skewered by the sudden emergence of a thick branch that tore through its scales. Cassidy laughed uncomfortably at the absurdity. She was cut off when another winged beast crashed into the *Dreamscape* and clawed at the deck. Kek fired a cannonball, knocking the creature off the ship.

The *Dreamscape* spun wildly on the strange course it was forced to follow. Cassidy forced herself to take a step toward the helm, helping Nieves steer a straight course. As the storm continued to unfold, Cassidy could see its path was a spiral, and at the heart of it was the ship where Miria had been taken.

"There!" she yelled over the gale. She forced the wheel hard to port. The ship lurched to the side, still encircling the dragon ship, but coming closer with each revolution. A living dragon rammed into their broadside, knocking them askew to be dragged by the air currents for a time, but Cassidy straightened the ship out. When the *Dreamscape* drew near the other ship, Cassidy could see Miria. The princess had a sword in hand and was crossing blades with a figure in a strange cloak.

"We need to get her," Cassidy yelled over the wind and explosions.

"But how?" Nieves shouted back.

She looked at the distance between them and considered the speed they were forced to encircle the black vessel. They could never fly close enough for Miria to jump. Cassidy watched as the princess, for all her skill, took a cut to the arm.

Boom.

Something sent tremors through the air, distorting the path around the strange ship. Cassidy looked down to the Dragon's Nest and saw a swarm of dragons spewing forth as an expanse of white light emanated at the base of the shifting pillar. *Something* was following the dragons out of that light. Something *massive*. Whatever it was, it was covered in gray scales that made Cassidy think of mountains. It opened its mighty maw, and three of the nascent dragons disappeared into the cavernous depths.

"*What the fuck is that?*" Cassidy shrieked.

"That is a leviathan," Hymn said, awe heavy in her voice.

"That's just its head," Kek declared. Cassidy realized he was right as more of the creature emerged from the light. Dragons fled, scrambling and flying into ships in their attempts to escape the impossible jaws. The leviathan cracked open a burning ship with one bite for no other reason Cassidy could see than the ship had been in its way, and it kept going.

Cassidy forced her attention away from the creature and back to Mira, who was being driven back by her mysterious opponent. She knew the ship wouldn't be able to remain in place long enough for them to extract her. *It doesn't have to!* She realized. "Nieves, get as close as you can. Kek, come with me!" She and Kek descended the ladder to the lower deck, and Hymn floated behind them. Lierre was surrounded by the corpses of baby dragons – no larger than dogs and covered in blood.

"Captain?" she asked, "I would really like to know what the *fuck* is going on!"

"Later," Cassidy promised. "Get a harness on me."

"A harness? Aye, Captain."

As Cassidy was being secured, she said to Kek, "I need a harpoon in the deck of that ship."

"Aye, Captain," Kek answered, taking his place on the harpoon gun." His first shot grazed off the dragon ship's deck, sending the harpoon careening uselessly to one side. He disconnected it. The second shot was intercepted by a piece of flying debris.

"Kek, if you don't make that next shot, I'm docking your pay for a year," Cassidy warned over the commotion.

Kek barked a forced laugh. "Alright, alright, one rescued princess, coming right up!" He fired. This time, the harpoon stuck in the decking of the other ship.

"Hymn, can you keep me balanced?"

The Fae hesitated; her mouth quirked in an uncomfortable frown. "I will do what I can," she said reluctantly, "but I cannot follow you to that ship."

Cassidy swallowed a lump in her throat. *I'm no Elyia Asier,* she thought, *but she raised me, and I can't disappoint her now.* She started at a run. She jumped. She threw her arms around the rope and pulled herself tight against it. Her ribs protested through the veil of the power she held, and she almost slipped. She kept her grip, however, even when the blood that dripped from her face started to slick the rope under her hands. She slowly pulled her way over to the other ship. The rope sprung taut as the winds buckled and pushed the *Dreamscape* away, and Cassidy was nearly bucked off. Terror sucked what little warmth was left from her insides.

She reminded herself of her harness, and of Hymn, and took a steadying breath. Confidence slowly crept its way back into her heart, enough to grip the rope and begin swinging her legs. She ignored the pain in her ribs and arched her body as much as she could bear. The sounds they made were miserable, and she felt tremors of pain snaking through her entire body. When she felt the arc in her swing would give her enough momentum, she let go. She felt cast adrift in the storm. Debris and dirt and blood and rain swept past her.

When she hit the opposing deck, relief flooded her so rapidly she nearly dropped the Fae power coursing through her. She had only lost it for a fleeting moment, and yet she was almost consumed by a rush of agonizing pain that paralyzed her. Her thoughts were a scrambling mess of thrashing chaos trying to put the pain back behind the dam.

Miria was still fighting the cloaked figure. She was losing; the princess had taken several cuts and one hand was hanging uselessly at her side, clearly broken even from Cassidy's vantage through the storm. The stranger lifted a sword high for a strike that threatened to take Miria's good hand, but Cassidy rose to her feet and charged. The stranger flowed easily, shifting the attack that had been leveled against Miria to turn and block Cassidy's strike. The shroud flapped wildly in the gale, pressing tight against its wearer. Cassidy thought the figure behind the veil was quite feminine. She tilted her head quizzically as she effortlessly pushed Cassidy's blade aside. *How did she know when I was attacking?* Cassidy wondered.

This Daughter of Daen had the upper hand. Cassidy needed to tip the scales. She tensed, reaching out with her Fae-given sense for iron, to set off the enemy's blade – surely having her sword spontaneously combust would throw her off balance. But the combined tasks of holding her body together and searching for the enemy's weapon was tearing her mind apart. She felt as though her skull would burst from the strain.

The stranger flourished her weapon, and Cassidy barely stepped back in time to avoid the worst of it. As the thin blade of her opponent flicked across her cheek, Cassidy realized the blade was not iron at all, but orichalcum – the iridescent and light-weight metal found in dragon bones – before striking her in the jaw with the pommel of her sword. Cassidy staggered, struggling to keep both her footing and the staggering Fae pressure in her head.

Miria struck at the cloaked woman's back. The mysterious figure pirouetted, and in one smooth motion, parried a killing strike from Miria, and continued her turn to turn Cassidy's blade away from her back.

Cassidy spat. It was a losing battle. They had to retreat, but where? They were on an enemy vessel in a storm. Cassidy felt the tug of her harness when she tried to match the stranger's stalking steps.

"Miria!" she called out, "Do you remember what I taught you when we sparred?" The princess nodded. "Show me!" They ran together at the stranger, each dropping to trip one of her legs out from under her. The stranger jumped over the attacks effortlessly, but Cassidy hadn't been after her. She released her sword, threw her arms around Miria, and rolled off the side of the ship.

As they swung wildly from the momentum, Cassidy felt her reservoir of power waver and the pain creeping in every few seconds. She let out a yelp as the princess squeezed her ribs. "No matter what happens," Cassidy breathed into Miria's ear, "do not let go of me, no matter how much I scream. Do you understand?" The princess nodded into Cassidy's shoulder. Cassidy rested her head on that of the princess and realized she was bleeding down Miria's back. They were being battered by the storm, but up above, Cassidy felt the winch pull them up. She gave a relieved sigh before she lowered her eyes and looked below. Vines shot up and ensnared them, and the thorns that dug into their legs pulled them with such force it stopped the winch. Cassidy and Miria shared a loud, harmonized scream.

Boom.

Cassidy felt the hilt of Miria's sword against her back. "Miria, cut the vines," she said.

"You said not to let go," Miria said.

"It's okay," Cassidy promised, "I've got you. I won't let go." The princess nodded and Cassidy held on tighter as the princess let go with her only good hand. The shift in weight struck Cassidy like Ander's fist all over again. She shut her bleary eyes and focused on the anger that had driven her across the sky. It was difficult to stoke the flames of hatred with Miria in her arms, but fear was a useful motivator, as well.

Their weight shifted again as Miria swung her arms to make the cut. Cassidy clenched her teeth as she ignited the sword. The flames quickly spread from blade to vines, and hungrily crawled down the tendrils to their source. Miria dropped her sword and used her hand to rip apart the dead remains of the plant that clung to them.

Above them, the winch began to lift them again but snagged. A pair of hands from above reached to pull them up. *Kek,* Cassidy noted. After a moment, they were rising faster. Lierre had joined. Faster still. Nieves. When they reached the lower deck, the hand that reached out and took Cassidy's was *Hymn's.* The Fae easily hoisted her up, even with Miria's weight added to her own. The others, as Cassidy had suspected, had been pulling on the harness. Cassidy fell to her knees and the tears that had been welling in her eyes burst forth like a damn and flooded her goggles.

"Cassandra," Hymn said urgently, "relief should come *after* escape."

Cassidy nodded, wiping the blood from her face. "You're right," she said. She climbed the ladder, and the pull of each rung felt like it would rip her ribs from her chest. She staggered to the helm and dizzily pawed for the telegraph.

It wasn't there.

"The ship reacts to you, here," Hymn whispered in her ear. "Guide it."

Like a dream, Cassidy thought wearily. She nodded and focused on *speed.* She imagined – no, she *willed* wind to fill the sails. She spun the wheel and trusted, *demanded* the ship would get them out of the storm's pull. She gripped the spokes so tightly it sent tremors through her. She felt every fleck of debris, every buffet of the wind, as though she were just another part of the *Dreamscape Voyager.*

She broke away from the storm. Slowly at first. Then she gathered speed.

Boom.

With one last explosion, the *Dreamscape Voyager*'s sails flared with excitement, propelled forward away from the epicenter of the storm. The blast sent them faster than she had ever flown before, the winds cutting at her skin, hot and cold air whipping around her. Ahead, the edge of the eldritch light came at them as though they were flying at a cliff face. When they crossed into the more natural sunlight, the *Dreamscape* shuddered and slowed. The engines roared as they suddenly came to life, and the sails above once more became a balloon. Cassidy looked behind them, expecting to see everything as it had been before, as though the entire experience had been a dream.

Instead, she saw the sky and the ground below were both filled with the burning wreckage of what had once been the fleet dedicated to the suppression of the Dragon's Nest. Of the nest itself, there was no sign, but instead a massive, twisted tree with dark leaves had overgrown the plateau, with roots and branches so convoluted and elaborate Cassidy almost mistook it for a forest. The tree had so completely consumed or destroyed the rock that Cassidy could hardly see it against the intricately woven foliage. Far below, where the roots had reached the sands, bright grass and vibrant flowers of every color had appeared without cause, heedless of the barren wasteland it bordered. The image was so incongruous Cassidy couldn't convince herself she was actually seeing it.

She looked away from the nightmare – surely that's all any of it was – and turned back to her crew. Hymn appeared again as a tiny ball of light. Miria was bloodied and leaning on Nieves for support. Kek and Lierre were covered in black powder and coal. And they were all looking to her. What did they think she could give them? Answers? She didn't understand anything that had happened.

She pulled her goggles off and started to cry. The reservoir of power that had sustained her had run dry. She fell to her knees and was blinded by raw, unending pain. But beyond it, she felt the warmth of her crew, their arms thrown around her. It did nothing to dull the pain, to make it bearable, but she was grateful for them all the same, until she couldn't think about anything anymore.

CHAPTER FORTY-FIVE

"How did she do it?" Cassidy asked aloud as she stared up at the ceiling of Asier's – of *her* – cabin. She sighed, which sent a spike of pain through her ribs and she stopped breathing for several heartbeats. It turned out that running and fighting did nothing to improve her condition – *who'd have thought,* she thought sardonically – and even after taking poppy milk, the pain was still potent if she moved or breathed wrong.

"You should be more careful," Hymn advised. The Fae was floating lazily over Cassidy's head, a drifting blue light in her hazy vision.

Cassidy ignored the Fae. She closed her eyes and saw her crew, looking to her for answers, for a course of action. How could they look at her and think she knew what she was doing? How could *she* have thought she knew what she was doing? She did the best she could. She had to. Her crew was counting on her. *Damn them for fools,* Cassidy thought. She couldn't replace Asier. Asier always knew what to do. If Asier had been with them, they would have caught the *Second Chance* before whatever it was that happened at the Dragon's Nest. No, if Asier had still been with them, Miria never would have been taken in the first place. Cassidy was a failure of a captain. She groaned.

In a moment of blind reflex, she tried to sit to find a more comfortable position only for her ribs to protest. She yelped and fell back to bed. She spewed every curse she knew in all three languages and closed her eyes. Right now, the *Dreamscape* was sailing east with no particular destination – Cassidy had ordered they put as many miles as they could from the mess at the Dragon's Nest. Asier would have known where to go. She always knew.

"How could she always be so *sure?*" Cassidy whispered. She couldn't take lying down any longer. She tapped into the strange Fae power again. It came on her slowly, like ice water in her veins. The pain in her chest became distant and numb, and her vision became clear and sober. She pulled herself out of bed.

"You cannot heal if you continue to strain your –" the Fae began, but Cassidy cut her off.

"I don't care! I can't stand to lie down!"

"Perhaps if you asked Nieves to give you –"

"I've had enough poppy milk, thank you very much! I can't stand it, Hymn." She began to pace. "How can they look at me and see a captain? I don't know what to do." Her steps took her to the table bolted in the middle of the cabin, and she took hold of a decorative box that had fallen on its side. She opened it, revealing a silver pocket-watch. Cassidy had almost forgotten the thing – she, Kek, Lierre, and Nieves had bought it years ago for the captain as a 'thank you' for the life she had given them. Asier had used it every day, except apparently the day she had died.

Cassidy stared at the thing for a moment. "I wish you were here," she whispered. "If I could trade this damn watch, the bed, every last thing I own . . ." she knew that was stupid, but it was all she had. She let out a screech and threw the box containing the watch across the room. It hit the captain's writing desk and knocked over a book and some paperweights.

A voice – Kek's – called from outside. "Captain? Are you okay?"

"I'm fine!" Cassidy snapped before cradling her head in her hands. The pressure of holding the power was giving her a headache, but she couldn't bear to let it go, to be bedridden and in agony. She stared down at the table and blood began to drip from her face onto the wood. She wiped her nose once and almost completely painted her hand.

"Cassandra," Hymn said.

Cassidy felt like weeping. "What?"

"This is addressed to you."

Cassidy lifted her head and looked where Hymn was hovering. The Fae had picked up Asier's journal and was carrying it over to her. Cassidy took the book gingerly from the Fae's grip and made her way back to the bed. The book wasn't very large, but it felt heavy in her hands. *Addressed to me?*

She opened the cover with trembling hands and looked at the first entry, which was dated eleven years ago, on the day Cassidy first came on as Asier's First Mate.

> *Cassandra,*
> *Now that you're reading this, then it's been ten years or so since I took you aboard, and now I am dead. It feels so strange to admit, even on paper, that I've always known exactly when and how my life would*

end. Well, not always. Since I was nine or ten. You see, when I was a little girl living in Revehaven, I was dared by some friends to touch the mountainside. I did more than that. I climbed down the fucking thing. And when I did, I found a cave.

Inside that cave, I think I found where our world met the Dreamscape, and there I found a Fae imprisoned in an old oil lamp. Her name was Len, and she set me down the path that defined my life. She promised me a gift in exchange for freeing her. Well, what better way to get a ten-year-old to do anything?

Of course I freed her. And in exchange, she showed me the death that awaited me, killed by a man I still don't know, though I see his face every night when I sleep. And I feel that destiny call for me, pulling me toward it with every choice I face, counting down like sand in an hourglass. I feel so stupid writing this, since I've only just met you, but I believe by the time you read this you'll trust me. You see, I know you'll be there when I die, and I know you'll survive, along with four others. I've seen it.

I think I'll use this journal to chronicle my thoughts of our adventures together.

Elyia Asier

Cassidy blinked. She wondered if she had imagined the words passing in front of her eyes in some sort of poppy-induced stupor. She read it again, and again, and a fourth time, but the words didn't change. She read it a fifth time just to be sure. "She knew?" Cassidy asked weakly. "She *knew?*" She thought back to the day they had last encountered the *Scorpion*. Asier had been so sure something was going to happen. That thought led to another, to the day they had first met Zayne Balthine and his crew. She had believed Asier's distrust and behavior was because the Daughters of Daen were mercenaries, but *she knew*. Cassidy felt a sick pit in her stomach. She hesitantly turned the page to the next entry, which was dated about a week later.

Cassidy,

Today, you asked me why I left the empress' service. I'm sorry I couldn't tell you when you asked, but it was too painful. Still, I feel the need to tell you, just so my side of the story isn't lost with me. I guess it's coming on eight years ago, now. I suppose we should begin with how I came into her service in the first place.

As you know, as everyone knows, I pledged my loyalty to Empress Shahira when I was younger than you – fourteen, I think. Back then, Shahira was still a princess. I was trespassing in the palace, masquerading as a serving girl. I had done it a few times by that point because it was fun. There were so many faces coming and going that no one ever thought anything of me. But that day, I felt the pull of destiny, the lingering, almost physical memory of what Len had shown me. It was a powerful tug that I'd grown to rely on. I knew that if I followed it, I would be safe, because it was leading me to a fate I knew to be far away. So, I followed it, and in doing so, I discovered an assassin. Certain in the infallibility of my fate, I took a bullet meant for Shahira.

When I woke up, it was in the palace, and the princess herself was looking over me, smiling. In that moment I fell in love. Yes, I, a lowly daughter of a seamstress, had fallen in love with a princess. I'll spare you the flowery, memory-sweetened descriptions of what she was like, just know that I loved her. When I recovered, I swore fealty and became her bodyguard. I learned to fight with the best of her mother's soldiers and lords, and I was happy. When she was crowned Empress, I was at her side. Rumor about the palace said she even took me to bed. Rumor, as it happens, was right.

The war with Castilyn started not with assassins, as is oft mentioned – though they did come later – but with the Dread Hounds. Oh, you'll probably think I made that up, but I swear it's true. Queen Isabel had invoked Faeorn herself to send the Dread Hounds. I saved the Empress from the fucking Dread Hounds themselves! Together she and I escaped, and I did the unthinkable; we descended into the forest beneath Revehaven, and I challenged the goddess Faeorn. I told her that unless she bested me, she could not touch the Empress. The goddess marveled at my audacity, but she accepted the terms. Thrice afterward I found myself faced with her attacks. Each attack was at random, but always when I was alone.

Shahira praised me for my strength and loyalty and courage and showered me with love. But it was a hollow victory for me, and each kiss she laid upon me burned with guilt. For you see, I only challenged Faeorn because I knew she could never take my life; I knew I would die by other means. My courage was never tested, nor was my loyalty, because I never once had to risk my own life.

Still, I loved her. When the war was not going well, Shahira found she could not trust her own admirals, nor could she believe Isabel's attempt at invoking the divine were finished. So, against the warnings of all her advisers — myself included — she made me an honorary admiral, in spite of my youth and complete lack of experience and gave me the right of conscription.

The entry continued for some time, retelling what Asier had already said and implied about the time following her return to Revehaven. She still felt a pang of sympathy for her captain, but it was overridden by the burning thought repeating in her head. *She knew!*

Cassidy's hands shook as she began to flip through the journal, tears filling her eyes as each entry opened with a note of what had happened that day to give her context. Many entries amounted to Asier asking Cassidy not to forget something, like the sense of wonder Asier saw in her eyes when she first saw Arrelan, or what she saw the day she vouched for Nieves and invited her aboard. She struggled to breathe as she advanced through the entries. She had to stop several times to take a drink. She started with water to fight the dehydration, but eventually she turned to the captain's personal cabinet. She never liked brandy like Asier had, but it didn't matter. She drank until her thirst was quenched and then she drank some more.

Asier had left years of reflection for Cassidy, and each one contained double meanings and talk of destiny that threatened to crush her.

> *Cassidy,*
> *It's the night after we left Revehaven with our crew numbering one extra princess and a Fae. So, you know now that I do, in fact, know why Faeorn was probably after you. Put simply, she wasn't. She was after me. I'd bet you anything. And for that, I am so sorry that you got pulled into this mess. I wondered if she had given up, but an old adage I'd forgotten is that the gods can afford to be patient. I'm glad you're recovering, and I hope that your new friend, Hymn, proves to be just that.*
> *Elyia Asier.*

Cassidy decided to forgo drinking from a glass and put the bottle right to her lips. She read a few more entries.

> *Cassidy,*

Today, we met my killer for the first time. Since you're reading this, you already know who I mean. It was surreal, seeing this man and knowing someday he will kill me. I'm honestly racking my thoughts trying to think what will drive him. He seems like a nice enough sort, for a mercenary. There's a pain in his eyes, I think, and I feel I should pity him, but when faced with him, I can't get past the fact that his is the face that's haunted me since I was a little girl.

Several entries later, Cassidy found a short, undated entry, but knew the day immediately.

So that's why. I feel blindsided. I won't let that bastard take her from me. She may not be my daughter, but damn it all, she's as good as.

Cassidy read on. A later entry was written with a sloppy hand, suggesting Asier had been drinking.

Cassidy,
For the first time in my life, I don't know what to do. If we go to Sanarhal, I die. But if we go anywhere else, I have no idea what will happen. It's always been so simple when it was far away. But I've followed this course so long, it was bound to end. I don't want to die, life is too sweet, but I can't remember life without the safety of a destiny to steer toward. I don't know if I could handle the mystery.
So, there it is. I put the decision out of my hands, and without any prodding on my part, Sanarhal is where we are bound. It's honestly a relief, if I'm honest, to think that it's just the way things have to be, that it's not a choice but fate.

Cassidy's hands shook and she wanted to tear the journal in half. Tears tumbled out of her eyes as blood dripped out of her nose, both splattering the pages as she turned to the final entry.

Today's the day I face my destiny.
I'm sorry about all of this. But it's for the best. The crew deserves a better captain, and Cassidy, I believe that captain is you. You're everything I could never be. Honorable, true, and selfless. You have the makings of greatness, and I believe you'll forge a destiny that will outshine my legend, and you'll do it without burdening yourself with prophecy.

Cassidy had exhausted her tears and was staring at the page, eyes burning, when she noticed something hastily scribbled at the bottom.

One last thing; Do not trust Len!

Cassidy took a swig of brandy as she considered everything she had read. "She lied to me," she whispered into the bottle. "She lied to *us*." That brought to mind Djian's comment in the Dreamscape. In spite of the Fae's denial, Cassidy had figured when the Djian had referred to 'the deceiver,' she had meant Hymn. Now, however, she thought maybe Asier was the deceiver; Fae were apparently good at rooting out lies. "After everything we went through, she left us *on purpose*. She *abandoned* us!"

The sound of blood dripping on the pages of the journal snapped Cassidy's attention back to where she was. She raised the book, poised to throw it as she had the watch. But she didn't. Instead, she set it down by her side, still open to the last entry, and buried her face in her hands, wiping away blood and tears in equal measure. She felt a warmth on her neck. She turned to see Hymn had roosted on her shoulder.

"I am sorry it was not the answer you wanted," she said quietly.

"No, it wasn't" said Cassidy. "But it was the answer I asked for, wasn't it?" She tried to laugh, but it came out as a sob. "I always thought she was so amazing. I wanted to be just like her. So brave. So perfect. So sure. But now I learn she was just . . . just . . . a liar!"

"She did not lie about everything," Hymn argued. "When she said she loved you, she meant it. I believe she would have done anything –"

"If that were true, she wouldn't have died!" Cassidy snapped. "She said it herself, all she had to do was tell us to go anywhere in the world that wasn't Sanarhal! But when I . . . When I said, 'let's go to Sanarhal' –" Cassidy's breath hitched. She clutched a handful of bed sheets and tried to blink away her tears. "She just . . . she smiled. Oh, gods, I could have stopped it."

Cassidy's sobbing caused short bursts of pain in her chest to break through the wall of the power's numbness. She laid back and tried to steady herself. Hymn hovered in roughly the same place she had been. "She believed you would be better off without her," the Fae said.

"So, she's a fucking idiot on top of a lying bitch!" Cassidy regretted the words as soon as they were out of her mouth. Nothing seemed right. It couldn't be real. She tried to remember every moment she could of her captain, a woman she'd admired and loved. She tried to recapture the memories of Elyia Asier before this revelation. But every silver moment was tarnished with context. Every sentimental discussion had been deliberately chosen to ensure nothing was left unsaid. Every heroic deed had been selfishly carried out in the name of a defined future. Every step of their voyage, of their *lives* had been calculated and weighed against the dream shown to a child.

"Do you really think that?"

"No," she amended. "I don't know. I just . . . I thought she was happy. I was. So were the others. Why would she throw it away?"

"She was always so certain, was she not?" Hymn asked. There was something odd about her tone, but Cassidy was too tired and confused to place it.

"She was," Cassidy agreed.

"What do you think would have happened, then, had she not embraced her destiny?"

"What do you mean?"

Hymn floated a short distance away, forcing Cassidy to sit up to follow her with her eyes. "She always knew the course of action that would lead her where her story ended. As long as she followed the current, little could surprise her. She was willing to face great peril because she knew she would not fall to it. And you saw her confidence and you were inspired. What do you think would have happened had she not battled the Scorpion of the Desert?" The answer started to form in Cassidy's mind, but she didn't want to think it. "You would have seen her falter. You would have seen her fear, seen her doubt."

"Would that really be so bad?" Cassidy demanded. "That's part of life! I would be . . . the whole crew would be there for her!"

"It does not seem so bad, from where you sit," said Hymn. "You must remember, however, that the Dreamscape Voyager never had to *live* with uncertainty. She would not know how. You, on the other hand, have learned to live with it. You endure, and you have done what you could to carve your own destiny out of it. Thus, it is as she said; you are stronger than she could ever be." The words struck a chord in Cassidy's mind. She hated to consider it, to think ill of her captain, but at the same time, there was a *rightness* to it. The future was as unsure and frightening as it had ever been, but for once, Cassidy considered that a blessing.

She had no way of knowing if the choices she would make were right or wrong, but she could make them honestly. Asier had forged a path to an exact point, not caring of the devastation she left in her wake, but Cassidy would do right by her crew. She would act for *their* sakes. And maybe, that was what Asier had hoped for her, in the end.

She put her hands on the bed to push herself up, stopping when she remembered the journal. She glanced at the last line again. "Hymn? Do you know anything about a Fae named Len?"

Hymn's colors shifted from blue to red, and the light seemed to emit a sonorous tone. She hovered in silence for a few heartbeats, then forcibly returned to her usual color. "You would be hard pressed to find any amongst my kind who do not at least know *of* Len. Len is a monster, a betrayer, a murderer. She is also a coward who would wear any mask she felt was necessary to escape justice. She was imprisoned in an age long past, in a land far from here, for atrocities committed in the name of the one you call the Desert Goddess."

"So, why would the captain try to warn me about her?"

"A formerly imprisoned Fae who manipulated her for reasons unknown to her?" Hymn asked. "I believe in a world where the people are as mistrustful of the Fair Folk as they are here, that would be reason enough for some. Perhaps she had time to think about it, before the end."

"I guess," Cassidy said slowly. The note still stood out to her, amidst all else she learned. It seemed out of place. But maybe that was the brandy talking. She forced herself to her feet. "I need to talk to the crew."

"You *need* to rest," insisted Hymn. "You cannot heal if you keep pushing yourself to your breaking point."

"I'll rest after I've had a chance to talk to the others. I promise."

When she opened the door, the crew was gathered outside, standing in a circle. Kek had his back to her and was the one speaking. "I'm just saying, she doesn't seem to *want* the job, maybe *I* should be captain?"

Cassidy snorted. "Sorry, Valani, but you made me captain. No returns, no exchanges."

All eyes turned to her. "Captain!" Kek exclaimed. "It was just . . . I mean . . . you know, –"

"Aye, I know," she replied. "But it occurs to me. A captain needs a first mate, and I've been neglecting my duties on that score. So, congratulations on your promotion, Kekarian."

Kek blinked. "Oh – thank you," he said breathlessly.

"Don't sound so excited," Cassidy teased. "As for the rest of you – Miria, how's your hand?"

Miria looked at the cast on her hand, as if she had forgotten it was broken. "It hurts. A lot. Asier hadn't lied about that."

"I still can't believe you broke your own wrist," Kek muttered in disgust.

"I had to escape somehow," Miria argued. "I almost managed to steal their skiff, but the big man caught me before I could get it untied."

"I'm so proud of you," said Cassidy. She furrowed her brow as a thought struck her. "How did you know the Royal Guards were imposters?"

Miria gave a wry grin. "You mean, besides the fact that I didn't recognize them? They said the password was amber peonies."

"It wasn't? But I remember the ones sent to meet Captain Asier said–"

"There never was a *password*," the princess explained. "Amber peonies are a rare variant of the flower that Captain Asier adored. It wasn't a password; it was a *bribe*."

Cassidy stood dumbstruck for a moment. The implication that Asier's conversation with the Royal Guard had been overheard, or otherwise shared with the mercenaries unsettled her. Then she imagined the diminutive mercenary overanalyzing the invitation, and she burst into a laugh. She stopped abruptly when a sharp pain shot through her ribs. Nieves moved as if to catch her, but she steadied herself. She took a deep breath and turned her mind to business.

"Lierre, how far can we travel on the coal we have?"

"I'd say a thousand miles, if we're being careful," said the engineer.

"Nieves, until Miria recovers, you and Kek take shifts at the helm. Set course for Nasradaan."

Kek and Nieves shared a smile before they saluted Cassidy. "Captain!" they saluted unanimously as they went to their posts.

Lierre saluted as well. "I best check on the engines, then," she said. "I'll make sure it's a smooth run, so try to get all the rest you can, Captain."

"I don't think I can avoid it much longer," Cassidy admitted. She wiped her nose just as she felt another trickle of blood coming.

Miria lingered after the others had gone. "I never thanked you for coming for me."

Cassidy smiled. "You said it yourself. We're sisters. I'd do it twice over."

Miria raised an eyebrow. "Just twice, captain?"

Cassidy snorted. "I don't think my ribs could handle much more." She ruffled the princess' hair. "Now run along. You may be on light duty, but that doesn't mean you're off the hook. Rotate in a third shift at the helm, if you think you can steer with one hand."

"Aye, Captain." Miria said, saluting like the others had before taking her leave.

Hymn landed on Cassidy's shoulder. "Just now," she said, "you sounded like a leader, Cassidy."

Cassidy felt her smile deepen. "You know what? For the first time, I felt like one." She made her way back to her cabin but turned to take one last look at the horizon. She saw the silhouette of a dragon flying across the sun and wondered what the future would hold. She wondered at the horrors she had witnessed at the nest, at what the Daughters of Daen had wanted to accomplish with it.

As the pain crept back into her awareness, she decided it wasn't worth worrying about now. She would face whatever the future brought her way, and she would do it with her crew at her side.

EPILOGUE

Another song about some far-off tragedy played in the tavern. Sad notes befitting the shabby and poorly lit surroundings drifted effortlessly from Nanette's fingers as she played what came to mind. The turnout was pitiful – five sailors drinking beer and three locals serving it. Nanette supposed she should have moved on to a fresher roost, but if she were honest with herself – *really* honest with herself – busking in one tavern was the same as another. She wondered why she even bothered. What good was the money with nowhere to go with it? Word on the docks – and by extension, word in the Empire – was that when the *Scorpion* sank, so did her entire crew. As far as Dardan – or anyone else with any interest in such things – would know, that included Nanette Adarin, and she wasn't sure she even wanted to correct the notion.

She could change her name, she supposed. She was pretty attached to the one she was born with, though. She had no shortage of skills she could apply to a new life, but she couldn't see herself finding anything as exciting as mercenary work. True, it had never been an easy job, and she'd done a lot of things she wasn't proud of, but what if she found a different crew? One not associated with the Daughters of Daen? *No,* she decided. *It wouldn't be the same without Zayne.* She still felt the sting of his betrayal the day he had set sail without her. *Bastard,* she thought bitterly.

"Wench," yelled one of the patrons – a burly man with a mustache that swallowed half his face. "Play a different song already."

Nanette's fingers stopped dead on the strings. "What did you call me?"

"You heard me, I called you a –" Before he could finish, Nanette dropped her lute, pulled a knife from her sleeve and threw it. The blade knocked the man's beer from his hand, and it spilled onto his lap. One of his drinking partners laughed. The man turned a bright shade of pink and his nostrils flared. He rose to his feet and pulled a sword from his belt. "Just for that, we're gonna teach you a lesson." His compatriots made noises of general agreement. It was probably no coincidence that the bar staff had gone into the back room. Clearly, they didn't want to become witnesses in an altercation.

417

Nanette reached behind her stool and took up her sword. The man looked somewhat taken aback to see her armed, but unfortunately, he wasn't so surprised as to back down.

"Well, if you want to dance," Nanette offered, throwing her scabbard away, "I'll teach you the steps."

"Arrogant bitch," the man snapped. He charged at her with surprising speed, but nothing that worried her. Nanette sidestepped an overhand blow that cleaved the stool she had been sitting on in two. She flicked her wrist, cutting the man's knee before she ducked under a backhanded strike. She pulled a knife from her boot and slammed it up into the man's armpit, eliciting a scream. He dropped his sword and she pinned his other hand to the floor with her sword.

"Do you yield?" she asked.

He sneered and yelled to his friends, "Stop gawking! Kill her!"

Nanette heard the familiar sound of pistol hammers being cocked. She counted five, and sure enough, when she looked up, four men each held a gun trained at her with the last man in the row pointing two. She felt her shoulders slump and she let out a dejected sigh. After everything she'd been through, would she really die at the hand a few nameless drunks in the ass-end of the Empire over name-calling?

"Put those guns down," called a pair of harmonized voices from the back of the room. The sailors looked around to see their new challengers and Nanette peered through the gloom to get a look herself. Only one shadow moved through the darkness between candles. It was clearly a man's silhouette and when he stepped into the light, Nanette saw a streak of silver hair among long sheets of silky black. His gait was hauntingly familiar. *No,* she told herself, *you're just imagining it.*

"Are you deaf?" A cold chill ran down Nanette's spine. She could see only one man, yet she heard the voices of two, both coming from the same spot. "I said put those guns down."

One of the sailors took a hesitant step toward the figure in the dark. "W- we don't take orders from you!"

The stranger made an odd sound that might have been a parody of a laugh. The shadow moved like a blur and one sailor's pistol went off. Blood and brains splattered in Nanette's direction. There was a scream as the sailor fell to the ground and the shadow moved again. She heard the distinctive *crack* that often accompanied a broken neck. It was followed by the *thud* of a second body crumpling to the floor.

One of the sailors dropped his gun in fright and fell flat on the floor with his hands over his head. The other stared dumbly as a three-foot piece of iron suddenly shared space with his heart.

After the stranger withdrew his sword, his victim folded like a stack of cards. He kicked the man who had surrendered and with his unsettling voices said, "Get out of here, and spread word that your friends deserved their fates."

Nanette stared, dumbfounded, as the man scrambled to his feet and ran away. She turned to the silhouette. He sheathed his sword, and Nanette saw the hilt catch the light. The pommel had taken damage – it was blackened from powder burn, and part of the decorative piece had broken off completely – but Nanette would have recognized the falcon anywhere. She was carrying its twin, after all.

"Zayne?" she whispered. Her voice cracked a little, but she didn't care. "Is that really you?"

The figure stepped into the light. Something in Nanette's mind swam. Even with half his face covered by a black mask, even with a silver streak in his hair, Nanette could never mistake her best friend.

Zayne Balthine was standing in front of her. As ever, his favorite coat was weighed down by the excess of supplies he kept on his person, but now it was also soaked, as though he had pulled it out . . . *of a lake,* she thought with a sense of awe and a little fear.

It was not just the mask and his state of dress that made Nanette uncertain, however. Rising off him like steam, settling around him like mist, was something Nanette had never seen before. It took her several moments of staring to realize it was *color*. It was captivating, yet so unnatural, Nanette couldn't help but stare while some distant part of her mind screamed at her to back away.

Zayne took a step toward her, then another, and soon he was close enough Nanette could see his exposed eye. At first glance, it looked as dark as it always had, but in its depths, she could see strange mixes of colors dancing in the shadows. "It's good to see you, Nanette." A strange look crossed the part of his face she could see – was it regret? Sorrow? It vanished quickly, however, giving way to fierce determination. "We need a new crew," he said in his two voices: one unfamiliar and strong, and the other she had always known. "The *Scorpion* is ready to fly again."

ACKNOWLEDGEMENTS

I know it sounds cliché, but there are too many people to thank to address everyone who supported or inspired me, so I'll keep this as brief as I can.

First, I would like to thank Miss Robyn Huss, as without her edits this book wouldn't have been even remotely presentable. I would like to thank all my alpha and beta readers, but especially Andy and Evan for your constant feedback and support. Of course, it would be irresponsible of me not to ~~blame~~ thank my parents for putting me down this path in the first place.

And thank you to Fabrice Bertolotto for the beautiful cover art.

ABOUT THE AUTHOR

Vincent E.M. Thorn was born in Wyoming, where there was nothing to do but watch movies and read books. As a result, he became addicted to stories, which inevitably led to him becoming a writer. He now lives in the metro-Atlanta area. *Skies of the Empire* is his debut novel.